Seeking
Nibbana
in
Sri Lanka

A Novel by
Jason Siff

Vajra Publications
www.vajrabooks.com.np

Published by
Vajra Publications
Kathmandu, Nepal

Distributor
Vajra Book Shop
Jyatha, Thamel
P.O. Box 21779, Kathmandu, Nepal
Tel.: 977-1-4220562, Fax: 977-1-4246536
e-mail: bidur_la@mos.com.np
www.vajrabooks.com.np

© 2008 Jason Siff

ISBN 978-9937-506-25-0

Printed in Nepal

Nibbana is the Pali equivalent to the Sanskrit word, nirvana. It is best to keep the word undefined, as any definition of nibbana just leads to a concept of what it is. And it is not a concept. It is not even an "it."

Thus the following quotation:

> "Purification (nibbana) does not come about through what you believe, from having committed sacred teachings to memory, from experiential knowledge, or by the taking up of vows. Conversely, it is not a result of simply rejecting those beliefs, teachings, experiences, or precepts. Abandoning each of these extremes, and not taking them up again, one becomes peaceful and does not long for anything more in this life or any other."

The Buddha, from the *Magandiya Sutta*
of the Sutta Nipata
(translated by the author)

Part One

The Meditation Master
and
His Student

CHAPTER 1

The meditation master lives in a remote jungle on the island of Sri Lanka. He was an accomplished Buddhist scholar as a young man, but now he is widely recognized as a meditation master of the highest order. Everyone who has heard of him likes to think of him as an arhat, one who has uprooted all sense of selfhood and eliminated all forms of craving, and has arrived at the pinnacle of inner peace: nibbana.

Despite his reputation, he has never been invited to the towns or the big cities where he could teach hundreds of people. A common monk can teach beginners. A master, it is widely believed, should only give his time to the most advanced students, the ones who are perched on the edge of entering the stream to full awakening. Thus, it is that his next student, an American, who has lived five years in Sri Lanka, decides it is time for him to seek out the meditation master, under whose superior guidance he believes he will eventually put an end to greed, hatred, and delusion, and arrive at that very same nibbana.

This student, an ordained Buddhist monk, a *bhikkhu* to be precise, goes by the name of Sumana. He has a pleasant disposition, as his name suggests. After having spent much of his time in Sri Lanka at the meditation center monastery where he first decided to become a bhikkhu, he sets out on foot to travel the fifty odd miles to the master's hermitage. It will take him at least three days to reach the jungle hermitage, but that does not deter him. Neither is he deterred by the remoteness of it, the poverty of it, nor the dangers of living there. For there will be no electricity, no running water, thus no bathroom with a flush toilet, and no hot showers.

He has heard from a fellow foreign monk that the meditation master's hermitage is so deep in the jungle that few villagers are willing to bring food for the monks and that any monks living there have to walk miles to one of the neighboring villages for alms. Because of this seclusion from the rest of the world, Sumana surmises that the meditation master and he will be lucky to eat every day. Sumana embraces the idea of fasting for days as necessary for the attainment of nibbana, though the thought of going more than two days without a meal worries him.

The meditation master's reputed arhatship, combined with the notion that he lives an austere life aloof from worldly concerns, greatly inspires Sumana as he makes his long journey to the jungle hermitage. Each imagined inconvenience and every conceivable danger serve to bolster his determination to stay there for as long as it takes, for he believes with all his heart that such conditions are essential in his search for nibbana. His fear is not of poisonous snakes, which there is said to be many in that part of the jungle, but of poisonous thoughts keeping him stuck on the wheel of existence. Lack of food and drinking water frighten him less than the thoughts of sensual pleasures that sometimes catch hold of his mind and pull him astray. He is certain that he wants to make an end to the round of rebirths right now, before he turns thirty, and then he can face anything in life with calm equanimity, knowing exactly what to do, his peace of mind utterly unshakable.

Sumana walks barefoot, as that is what he has heard an ardent bhikkhu does on such journeys. He carries a brown cloth bowl-bag with his bhikkhu's double robe in it, a barber's razor, a toothbrush, a watch, his passport and visa papers, and at the very bottom, his black lacquered iron alms bowl, the most prized of his meager possessions. The sun beats down on his shaved head fiercely and he resists the temptation to put a cloth over it to protect his skin. Each day his head gets more and more sun burnt as he walks the highways through towns, and then the footpaths through miles of rice paddy broken up by old rubber plantations and patches of uncultivated jungle, until he reaches the border of the great jungle where the meditation master lives. There he stops at a small village to get directions.

The villagers decide for him that it is too dangerous for the young white-skinned bhikkhu to go alone into the jungle, so they choose a guide for him and insist that he spend the night in the village. He is told he would lose his way and perish before ever reaching his goal if he does not follow their advice. Sumana accepts their hospitality and retires for the night in a tiny thatched hut specially prepared for him.

CHAPTER 2

The villagers are early risers, and once Sumana hears voices shouting and exclaiming in the high-pitched tone of Sinhalese women, he comes out of a deep sleep. He does not pause a second upon waking up. He hastily wraps himself in his outer robe, grabs his bowl-bag, and runs outside to search for the guide.

From the night before, Sumana recalls what the guide looks like. He looks young, at least to Sumana's eyes, but in truth, he is really quite a few years older than Sumana. He is thin and tall, almost Sumana's height, which is a gangling 6'2", with dark smooth skin and straight black hair, cropped short, dappled with bright silver hairs. He speaks good English, which he learned as a young man at a Jesuit boarding school in Colombo.

There are dogs and chickens moving about, scouring the ground for food, and he imagines that all these creatures are starving and desperate for even the smallest grain just as he is desperate to find his guide into the depths of the jungle. He yearns to be with the meditation master right now. He needs a master to help him find inner calmness and clarity, believing that he can't do that for himself, for he is in a state of panic. He blames the villagers for causing this panic within him. The morning hours would be different if he were back in the monastery. There would be no commotion, no chaos and unfamiliar sights to greet his waking eyes and ears; instead, he would be sitting in meditation, his mind moving freely in and out of sleep, lulled by the morning songs of the birds in the trees outside his hut.

The guide finds Sumana looking anxiously at a crowded row of four thatched huts, each one housing a whole family. A tap on the shoulder startles Sumana, though he tries to disguise it by making his body stiff and his face appear blank and serene. This is an old monk's habit, which he has seen hundreds of times in Sinhalese monks and has successfully learned to imitate. Only it does not become genuine just because it has become habitual. He can't hold the blank stiffness for long. Within a minute, his anxiousness reasserts itself with concern about having enough time to reach the meditation master's hermitage before twelve noon, for he can't eat after noon. Sumana begins to speak, controlling his intonation, slowing his speech down into some kind of hypnotic rhythm. He tells the guide that they can't waste any time. As he speaks however, he has to fight back his anxiety and keep his face as stiff as he possibly can.

All this effort at self-control is unnecessary. The guide only sees a white-skinned man, who is tall and thin, with light-colored features, and an oval face. Because Sumana is from a more developed country and has so intelligently adopted Sinhalese Buddhism over any of the other world religions, the guide is proud to be in his company. When someone from a Western country comes to realize the greatness of the Buddha's teaching, and along with it, the Sinhalese mind, there is a sense of rightness, of victory over the forces of ignorance. And the greatest triumph is the Western bhikkhu who commits himself to the selfless pursuit of nibbana by going to the forest to learn from an authentic Sinhalese meditation master.

The grand stature of Sumana's quest is thus well understood and respected by the Sinhalese villagers. Thus when they are ready to leave, people bring them bags and baskets of fruit, vegetables, prepared foods, oils and tonics, stationery and other necessities to take with them to the meditation master's hermitage.

There are far too many gifts for the guide to carry alone, since a monk like Sumana can't help him carry anything, so he must get help from some of the young men of the village. Two brothers in their mid-teens volunteer as porters for this journey. With strong young bodies and youthful energy, they are perfect for the task.

Sumana speaks a little Sinhala, having picked up some common phrases and words from the Sinhalese monks at his home monastery. But he has difficulty forming sentences in Sinhala, so they speak mostly in English during the journey. The two young men from the village occasionally try to ask Sumana questions in Sinhala, and the guide often has to translate.

For the first half hour of their journey, the guide entertains Sumana with a story about the founder of the meditation master's hermitage, who was also a renowned meditation master. The guide begins by telling Sumana that there is a cave on the hermitage's grounds, where the hermitage's founding monk lived over fifty years ago.

The Buddha's monastic order arrived on this island, from India, over two thousand years ago, and has gone through several periods of decline and revival. Fifty to a hundred years ago, during one such revival, it was common for a solitary bhikkhu to go into the jungle and find a cave to live in for the rest of his life. These monks often did not live into old age, but that was not important to them or the Sinhalese lay Buddhist community. What made them special was the sincerity of their quest for nibbana, combined with the austerity of their lives. They were revered as true bhikkhus, and offering them food, shelter, and clothing was the greatest privilege a layperson could have.

The monk who founded the meditation master's hermitage was of that stature. His name was Atakkachari, which means, "he who lives in the realm of no thought." He was thirty when he first arrived and lived there for ten years. For many years, the story goes, he was quite healthy, and every other day he would walk to a nearby village, receive his morning alms, which was usually very little because he used a hollowed out coconut shell as an alms bowl. Then he would walk back to his cave, where he would eat his meal slowly and mindfully,

throwing away all of the leftovers when he was done.
Occasionally, when he remained in his cave, a group of local
villagers would come and bring him prepared food. No other
bhikkhu lived there with him, nor did any laymen. He was
completely alone, and died completely alone. No one knew he
was dead until several days after the fact, when a large group
of laypeople came to his cave on the full-moon day. They found
him seated in meditation, his eyes wide open, not focusing on
anything. One of the men put his ear to Atakkachari's heart
and could hear no heartbeat. A discussion ensued whether or
not he was meditating in the state of "the cessation of perception and feeling," where it is believed the heart stops for as long
as one is in it. But in that state one does not smell, and may
even have a flowery scent, while Venerable Atakkachari's body
was already starting to putrefy. Still, everyone believed that he
was a fully liberated arhat and that he had entered nibbana
upon "the breaking up of his body."

The word of Venerable Atakkachari's passing spread to
the towns and villages all over that part of the island. A big
funeral was planned and hundreds of people attended it. They
cleared a large area of land and built a funeral pyre with the
wood. A group of monks carried the body on a plank. As they
walked carrying the body, hundreds of young women bowed
to the revered Atakkachari, their long black hair covering the
ground, making a carpet for the bhikkhus to walk on. There
were many other signs of devotion from those assembled.
Many presented flowers to the corpse as it passed by, while
others chanted, reciting the appropriate suttas (discourses or
poems of the Buddha's). When the body was placed on the
pyre, a crowd rushed up to it to touch the robes and exposed
feet of an arhat before his body was incinerated. After the
stack of wood beneath the body was lit, the flames climbed
high into the sky and the corpse was said to emanate a brilliant
white light. Some who saw it were changed for life, and from
that time on became devout supporters of bhikkhus. A few
even joined the monastic order. After that a group of villagers
decided to build two huts on the cleared land and construct a
cistern over a nearby spring. In another part of the hermitage,

a memorial would be built to house the charred remains of Atakkachari's bones and teeth. They would make this place into a hermitage for those rare monks who are determined to arrive at nibbana in this very life. Everyone agreed to name it Atakkachari Arañña, the forest hermitage of Atakkachari.

That is, in summary, the story the guide told him. Sumana was captivated by the vision of a bhikkhu living alone in a cave and attaining nibbana. The part about his death made him sad at first, but then the whole thing about hundreds of women forming a carpet of hair for the monks to walk on struck him as an exaggeration, as did the part about the corpse emanating a bright white light. He is familiar with the Sinhalese tendency to over-embellish a story to make it seem grander and more significant than it really was.

Sumana has been conscious all along that they have not been following a real trail, but was so engrossed in the story and his thoughts about it, that he failed to register much concern. Now that the story is over, he begins to feel some anxiety about this. They have been creating their own trails through the jungle, and he recalls having hiked up and down a couple of hills. Whenever they reached the top of a hill, the guide would pause in his story telling to climb up a tree to get an unobstructed look at the land below. Then they would often make a slight adjustment in their course, creating another thin trail supposedly leading in the right direction.

Sumana thoughts about getting lost in the jungle become more frequent and fearful. He now seriously doubts if the guide knows the way to the master's hermitage. But he is unsure how to state his concern. Finally, after nearly half an hour of haphazard meandering through an obviously unvisited swath of jungle, he succumbs to his exasperation at what seems to him useless, counterproductive wandering in the bush, and asks the guide the question that has been on his mind.

"Are you sure you can locate his hermitage in this vast jungle?"

"It is here. I know it is near," the guide replies.

"Have you ever met the meditation master?"

The guide stops and turns around to face Sumana. He does not believe he is being asked such a question. "Of course the meditation master knows me. I have brought him offerings every year for the past twenty years."

"Then why do you seem not to know if we are going in the right direction?"

"In the jungle, paths get overgrown in a matter of days. You must then rely on landmarks and what you remember from previous journeys."

That answer makes perfect sense to Sumana. Perhaps this guide has studied under the meditation master. Sumana pictures pathways in his mind, ones leading to pleasurable and peaceful states of consciousness, having become overgrown with fearful and obsessive thoughts. At that time, he reasons, he could look for the landmarks and signs that have led him to a kind of the inner peace he has known before.

They continue walking in silence. The jungle all around them is mostly silent, too. Sumana, now much less concerned about getting lost in the jungle, moves his attention to the life within the jungle. He has heard that there are poisonous snakes everywhere, on the ground and in trees. All of a sudden, he finds himself very alert and tense, imagining a possible snake hiding in the grass, or above him in a tree. His walking becomes clumsy, his face turns pale, and it is hard for him to breathe. Then the guide turns around and motions him to stop. A burst of fear shoots up through his whole body. Has the guide seen a snake?

"Do you hear that?" the guide says to Sumana, who is out of breath and therefore unable to speak. When he does not get a response from the white-skinned monk, he asks the two young men from his village the same question, this time in Sinhala. All of them stand motionless, listening for something. Sumana listens for a sound a snake might make, the two young Sri Lankan villagers listen for some sound they have never heard before, while the guide listens to the periodic sound of water splashing on rocks.

"Hear that?" he says. "The meditation master is not far."

Sumana and the two young men look at each other, wondering how the guide knows that the meditation master is nearby. As they get closer however, the sound of water hitting the ground becomes more audible, and all of them recognize it. The meditation master is taking his morning bath. Soon they are in a clearing where they can see a stone cistern and a monk, dressed only in his under-robe, which is worn like a sarong, being a single piece of brown cloth that is folded several times in front and held in place by more folds from the top. It is wet and sticks to his thin waist and legs.

The monk appears to be middle-aged, a good deal younger than Sumana expected. He is also much shorter than Sumana imagined he would be. His shaven head — glistening brown, beaded with sunlit droplets of water — is pleasantly shaped, more oval than round, creating an aura of serene wisdom. His facial features are in proportion to the overall shape and size of his head: his eyes, ears, mouth, and nose are all perfectly laid out. Soon Sumana is not seeing the master's head in the distance, but some recollection of a Buddha statue.

The meditation master pulls up a metal bucket with a rope attached to its handle, sets it on the ground and then lifts the bucket over his head and empties the water on his shaven head. It cascades down his body, creating the impression of a transparent egg encompassing his body for an instant before vanishing with a loud splash.

Sumana is transfixed by the spectacle of the meditation master bathing out in the open. He has also bathed in the open, but he has never watched another monk do it from a distance before. It strikes him as being a most ancient way of bathing, as how it was done during the time of the Buddha. Sumana's mind habitually looks for ways to identify with the Buddha's time, believing that such fantasies are part of the bhikkhu's life. Whether or not the monks of the Buddha's time actually bathed this way does not matter to him. He is not an historian, but a monk seeking liberation. If an illusion aids in his pursuit of liberation, he sees no reason to dispel it.

The guide and the two young villagers pull their attention away from the meditation master and talk very softly amongst themselves. Sumana is at first distracted by their voices. But when they are done talking, the guide explains to him that now is not an auspicious time to approach the meditation master. They should stay where they are until he has finished bathing and has put on his outer robe. Then when he is fully dressed, they should approach him with their baskets of food and other offerings. That will be the perfect time to gain the most merit.

This way of looking at things has become very familiar to Sumana. It boils down to how to get the most spiritual profit for your material investment. It is widely believed among Sinhalese Buddhists that the same good actions can produce varying degrees of merit depending on whom they are done for and at what time they are done. Thus, giving alms food to an arhat will produce greater merit, greater spiritual profit, than giving the same food to an unenlightened monk, though that will produce more merit than giving the same food to a poor person truly in need of sustenance. Giving food to someone who has just emerged from a state of higher consciousness is supposed to produce more merit than giving the same food to the same person at some other time. This is how lay Buddhists all over Sri Lanka think, and Sumana sees clearly how this way of thinking makes his life more secure.

The meditation master soon finishes bathing, leaving the cistern with his bucket. Sumana, the guide, and the two young men wait about five minutes before going to the master's hut. As they approach the hut, they see the meditation master fully dressed in a thick dark brown robe, sitting on a stool in front of his hut. His eyes are closed and his head is tilted upwards at the sun. To Sumana's mind, he is drying off in the sun. To the three Sinhalese men, he is in a profound meditative state that can bring them great merit if they do not disturb it. They decide to wait and give him their gifts immediately after he emerges from it. Several minutes pass and the four of them stand silently observing the meditation master. They see mosquitoes buzzing around his face, but none landing on his skin. Sumana marvels at this miracle. They feel a breeze occasionally blow through the clearing where they're standing, and the guide remarks how the master's robes are not touched by the wind, as if this were not his physical body, but a mind-made one before them.

Then the master's eyes open and he looks across at the four visitors. He smiles. He has all of his teeth, a rarity amongst Sinhalese monks at the master's age, which Sumana now places at near fifty. His face beams with light and friendship. He does not rise from his stool, waiting for them to approach and bow before him, which they all do. Sumana the monk goes first, asking for compassion, followed by the other three who ask for nothing, though they anticipate how much merit today's offerings will bring. The guide gestures to the bags and baskets and then asks the meditation master if he would kindly accept alms from them today. The master says he would, but first he would like to learn more about the white-skinned monk.

Sumana approaches the meditation master again, sitting down cross-legged on the ground in front of him. He looks up into the master's dark brown eyes and imagines that he is seated in front of the Buddha and it is now his time to receive that teaching that will result in the end of suffering, the final severing of all rebirth, nibbana. The meditation master speaks first.

His voice is deep and calm, and his English is crisp and clear. He says, "Venerable monk, I am Aggachitta Thera, a monk of twenty-five rains. Have you come for meditation instruction?"

"Yes, Bhante," Sumana says in a soft, breathy voice.

"Then what is your name and who is your preceptor?"

"I am Sumana Bhikkhu. My preceptor is Dhammaphala, a Nayaka Thera of the Shwe Jin Nikaya," he says with a tone of pride at his distinguished pedigree.

"I too am of the Shwe Jin Nikaya. It is a noble Burmese ordination. I studied in Burma. Did you know that?"

Sumana didn't know that. Actually, he doesn't know anything about the meditation master, Venerable Aggachitta, except that he's a reputed arhat and the greatest living teacher in Sri Lanka.

"Before I became a monk," Aggachitta continues, "I was a student at Peradineya, the University in Kandy. After I had completed my doctoral thesis on conditionality, I was offered the opportunity to go to Burma and study the commentaries on the *abhidharma*. It was there in Burma that I first meditated at a large meditation center, and soon after ordained as a bhikkhu. I returned to Sri Lanka. Instead of taking up a teaching post at the university, I left for the forest. I have lived alone, except for the occasional student, for the past twenty-five years."

Sumana doesn't quite know what to make of the meditation master's description of his background. It doesn't seem extraordinary to him: college, writing a dissertation on something obscure, a Burmese meditation center, and then going to the forest. It sounds as though the meditation master has barely lived, though that should be a good thing for someone who has attained nibbana. Sumana did have a life of sensual pleasure and intimate relationships between the ages of eighteen and twenty-four, before he decided to become a monk. He believes this will make it harder for him to progress on the path to nibbana. He too has gone to college, but only enough to satisfy his parents so that he could leave his country and search for liberation in the East. He read a few popular books on Buddhism before setting out on his quest, never attempting anything scholarly. The idea of learning Pali and studying the early discourses of the Buddha has not appealed to him. It is too much of a burden to take on. Besides, he has heard that study is not necessary for full awakening, and that it can even become an impediment.

For a brief moment, as he sits in front of the meditation master, he feels stupid and inadequate. Then it occurs to him that he may not get the kind of teaching he has dreamed about from the meditation master. Instead of fasting, long hours of sitting meditation, depriving his body of sleep and exercise, he may now be in store for long hours devoted to the study and contemplation of Buddhist philosophy. Nibbana now seems to him to be utterly unattainable.

Aggachitta watches the expressions that flit across Sumana's face, acutely aware of the white-skinned monk's drop in enthusiasm and apparent confusion. He certainly expected a very different response to this summary of his life. Then it dawns on him that this monk must feel intimidated by what he has just heard, as if he will be required to do all that Aggachitta has done in order to become a renowned meditation master.

The silence between them grows longer, bordering on the uncomfortable for Sumana, but not so for the master. His mind goes to the memory of his dissertation on conditionality and his intellect adroitly latches on to the conundrum of Buddhist causality. Simply put, in order for there to be no self, the basic principle of the Buddha's original teaching on conditionality has to be violated. This principle, which states that "when one thing arises, so does another," describing a link between two things, a connection that can't be severed, is violated by the theory of momentariness, which states, "when one state of consciousness vanishes, another state immediately arises." In his thesis, Aggachitta proves that the doctrine of momentariness is essential in preserving the doctrine of no-self from being corrupted with views of self. Then he goes on to state that the original formulation of conditionality was in no uncertain terms only meant to cover the cycle of renewed existence and not operations in the mental present moment.

Just as he completes this last train of thought, Sumana addresses him.

"Venerable Aggachitta, I would like to bathe. Where will I be staying? And, is there a bucket I can use?"

Aggachitta motions to the guide and speaks to him in Sinhala. The guide understands well what is asked of him, instructing Sumana to come with him to a nearby thatched hut. Sumana follows the guide, leaving Venerable Aggachitta alone with the two young men from the village.

The meditation master doesn't have any reason to talk to the two young men and so remains silent. They stand with their wiry bodies swaying, their arms dangling and then moving to point at birds and plants that they notice in their distracted moments, which soon become each moment. The constant movements of the two men begin to disrupt his inward reflection, so he asks them to go prepare the dining area for today's *dana*. Dana is a Pali word that means both the quality of generosity and the gift one gives, and refers to the meals that are given to monks and nuns in Sri Lanka.

Once Aggachitta's intellect is engaged, he can't just disengage it. He now wishes he had explained the subtleties of conditionality to the white-skinned monk, laying out the thesis of his student years, and then adding to it the refinements of over two decades of meditation. Conditionality, sometimes referred to as Buddhist causality, still interests him greatly, and he has had half a mind to write a book about it. But to his present way of thinking, books on ideas are counterproductive. They just give people more concepts to cling to, and thus more concepts to abandon, while at the same time making the act of abandoning them harder, for the habit of identifying oneself with one's beliefs has been further fed and reinforced. So it is better that he decided not to elaborate for Sumana. On this point, he agrees with his Burmese meditation teachers: during the intensive meditation retreat, there should be no reading, no writing, and no talking to other meditators. But then the Burmese teachers would tend to give a dharma talk everyday to all the meditators present, feeding them with new concepts. Aggachitta does not agree with that approach. He teaches only one person at a time, giving that person what he believes he needs at that time.

It has been a great sacrifice for him to refrain from scholarly pursuits. Out here in the jungle, away from libraries and the company of other scholarly monks, he has been starving his intellect. He believes he has been purifying his mind by not using it in any ambitious way. But he occasionally thirsts for knowledge from outside. And why not? He has been out of the mainstream of Buddhist scholarship for the past twenty-five years. In some respects, he is still the young man who was to have become a university professor and written many articles and books on Buddhism.

Here he has lived in solitude, a self-imposed exile, having denied himself a life where he could have flourished. Whenever his mind goes back to the past and lands on this particular crossroad, he usually averts his attention. But not today, with this new monk arriving. Somehow, it is important for him to look at this crossroad a little longer than usual, as if it contains some kind of wisdom, even though he has thoroughly convinced himself that much of what he had thought, said, and done in his past was based on ignorance and not wisdom. Could that also apply to his decision to become a bhikkhu?

Here is how that decision was made. He received an invitation, along with a small stipend, to study the *abhidharma*, a highly systematic formulation of the Buddha's teaching, in a Burmese monastic university, which just happened to have a meditation center attached to it. When he arrived in Burma, the head monk and president of the university suggested that he spend a month in a silent meditation retreat before pursuing his studies. This idea appealed to him. It sounded like a much-needed rest before the real work was to begin.

He was given a bed in the large dorm room where the Burmese laymen were housed. There was a nail on the wall for him to hang one shirt, and everything else had to be stored under his bed. He hardly spent anytime in the dorm room, except to sleep a few hours each night. The rest of his time was predominantly spent in the meditation hall. One hour of sitting, followed by one hour of walking, all day long, with an-hour meal break at eleven each morning.

Once he started meditating, he found he could do it. More than that, he found that he was good at it. He could sit still for an hour without much pain or restlessness. His mind quieted down quickly. For long periods, he was able to note every moment of his experience. There were days when he saw fantastic images, bright lights, and felt his mind dive through bursts of bliss and waves of serenity. Then he came to a long stretch of discomfort and irritation, and he longed to leave this world of pain and sorrow. It was then that he decided to become a bhikkhu and pursue this path of meditation to its end.

His teacher approved of his decision, but cautioned him to wait until the full thirty days had passed. He was given the impression that there was more in store for him if he continued as a layman. He resumed his meditation practice with even greater effort, sleeping only a couple of hours a night, determined as he was to get through this sea of pain and arrive at the other shore.

Soon he was sustaining very peaceful and deep states of mind for extended periods of time. His mind became clear: his thoughts were slowed down and magnified several times, slipping into oblivion each time he put his attention on them. Then one day, all of a sudden, he saw his mind knowing one thing after another: an internal image, a physical sensation, a sound, and then a thought, flashing on one thing, its vanishing, and the arising of the next thing. Within this experience, as an integral part of it, was a wordless understanding of no-self. And for the briefest of moments, his mind vanished. As his consciousness returned, it was flooded with light, floating on a bed of tranquility.

When he told this to his teacher, he was told that he had attained the path and the fruit. He was now a *sotapanna*, a stream-enterer, one who is destined to attain nibbana within seven lifetimes. Shortly thereafter he ordained as a bhikkhu and was given the name, Aggachitta, which means, "the highest consciousness."

From that time on, he has dedicated his life to the attainment of nibbana, but he does not know how far along the path he truly is. For all he knows he could still be a sotapanna, though he feels at times that he has progressed much further than that. He has wondered if he has advanced to the next path and fruit, which would make him a *sakadagami*, one who is destined to attain nibbana in his next lifetime. One thing is certain in this regard. He knows he is not an arhat.

CHAPTER
3

Sumana and the guide leave Sumana's hut together. Sumana carries a bar of soap and an orange towel, while the guide carries a dented old metal bucket, which is missing its handle and has a few holes in it. Sumana voices the urge to ask Venerable Aggachitta if he can use the new bucket, but the guide persuades him not to. These buckets can be very personal possessions for monks, and asking Aggachitta might put Sumana in an awkward position. This sounds reasonable to Sumana, for he has seen firsthand how Sinhalese monks will keep a bathing bucket in their rooms. Maybe this has something to do with the communal nature of most property in Sri Lankan Buddhist monasteries. Since a Buddhist monk doesn't own any possession apart from an alms bowl and robes, anything given to him rightly belongs to the whole community, and the only way to secure the continual use of something, such as a bucket, is to keep it in your quarters. Thus, communal property in Buddhist monasteries can paradoxically give rise to possessiveness. That is not to think that the meditation master is possessive over his bucket, for that is unthinkable for an arhat. But it can lead to some kind of misunderstanding regarding the respect Sumana should have for him. A little matter such as borrowing a senior monk's bathing bucket and not returning it can disrupt the very core of monastic harmony. Sumana doesn't want to do anything like that, especially on his first day. The leaky old bucket will just have to do.

Sumana follows the guide the short distance to the cistern. While the guide disappears behind some bushes to change his clothes, Sumana decides to get a better look at the cistern. It is rectangular, about twelve feet by six feet, made of rocks that appear to be cemented together to become watertight. The bathing area is also made of rocks cemented together, laid into the cement as they were found. Some are sharp, others round and bumpy, and yet others are soft and slippery when wet. Sumana feels unsteady as he kneels in the bathing area looking down into the cistern, which is filled with algae, leaves, and other organic debris. The guide reappears and sets the bucket down on the rocks near Sumana. Sumana looks up at him and notices that he is wearing only a pair of bathing trunks. Sumana turns his head away and walks over to a stone bench where he takes off his outer robe and sets it down. Monks do not where shirts under their outer robes, so when they take them off, they are naked from the waist up; while from the waist down they are clothed in an under-robe, which, on Sumana, hangs down to his ankles like a stiff cotton skirt.

As Sumana approaches the cistern, glancing a few times at the guide's body, he begins to feel sexually uncomfortable, though he would have a hard time putting that feeling into words. His discomfort arises predominantly as images, not of the thin dark smooth body of the guide, but of memories of being on a beach and seeing women in bikinis, their tanning bodies glistening with lotion in the sunlight. He sees one woman after another, three in all, until a stone stabs him in the arch of his foot, the pain breaking him free from the fascination of those images with an "ouch!"

The guide looks over at him and chuckles to himself before dumping a bucket of water over his head. The splash that follows is nothing like the splashes made by the master's bucket. There is barely any water on the ground. Upon watching the guide, Sumana realizes that this is not going to be an easy and quick bath, but that it is going to require twice as much bending and lifting than it would with an intact bucket. He decides not to use soap this time. That would cut down the number of bucketfuls to less than three, which is all he feels up to today. He is exhausted from the journey through the jungle and the strain of meeting the meditation master. What he needs right now is a nice warm shower, not this kind of strenuous outdoor bathing.

While the guide applies soap all over his body, Sumana takes the bucket from him and lowers it down into the water. Sumana holds the bucket by its rim with one hand and pushes away some leaves floating on the water's surface with the other, scooping up some clean water and then bringing the bucket up to set it down on the ground. It begins to leak from several places, so he jumps to his feet, reaches down for the bucket and lifts it over his head, releasing a nice gush of cold, sweet water that blissfully flows down his face and caresses his body. He shakes his head and wipes his face with both hands, opening his eyes. His body has cooled down and his mind has dropped some of the weight it has been carrying. He is able to get in two more bucketfuls before the guide asks him for the bucket back. Sumana gladly gives the guide the bucket as he walks over to the bench where his robe is and sits down.

For the first time on this journey to the meditation master, Sumana is truly relaxed. The turmoil within has cooled and he feels refreshed. When he puts on his outer robe, he believes himself worthy of being the meditation master's student. The only fear he has now is whether he can prove his worthiness to the master.

CHAPTER
4

On one side of the dining hut, which is an open-air hut with a thatched roof, there is a bench with a spittoon at both ends. On the other side is a wooden dining room table with large plastic bowls containing overcooked potatoes and onions, red rice, gotu kola leaves, chickpeas cooked into a dull yellow mash, and some kind of peppered fish cut into cubes. The two monks, Sumana and Aggachitta, sit on the bench, while the guide and the two young men pick up one bowl each and proceed to place spoonfuls of food into the large black metal alms bowls resting on the laps of the two monks. The monks' bowls slowly fill with food until, without any ritual, Aggachitta begins eating with Sumana soon following his lead.

Sumana is a slow eater. In his five years in Sri Lanka, he has never adopted the habit of eating like a Sinhalese monk. Few foreigners ever do. Aggachitta, though he is reputed to be an arhat, and therefore in Sumana's opinion should be always mindful, eats his food at break-neck speed. Sumana, on the other hand, slowly mixes up all of his food in his bowl with his right hand, for he believes that a true forest monk should follow the custom of combining all the food in his bowl as a way not to become attached to any one particular flavor. When it is all thoroughly blended into one large unappetizing mound, Sumana self-consciously begins eating, hoping that Aggachitta will notice how austere and mindful he is. Aggachitta ignores Sumana and is just about finished eating when Sumana finally takes his first bite.

Immediately upon finishing eating, Aggachitta silently excuses himself to take his afternoon nap. The custom amongst Buddhist monks is that the moment the senior-most monk stops eating all the other monks have to stop. Sumana, therefore, must stop eating even though he has only eaten one-quarter of the food in his bowl. This is not a rigid rule in all monasteries, but it is observed scrupulously by ardent bhikkhus such as Sumana. Sumana is not as bothered by this abrupt ending of the last meal of the day as he would normally be. He is tired from the long journey and welcomes a nap. He holds his hands over the spittoon to his right, waiting for one of the laymen to bring over a pitcher of water. The guide comes to him and pours water over his hands, rinsing them of all remaining food. Sumana then wipes his hands with his orange handkerchief and gets up from the bench, leaving the dining hut for his own. Upon arriving in his hut, he lies down on the fiber mattress and swiftly goes to sleep.

The meditation master and his student both nap for over an hour, with Sumana waking first. He does not know what he should be doing, so he gets up, puts on his outer robe and makes his way back to the dining hut.

He finds the dining hut cleaned and empty, except for a few goods neatly piled on the table: five exercise books, some pens and pencils, a new flashlight with three sets of batteries for it, about twenty bars of soap, one brand new outer robe, two new under-robes, about ten boxes of candles, five boxes of matches, ten mosquito repelling coils, and a tin of quality estate grown tea. They could not leave the monks any food, since bhikkhus are not allowed to store food for future meals, but tea is all right. Sumana decides he will make a pot of tea, so he goes over to the kerosene stove, lights it, and places a pot of water on it. He squats by the stove as he waits for the water to boil.

Aggachitta wanders over to the dining hut after his nap, finding the new monk near the stove, boiling water for tea. He is pleased to see that Sumana has discovered one of his new responsibilities without having to be told. He now hopes that the other responsibilities will similarly be discovered, for he dislikes "running" the hermitage, even though most of the time he is the only monk here. In many respects he prefers being alone. Seeing this new monk here, who is now under his tutelage, makes him somewhat uncomfortable. An obligation to teach, to administer, to guide, to herd, to please, to comfort and bolster, and then also to serve as a model, all amount to one great responsibility he will have to carry around once more. He groans internally under the remembered weight of past students.

"When you have made us tea," Aggachitta says, "we should talk."

Sumana looks over his shoulder at Aggachitta standing next to him and nods his head. The water boils and Sumana searches frantically for a cloth to grab the hot pot handle. Not finding one, he uses the bottom of his robe. He limps over to the table, for his robe is now wrapped closely around his legs, and sets the pot down carefully. Then he looks around for a teapot to put the tea and water in, and once again not finding one, he decides to put the tea into the hot water, even though that will most likely stain the pot.

Aggachitta watches all this wondering what Sumana could be looking for, since he always uses a handkerchief, or a part of his robe — though never the bottom hem — to grab the pot handle, and he always measures the tea leaves into the pot of water. It thus surprises him that Sumana is new to making tea. Aggachitta wonders, "How much experience living in the world does this young man have? Was he brought up in a wealthy house with servants?"

Aggachitta has taught three students from Western countries before. The first was a young man who fancied himself a poet with a mystical bent, and soon found Aggachitta's style of teaching too dry, leaving him, and Sri Lanka, to become a Tibetan Buddhist in India. The next was an abstract painter before becoming a bhikkhu. His mind was very scattered and he had a hard time meditating. In the end, he realized that he had to paint, for it gave true meaning to his life, and so left the jungle for a monastery in the hill country where he could have a studio. Aggachitta has heard that this monk's paintings have been on exhibit in Colombo, and that he has shifted from abstract painting to representational expressionism because of his time spent under the meditation master's guidance. The third foreign bhikkhu was a student of Sanskrit and Indian philosophy before he became a monk. Aggachitta delighted in the intellectual discussions they would have and soon forgot that the monk had come to learn meditation, leaving him much to his own devices, which later turned out not to be such a good idea. For this monk, though in Buddhist robes, was deep down a believer in Vedanta. Aggachitta realized that this Western monk was an incurable Vedantist only after about a month, when all he heard from him was talk of experiencing Oneness, merging with the Divine, and dwelling in the Eternal Present. Aggachitta felt he needed to correct this monk's erroneous views on the nature of reality, so their friendly philosophical talks turned into heated debates. Then one day the monk left without saying a word and was never heard from again. It is rumored that he left for India and has become a devotee of a famous Swami there.

Now here is another foreign monk, another unpredictable individual no Sinhalese, not even an accomplished meditation master, could truly understand. Ah hah! This is where the weight of responsibility comes from! Just at that moment, Sumana hands him a cup of tea.

"Sit down, young bhikkhu," Aggachitta says in a gentle tone of voice, motioning to the bare ground in front of him. Sumana looks at the spot where he is supposed to sit and then looks around for a cushion or a mat. He finds a small straw mat and brings it over to the spot, laying it down carefully. Then he goes to get his own cup of tea from the table. Finally, he sits down in front of Aggachitta, who has already finished his cup of tea.

"I would like to know more about you. Tell me, what sort of meditation instruction have you received?"

Sumana takes two sips of tea before setting his cup down, fumbling with it and upsetting the liquid as he tries to situate it on the uneven earth. When the teacup is finally balanced and steady, he answers his teacher.

"I have been instructed to observe my abdomen as I breathe in and out, and at the same time note each rising of the abdomen as 'rising, rising' and each falling as 'falling, falling.'"

"What about the other sense doors?" Aggachitta asks.

"I have been noting hearing as 'hearing, hearing,' seeing as 'seeing, seeing,' and thinking as 'thinking, thinking.'"

"Well then, what have you learned from practicing this particular technique?"

Sumana has to reflect a few moments before answering. He believes that the answer to this question is somehow very important, for his previous meditation teacher would ask him a similar question before giving him the next set of instructions.

He says, "I have learned that there is only rising and falling, which is the arising and passing away of each experience. That is the true nature of things."

Venerable Aggachitta suddenly feels great compassion for this young man. He can hear that Sumana's previous teacher coached the poor boy into viewing his meditation experiences all in the same way. Even if he has actually come to this "knowledge of impermanence" on his own, which the meditation master sincerely doubts, the language he uses to describe it surely comes from his previous teacher.

The meditation master speaks without any reservation, absolutely certain about the teaching he is about to give Sumana.

"You will have to start from the beginning. What you have done up until now has been of use, but it must be abandoned for you to go any further."

The meditation master decides to give him the most basic of meditation instructions.

"Just sit."

Sumana's mind is instantly flooded with questions: How should I sit? When and where should I sit? How long should I sit? What do I do when I *just sit*? Do I become aware of breathing, of sounds, of thoughts, of sensations?

Venerable Aggachitta can see the anxious confusion on his face. He lets it go on for a little while before interrupting Sumana's internal search for answers with what he thinks will answer all of his unspoken questions.

"By just sitting," the meditation master says, "I mean just that. Do nothing but sit when you sit in meditation. Then tell me what happens."

"That's it?" Sumana exclaims.

"That's it for now," the meditation master replies. "I'll see you tomorrow morning."

Aggachitta then gets up from the bench and walks out of the dining hut. On his way back to his hut, he hopes that the young monk figures out that another of his responsibilities is to wash the cups and scour the kettle.

CHAPTER
5

Sumana cleans the cups and the kettle and then goes to his hut to meditate. Before sitting down in meditation, he decides to make a meditation area in his room. He has become accustomed to sitting on a large, square cotton stuffed meditation mat called a "zabuton" in Zen circles, but there's none here. The two obvious alternatives are the coconut fiber mattress and the loosely stuffed cotton pillow. He doesn't want to meditate on his mattress, afraid that he might be tempted to lie down during meditation. Nor does he want to use his pillow, for he is repulsed by the idea of resting his face on something at night that he's been sitting on all day. There has to be a better solution.

What if he sat on his double robe? It is a completely useless article of clothing in this tropical climate. He's only worn it once while visiting a monastery in the central mountains. But the double robe is supposed to be a bhikkhu's most important possession after his alms bowl. There are specific monastic rules, observed continuously for centuries, regarding this special robe, though there aren't any that come to mind which prohibit its use as a meditation cushion. It is thick, heavy, sturdy — an awful burden to keep track of and carry everywhere he goes. It would make a perfect mat. When he has it folded to the right size, he lays it down on the ground opposite his bed, admiring the padded square fabric and his own ingenuity for a moment, before sitting down on it cross-legged.

Then he remembers that he needs to keep track of time in his meditation sittings, so he gets up and finds his wristwatch, placing it on the bed in plain view. He is now ready to begin a meditation sitting, and so resumes a cross-legged position. During the sitting, he occasionally opens his eyes to peek at the time. Usually only about ten minutes pass between peeks. Nothing of any interest is happening. His mind just goes on talking about the meditation master, going over details of the day, trying to figure out what the master might think of him. Then there are times when he thinks about himself, why he has chosen to become a monk, what he left behind and what he imagines to find in his future. It occurs to him towards the end of the sitting that by just sitting like this, he does a lot more thinking. Perhaps he's doing it incorrectly. But how can you mess up an instruction to just sit? The only way would be to try to do something other than just sit, such as recite a mantra, or stay with the breath, or any of the number of techniques he is familiar with. In fact, it is much harder to just sit.

The first hour of meditation ends and he gets up to walk around. It doesn't seem to him that he was just meditating, for there were no periods of feeling his mind settle down and become calm. But he does feel slightly different than he did before he sat down to meditate. He feels less driven, not so goal-oriented. It is subtle however, and he can't trust it. He still concludes that this kind of meditation doesn't seem to do anything — it is completely aimless!

When he sits down again for another hour of meditation, he continues this train of thought. Since this way of meditating has no goal, it is free of concepts about what it accomplishes. For if there are concepts about it, the master would have mentioned them, just as all his other teachers have done in the past. When he learned to note "rising, rising" and "falling, falling" as a way to observe his breath at the abdomen, his teacher informed him that each "rising" is an "arising" and each "falling" a "vanishing" of that arising, which confused him at first. But after a while he began to see things in exactly that way in each and every meditation sitting. And then he began to see it in everything: in eating, walking, bathing, and talking. The whole world was filled with risings and fallings, going on all the time. What a powerful experience! And it all came from following that one instruction, with that single concept embedded in it.

Now, though, here he is meditating with an instruction that contains no concepts. There's nothing for him to apply to everything in his world. He's just sitting, and begins to drift off. His previous teacher warned him repeatedly against drifting off in meditation. He hears his old teacher say, "It is not being mindful" three times. On the third time the words "not being" echo in his mind, rippling in waves of mind-sound, pulling him in and then throwing him back into his body, where he lands in an explosion of cool pleasurable sensations. His eyes open spontaneously, and he takes a calm look around his hut, his attention going from his bed to his bowl, and finally resting on his bag for a few moments before he closes his eyes again.

There are periods of just being aware of his body sitting. He knows this by feeling the contact of his rear against the mat. When his mind loses concentration on just sitting, it often rests in a yellow-orange light, which sometimes grows brighter, engulfing his mind, or dimmer, where it tends to break up into a multitude of dots of light set against a black background. No new images or words arise during these brief periods of being in the yellow-orange light. He feels tranquil and experiences his mind as being empty and settled. But when his attention stays on his body for longer than a couple of minutes, he begins to have more ordinary thoughts, ones about what will happen tomorrow and the next day. He notices a particular vibration behind these thoughts, but can't readily name it. "Anxiety" is too broad, and so is fear, though the vibrations could be emanating from such emotions. He sits with this barely discernible vibrating feeling for several seconds before it vanishes. Immediately after its vanishing, he finds his mind engulfed in the yellow-orange light again. He makes a connection between the vanishing of the emotional vibration and his experiences of mind engulfed by light. One leads to the other; the arising of the light occurs upon the ceasing of the feeling. He makes a mental note to ask the meditation master about this. Then he has a short fantasy of imagining telling this to Venerable Aggachitta and receiving some kind of praise for his insight. But that thought doesn't last long and he's once again aware of just sitting. He opens his eyes and looks at his watch. It takes him a few seconds to realize that over an hour has passed. He ends the sitting.

With a good sitting under his belt, Sumana decides to go for a walk around the hermitage. He wants to find the cave where Venerable Atakkachari attained nibbana. Perhaps he could meditate there. Some monks have told him that caves house a kind of spiritual energy, while others say caves protect one from negative thoughts and influences. His meditation is going well so far, and meditating in a cave can only improve his sittings. It may even be the key to the attainment of nibbana.

He doesn't have to walk much further than a quarter of a mile to reach the hill where the cave is. The hill rises only a couple hundred feet, and near the top of it he sees three large slabs that form a triangular opening. When he reaches it, he kneels on the bottom slab and sees a brown cloth ripped from a ragged monk's robe attached somehow to the top of the opening. He lifts it up with one hand and with the other holds a flashlight, shining the light inside. He can't smell any animals and sees no snakes or any other creatures. But what he does see takes him by surprise.

The cave has furniture in it. There are a couple of chairs, a nightstand, a bed, and a desk. In the far corner near the bed is a wooden chest. As Sumana walks around the interior of the cave, his back hunched due to the low ceiling, he surmises that the cave is used as the meditation master's study. He goes over to the chest and lifts its lid. Inside are books, some with hard covers but mostly paperbacks, many of which are yellowed and water-damaged. He kneels beside the chest of books, lifting one after another, illuminating the covers with his flashlight so that he can read the author's name and title. His mind leaps to the conviction that these books belong to the meditation master, and were part of his undergraduate studies in the liberal arts. A few books stand out, ones that he has never heard of, which may have been part of the meditation master's graduate studies.

Sumana looks around from where he kneels to see if there is another form of light in the cave, since surely there has to be if this is the master's private study. Over on the nightstand he notices a small kerosene lantern with a little oil left in it. Now all he needs is to find some matches. As he moves about the cave searching for matches, he hears someone approaching the entrance of the cave, and is transfixed by fear as to who that could be. The cloth at the entrance is lifted up, letting in the rays of the setting sun. Soon enough, the cloth curtain drops and a man enters the cave, shining a flashlight in Sumana's direction. Sumana's heart races as his body becomes even more rigid and still. He is certain the man is the meditation master.

The man turns the flashlight on his own face, illuminating it from below his chin. He is a thin young man of average height, with dark skin and short-cropped hair. His nose is narrow, and his eyes are set far apart, while his forehead is broad and flat. He approaches Sumana and kneels before the monk, as all devout Buddhist lay people do in Sri Lanka, with knees and elbows on the ground, and palms pressed together in a salutation. Sumana turns around and stands up as much as he can, facing the young man. After the young man finishes, Sumana asks him who he is. He says he is the temple boy, and then he points to the other side of the cave, to the left of the entrance, where there is a freestanding wooden cabinet. It is here that certain food offerings are stored. Now Sumana understands.

This cave is not officially part of the hermitage that is reserved only for bhikkhus. Thus, a layman can live in it and store food for the bhikkhus. This thought comforts Sumana, for he has never lived in a monastery without such an arrangement, which is absolutely necessary in times of illness and scarcity.

Unexpectedly Sumana imagines that the meditation master might walk in on them; for all he knows, this is the master's study, and he could be here any minute. For some unknown reason, he dreads the meditation master seeing him in the cave. This makes him anxious to leave. He slowly makes his way out, leaving the young man baffled by his sudden, silent departure.

Sumana begins to feel a sense of relief once he is sufficiently down the hill for it to appear to any onlooker that he is just out for a stroll on the hermitage grounds. Taking a meandering path back to his hut, Sumana reviews the events of the day. It has been an extremely full day. Things have turned out all right. That has been his way of summarizing events. He does not bother to look much deeper. Instead, he decides, as the sunset fades into twilight, that once he is back inside his hut, he will retire for the night. He promises himself that he will wake up before dawn and begin the new day with a long meditation sitting. And so, upon entering his hut, he plops down on the fiber mattress, which pricks him a little, but not enough to rouse him from the clutches of ensuing sleep.

CHAPTER
6

Sumana sleeps deeply, softly, peacefully throughout the night. When he awakes at dawn, he feels refreshed. The jungle is quiet at first. He is just getting seated on his double robe, adjusting his posture and placing one hand on top of the other in his lap, when the cries of birds — hundreds of birds, singing at the first light of day — break through the quiet of his mind. He is irritated by how loud the birds are, how shrill some of them sound, and wishes that the volume could be turned down. When he closes his eyes and tries to put his attention on just sitting, the discordant bird sounds seem amplified, and he feels goaded to jump up and stamp out the door to yell at those inconsiderate birds to shut the hell up!

He suppresses that impulse, not by soothing himself with words, but by tensing his body and forcing himself to stay rooted in his meditation posture. He then tries to locate where the different bird sounds are coming from. Some of the birds are near his hut, chirping furiously above his right ear. Then there are whistling bird sounds that seem to fill the whole sky above the roof of his hut. Soon he has pinpointed the direction and approximate distances of many of the birds. In the course of making this mental map of the various sounds, he feels the tension in his body begin to lessen. His anger at the birds also dies down. His body relaxes even more. His trunk caves in a bit and his arms make a wider circle in front of him. His breathing slows down. Sleepiness returns. The volume of the birds is reduced further and further into dead silence as his mind turns inward.

At first he is caught off-guard by the onset of sleepiness, as he was feeling well rested when he began the sitting. Maybe it is not sleepiness. But it certainly feels like it. His head droops and his body leans forward even more. It feels as if his body will tip over any minute. Then he has a giddy sensation of falling forward, but his body does not move. It is as though he falls forward through his body for a second and then is snapped back into it. This startles him fully awake. He is determined to sit up straight so as not to have it happen again. A minute or so later, the drowsiness returns, his body is hunched over again and he can feel himself once again falling forward. But this time he does not fall through his body. He just vanishes for a second and then abruptly returns to awareness. He opens his eyes. The light is bluish and it is hard to make out the forms of things around him. He does not feel tired anymore. He straightens up and, shutting his eyes, makes an even stronger determination not to let his mind drop off in this strange way again. He places his attention on the sound of the birds outside, even though the external noise has quieted down considerably. He soon finds his mind getting drowsy again. Within a few seconds, his chin is resting on his chest. A gurgling sound, coming from his own throat, enters into his awareness, and he wonders how long he has been asleep. He scolds himself for not being able to stay awake. Then, without a clear intention to do so, he gets up and makes his way outdoors. Only then does it occur to him that a cup of tea might help him stay awake.

The jungle is truly beautiful and mysterious in the early morning twilight. He doesn't know the names of the tropical trees and plants, but they all seem thick and full, which arouses a sense of awe and appreciation of his surroundings. The world he walks through is a primeval garden, no different from the jungles of the Buddha's time. The same plants, the same birds, the same snakes, insects, and mammals seen by the bhikkhus of olden times are right here with him. It is barely light enough to see if a snake were in his path. This thought sends a burst of fear right through him. He stops in his tracks, anxiously scanning the ground in front of him. He sees no snakes, but he feels the fear of snakes hover between his chest and thighs. As he walks towards the dining hut, the sensation of fear stays around his belly, and so he puts his attention there as a way to keep it from spreading to other parts of his body.

As he approaches the dining hut, he notices a light coming from it. The hut seems flimsy and insubstantial next to the hardy jungle foliage. It has no walls, just pillars, one at each corner, made out of logs cemented in the ground, supporting a thatched roof.

The light is coming from a kerosene lantern. Near the lantern, Sumana can see the temple boy squatting in front of the kerosene stove. He is boiling water in the kettle. As Sumana enters the dining hut, the temple boy looks up at him with a smile, greeting him with hands clasped together in reverence, which lasts for a moment before he brings his attention back to the kettle.

Sumana watches him make tea as if in a daze. Next to the stove is a cup containing white powder and water, which the boy picks up and stirs with a spoon. Squatting near the stove, he opens the tin of tea and reaches inside it with his free hand, pulling out a large clump of tealeaves. He puts the tea in the pot of water, which just now begins to boil. He opens an old cocoa tin and, using the same spoon, adds a spoonful of sugar to the kettle. He adds a few more teaspoons of sugar, turns the stove off, and only then pours the cup of milk into it. He lets it sit as he gets up and goes over to the table where some teacups and saucers are.

The temple boy brings Sumana a cup of tea, silently offering it to him, holding the cup in both hands with its handle facing Sumana. Still in a daze, he wraps his index finger around the porcelain handle as the boy lets go. The cup dangles in his hand, almost spilling over until Sumana tightens his grip. He is about to lift the teacup to his lips when he recalls the rule against monks eating or drinking while standing up. He catches himself in time and carries the tea over to the bench reserved for monks. He sits down, setting his tea on the bench next to him. The temple boy pulls up a mat and sits down on the ground in front of him, just as he did the day before with the meditation master.

He takes his first sip of tea and relishes the pleasant taste. He enjoys milk tea more than any other Sri Lankan beverage, especially in the morning, when the air is still cool enough to make drinking a hot beverage pleasurable. He so relishes the flavor and sensations created by sipping tea that he hopes to be left alone in silence. But that is not going to happen.

The temple boy introduces himself, speaking in good English without much of an accent.

"Yesterday we met only briefly. My name is Rahula." He looks to Sumana for some sort of reciprocal reply, such as, "Hello, my name is Sumana. I am pleased to meet you." But no such reply comes his way.

Rahula adds, "Venerable Aggachitta is my teacher too."

This wakes Sumana up a bit. He looks more closely at the young man seated on the ground. He sees a healthy, handsome, though somewhat awkward eighteen-year old. Rahula's eyes are bright, creating the impression of him being an aware and intelligent individual. When Sumana focuses on Rahula's smile, he senses the young man's friendliness and concern for others. Sumana then returns his attention to his cup of tea, taking the last few remaining gulps. He hopes that the temple boy will refill his cup without being coaxed, but instead he continues with his story.

"I was supposed to attend university this year, but the civil war has made the colleges dangerous. That's why I'm here. Venerable Aggachitta is teaching me about the monk's life while at the same time tutoring me in various subjects. Would you like to discuss the Buddha's teaching?"

Sumana knows all too well that a young man like this would have a considerable advantage over him when it comes to discussing the Buddha's teaching. Not only can a Sri Lankan with a complete high school education read the Pali Canon in Sinhalese and English, but he would also be familiar with many Pali words and phrases from having memorized suttas in his childhood. This young man has all the background to delve deeper into the Buddha's teaching. But for some reason that seldom happens among the Sinhalese. Sumana has heard from foreign monks who have lived here much longer than he has that few Sinhalese monks ever question the Buddha's teaching deeply or make their own inquiries into what the Buddha actually meant.

The meditation master doesn't seem to be that kind of Sinhalese monk. Perhaps his other student is also different. Sumana is becoming a little curious about the temple boy, whose name he can't seem to remember, though his main focus is on whether the young man will notice that his teacup is empty and in need of a refill.

"What do you think?" Rahula asks after the long period of silence.

"Is there any more tea?" Sumana asks, not fully conscious of what he is doing.

"Let me get you some," Rahula says, happy to be of service, uplifted by being given this new monk's undivided attention for a moment.

With his second cup of tea in his hands, Sumana feels at ease. Now he can concentrate on what the young man was saying. It had something to do with discussing the Buddha's teaching, but it is too early in the morning for Sumana to strain his mind on what little he actually knows of the Buddha's teaching. Perhaps asking the young man a few personal questions will do instead.

"When are you going to become a monk?"

Rahula replies, "I don't know yet. My family may someday need me to earn money for their survival."

"What does your father do?"

"He's a schoolteacher and may be a headmaster one day. My mother teaches at a finishing school for girls."

"Surely your parents will have a pension and be able to take care of themselves."

"I hadn't looked at it that way." Rahula replies.

"Then what's stopping you?"

Rahula blushes. Sumana guesses that it has to do with a woman. That's the main reason why men don't become monks: they're in love with a woman. At least that is what most of his fellow bhikkhus have led him to believe.

Rahula looks away, and then back up at Sumana. He feels uneasy about trusting this monk with his secret. He's not even told the meditation master about his girlfriend in Colombo. There's a good reason for that. He's not sure if the meditation master will tell his parents if he confides in him. For the meditation master is his father's older brother and would feel obligated to pass on such information.

Rahula takes Sumana's teacup with some tea still left in it, and then goes outside the hut to wash it along with his cup. Sumana is finally left alone, but without the company of Rahula, or even his cherished cup of milk tea, it feels more like being deserted than just being alone.

CHAPTER
7

Sumana is about to leave the dining hut when the meditation master appears. The meditation master is not surprised to see Sumana here, as all the foreign monks have been early risers, coming to the morning dana at the crack of dawn, when bhikkhus are once again allowed to eat food. Between dawn and noon, a bhikkhu can eat as much and as often as he likes. Some bhikkhus eat three or four meals within the allowed time, while others just eat once. Aggachitta prefers to eat twice, for then he can eat less at the second meal. Sumana also prefers to eat twice before noon, but if he could, he would also like an evening snack, for usually he goes to bed early as a way to take his mind off how hungry he is.

Aggachitta sits down on the bench next to Sumana. He does not say hello. Monks often do not greet each other when they meet for meals, and this is not taken as a sign of disrespect or of harboring ill will, but as respecting the ideal of a true bhikkhu who is perfectly silent and aloof as he waits patiently for dana. Rahula brings Aggachitta a cup of milk tea and a saucer. Aggachitta takes the cup and saucer and pours some of the tea out of the cup and onto the saucer. He then drinks the tea by placing the saucer up to his lips and tilting it so that the liquid flows downward into his mouth. He does this several times in complete silence. Sumana glances at him a couple of times, and marvels at how Aggachitta can drink tea this way without spilling any on his robes.

When Aggachitta finishes his morning tea, he turns around to face Sumana and asks him, "Did you sleep well?"

Sumana replies, "Yes, Bhante."

That is the extent of their conversation. During this kind of waiting, they are not supposed to meditate, chat, read, or fidget; in short, they are not to do anything except sit in complete silence. Sumana always finds waiting for dana to be excruciating. Sometimes, like today, he can sit with his impatience and look at it with compassion, though it hurts to do so. His body seems to tighten, and he wants to move his limbs or shout at the temple boy to hurry up. Then he slips into a brief period of sadness about the state of turmoil he was just in and gently reassures himself that food is indeed coming.

But Venerable Aggachitta has no difficulty waiting for anything. He also doesn't meditate during such times, for he doesn't want to enter into a deep state of consciousness only to be pulled out of it when presented with some unappetizing dish. Too often, it has happened that he lost his appetite from having meditated before eating, so he has become accustomed to putting his attention on other things. He actually has a great deal to think about with this new foreign monk here. He goes through a series of plans for the day, such as when to talk to Sumana about his meditation sittings, when to discuss with Rahula his plans and studies, and when to shave, bathe, wash his robes, and sweep the leaves around his hut. He sees the day before him on a checkerboard, with pieces placed in a row on the diagonal, everything he has to do put in a perfect line, and then his mind picks up one piece after another, clearing the board. Thus, he knows he can accomplish each thing today within the allotted time, for there are also the hours of meditation, the main meal just before noon, and the afternoon nap, the three mainstays of his life. Right at this moment, a disdain forms for the other work he has to do. He would rather meditate for the rest of the day. A familiar inner tension arises around this conflict. His natural tendency towards inwardness rebels against having to do things in the world. The active life and the meditative life have never really gotten along well in Aggachitta's psyche, and this tension produces a profound resistance to the work and responsibility of running the hermitage. He notices a longing arise within him, a fantasy about having the way of life of Venerable Atakkachari, the hermitage's founder, completely free from all this planning, managing, and teaching.

With a hint of shame, he considers why he is here waiting for the morning meal in the first place. He only needs to eat once a day. But that single meal often leads to indigestion and heartburn from having eaten too much at one sitting. Still, he could be using this time to meditate instead of waiting around for some typical oily, starchy breakfast.

Finally, Rahula has finished preparing the morning meal of leftover red rice drenched in a coconut oil sauce with some chunks of potato in it. Along with the main course, each bhikkhu gets a banana and half of a small papaya. Rahula carefully lays the food out on two large metal plates, with inch-high rims that keep the coconut sauce from overflowing onto the bhikkhus' robes. He first serves Venerable Aggachitta and then goes back to the table to get Sumana's plate. Both bhikkhus eat with their plates on their laps, holding them steady with their left hands as they mix the rice and potatoes into a mush with their right hands. Venerable Aggachitta eats slower this time, while Sumana eats faster, propelled by hunger. They both finish at about the same time. Rahula then takes their plates, which are both wiped clean of food, having only a banana peel and an empty papaya skin on each. Rahula brings over a pitcher of water and the bhikkhus move their respective spittoons from the side of the bench to directly in front of them. First Aggachitta, and then Sumana, hold out both hands over a spittoon as Rahula pours water over them from the pitcher. They dry their hands on handkerchiefs they have with them, wiping off their lips before putting the handkerchiefs away. Venerable Aggachitta now rises and leaves the dining hut without saying a word. Sumana does the same a moment later. Here is another morning meal under the belt, executed perfectly by two bhikkhus and their attendant, all of whom share the same ideals. Each day, from now on, there should be no deviating from this routine, unless, of course, something unexpected happens.

CHAPTER
8

Sumana goes to his hut to fetch the old bucket, into which he puts a towel, a bar of soap, his toothbrush and a small container of tooth powder. He feels incredibly mindful after breakfast. To him mindfulness is being totally absorbed in the present moment, where each and every little thing is known and observed in the three phases of arising, persisting, and passing away. All around him, the sights and sounds of the jungle do this cosmic dance of arising, persisting, and passing away. Not only that, but also every sense impression seems to last only a second before vanishing.

He feels each sharp pebble stab his feet as he walks barefoot along the dirt path to the outhouse, which is located not far from the cistern. He hears fewer sounds than earlier in the morning, but sees more birds sitting in tree branches or flying by in front of him. Mosquitoes hover around his exposed arms, right shoulder, face, and feet, and when one lands and sinks its proboscis into his skin, he imagines he can feel it suck out his blood, for he sees this picture vividly in his mind whenever a mosquito buzzes nearby. But he is only conscious of all the new bites when comfortably squatting in the outhouse.

Sumana has become accustomed to using Asian toilets, crossing over culturally to prefer them to their Western counterparts. This one is not as primitive as he anticipated for it being out in the jungle. There is a cement base with raised cement pads on both sides of the hole for his feet to grip as he squats. Just in reach of his right hand is an old, bent round cocoa tin with water in it. Everything he needs is right there. He is able to relax, balancing himself on the balls of his feet, but after a few minutes, just before he's finished, he gets a slight cramp in his calves and his legs begin to shake all the way down to his ankles. This frightens him a little, as if he were going to collapse right there in the outhouse and not be able to get up. This fear prompts him to hurry up and finish. He cleans himself with water from the cocoa tin, and then, in agony, rises and grabs hold of the door. He pulls himself upright, moves his legs, and then opens the door. The idea comes to him to bring a bucketful of water to clean the latrine more thoroughly, so the next person using it would not encounter any offensive odors.

Sumana ambles over to the cistern, which is not more than fifty yards from the outhouse. When he gets there, he immediately begins washing his hands. With his hands washed and dried, he then brushes his teeth. He takes his time brushing his teeth, making sure he gets into the gums and behind each tooth. One thing that he wants to avoid is getting dental work done while in Sri Lanka. The most common treatment for anything more than a surface cavity is extraction, and he would like to keep all his teeth until his deathbed if he could. After he finishes working on his teeth, he remembers to fill the bucket to bring it to the outhouse. Since the bucket leaks, his plan is to run with it all the way to the outhouse, quickly pull open the door, and fling the water down the hole.

So he fills the bucket and tries to hold it in such a way as to plug as many leaks as he can. Then he runs with it, like a running back dodging would-be tacklers to make a mad dash to the goal line. He reaches the outhouse door out of breath, but with three-quarters of the bucketful of water still intact. He quickly yanks open the door, and throws the water with great force at where he remembers the hole to be. He is suddenly thrown back by an ear-piercing yell.

Sumana freezes. He shuts the door and walks back to the cistern in a daze. He wonders who it can be. Quickly — or rather conveniently — ruling out the meditation master, for he can't imagine that an arhat would yell like that. It has to be Rahula, or some villager who has just arrived. Still, that does not put him at ease. For what if the meditation master finds out about it and concludes that Sumana is not mindful enough to be his student. This thought makes Sumana extremely anxious. He feels the urge to flee the scene, especially before the person in the outhouse comes out, for perhaps he won't be recognized and this whole thing can be a mystery, since he needn't say anything about it. It isn't an offense a bhikkhu would have to confess.

He goes back to the cistern and collects all of his toiletries, stuffing everything into his bucket, and takes a longer path through the dense brush to his hut, one that he believes he won't be spotted by anyone.

Aggachitta returns directly to his hut after breakfast. He has a washbasin and a mirror in his hut, as well as a gallon water dispenser. He takes out his barber's razor and a sharpening stone and proceeds to hone the edge of his blade. He slaps the blade a few times across a piece of leather stretched out for that purpose. He mixes up some shaving lather in a shaving cup with a brush and then lavishly applies it all over his head. Looking into the mirror, he begins by shaving the right side of his head, then the left side, and then the top. Then there is the tricky part of shaving the back of his head. Some monks shy away from doing this altogether, usually asking one of their fellow monks to shave it for them, but Aggachitta has lived alone for twenty-five years, and so has figured out a way to do this without leaving any hair uncut and without cutting into his scalp. He simply uses a second mirror, holding it with his left hand behind his head. While looking at the reflection of the back of his head in the mirror in front of him, he carefully moves the blade with his right hand, scraping off all the stubble from the crown of his head to the back of his neck.

With his head fully cleansed of hair, shiny and smooth, Aggachitta takes his new metal bucket, a towel, a bar of soap, and a stick that is used as a toothbrush. On his way to the cistern, he becomes aware of the need to relieve himself. He finds the outhouse empty, and after positioning himself over the hole, he notices that the tin of water used to wash oneself afterwards is empty as well. He surmises that the foreign monk was there before him, for his nephew, Rahula, would never leave the tin empty. This bothers him more and more as he squats, for he wishes he had checked the tin when he could have gone and filled it. He is just getting started when he hears the door of the outhouse open. He is ready to say something to the intruder like "Just a minute," but before he can get the words out, with his mouth wide open, a gush of cold water streams all over him. Shocked by this, he yells. It is an involuntary yell. But he does notice that as the water saturates his robes and drips down his face, his mind seethes with some kind of unfriendly — if not downright hostile — feeling, which brings up thoughts of getting up and rushing out to accost whoever has done this to him.

Then, all of a sudden, he begins to laugh, just as uncontrollably as the yell before it. It is not compassion that eliminates all negative feeling in his mind for the person who has done this to him, but laughter at what an absurd and ridiculous thing it is, as though it happened to someone other than himself. He does not feel defiled, no, he has been cleansed. And he laughs out loud at that play of words.

When he finishes he is once again aware that someone has not refilled the water tin in the outhouse. He resolves that he must mention this in some way as to not give away that it was he who was in the outhouse when someone, his new student most likely, threw water into it to clean it. For it would be too shameful to admit to a junior monk, one's new student no less, that one was made a fool of in such a way. It's not dignified to acknowledge that such things happen to one's self. But for it to happen to someone else, well, then it's all right to laugh at that poor fool. And Aggachitta chuckles some more as he leaves the outhouse with his bucket in hand, mumbling to himself, "that poor fool," over and over again, replaying in his mind the picture of some other monk squatting in the outhouse and being surprised by a bucket of water thrown in his face.

CHAPTER
9

By the time Sumana finally reaches his hut he's in a full blown panic. He fears that if the meditation master finds out about this, he will be expelled from the hermitage, possibly even from the monastic order.

Sumana feels he needs guidance now more than ever, but there's no one to ask for help. He's just going to have to sit with his anxiety. So he brushes off his double robe and flattens it on the ground in his hut and sits down on it. He begins by trying to hold himself still. That only increases his already high level of tension and tightens his muscles even more. He tells himself to relax repeatedly, and then begins telling himself that everything is going to turn out all right. That works somewhat, as his breathing slows down and he experiences freedom from shame about what he did for several seconds at a stretch, though this has almost no effect on the fear and anxiety he's feeling. Then he places his attention on the fear in his chest, which soon intensifies and becomes unbearable. He wants to get up and move about. In a flash, he's pacing about his hut.

He only has enough space to walk four paces in one direction, then turn around, and go in the other direction. This proves too constraining for him. After only a few minutes, he goes outside and starts pacing in front of his hut. That feels better. The air is still cool, though the sun is beginning to shine through from above the trees, and there are just enough distractions for him not to get completely absorbed in his thoughts. He walks at a vigorous clip, going about twenty paces in one direction before turning around and doing the same in the opposite direction.

As he walks, he becomes acutely aware of how his panic is shifting into pulses of fear, each one reverberating for a couple of seconds, dying out for a fraction of a second, and then returning. These pulses would normally be experienced as a continuous wave of fear if not looked at minutely, as he is now able to do. The more he observes this pattern, the longer the gap between the ending of one pulsation of fear and the arising of the next one. He stops and stands still for a few moments to concentrate on the next pulsation of fear. As he does this, he notices a mental shell form around it. Focusing on the shell covering each pulsation of fear drains it of fear. His walking slows down of its own accord and he is easily able to keep his attention on the soles of his feet for several minutes at a time. Only occasionally does he recall the incident at the outhouse. Moreover, when he does, it doesn't trouble him in the least. He's completely absorbed on each movement of his feet to the exclusion of everything else. One could say that he's deep in meditation.

Aggachitta has bathed, dried himself off, and dropped off his towel and bucket in his hut before going up to the cave. He usually meets his nephew, Rahula, around this time of day. The young man is in a state of confusion about his life and needs to come to a decision about it. Aggachitta would like to see the young man choose the bhikkhu's life, though he knows that his brother and sister-in-law would be devastated if he did. Rahula is their only son; and besides that, he is their brightest and most gifted child. They also have three girls who are younger than Rahula. Though they are pretty, full of spirit and growing up with a solid English education, they're not exceptional students. Rahula, on the other hand, has always been a good student, and could someday be an engineer, a doctor, or a barrister if he were so motivated.

Aggachitta fondly thinks about how his nephew has inherited his intelligence. Perhaps Rahula would take up

Buddhist scholarship, for that is also a very well respected profession. Maybe that is the middle way through this: Rahula should not be encouraged to become a monk but a university scholar. Aggachitta thinks of his own life in this respect and feels joy at the prospect of his nephew living the life he left behind.

Rahula is in the cave waiting for him when he arrives. Aggachitta sits in a chair, while Rahula sits in front of him on the ground. They look at each other for a moment, smiling and grinning back and forth several times.

"So," Aggachitta asks, "where are you today in your thoughts about life?"

Rahula pauses a moment and replies, "I am more inclined towards becoming a bhikkhu than anything else right now."

Aggachitta knows he has to be careful here, so he says, "That is how it looks to you today. What has it been? Six weeks here? Of course, you want to become a bhikkhu. You have seen how good we have it."

Aggachitta chuckles and Rahula smiles and allows a soft, short laugh.

"Now," Aggachitta continues, "I think we should begin with a serious study of literature. I want you to read one book as carefully as you can and write a ten page paper on it." This kind of assignment reminds Aggachitta of his teaching days, before he left the University for Burma, when he taught philosophy to a class of freshman.

"What do you suggest I read?" Rahula asks.

"Anything," Aggachitta replies. "Just hunt around in that chest of books over there and find something that interests you. It's all university-level reading material in that chest."

"All right, uncle."

"Good then, we'll continue this dialog about your life at a later time. Ordaining is a big step, one that should not be entered upon and then abandoned. Besides, you have time. Make good use of it."

They smile at each other and then Aggachitta gets up and exits the cave. Rahula waits for him to leave before going over to the trunk. He rummages around in it, pulling out four books he has had his eye on for some time. He doesn't know which one he wants to read and wishes he had pulled them out sooner and gotten his uncle's opinion. He only wants to act in a way that would please his uncle, and thus please his parents.

But then, what of the girl he was secretly meeting in the library after school, the one who daily receives his carefully drafted letters? He suddenly feels an apprehension that his parents have found out about her and that is why they have sent him here. But that is not the case. His parents wanted him out of Colombo because they feared the civil unrest would get worse. They didn't tell him this directly, though he overheard them discussing their fears for his safety on a couple of occasions. Never did he hear them suspect he had a secret girlfriend, but now it occurs to him that they might have suspected something of that sort.

Then again, this retreat in the jungle is a place for him to be with men, in an ancient brotherhood, where many a boy before him has made the transition to manhood. If he can find meaning and value in this way of life, he too might someday become one of them. On the other hand, he can go to college and fulfill his parents' expectations for him. It is really a very tough decision to make. And his uncle's way of dealing with it is to have him write a book report. He smiles at this realization.

CHAPTER
10

After Sumana thinks he's finished an hour of walking meditation, he goes inside his hut to sit in meditation. This time it is easy for him to meditate. He quickly becomes tranquil and in no time falls asleep. There's no question in his mind that it's indeed sleep, for he's awakened by his own snoring. He gets up from the ground, looks at the watch near his bed and sees that it's almost ten o'clock. Dana is usually served at eleven, or, at the latest eleven-thirty. He has only an hour before eating, which is just enough time to bathe and get ready.

This time bathing is easy. He's the only one using the old bucket and it works just fine once he gets into the flow of dunking it, lifting it, dumping it. He's able to get a good lather of soap on his body, rinsing it off before it dries and forms a hard film. Everything goes so smoothly that he finds himself back at his hut at ten-thirty with nothing else to do. Instead of meditating, for he has done enough for one morning in his opinion, he decides to go to the cave and see if he can get some supplies. On the way to the cave, he makes a list in his mind: insect repellent, mosquito coils, a mosquito net, some tissues, a mirror, another bucket or a basin that does not leak, a water container, and a water filter.

When he gets to the entrance of the cave, he shouts, "Anyone inside!"

Rahula hears him and yells back that Sumana is welcome to come in. Sumana steps into the cave to find Rahula next to the chest of books, with four books on the ground in front of him.

"Will you help me decide?" Rahula asks.

Sumana kneels down close to the books and looks them over. But before he gets too involved in this, he wants to collect all of his supplies. Otherwise, he may forget something important. So he rises and walks over to the closet, and begins rummaging around inside of it. Rahula isn't sure what to make of his behavior.

Sumana pulls one thing after another out of the closet, making a pile on the ground. He has all the things on his list except for the water filter, the new bucket, and the water dispenser. Perhaps he should ask Rahula where the missing things are kept. But when he looks over at Rahula to ask him, the young man is pouting. Sumana wonders what he could have done to upset him, but instead of asking him that, Sumana once again approaches the books and kneels down to look at them.

They are mostly paperback books, published in England or America a couple of decades ago. He recognizes one book he has read and another he saw the movie of. The book he read is *The Stranger* by Camus. He thought it was a sick, depraved story. He doesn't like stories where people are murdered. The other book he is familiar with is *The Woman in the Dunes*. He remembers seeing the movie on a date with a female film student he went out with briefly. She recommended the film and raved about it to him. When he saw it, it made almost no sense whatsoever. All he really can recall from it are scenes of moving, flowing sand and the occasional beetle. The woman and the man in the story were not the least bit memorable.

Of the two books completely new to him, one immediately catches his attention. It is called *Hunger*. The title in itself evokes much feeling. He knows hunger; it's what brought him to Buddhism. He has always been hungry, not just for food, but entertainment, conversation, sex, intoxication, anything that has at one time created a moment of joy in his life. This same hunger led him to try meditation. And, for a moment, on his first retreat, he did find joy in meditation. Then he attended meditation sittings and went on retreats whenever he could.

He would usually find a moment of joy here and there that kept him returning to meditation. Then the moments of joy turned into long periods of pleasure. The hunger for that pleasure got so strong that he decided to devote his life to satisfying it, and that is the real reason he came to Sri Lanka to become a bhikkhu. Since becoming a bhikkhu, however, he has known the hunger that comes from depriving himself of things and experiences that he could easily have were he not a bhikkhu.

This book interests him and he would have asked to borrow it if, in his pursuit of nibbana, he hadn't given up reading. It is commonly believed in the community of bhikkhus who are ardently seeking nibbana that reading, especially stories, leads to more craving and delusion. Therefore, Sumana would not read such a book under any circumstance. But he would help Rahula pick one out.

"Of these four," Sumana says, "I would suggest you read *The Woman in the Dunes*."

"Have you read it?" Rahula asks.

"No, but I know what it is about."

"What about this one?" Rahula says, holding up the fourth book, called *The Abyss*, which was written by a woman.

"I have never heard of it," Sumana replies.

"It says here it is about an alchemist," Rahula says.

Sumana does not know what to say. He has never been interested in alchemy. What would the Buddha have said about alchemy? He imagines that the Buddha would have considered it a form of magic and thus would have prohibited bhikkhus from practicing it.

"You shouldn't read that!" Sumana exclaims.

Rahula is happy that he is getting definite, genuine responses out of Sumana. In deference to Sumana's opinion, he decides to read *The Woman in the Dunes*.

CHAPTER
11

Sumana leaves the cave after this exchange, so that Rahula can get the leftovers from yesterday's meal ready to be served. Sumana returns to his hut with about twenty minutes to kill before mealtime, and so decides to meditate. Sitting for twenty minutes is easy, and it is the perfect way to make time pass. He once again sits cross-legged on his double robe, and starts by putting his attention on his sitting posture. He is getting used to meditating in this way, just sitting, though he still is not too sure if he is actually doing it right. He will have to ask the meditation master that, and thinks briefly of some roundabout way of posing the question.

After a couple of minutes, his mind drops that train of thought and starts to wander all over the place. He recalls hearing his previous teacher, Venerable Dhammaphala, say that the awakened mind is homeless, like a bhikkhu who lives on alms food. That image has never made sense, for it resembles his familiar mind, which is always on the move. He probably misunderstood what his teacher meant. There is something in this general territory he's beginning to understand with each successive sitting. The mind, when given freedom, isn't wholly irresponsible, degenerate, acting on impure thoughts and feelings. No, it's actually somewhat reliable. It does become settled eventually. It does divest itself of useless, distracting thoughts, and it can touch upon new unplumbed depths. What he begins to comprehend is that his mind is not as he had previously believed it to be.

In the back of his mind he still believes he's just killing some time before lunch, and is caught off-guard when his mind suddenly becomes settled, then deeply tranquil, and then it's as though he were suspended in a bubble, weightless, empty, expansive. If there's a self, an identity that's him observing all of this, it's a small speck no larger than a grain of sand lodged somewhere near the center of the bubble. There is no body. So what is sitting? He ponders that question and knows the answer, but words fail to form around it, so he drops the need to conceptualize and just rests in the bubble. It's like some kind of liquid, and he associates it with consciousness. He thinks that what he's seeing is consciousness, though he knows that's not true. What he sees and feels is how consciousness might manifest itself to the senses, but still that's not consciousness. What consciousness is eludes him and yet it stares him right in the face. "No definite thing," he hears his mind say. And he understands that consciousness can't be a definite thing, nor can it be nothing. It's somewhere in between those two extremes. It can't be separated from thought, feeling, perception, sensation or any of the ways by which it can be known, but it's also not a thought, a feeling, a perception, nor a sensation.

His mind can probe no further, so he rests, his mind going even deeper, almost slipping away from being conscious, and then he feels a reverberation beginning in his chest and spreading throughout his body, tingling all the way down. His breathing quickens rapidly — it had slowed down considerably during this meditation — and an identity, one he recognizes as himself, rises to the surface. He knows one thing with utmost clarity. He is hungry.

He uncrosses his legs and gets up off the ground. Once standing, he straightens his robe, patting it down with both hands. He goes over to the table, and picks up his alms bowl and carries it in the crook of his right arm like a football. He leaves his hut and walks solemnly to the dining hut.

At the dining hut, he sees Aggachitta already sitting with his bowl in his lap. Sumana notices for the first time how big

Aggachitta's alms bowl is. It is the largest one he has ever seen, about one and half times larger than his bowl. It must come in handy when Aggachitta has to walk several miles for alms, since he can put several packets of food in it and still have room for all sorts of requisites.

Rahula has placed all of the food that was left over from yesterday's meal into separate bowls. It is exactly the same selection of food, minus the fish. The rice, vegetables, and chickpeas have all lost their flavor. Aggachitta eats slower today, and Sumana soon becomes unenthusiastic about the meal. When the meal is over, Aggachitta reminds Sumana to meet him in the dining hut for meditation instruction after the midday nap.

Rahula usually enjoys his after-lunch routine. When he finishes cleaning up the dining hut, he gathers up the leftovers and puts them into a plastic bag, which he empties in some nearby bushes. His next stop is his uncle's hut. He stealthily opens the light wooden door, making sure not to wake Aggachitta, who is lying on his bed on his back snoring. He takes long strides into the room, careful not to step on anything that would make a sound. The bucket is where it always is. He grabs it by the handle, which rattles a little, and then lifts it up to his chest to hold it still as he walks the few long paces to the door, and soon enough, he is in the bright noonday sun going down the path to the cistern.

It only takes him a couple of minutes to reach the cistern. He begins by stripping down to his swimming trunks, doing so with great anticipation, as the anticipation of dousing his body with bucketfuls of cool water excites him, as it does most Sinhalese who live at lower elevations. In this tropical climate, one perspires freely all day long.

Rahula thoroughly cools his body down with several bucketfuls of water. To enhance his enjoyment, he then stands in the shade, letting the water evaporate slowly, fanned by gentle breezes, cooling him down even more. He basks in a feeling of joy at this simple way of life. Then he returns to the cistern and soaps up completely, lathering his hair and rubbing soap on his feet and in-between his toes, dousing his body with water in stages, his feet first, his head next, followed by his trunk, arms, thighs, and finally the places protected by the cloth of his shorts. He ends with a few more bucketfuls over his entire body. The whole experience of water rushing down from the top of his head to the tops of his feet, wrapping him in a heavenly coolness, is what he would describe as bliss. When done he returns to the cool shade and begins drying his hair and body with a towel. This whole ritual takes almost half an hour, and is the happiest time of day for Rahula.

Once back in the cave, he becomes aware that he has no responsibilities for the rest of the day. His time is now his own. He decides that he will start reading that book. First, he lights the oil lantern and then he opens the book to the first chapter and begins reading. The English is not too difficult and the sentences are nice and short. After the initial two paragraphs, he feels that he can go on without encountering too much difficulty, and if he does, he has an English-Sinhalese dictionary at hand.

The Woman in the Dunes is about a Japanese man who collects insects. This man is a schoolteacher. He is interested in finding a particular kind of sand beetle. He travels by train to the coast, in a remote region, to search the sand dunes for it. He never returns home. Some people believe he ran off with a woman, committed suicide, was abducted, or simply became fed up with the world.

The story makes Rahula think about his uncle the meditation master. He has never really known his uncle until now. When he was a young boy, he saw his uncle as some kind of godlike being living alone in the jungle, possessing great spiritual powers, a giant among men. These ideas were fed by stories he had heard from his father's friends and the monks at the local temple. While growing up he had thought that he would never see his uncle, that his uncle was beyond reach, having disappeared in the jungle. Then, when he was eleven years old, his father took him to meet his uncle. What he saw was a bhikkhu much like any of the other monks he had met. There was nothing special about him and Rahula kept asking his father if this man truly was his uncle, for he thought that perhaps his real uncle had died in the jungle practicing austerities, and that this monk was an impostor.

Rahula breaks off this reminiscence and begins thinking about his own choice to live in the jungle. Is he trying to escape the world? Alternatively, is he like the man in the story, looking for something rare and exotic, disappearing from the world while not meaning to? Neither of these scenarios fits his situation, partly because he is mostly ignorant about what his situation is. If he is neither escaping from something unpleasant nor seeking something pleasant, then what is creating his present situation?

Rahula has to read on. The schoolteacher gets off the train and makes his way towards the seashore, walking through the village. Past the village, he walks along the dunes, noticing that there are houses sunk in gigantic holes within the dunes. He searches for the elusive beetle, hunting for it among the dunes, for he believes it dwells in the sand.

The man doesn't find anything on the first day and needs a place to sleep for the night. The villagers arrange for him to be the house-guest of one of the village women. The woman lives in one of the submerged houses he saw earlier that day. The man believes he's just going to get a good night's sleep and leave in the morning. Instead, the woman stays up all night shoveling sand into buckets that are then hoisted up to the surface to be carried away on jeeps. The man rebels against helping her, and tries to sleep. When he awakes, he sees the woman lying on her back, naked except for a towel over her face, with a thin layer of sand covering her young body. There is a drawing of this in the book, which Rahula stares at for several seconds before closing the book and putting it down.

Rahula has been carefully shielded from talk about sex, explicit movies, and nude photos. He has matured late, as have many of his friends, and at eighteen is more like an adolescent in these matters. He's aroused by the image of the naked woman in the book, but can't see his feelings as being part of his budding sexuality. Instead, he feels anxious and uncomfortable, as if there is something wrong with this kind of stimulation, these strange physical sensations. In fighting this discomfort, he tells himself he doesn't love this woman in the book, though her image makes him feel this way. Even his girlfriend, who is flesh and blood, has never made him feel this kind of excitement. However, he isn't sure he loves her either.

He tries not to continue thinking about this. The monks at the local temple told him that the mere sight of a woman could bring about lustful thoughts, so monks should not look directly at a woman. They may become overpowered by desires and break their vows. Rahula did not know what they were talking about, for lust was just a word to him then. Now he knows.

He picks up the book and starts reading from where he left off. In the back of his mind, he hopes that this isn't the only stimulating part of the book.

CHAPTER
12

Sumana's nap is uneventful. He rarely dreams in the afternoon. What usually happens is that he lies down on his bed and starts thinking about something that at the time feels important, convinced that his thoughts will keep him from falling asleep. Then he gets a little drowsy and his thoughts radiate from his head toward a white ball of light that is above his head and outside of his body. This would most certainly strike him as highly unusual if he were ever fully conscious during it, but as soon as it starts he's drawn into a state of deep sleep, which usually lasts for about forty-five minutes. When he wakes up, he feels as though he has gotten a full night's rest.

Like yesterday, he arrives at the dining hut before Aggachitta. He immediately lights the stove and puts the kettle of water on it to boil. He's much more relaxed today, since he knows what he's supposed to be doing. He makes the tea, pours himself a cup, and waits for the meditation master to appear. This kind of waiting is not unpleasant. He's glad that Aggachitta is late. It gives him extra time to go over in his mind what has happened during his meditation sittings.

Aggachitta enters the dining hut and pours himself a cup of tea. He would have preferred it if there were a layman present to offer him tea, as it is more proper when done that way. The white-skinned bhikkhu could offer him his tea, but according to the monastic rules that would be practically the same as getting it himself. Sometimes the rules are just so cumbersome and seemingly senseless that Aggachitta perceives them as an oppressive force in his life. The two hundred and twenty-seven rules are supposed to aid in arriving at freedom from worry and care, though they seem to produce so many new worries and cares that they often interfere with the practice of meditation and honest self-reflection.

Aggachitta sits on the bench and Sumana remains seated on the ground in front of him. They sip their tea in silence for several minutes.

Then Aggachitta asks Sumana a question. "How many times have you meditated since I gave you the instruction to just sit?"

Sumana counts the times and says, "I sat a couple of times yesterday afternoon, once before breakfast, did walking meditation after breakfast for an hour, sat for a little while after that, bathed, and then sat again before the main meal."

Aggachitta thinks that Sumana must be restless and lazy to have sat so few times since they last talked, so he asks him.

"Have you been restless, distracted?"

Sumana, unsure as to how much restlessness is acceptable to his new teacher, replies, "Not that much."

"Then what has gone on in your sittings?"

Sumana pauses a moment, thankful that he had a few minutes alone to recollect his meditation sittings before Aggachitta arrived.

"The first sitting," he begins, "was not very good. My mind was running on and on about all sorts of things. Though after the sitting, I felt more relaxed. Then I sat right after that. The second sitting was better. I was focusing on just sitting, but I was not sure if it was the words 'just sitting' or my sitting posture. Soon I got very relaxed and drowsy, and I began to think that I was not being mindful. Then, all of a sudden, I heard the words 'not being.' I was drawn deep inside my mind. It lasted only a few seconds and then I was flung back into my body and opened my eyes. My body was filled with tingling sensations."

The meditation master feels the impulse to interrupt Sumana and ask him some questions about this experience. He is sure he knows what Sumana has stumbled upon in his second meditation sitting, and wants to convey that information to him. Nevertheless, he checks this impulse. When Sumana looks into his eyes for some sort of confirmation, Aggachitta simply tells him to continue.

"Then I became very calm and sat with an awareness of just sitting. I saw a yellow-orange light that would cover my field of inner vision for a period of time and then break up into smaller dots of light. I had thoughts at times, but never along with the yellow-orange light."

Sumana stops talking and looks at Venerable Aggachitta, trying to see if this sitting impresses the meditation master or not. Aggachitta's expression is inscrutable. There is nothing for Sumana to make of it, except, of course, that the meditation master has heard these kinds of meditation experiences before. Perhaps he regards Sumana's experiences as *delusions*, or *corruptions of insight*, as his previous teacher did. Infusing himself with additional courage, Sumana goes on to relate his last couple of sittings.

"The sitting before the morning meal was difficult at first. I was very much aware of the sounds of the birds. I felt irritation at them. But after a few minutes, I began to get sleepy and the sounds no longer bothered me. Then I had this strange experience! I was sitting with my back curved and my head drooped, but I was still awake, though barely. As I sat hunched over like that, I fell through my body. It was the strangest sensation. I awoke with a jolt and wondered what had happened. I decided to sit straight again and soon I was feeling sleepy, hunched over as before, but this time, instead of falling through my body, I just vanished for a second, returning with a gentler jolt than before. I opened my eyes and looked around, and made a firm determination for it not to happen again. I tried to keep awake in the sitting, mostly listening to the bird sounds, but soon I fell asleep for a long time."

Sumana expects the meditation master to concur with his assessment that this was not a very good sitting and that Sumana's efforts to remain awake were admirable. Aggachitta just sits there thinking to himself. He's not about to make any comments until he's heard all of Sumana's sittings. When Sumana has said his fill, then it will be the right time for Aggachitta to impart his wisdom.

Sumana has a sheepish look, wondering what to do now. Aggachitta smiles in a reserved way and makes a gesture with his hands to say, "Please continue."

Sumana regains some of his confidence and sets out to complete his narrative. "The next sitting, well, was walking meditation." Then he pauses, for he remembers the incident at the outhouse. He does not want to give any sign or indication that he could have been the one who unmindfully threw water into the latrine, just in case Aggachitta was there. Therefore, he adjusts what happened just a little.

"I walked for an hour. At first, I was experiencing the hindrance of restlessness and worry. I walked very fast back and forth. Then, after a while, I became aware of feeling fear as pulsating sensations that lasted only a few seconds before vanishing. The sensations soon became empty of fear, and then vanished altogether. After that, I sat and nothing much happened. I became relaxed and seemed to fall asleep.

"Then," he adds, somewhat excited, "the next sitting was the best of them all. I experienced myself as a bubble sitting. I did not feel my body at all. There was just my mind, and it felt like water. My thoughts were about consciousness, that it was no definite thing. I stayed with that for about half an hour until I knew it was time for dana."

Aggachitta waits for Sumana to say more, but Sumana sits with a confused expression on his face, waiting uncomfortably for Aggachitta to speak.

Aggachitta considers which experiences he will comment on first, and which he will save for later or not comment on at all. It is clear to him that Sumana was completely honest about his sittings. They sounded like genuine meditation experiences, ones that someone would encounter after a month or so of intensive meditation practice. That it has taken Sumana over five years to reach this point in his meditation practice is not surprising, since he was given inadequate instruction from his previous teachers. Now could be a turning point, so Aggachitta wants to be sure that he gives Sumana the best possible instruction.

"Well, young monk," Aggachitta begins, "it appears that your *samadhi* is high, your *sati* goes from medium to high, and your *viriya* is low. That is how it seems to me in terms of the five faculties."

Sumana is bewildered by Aggachitta's use of Pali words and so asks the meditation master to explain what those terms mean. Aggachitta can't quite believe that the foreign monk does not know even the simplest and most common-place Pali words. He begins to explain them.

"Samadhi refers to the deepening tranquility you experience, which pushes out the hindrances and enables the mind to become inwardly focused. Too much samadhi, when not balanced by viriya, that is, energy, leads towards sleepiness."

"You must have heard of sati?" Aggachitta looks at Sumana to see if this is true, but from Sumana's blank expression concludes that he does not even know that much. Sumana has in fact heard these terms before, but remains silent as a way to learn new meanings of these words and not expose his faulty knowledge of Pali.

"Well, anyway," Aggachitta continues, "sati refers to how aware you are of things. When it is high, your mind is clear and able to note each moment exactly as it is, from its arising to its passing away. When it is in the middle, as in your sittings, the mind is able to catch things clearly for short periods, but ends up being distracted on occasion, pulled away from the predominant objects of awareness."

Sumana looks even more confused, so Aggachitta, instead of feeling the need to offer more thorough explanations, realizes that he should never have begun this type of interpretation in the first place.

He says, "I know that the five faculties can be quite complex, and it is only one way of looking at one's sittings."

"What are the other two faculties?" Sumana asks.

"Well, the other two are *saddha* and *pañña*, faith and wisdom," Aggachitta says, deciding to leave it at that.

Sumana then asks, "At what levels were they in my sittings?"

This question forces Aggachitta to think more about what he can remember of Sumana's sittings. It is a good question, and he wants to give Sumana all the knowledge he can at this time. So he sits quietly, absorbed in thought. It then occurs to him that perhaps this system of the five faculties actually amounts to nothing more than an intellectual model made up by some brilliant bhikkhu ages ago as a way to measure and assess meditative experiences without resorting to theories of divine intervention, psychic powers, or mystical revelations.

Saddha, or faith, is trust in the Buddha's teaching, while pañña, or wisdom, is direct knowledge of that teaching. These two faculties counter erroneous views and set the meditator on the true path to nibbana. How can one assess them? When they are absent, the meditator easily falls into believing false views around self, God, and the nature of existence. When they are present, the meditator trusts the teaching and learns from following it. All that Aggachitta can say about Sumana's sittings is that he heard no obvious false views, and so faith and wisdom must have been present to some degree.

"Young monk, it sounds as though faith and wisdom were present in your meditations. It is enough that the five faculties are present."

"Then am I doing it right?" Sumana asks.

This is the first time a student has asked him this question. Aggachitta brushes it off as an irrelevant question, for as he construes meditation, it is not about a self that does something correctly or not, but about a consciousness that flows along, awakening to its inner world and knowing that world as it is.

He thus gives Sumana a token reply, "Your meditation practice is going just fine."

"What should I do now?"

"Just continue sitting."

Sumana is disappointed by this reply. Aggachitta should be able to see that he needs more than that.

Aggachitta senses that Sumana needs some inspirational parting words. "As the Buddha said to the wandering sage Bahiya: 'in the seen is only the seen, in the heard only the heard, in the sensed only the sensed, and in the cognized only the cognized. There is neither being here nor there, faraway, nor in between. That is the final end of suffering.'"

Beaming with joy at the beauty of the Buddha's conceptualization, Aggachitta rises from the bench and leaves Sumana to contemplate what he has heard. It is a great teaching, and Aggachitta lets it slosh about in his mind, like a child with hard candy in his mouth, as he leaves the dining hut. Before he has reached the perimeter of the hut, he remembers something important he has to tell his new student. He turns around and says in a soft, pleasant voice, "Next time you use the latrine, please remember to fill the tin when you are finished." Then he walks away.

With a rush of anxiety, Sumana is now certain that the person he threw the bucketful of water at was his teacher. He sees Aggachitta's great compassion in allowing him to stay on at the hermitage. This relieves his anxiety somewhat. He resolves to follow the meditation master's instructions to the letter and thus prove himself worthy. Now, if he can only remember what they were.

Aggachitta believes he can come away from an interview with an individual student with enough information to think about, and eventually figure out, how the truths of the Buddha's teaching are found in that student's sittings. In front of the student, he can't concentrate to the degree necessary on what he is hearing. Once he is alone in his hut, he can examine the student's sittings for hours, breaking them down, seeing, he believes, how that person's mind operates. He fancies himself at times to be rather like a scientist, though he's not a man of science; the empirical method doesn't quite mesh with his philosophical temperament. He's only interested in facts in so far as they support his own theories or spur an investigation into evaluating or reformulating one of those theories.

Aggachitta will often conduct such contemplations while seated for meditation. He sits on a cushion opposite his bed. His back is slumped over a little, his hands are on his lap, the right hand resting on the left one, and his eyes are closed, though a small amount of light leaks in underneath his eyelids. He doesn't bother to put his attention on any particular meditation subject. Instead, he sits and lets his mind do what it does best: think.

Thinking, he focuses his intellect on Sumana's sittings. What ñana is his student in? He knows that ñana originally meant knowledge, but here he uses the word as his Burmese teachers instructed him. It means stage. What stage is Sumana in? Is he at number four, five, or six? For his sittings have the markers for all of these stages. What if he is going up the scale, from four to six, and then sliding back down. It is known to happen. If Aggachitta had gotten him as a beginner, then he believes he could surely tell.

Here is the problem: what if these stages are also fabrications concocted by a brilliant theorist over a thousand years ago and don't really exist? What if there is actually no way to plot a meditator's path to nibbana? Worse yet, all those who believe they have attained nibbana by going through these stages could be deluded about their attainment. Suppose someone goes through all of these stages and actually attains nibbana. Does that mean the stages are true, or does it mean that one can attain nibbana despite going through these stages?

This type of thinking is always circular for him. When he would reach this point, where he questions whether anyone attains nibbana through the Burmese method and its reliance on stages, he would pull back and bring his attention to something less stressful. He doesn't want his questioning mind to chip away at the protective covering he has placed over his attainment of sotapanna, the entering of the stream to full awakening, over twenty-five years ago. Without that attainment, he would be a failure, a misguided teacher, one who is still capable of incarnating in lower realms of existence. He will not let his mind probe any further into the validity of his attainment, for that would surely indicate the presence of the fetter of doubt, which is a state of mind he should be beyond experiencing ever again if he truly is a sotapanna.

What if the stages, the five faculties, and all the ways Buddhist meditation masters are taught to interpret meditation experience are merely intellectual constructs having no basis in fact? Then there would be no way to determine a meditator's progress towards nibbana, though there may still be a way to note, discern, and assess progress. It may look something like what the Buddha said to Bahiya. "In the seen there is only the seen." By just looking at each experience, one with knowledge could discern if it is more developed and refined than a previous one like it. There would be no interpretation then, but rather just the comparison of two or more actual experiences, and an understanding of which one is more advanced or of greater benefit.

This approach appears delightfully simple to Aggachitta's mind. He then wants to try it out. He recalls that Sumana mentioned sleepiness several times in his meditation sittings, and then, in his last sitting, he said that he was in his mind as though it were a bubble of water. Suppose the bubble experience is a progression from his earlier experiences of drifting towards sleep, waking up, and then going again towards sleep. Then instead of passing through stages in his sittings, Sumana's consciousness is developing new states of mind superior to his old, customary ones. That is what progress in meditation truly means!

With that new understanding, all thinking stops and his mind dips into a still realm of being for a long stretch of time.

CHAPTER
13

Sumana returns to his hut to meditate after his interview with the meditation master. When he gets there, he realizes that he does not feel like meditating. Still, he sits down on his double robe and begins to meditate. He becomes aware of a feeling of resignation, one that comes from losing his initial resistance to sitting, though it too feels like some kind of resistance, as if by being resigned to meditating he's allowing his resistance to sneak in under the guise of apathy. When his mind catches its own devious machinations, his apathy vanishes, and he experiences a mental energy that wakes him up. This must be viriya, effort, he thinks; and he believes his sati must be very high too. He is very pleased with himself for using Pali words, and pats himself on the back at having applied the meditation master's teaching.

He begins to notice such an increase in sati that it's as if someone other than himself is meditating. His mind speeds up and he notices an itch on his neck spread out, tingle around the edges, and then become a dull sensation, all in a matter of seconds. The same occurs when he hears a branch in a tree above his hut rustled by a bird. The sound of it is instantly apprehended, and each phase of the sound is chopped into minute segments of sound. Every sound, sensation, and thought comes and goes quickly and, to his astonishment, he sees everything clearly arising, persisting briefly, and then vanishing altogether.

This lasts about ten minutes. When it ends, and his mind returns to its normal pace of perception, he starts to have moments where he is completely aware of something and then in the blink of an eye, he is aware of nothing for a brief moment. It feels as though his mind turns itself off for a moment, and then quickly turns itself back on. Nothing changes however. He doesn't feel anything from these experiences of his mind stopping and restarting. After a while, the entertainment wears off and it begins to annoy him, so he decides to get up and take a walk.

Sumana has by now seen most of the hermitage. Thus, he feels the urge to walk somewhere he hasn't ventured yet. He sees a hill not far from his hut, though outside of the hermitage grounds, or so he supposes. He can't really tell, because there's no fence or any other marker around the hermitage. A small trail goes from his hut in the direction of the hill and he follows it.

It is an easy enough walk, mostly level, with dense jungle growth on either side of the cleared footpath. When he reaches the hill, the trail veers to the left, and Sumana follows it assuming that it would be a gentle rise leading to the top. Instead, it keeps veering around the hill on level ground. He stays on it, anticipating it to slope upwards, but it keeps going until he is on the other side of the hill. There he arrives at a small valley of tall grasses. Near the base of the hill is a four-foot high mound made of cement. It has a bronze plate on one side with a name and set of dates etched into it. Sumana concludes it must be the burial mound of the hermitage's founder, Venerable Atakkachari.

He stands looking at it for some time, recalling the story of this great bhikkhu. He becomes conscious of a hissing sound that comes and goes periodically, which he is unable to identify until, on the other side of the mound, a cobra springs up with its hood open and fangs glaring. Fear shoots up through him and he freezes. He stands completely still as the cobra eyes him, shifting its gaze constantly. The snake backs down, returning its upper body to the ground and slithers off in the opposite direction.

Sumana stands motionless, waiting a few minutes before he considers it safe enough to move. When he does move, his legs are stiff. He wants to sit down, but knows he can't if the cobra is still in the vicinity. So he returns by the path he came, walking very cautiously, scanning the ground carefully for any sign of the snake.

When he's safely inside his hut, he plops down on his bed. Lying on his back, he breathes a sigh of relief. He closes his eyes and sees the cobra's head. It is a beautiful creature, but its eyes have a dull, dumb look in them. Its show of hostility seems to Sumana to be anger stemming from pain, not from a desire to kill another living being. He's surprised to find he recalls the cobra in this compassionate way, while at the same time he's a bit concerned that the thought of his life being in danger is altogether absent from his mind. Try as he may to bring his fear and sense of mortal danger back to consciousness, all he manages to retrieve is that first rush of fear at seeing the cobra not more than three feet from him. But when he peers into the serpent's face as he remembers it, all he sees is a dumb, blind rage that speaks of a snake's pain and not his own.

He spends some time thinking about what it would be like to be a cobra and is grateful that he wasn't born one, for he wouldn't like an existence where he has to kill in order to eat, where he is hunted by men and mongooses, never entirely safe from capture or extermination. Then he recalls the sculptures he has seen of the Buddha with a cobra fanned out over his head like an umbrella.

Sumana does not know the story of the cobra and the Buddha, but he believes he now knows what those sculptures mean. He gets up off the bed and sits in meditation. When he shuts his eyes, the cobra reappears behind them. It looks at him, and then he turns the image around, having the cobra look in the same direction as his eyes. The cobra's eyes are his eyes, the cobra's hood his brain, and its body his spine. Soon, the distinction between Sumana and the cobra seems to evaporate and he begins to understand the cobra's pain.

It lives all alone. It lives frightened much of the time. It has the power to kill and harm, and is forced to use it out of hunger and fear. It's seldom content and never at peace. It has to keep moving, or else other creatures will kill it. In so many ways its suffering is no different from Sumana's, for he too is all alone, frightened, seldom content, restless, and has the power to harm if he so chooses.

The cobra has dumb, lusterless eyes. It's an ignorant creature. Whereas Sumana can overcome his ignorance, arrive at calm and inner peace, leave this world of fear behind and enter into nibbana.

In a flash of insight that exposes an incomprehensible happiness within it, Sumana believes he can do it.

He knows nibbana exists.

He sits with a strange feeling that the cobra above the Buddha's head was not a snake after all. Rather, it was the world the Great Sage had left behind when he attained nibbana.

Part Two

Consciousness and Conditionality

CHAPTER
14

The following morning Sumana comes to the dining hut as Aggachitta sips his morning cup of tea. Rahula is there, but there is no food for breakfast. Sumana has been experiencing an inexplicable serenity since waking up this morning, sitting in meditation for over an hour, entirely at peace with himself and his surroundings. Now he will have to fast longer than he wishes. His mind loses its serenity and takes a turn towards sluggishness and apathy, with a tinge of hurt, as if the absence of breakfast is somehow a punishment. Uppermost in his mind is the idea that he's bad because he's hungry. He sees himself as his greed. And greed is bad.

Sumana sits down on the bench next to Aggachitta. Rahula hastily brings him a cup of steaming hot milk tea.

Aggachitta turns to him and says, "Today we must go to the nearest village for alms."

Not only is he to be deprived of breakfast, but now he's going to have to walk several miles through the jungle on an empty stomach. Sumana experiences a huge wave of exhaustion come over him just thinking about this journey.

He asks, "Venerable Aggachitta, won't we have to leave soon?"

Aggachitta remains silent, as though he has not heard the young monk. He doesn't like impatience in others. He hurries for no one. He reasons that if he doesn't answer Sumana, then he can take his time and leave on alms round at a reasonable hour, such as ten in the morning.

Sumana puts his attention on his milk tea now that he realizes that this might be his only meal until just before noon. He then considers that he could always go back to sleep and wake up again, start the day closer to meal time, but then he will still have to walk several miles for food. Maybe Rahula can show him the way to the village so that he could leave early, since Aggachitta seems, in his silence, inclined to leave late and perhaps even arrive too late for alms. It strikes Sumana just then that breaking the rule about not eating after noon is a grave offense, when in truth it is a rather minor transgression. What makes it appear more serious than it should be is that he's been told it's one of the ten main precepts which a sotapanna never breaks.

Aggachitta can feel Sumana's agitation move along the bench where they both sit, mildly shaking it.

"It is all right," he says, "we will leave at ten and have plenty of time."

Sumana is now convinced that he won't get to eat today, which pushes him further into a dejected state of mind. He leaves the dining hut before finishing his tea and heads straight to his hut where he plans to lie down and go back to sleep.

Aggachitta stays in the dining hut for quite some time after Sumana leaves. He decides to have another cup of tea and have a chat with his nephew, who is now sitting on the ground in front of him, also sipping tea.

"Well, have you chosen a book yet?" Aggachitta asks.

Rahula smiles and nods his head. He is both gleeful and embarrassed.

"What then have you chosen?"

Shyly Rahula says, "A book called *The Woman in the Dunes.*"

"I have not heard of it," Aggachitta says.

He has never really looked through the chest of donated books, left to the hermitage by the family of an English teacher at the university in Kandy who was killed in a terrorist bombing. Aggachitta has no idea why this teacher's family donated his collection of literature to a forest hermitage where monks don't read such books, but he safely assumes that these books were given to gain the most merit.

"Tell me something about the story."

"Well, uncle, it is about a man who is kept captive in a house with a woman who lives in a giant hole in the sand from which there is no escape." Rahula rattles off this sentence with great assurance and skill. He composed it last night in case his uncle asked this very question.

"That sounds interesting," Aggachitta replies, thinking that this is a fanciful story, and highly improbable.

"What kind of book is it?"

"Uncle, it is existentialist, I think."

Aggachitta is pleased to hear Rahula use such a word to describe a book. Maybe he is an adult after all.

"I know a little something about existentialism from my days at the University. I read Sartre, Heidegger, Husserl, among others. I actually found them interesting up to a point. But existentialist fiction is either too dark or too senseless and trivial for my taste."

"This book is different," Rahula says. "Maybe it is not existentialist, but rather, a book on what existence is."

This remark pleases Aggachitta. It shows that his nephew can differentiate between a school of thought and a subject of inquiry. It reminds him of his undergraduate years when he learned the philosophies of the various Buddhist schools and then went further to inquire on his own into the true meanings of the Buddha's words.

"And what does this story say about existence?"

Rahula squirms uncomfortably at this question. Perhaps it is still beyond his budding intellect to answer. However, after a moment of thought, Rahula comes up with something original.

"Existence is a trap."

"That is exactly what the Buddha taught!" Aggachitta exclaims, happy that Rahula has figured this out from his reading.

"This book sounds good. Keep reading. We will discuss this book again, once you have made some progress."

Aggachitta is about to rise from his seat when they hear some men talking in the near distance. The voices are jolly, friendly, animated. Aggachitta looks around him, trying to catch a glimpse of who it is that is coming his way, but fails to get the right angle to see the approaching men. One of the voices, the loudest one, begins to sound familiar to him, and when the men reach the dining hut, Aggachitta is not surprised to see Venerable Maggaphala, a fellow bhikkhu who ordained some months after he did. He also became a bhikkhu after completing his studies. But Maggaphala is not a Buddhist scholar; his field is Shakespeare. However, he's not someone who goes around quoting Shakespeare's words. For him, Shakespeare is a master of the human psyche, opening doors of understanding on how people truly think, feel, and behave.

Maggaphala enters the dining hut and goes over to bow to Aggachitta. He is a large, robust man, with a big head and a double chin. His features are monstrously unattractive, reminding one of Indian paintings of demons. Since Sri Lanka is a land of demons for the Hindus, perhaps they modeled these grotesque images after seeing people like Maggaphala. Regardless of his appearance, his disposition is warm, jovial, and he is socially stimulating. After Maggaphala rises from bowing to Aggachitta, he stands up and adjusts his robe from the cumbersome away-from-the-monastery fold to the leisurely one-shoulder-bared in-the-monastery fold. He has a huge smile on his face. Aggachitta can feel Maggaphala's joy at seeing him again. It warms Aggachitta's heart to have a visitor like this, one who asks nothing of him, who simply gives him the pleasure of good company.

They sit next to each other on the bench, smiling as they greet each other, while the four laymen who arrived with Maggaphala perform their customary bows to the two bhikkhus.

The laymen then unpack some bread and butter and a few hard-boiled eggs to serve the monks. This is not a common breakfast in Sri Lanka, but it is easy to prepare and transport. The monks eat in silence, and as they do, Rahula brews up some more tea for everyone. When they have eaten, the laymen go with Rahula for a tour of the hermitage and then to the cistern to wash up.

The two old friends then start talking about bhikkhus they know in common. Maggaphala is a wellspring of gossip and soon Venerable Aggachitta knows pretty well all the comings and goings, the disrobings (monks leaving the order and returning to the lay life) and transgressions, and the ailments and treatments of various bhikkhus he has known over the years. After a few minutes, Aggachitta begins to tire of this kind of conversation. It is a strain for him to think about other people's lives. He would rather move on to ideas instead of people.

"Maggaphala," he asks, "have you ever thought about how most of our fellow bhikkhus live the first two noble truths without knowing the path to end them?"

"We all suffer and desire, Venerable Aggachitta, but that does not mean we do not know the path."

Aggachitta feels energized by his friend's response. "But ignorance of the path keeps fanning the fire of desire, creating the smoke of suffering, while wisdom douses that fire into smoldering embers."

Maggaphala laughs heartily at this analogy. "That is very poetic for a philosopher."

"Not really," Aggachitta says, somewhat abashed at this compliment. "The fire and smoke metaphor has been around in Buddhist logic since the scholastic period and can even be found in pre-Buddhist Brahmanic texts."

Maggaphala reflects on what a serious person his old friend is. He can't laugh, can't take joy in conversation, and is unable to accept any kind of compliment. But I will keep trying. Maggaphala just nods his head in response, conveying that he understands what Aggachitta is saying.

Then Maggaphala remembers the real reason behind this journey to Aggachitta's hermitage, though he now realizes —

being with his old friend —that he has missed his company and would have made this journey sooner if he had only been aware of it.

"The reason I came to see you is that I read an article that might interest you."

"What could possibly interest me?" Aggachitta asks rhetorically.

"I've got it in my shoulder bag." He reaches down into his orange cloth shoulder bag with an embroidered silk dharma wheel on it. He pulls out several pages stapled together.

"This article is titled, *Conditionality: A Structural Analysis of the Links of Dependent Arising.*"

Aggachitta is surprisingly curious, much more so than usual. He feels a sudden intense craving for this article in Maggaphala's hands.

"What is the author's thesis?" Aggachitta asks.

"You can read it for yourself. I brought you this copy to keep."

"Well, have you read it?"

"Yes," Maggaphala says hesitantly, "but I found it too advanced. I majored in literature, not philosophy, remember."

This confession pleases Aggachitta, for it states without ambiguity that he is the expert in this field.

"Who wrote it?"

"Here, you can look at it yourself," Maggaphala says as he hands over the sheets of paper.

Aggachitta takes the papers and squints as he reads the author's name. He is a Westerner, an Italian to be precise. He is not even a Ph.D., but a lowly B.A. How could this paper be a difficult work of scholarship? Is Maggaphala that uneducated about Buddhist philosophy after twenty-five years in robes?

While Aggachitta is presumably reading the first page of the article, Maggaphala says, "I know you might not think much of this article at first glance, seeing that the author is not one of our great Sinhalese scholars. Once you start reading it, he makes some very good observations. His thesis begins in such contrast to yours that I thought you might find it interesting, or even amusing."

Aggachitta smiles at the compliments that Maggaphala throws his way at the expense of this poor Italian writer. One thing that both men agree on is that a foreigner may be able to put the Buddha's teaching into good English, but that is all. Still, Aggachitta is curious about this article and begins reading the first paragraph.

He reads, "Dependent arising *(paticca-samuppada)* has traditionally been interpreted as a sequence of events that arise in linear fashion over a given period of time. This has led scholars to believe that they can separate the links in the chain of dependent arising and view each link as an isolated element. When the Buddha proclaimed, 'When this is, that is so,' did he mean, 'from this being so, that arose' or did he mean, 'this being so, that is'? I am of the opinion that he meant, 'this being so, that is.'"

Aggachitta frowns as he reads the last sentence. He does not agree with it, but for a moment, feels a particular kind of enjoyment he has not known for some time: the pleasure of following a brilliant line of reasoning through a dense and profound concept.

He puts the article down on the bench, deciding to save it for a quiet, private moment when he can fully relish the pleasure it will bring. Instead of complimenting the author, he feels contempt for the man: how can he be so smart and so ignorant at the same time? A counter-argument forms in his mind within an instant, and he feels indignant, if not a little self-righteous. He has to relate his argument to his friend, Maggaphala, who has been basking in the delight of giving his friend this article, but is not very interested in hearing Aggachitta's remarks on it right now.

Aggachitta says, "This foreigner clearly has no understanding of Pali grammar. The statement definitely reads, '*Imasmim sati, idam hoti; imassa uppada, idam uppajjati*: When this is, that is; from the arising of this, that arises.' Time is a key element. That is clear when the Buddha

says, 'From the arising of this, that arises.' How could someone
not see that?"

"Well, not all people are as well-schooled in this subject as
you. Perhaps you should write an article refuting his thesis."

"No, no, no," Aggachitta says, waving right hand as if to
push away the suggestion. "I am not one to write papers. I put
the teaching into practice."

"But such a perspective as yours, from years of meditation,
would surely revolutionize the field of causality. Just think
what a service it would do for scholars and monks seeking to
know exactly what the Buddha meant when he expounded this
deep and profound doctrine."

Aggachitta smiles once again, soaking in the praise, acting
out of habit with hand gestures to brush it off, but no matter
how much he shows that it is unwarranted, in his heart he sees
this kind of recognition as something he has been denying
himself for the past twenty-five years.

CHAPTER
15

On entering his hut, Sumana plops down on the bed. He turns over on his back, and decides he'll meditate lying down. If he falls asleep, there'll be no blame in that. Within a minute, he falls into his old meditation practice of keeping his attention on the rise and fall of his abdomen, except now he does so without noting each time his abdomen rises or falls. At some point his thoughts become disjointed and his attention leaves his abdomen altogether. A few minutes later, while in this state of unrelated and fragmented thoughts, he loses consciousness for a minute or so, returning to his body with a mild feeling of rapture. Following upon the rapture is a syrupy calm. If he were sitting, it would be soothing, but since he's lying down, it beckons towards sleep. The next time he loses consciousness, he begins to snore.

He emerges into a world of light and noise and people, the world he left behind in America. He sees a familiar street, lined with single-storied houses built in the fifties and sixties, though the cars parked in the driveways and along the curves are mostly newer models, like the Ford Taurus his mother drove him to the airport in when he left for India. He sees his mother, and then his father. Both appear younger than he knows them to be. They're not much older than he is now.

His parents look at him and don't see a monk. Sumana is wearing dark brown baggy cotton short pants and a bright orange T-shirt, the colors of his two robes. He is at the beach near their house in San Diego. No, not San Diego, he thinks.

Del Mar is where we lived. And we do not live in a single-storied house, but a condominium.

He's at the beach. It is crowded with people sitting on beach towels on the sand in small clusters, talking among themselves, sunbathing, reading, listening to music or sports on the radio, or playing board games. When he appears, all eyes are on him. He's an oddity: a Buddhist monk in baggy shorts and a T-shirt. He has a strong feeling that he now belongs with these people, that he is of their world, and no longer of the monk's world. To show that he's one of them, he runs to the surf and jumps into the waves. The water has no sensation of wetness to it. It feels very cold, and for a moment, all is dark and empty.

He wakes up in fear. He immediately checks his robes to make sure he's still a bhikkhu. Satisfied that he's still in robes, he looks around his hut, confirming to his senses that he's still in Sri Lanka. These dreams of being a layman living in America terrify him. He's heard other monks speak of having such dreams, though they're usually untroubled by their past selves coming back, whereas Sumana regards the past as his biggest obstacle to attaining nibbana.

On his ordination day, he vowed never to return to the lay life. He wanted a complete break with how he acted, how he thought, what he felt, and how he looked before becoming a bhikkhu. It was as though the old Sumana, "Simon" as he was known then (he always thought that his preceptor had just twisted his lay name into some Pali likeness when giving him his monk's name), was a pleasure-oriented, selfish, and lazy individual, who could never hope to make anything out of his life. Simon had no future, no options, and no potential. He was destined to work at mediocre semi-mindless jobs, have dull and unsatisfying relationships with women, and squander his free time seeking pleasure where there is none. Sumana the bhikkhu, on the other hand, is doing something with his life: he's doing the work to end all suffering, all future meaningless existence. If he were not a monk, he's certain that he would still be trapped in the futile existence he had left behind. That fact terrifies him more than anything.

These reflections, once put behind him, are purposely downplayed, as though they mean nothing. The image of being trapped, the frustration of it, brings a sense of urgency, which agitates him inwardly, causing him to spring from the bed. He straightens his robe, grabs his alms bowl, and bolts out of the hut, making his way quickly to the dining hut.

As he nears the dining hut, he can hear voices in conversation. At first, he thinks he hears Aggachitta and Rahula talking, but there is a new voice louder than the rest. When he gets there, he sees an elephant of a monk sitting on the bench next to Aggachitta. The single board of the bench sags under his weight. The appearance of this monk can only mean two things: laymen have come with dana; and Sumana will have to eat sitting on the ground, being the junior monk, as there is no way he could also fit on the bench even if he wanted to.

Sumana approaches the new monk and bows to him. This interrupts the conversation between the old friends, which displeases Aggachitta a little. Aggachitta was just beginning to outline his counter-argument to Maggaphala, who was politely half-listening. This foreign monk comes at the right time, and is the right kind of diversion for Maggaphala, as he always finds something in white-skinned monks that reminds him of his favorite Shakespeare characters and plays.

When Maggaphala first sees a young foreign bhikkhu, his mind immediately draws up a picture of that monk being a version of King Henry V of England, who was Prince Hal in his youth. The reason for this lies in Prince Hal's transformation into King Henry V. For Prince Hal was fond of spending time with lowlifes, such as Falstaff, pulling off practical jokes and living a debauched life. When his father was old and dying, he completely closed that chapter of his life, distancing himself from those who were once his dear friends. He made such a decisive break from his past that it was hard to imagine King Henry V was once Prince Hal.

To Maggaphala's thinking, all white-skinned monks have wild pasts that are well hidden under the austere robes, the shaven heads, the humble bowing and reverential gestures.

Monk-hood turns them into serious-minded adults, and Maggaphala sees this as a mask to cover what they truly are.

After concluding that Sumana is indeed this type of Western monk, Maggaphala then tries to find another Shakespearian character that captures the salient aspects of the young monk's personality.

He wonders if Sumana is a comic character or a tragic one. The awkwardness of Sumana's movements, his slowness and ineptness, give Maggaphala the impression that Sumana is indeed a comic figure. The comedies are not Maggaphala's strong point, but he can sort and shuffle the different characters without much difficulty, coming up with one that he now sees best suits his first impression. Sumana is that young nobleman in *A Midsummer Night's Dream* who rendezvous with his lover, goes to the forest, sleeps, and is given a love potion by mistake, whereby he falls in love with another woman, who treats his advances as a mockery of her, all the while scorning the woman he truly loves. This scenario strikes Maggaphala as more tragic than comic, for the character is a foolish man who symbolizes someone who thinks he knows what he's searching for, such as being in the forest to pursue his heart's desire, but once in the forest, has his head turned by the next fancy that crosses his path.

Such a man is Sumana. Maggaphala is sure of that before they have even exchanged a few words.

Maggaphala says, "Young bhikkhu, how do you like living in the jungle? Does it suit your aim?"

Sumana is surprised by Maggaphala's impeccable English and is taken aback by the directness of his question. He hesitates before answering.

"I like it very much here. I have all my requisites and I am with my teacher."

"What has my old friend been teaching you?" Maggaphala asks.

"He has taught me to just sit."

Maggaphala chuckles and then says, "So you are a meditator. That is a noble pastime. My old friend here is said to be one of the best teachers in Sri Lanka."

Then Maggaphala pauses in order to change his line of questioning. "What brought you here, to Sri Lanka, to the life of a bhikkhu?"

Sumana isn't prepared to answer such a personal question. He doesn't like being put on the spot like this in front of Aggachitta.

"My story isn't very interesting."

"I'm sure it's quite interesting," Maggaphala replies. "Go on. Tell us how you came to be a monk."

"I wanted to become liberated. That's all."

"The details, more details please," Maggaphala says.

"I went on a few vipassana retreats in America and attended a weekly sitting group. Then I wanted to pursue the path further, so I left for India. I didn't find much in India, so I decided to come to Sri Lanka, where I heard there are vipassana meditation centers where I could stay and meditate for several months. So I decided to check it out and liked it. I got to know some of the monks and decided to ordain."

"I'm sure there's much more to it than that."

"Not really."

"Your teacher didn't say that you had attained sotapanna or anything like that?" Maggaphala asks.

This probing question angers Sumana. He can't summon up a reply that would not be perceived as disrespectful, so he tries to recall what others have said when asked this irreverent question.

"It's against the rules to talk about such things."

"So he did tell you. Well, that's not unusual. So you are a changed man. And now you believe the only thing you have to do is go to the forest, meditate often, and you will attain nibbana. That's very noble indeed."

Sumana's rage rises to the surface. His face reddens and his fists clench. Inflamed words percolate up from his throat and hover around his tongue and jaws. He's one second from lashing out at this old, fat monk. He then looks over at Aggachitta and imagines what his teacher would think if he lost his temper. He swallows his rage in chunks, not saying a word.

Aggachitta, meanwhile, is lost in thought. He is absorbed on the subject of causality. He excuses himself, gets up, and walks out of the dining area, as if in a trance. Neither Sumana nor Maggaphala pay him much attention.

Maggaphala is the first one to break the tense silence. "My name is Maggaphala, by the way. Do you know what *maggaphala* means?"

"No."

"It means path and fruit. My teacher gave it to me because he thought I had become a sotapanna from having meditated under his guidance. For a few months, I also thought that. Then something happened to change my mind. A white-skinned monk, about your age then, came to the monastery for meditation instruction. He was very talkative, not very attentive or considerate, and, by my estimation, not terribly bright. After about a week, my teacher told him that he had attained the path and the fruit.

"I wondered how such a person could become a sotapanna in a week when it took me over a month. Then I wondered how such a person could attain it at all, especially as I noticed no significant change in this bhikkhu's behavior. He still talked all the time, about all sorts of nonsense. After about another week, this same bhikkhu went into a great depression and had to be taken to hospital. That convinced me my teacher had made a mistake. Soon after that, it occurred to me that undoubtedly he had made a mistake about my attainment as well.

"For the next three years I dedicated myself to meditation. In that time, I saw deeply into my mind and knew that I still had the fetters that the attainment of sotapanna should have eradicated. I finally abandoned the idea of being a sotapanna."

Sumana listens intently to Maggaphala's story, not making a comment or even a sound. He feels indignation and anger towards Maggaphala. Underneath this indignation however, lurks a fear, a dread of finding out that perhaps his teacher deceived him about being a sotapanna.

"Did anything like that happen to you?" Maggaphala asks.

There's no need for Sumana to answer. He can see it on his distraught face.

Maggaphala gets up from the bench. He yawns, stretching his whole body.

"Time for a midmorning nap," he says as he walks out of the dining area and in the direction of the cave, leaving Sumana to his distress.

Sumana frantically considers if he has been deceived. If so, then going to the forest to find nibbana may not work after all, since he truly may not be ready for it.

CHAPTER
16

Aggachitta walks to his hut, his mind preoccupied with thoughts of causality. Usually at this hour, he must put his attention on the morning routine of washing up, straightening up his room, and raking the leaves that have accumulated around his hut. These physical, worldly responsibilities make an intrusion, disrupting his thoughts for a moment before he exiles them with the words "not now." For now, he is climbing the great ladder of *paticca-samuppada*, dependent arising, or dependent origination, depending on the translator.

His mind holds onto the central link in the great chain, as if it held the key that will unlock his understanding. The pivotal causal link is an idea that he believes deep down is simply a mistake of choosing the wrong word, leading to the wrong ideas, thus dooming any serious investigation into causality. It is a joke played by the Buddha, or perhaps — granting the Buddha more respect — it is a puzzle.

He enters his hut and sits down at his desk. He has an exercise book and a pen ready to write down his thoughts. He writes the word that troubles him: *tanha*. What is it doing in the great chain of dependent arising? One of its many synonyms would be clearer in its place, and that is how it has mostly been translated, leaving the riddle unanswered. For it is easier to call it desire, longing, craving, passion, greed, or any number of recognizable causes for suffering than it is to call it by name. Tanha is thirst.

In the front of his mind, he holds the idea of thirst, peeling it carefully, separating it from all the associations built up around it over the centuries, looking into it to see if he can see its core.

Thirst only goes away by drinking liquid. It then returns sometime later, compelling one to consume more liquid. All animals that walk the earth know thirst. Without water, there would be no life. The ending of thirst, in a physical sense, is death. Was the Buddha speaking in metaphor? Why would he choose a metaphor in such an important philosophic statement, where that word is the key element? He couldn't really have meant thirst, for there's no possible way that the Buddha and his disciples never felt the need to drink water after they attained nibbana."

As much as his mind hates the idea, the only conclusion Aggachitta can reach right now is the same that countless Buddhist philosophers before him have reached, which is that thirst is indeed a metaphor. He cannot be satisfied with that explanation. Maybe the word has a particular connotation that has been lost over the ages. Then it would not be a metaphor, for he despises the use of metaphors in philosophical statements.

What modern connotations does the word thirst have? It conveys the search for something greater, or more stimulating, pleasure producing, than what one has already experienced, as in the sentence, "He thirsts for adventure."

Then he thinks about thirsting for fame, for wealth, for adoration, for power, and even for knowledge. It occurs to him that the central thread connecting all these objects is dissatisfaction with what one already has combined with an unstoppable momentum to get something greater than that.

Such thirsts are never truly satisfied. The object of thirst is not material; it does not have a specific size, shape, or weight. It can always grow beyond one's grasp.

This line of thought leads right into grasping, or clinging, which is the next link. It is another puzzling term. However, is he finished with thirst yet? He doesn't want to go on before he is. Just at that moment, he catches thirst in action. It's the thirst in his investigation that makes it impossible to hold onto what thirst is for any length of time. Instead of looking at thirst, he is thirsty. Thirsty to know what thirst is. He can't just be satisfied knowing what little he has come to know thirst to be. His mind is thirst-driven.

Aggachitta knows that all minds are thirst-driven in this way. Coming and going, that is all about thirst, as is the past, present, and future. The mind can't think a thought without being dissatisfied with it in some way to seek another thought. The same holds true with sensations, feelings, and perceptions. When one feels pleasure, one doesn't immediately grasp it tightly as the traditionalists believe. Instead one thirsts after another pleasurable experience, for once the present one is felt, it is no longer an object of satisfaction. Then what is grasping?

Now the puzzle has shifted to the next element, for Aggachitta believes he now understands what tanha is. That understanding is soon buried by tanha, just as when one digs a whole in the sand, the sand slips back in to any space that is cleared.

CHAPTER
17

Maggaphala stops at the outhouse before going up to the cave. His mind is heavy. He doesn't like the way he behaved towards Sumana. He was heavy-handed. He could have crushed Sumana's self-esteem by the insinuation of his attaining sotapanna being a deception, a contagious self-delusion.

As Maggaphala walks towards the cave, he imagines humankind being infected by a virus, a psycho-spiritual disease. This virus creates unfathomable and impenetrable delusion in the mind, making it impossible to see and understand things clearly. A miracle cure is discovered. It is manufactured worldwide and distributed free of charge. However, those who take it eventually find that the miracle cure creates its own new disease, one that is initially less harmful, though its long-term effects are still quite dreadful. Such a miracle cure was administered to him a quarter of a century ago when his teacher told him he was a sotapanna. Did Aggachitta get the same miracle cure, or did he get a purer batch of it, one that may have actually worked?

The climb up to the cave is a bit too strenuous for Maggaphala. He pants as he moves his heavy body up the small hill to the cave's entrance. Once inside, he plops down on one of the wooden chairs. His breathing is labored. His chest hurts. He wants to go back to his thoughts, but his body holds his attention a while longer. Aches appear around his shoulders and his knees. His calves feel tight. His body and mind are in agitated union, both victims of his heaviness of form and thought, neither under his control. This is suffering, he tells himself, only half believing it. The other half believes that when it passes, all will be fine.

His mind goes back to his previous train of thought. What is the disease I have discovered? What should I call it? Then again, what did the Buddha call it? He said it was ignorance. The so-called miracle cure, what is it called? They call it vipassana, thinking that they have discovered the one true path to nibbana. What would I call it? I have always liked the word *abhutaparikalpa*, even though it does come from Mahayana Buddhism. It gets at it best: imaginings that are not real, which are treated as real.

Innocent people go on a meditation retreat to find true liberation of mind, and instead they get an imaginary sense of being on the path to liberation. They believe it is real, for everyone around them believes in the medicine of the teachings they have received. They try to act liberated, promoting their views and practices while denouncing the ways of other teachers and religions. There it is. It is not just an abstract belief in what is not so as being so, but also a conceit about being one of the privileged few who are on the path to nibbana. Only they are not on the path to nibbana. How could they be?

Maggaphala's breathing moves from agitation to the verge of hyperventilation as he develops this train of thought. He senses a nebulous form of rage underneath his thoughts, but he does not know how to investigate it. He can't see any further into himself than he is prepared to know, and he has never been this far before. He surrenders to a sigh. He can think no more about this. Just then, Rahula enters the cave.

At first Rahula is unaware of his visitor, but as he goes over towards his bed, he hears Maggaphala breathing with difficulty. His initial reaction is fear, the kind that freezes one for a few moments. Then he looks over towards where he hears the breathing and notices the dim outline of a heavyset man in bhikkhu's robes sitting in a chair. From that he assumes that his visitor is his uncle's friend.

Rahula goes over and dutifully prostrates before Maggaphala, who has difficulty catching his breath well enough to speak, until he finally wheezes, "No need to do that."

Rahula sits on the ground not far from Maggaphala. He's not sure why he's sitting down, doing so more out of habit than anything else. This puts Maggaphala in the awkward position of speaking to Rahula at a time when having a conversation is the last thing on his mind.

"Young man, I understand that you are Venerable Aggachitta's nephew. Are you planning on becoming a bhikkhu like your uncle?"

"I'm not sure," Rahula says, pleased that he knows the answer to this question and doesn't feel at all embarrassed by it.

"Then what are you doing here? Wouldn't it be better for you to stay somewhere you can study or find work?"

"My parents sent me here. They are concerned about my welfare. People say the college campuses are not safe. Students are being killed and abducted all the time."

"It's not as bad as that," Maggaphala says, reassuringly enough, though he remembers reports of rebels, in the guise of students, assassinating teachers and administrators. When the troops come in, the campuses turn into bloody battlefields. What a horrible time to seek a higher education! Better to be safe in the jungle.

"How do you spend your time?" Maggaphala asks.

"I do some of the chores my uncle and the white-skinned monk can't do because they're bhikkhus. I have a lot of free time. Right now I'm reading a book."

"Oh, you are. What book is that?"

"*The Woman in the Dunes.*"

Maggaphala is familiar with this book. He studied it in graduate school and even wrote an essay on it.

"That is an advanced book. How are you coming along with it?"

"I've read about forty pages."

"Let me tell you something about that book. The first time
I read it I did not know what to make of it. Then I read it again
in order to write an essay on it. It started to make sense. The
man wasn't trapped in the house in the dunes. The woman
really wasn't keeping him for her own needs. That was a
delusion the man lived under. See, believing one is trapped in
a situation like that is often a delusion. We go off seeking to
discover something important, in this man's case, a new form
of sand beetle, and end up captive to a community that, by
nature, has its ways of keeping us an integral member. We only
call it a trap and rebel against it when we don't want to be a
member of that community, or live by the rules of that
community, though we are happy enough when the
community sees to it that our needs are met.

"It is the notion that the individual exists before
community that creates the sense of being trapped. Our
existence in isolation is the delusion the man lives under. The
truth of existence is that a person can't exist in isolation. When
he realizes he can go free and decides to stay, he is at peace
with his life. There is no more thirst. He awakes from the
dream of an individual existence apart from others to the real
world of being with others."

Maggaphala feels satisfied that he has captured the
essence of his essay of nearly three decades ago. Whether he
currently thinks that way is another question. For back then he
believed that social and political action brings about progressive social change. It was only later, when he became interested
in Buddhism, that he put his attention on individual growth as
a necessary requirement for expansive, long-term social
reform.

Today, however, as he thinks about the man's predicament
with the woman in the dunes, he glimpses a sociological
connection to his earlier thoughts on the miracle cure. When
someone is told that he has attained the path and fruit, and is
thus a sotapanna, he joins a community, a type of pseudo-
spiritual brotherhood. In those monasteries and meditation
centers where people are told they are sotapannas, an inner

circle forms. This special community usually has a hierarchy, whereby the head monk or teacher is considered the most spiritually advanced, and is either an arhat, or one attainment lower, an anagami. The junior teachers are often thought of as belonging to the next stage down, while everyone else in the club is a sotapanna, except for the occasional outstanding meditation student, who can rise to great heights and reflect favorably on his teacher. In these communities, no one can say what his attainment is, for that is against the rules, but he can have others hint at what he believes his attainment to be.

Yet the connection to the novel is hard for Maggaphala to pinpoint. Is a man held captive in a house with a woman in the dunes somehow like a man who lives in a monastery under the delusion that he is awakened? No matter how much you dig the sand, it just keeps returning. There's no way to climb walls of sand either. But that might not be the delusion of what is not so being so. It's just the delusion of being trapped. Maggaphala's thinking rarely ever gets this involved and tangled. It must be his contact with his old friend. He wonders if Aggachitta's more complex thoughts are clearer, more penetrating than his own. For his thoughts do not satisfy him. There are always too many ways to argue against any of his conclusions.

"Thank God! What the Buddha called Right View is not about being right about everything," he mumbles to himself as he begins to drift off in his chair. Soon he's snoring. Rahula quietly gets up and leaves.

Maggaphala's consciousness emerges from a momentary deep, peaceful sleep and into a dream-world continuation of his previous thoughts. He's on the dunes as one of the workman hoisting up buckets of sand from a submerged house. He looks down below at the house, expecting to see a thatched hut, but instead his vision rests on what looks like a white teepee. The teepee looks like a rhinoceros horn. Outside of it is a monk shoveling sand into a bucket. The monk glances up at him. He recognizes the monk. It is his old friend Aggachitta. Aggachitta lifts up the shiny new metal bucket above his head and tilts it, and instead of sand falling, water pours from it over his body. Maggaphala moves away and looks around him. Where he saw sand, he now sees water. Floating on the water are little rafts, each with a single monk seated in meditation. In the distance, he sees a shore. "That is the other shore." The land glows white. The white light spreads, engulfing him, and he feels serenely held as if he were a baby floating on a leaf in the water. "This is the Way of Delusion," another voice says. His mind then drifts back into a dark, deep sleep.

When he awakes, he begins thinking again about all these meditating monks with their false attainments adrift on rafts in the great ocean, imagining that they are heading towards the other shore. Somehow they are all tied together, which gives the appearance of going in the same direction, but in truth, they are equally tossed by the watery currents of their deluded minds. It may be possible at some time or another one of them cuts his ties with the group and goes off on his own. That is what Maggaphala has done. Perhaps that is all he has really done in all these years of being a monk. The other shore however, still glows far off in the distance. "Is it actually reachable?" Maggaphala says aloud to himself.

CHAPTER
18

Rahula leaves the cave and walks over to the dining hut. There he finds Sumana and the four laymen who came this morning. Sumana is just finishing a hard-boiled egg.

Sumana and Rahula have nothing to say to each other, and neither of them speaks to the four laymen. There is a stillness about this scene that lasts for about two minutes, when it is broken by Aggachitta walking at a quickened pace up the path towards them.

Aggachitta wears his robe draped around both shoulders, wrapped tightly around his body. He has his alms bowl in his right hand tucked under the folds of his robe. When Sumana looks up at him, he becomes immediately aware that Aggachitta is dressed to go on alms round. Sumana doesn't have his watch with him and can only guess at the time. He surmises it must be after ten o'clock and imagines them reaching the nearest village a few minutes before noon, with barely any time to collect alms and eat. He quickly chews the last piece of bread and then gets up from the bench to wrap himself up in his robe.

Sumana is putting the final twists in the fabric around his body to make it secure for a long journey, when Aggachitta announces that they will go to the town of the four laymen, and would the laymen like to accompany them. They ask about Venerable Maggaphala, and Rahula informs everyone that he is asleep in the cave.

"Then, Rahula, you will have to return with alms for him," Aggachitta says.

Rahula goes over to a small cupboard near the stove and pulls out a nylon shopping bag.

Now they are all ready.

Aggachitta walks in front with Sumana behind him. He leads them in the opposite direction from which Sumana arrived just two days earlier. This takes them past the monument where Sumana encountered the cobra. Beyond the monument, the jungle becomes quite dense. Aggachitta has to push aside branches as he walks. The six others follow him, doing the same. Sumana frets over the image he has of several miles of dense brush before they reach the nearest village. His feet are wet and full of mud, as he is not wearing sandals like the others. A branch hits him in the right eye, and he stops to check whether he can still see out of it. The five laymen, including Rahula, wait impatiently behind Sumana as he rubs his eye and then cups a hand over his other eye to make sure he still has vision. He is surprised to find that his right eye sees more clearly than his left one.

Aggachitta stops several paces ahead, wondering what has happened to everyone. He becomes conscious of his own impatience. He has this urge to get to the library in the monastery of the neighboring village and pull out some of the books he remembers seeing there but never had the need to read. Now he does. Now he is determined to set the record straight on the Buddha's teaching on conditionality.

Sumana and the others finally catch up with Aggachitta. The path gets easier a few yards up, as the ground is less damp and is covered with short grass. Then it opens out into a coconut plantation. They walk on a clearly defined trail through the evenly spaced coconut trees. Sumana is pleased that the journey has gotten easier, though he is soon surprised when it ends abruptly as they reach a dirt road with houses on it. They turn right on the dirt road and in no time arrive at a paved road flanked by shops and buildings, one of which is a two-storey whitewashed monastery.

Sumana is bewildered by what has happened. He was told that the hermitage was in a remote jungle, which is true when approached from the other side. Frankly, he is relieved to find the town so close. The isolation of the hermitage was starting to get to him. Now he knows that he can easily walk to other monasteries and houses of well-to-do devout laypeople for alms. Perhaps there are even other foreign monks in this town.

They walk up the steps of the monastery and go inside behind Aggachitta. A young monk greets them, bowing to Aggachitta. Aggachitta asks about the head monk and requests to see him. He is led down a hallway to the right. Sumana and the others are motioned to go down the hallway to the left where the dining hall is.

The dining hall is a large room the size of a well-equipped cafeteria. Along the walls to their right are benches laid out in an L-shape. Sumana hands his bowl to Rahula as he changes the fold of his robes to the more casual one-shoulder-bared look. He glances up and down the benches, where about thirty monks of all ages sit in the order of their ordination, and wonders to himself where he would fit in. This would take a considerable amount of discussion with the seated monks, so Sumana drops the idea of finding his proper place in the hierarchy and decides to sit down next to the last monk, who is just a young boy. Rahula brings him his bowl and Sumana motions him to hold it a while longer as he pulls out a handkerchief and places it in his lap, and then motions Rahula to hand him his bowl. Sumana sets it down squarely on the handkerchief over his thighs, testing the placement of his bowl, making sure it will not tip over with the weight of all the food it will be required to bear.

A group of laypeople forms a line at the opposite end of the L from Sumana. Each person holds a large dish of some kind of prepared food. Sumana looks up from his bowl to count how many dishes there are. With over ten counted, he returns his gaze to the black hollow bowl on his lap. He calculates that there will be at least two fish dishes, three vegetable dishes, and two kinds of rice. He is eager to find out what extra tasty morsels might be coming his way. As the food-givers near him, he has an urge to look up from his bowl and catch a glimpse of someone ladling something into one of his neighbor's bowls, just so he might know beforehand what kind of delicious treat to expect. They are ladling the food so fast into the monks' bowls, that whatever is at the end of each spoonful blurs before his short, furtive glances. When it is finally his turn, he keeps his eyes focused on the empty center of his bowl as one spoonful after another creates small mounds within it. The last layperson passes by and now he can put his right hand into his bowl and inspect the offerings of food there. He likes what he finds. When he lifts a piece of deep fried fish fillet to his mouth, he is filled with delight. The fish is delicious. So are the green beans and carrots, the lentils, the cubes of grilled fish, and the Sri Lankan red rice. Sumana eats like a man who has been starving for days.

Aggachitta sits in a large cushioned chair opposite an elderly bhikkhu seated in the same kind of chair. He speaks to the senior bhikkhu, Venerable Ananda, who has been the head of this monastery for as long as Aggachitta can remember.

"My needs are small. A room with a desk and a lamp would do just fine. I will only use it on occasion."

"We have many monks here these days. It may be difficult to locate an empty room for you."

"Do you have a quiet place where I can write and study?"

"We have a small library. It is not used much."

"That will do."

"Venerable Aggachitta, I am curious as to why a forest monk would need a room in town. Aren't your quarters ample for your needs?"

"I will be consulting books and writing down my thoughts. For that I need electric light and access to a good library of Buddhist texts."

"It must be a great work of scholarship you have planned. May I ask what you are writing?"

Aggachitta is a bit hesitant to share his secret ambition with Ananda. Ananda has been a monk for longer than Aggachitta has been alive. He has taught countless young monks the basics of Buddhism. Only his Buddhism, the standard Theravada Buddhism of Sri Lanka, is reduced to one list of concepts after another, which when memorized, give the appearances of having tapped the deeper truths of the Buddha's teaching, but are, in the final reckoning, just words. Aggachitta has disdain for such rigid distortions of the Buddha's message of liberation. Such bhikkhus will never understand the transcendent logic of Aggachitta's thought. Ananda's well-intentioned question, accompanied by a friendly smile, puts Aggachitta in a position he wishes he were not in, for now he is obliged to explain his radical way of thinking so that a stodgy concept-counter can grasp it.

"It is an involved work of philosophy. I have not done enough work to be able to summarize it yet. Let me just say that I explore the structural theory of conditionality and compare it with the more familiar sequential theory. I will attempt a highly refined delineation of causal elements found in the diverse chains of conditioned phenomena stated by the Buddha."

Having said this much, in this way, Aggachitta feels not so bad. He now hopes that Ananda will not want to discuss it further. With some other monk, like Maggaphala, he would more than welcome a discussion following such a statement.

"Your intelligence and wisdom have always impressed me, Venerable Aggachitta. It sounds like a worthy undertaking. Please use our library as often as you like and I will secure you a private room for your stay here. It is an honor to know you."

Aggachitta clasps his hands together, showing reverential respect toward Ananda, feeling truly appreciative of the elder bhikkhu's generosity and kindness. Venerable Ananda gets up from his chair and motions Aggachitta to follow him.

Ananda hobbles down the long hallway towards the dining hall, with Aggachitta on his heels. They enter the dining hall. Instead of sitting with the rest of the monks, who are engrossed in their meal, they go into a small room off the dining hall, a kind of breakfast nook, which has windows and a round table with chairs and plates. As soon as are they seated, lay-people come in and begin ladling food onto their plates.

After lunch, one of the temple monks, a tall young bhikkhu of Sumana's age, who goes by the name of Kusala, approaches Sumana and starts up a conversation in English. He's friendly enough, and certainly well meaning, but Sumana feels more disposed to napping than conversing. Sumana asks this monk if there is a place for him to rest. Kusala leads him down the same hallway he came, and then down the corridor leading to Ananda's office. From there they turn right down another long hallway to the library. It has a couple of folding tables with chairs and a long couch situated along one of the walls. There are bookcases stocked with many large hard-backed books on the wall opposite the couch.

Kusala then leaves, shutting the door behind him. Sumana gets comfortable on the couch, lying on his back. As his mind flows towards sleep, he recognizes that this is his second nap of the day. He tells himself it is all right after a large meal. He relives the meal, trying to recall the splendid tastes, but his palate is overwhelmed by the numbing cold of the chocolate ice cream he had for dessert. Awareness of his cold mouth, tongue and throat gives him a slight chill. A fear arises, one that he immediately uncovers as a fear of dreaming, for he does not want to go back to the lay life again. He likes the monk's life best after a sumptuous meal and a satisfying rest. All he wants is for his mind to go blank, to be empty for twenty or thirty refreshing minutes. As he lies on his back, waiting to dissolve into nothingness, he knows a moment of pure contentment. This is the life!

Aggachitta finishes his meal, refusing dessert, though Ananda attempts to persuade him to try the avocado mixed with sweet treacle.

"It is better than ice cream," he says.

Aggachitta knows that the main reason the old monk likes it is that he does not have to chew it. All he has to do is spoon the greenish brown pudding up to his mouth and swish it back and forth a couple of times and then swallow. It is a toothless operation, perfect for a man who has lost all his teeth.

Aggachitta thirsts for something else, now that the obligatory meal is past. He excuses himself, bowing to Ananda, who has a beatific smile covering a mouth full of sweetened avocado. The old monk swallows and then says, "Join me for tea at two. I have some ideas on conditionality too."

The invitation for tea is to be expected, but the notion that Venerable Ananda might have actual thoughts on conditionality catches Aggachitta off guard.

Aggachitta fumbles for words. "I must leave soon after tea. I have things to do at the hermitage. Perhaps we could talk some other time, when I have progressed further in my work."

"I am at your service," Ananda says. "It is a privilege to assist such a great scholar and renowned meditation master."

Aggachitta leaves Ananda and retraces his steps back to Ananda's office, and then turns right onto the hallway leading to the monastery's library. He wants to get down to work. His mind is bustling with thoughts about the links in the great chain of causation. He considers the relationship of sense impressions with the formation of cravings, digging into the intricate fashioning of pleasure and pain in all of this. Just as he reaches the door to the library, he has a revelation about the dissolution of pain and pleasure and the ending of thirst forever. He must hurry and write it down before it vanishes. Balancing that thought in his mind like a plate on his head, he opens the door to the library and goes to a table, which, as luck would have it, has a pad of paper and pencils on it. He sits down and begins to set down his understanding, but he is distracted by an unusual sound. Someone is snoring nearby. He is at once drawn to find out who it is, but pushes that impulse away and continues writing down his thoughts. His thoughts are punctuated with bursts of irritation at the person sleeping. Nonetheless, he gets them down and is relieved that he was able to do so with such a gross disturbance in the room.

He gets up from the desk and looks at the sleeping monk. It is Sumana, his student. He should have known. Western monks tend to treat these large danas like buffets, stuffing themselves unconscious. He has seen it before. The question now is whether he should wake Sumana and tell him to sleep elsewhere or should he find somewhere else to continue his writing. He decides in the best interest of the Buddha's teaching that he should wake Sumana. A library is a library. It is not a guest room.

Aggachitta rouses Sumana, who awakes groggy and disoriented, not recognizing Aggachitta, mistaking him for one of the temple monks he noticed at dana.

"You can't sleep here," Aggachitta calmly informs him.

"Why? I was told I could," Sumana says, annoyed and sluggish.

"You are mistaken," Aggachitta replies.

"Where can I take a nap?" Sumana asks, rubbing his eyes, but still not recognizing the Sinhalese face looking down at him.

Aggachitta knows this monastery fairly well, having stayed here often during his twenty years in the forest. Of all the rooms, the library is really the most logical place, because it is quiet and has a couch. However, after the laypeople have finished eating, Sumana would be able to sleep in the dining hall.

"Try the dining hall."

Now Sumana is able to take a good look at the man speaking to him and is startled to realize that it's his teacher. He knows he's been terribly disrespectful, and with such knowledge of his inappropriate behavior, feels intensely embarrassed. He jumps up off the couch and says, "I'm sorry, Venerable Aggachitta. I didn't recognize you. Your suggestion sounds good. I'll go to the dining hall straight away."

Sumana hurries out of the room. He is still groggy, but not really so tired any more. He's in a more or less lethargic haze, one that often follows overeating. He takes a wrong turn, which leads him into the belly of the monastery, where there is a courtyard bounded by rows of rooms like an apartment building. In the middle of the courtyard is a fenced-in grassy area where there are several pet rabbits. Sumana leans against the fence and watches one rabbit after another, wishing for one of the furry creatures to come close enough for him to pet.

Someone taps him on the shoulder. It is Kusala. Next to him is Rahula with a full shopping bag of food morsels wrapped in newspaper.

"We should get back to the hermitage," Rahula says.

"What's the hurry?" Sumana says, not because he particularly wants to stay, but more from a desire to rest, relax, be in the world a little while longer.

Kusala interjects, "White-skinned nun lives in house in town."

Sumana turns around to look at him. He is a handsome monk, seemingly healthy and happy, the kind of Sinhalese monk Sumana can see becoming his friend.

"Where does this white-skinned nun stay?" Sumana asks.

"I show you. Not far. You want go there?"

Sumana looks at Rahula, trying to gauge his interest in this adventure. He is fully aware that not only does he need Rahula to lead him back to the forest hermitage, but he also has to have a layman present whenever he is alone with a woman, and so must have him come along. Rahula's blank expression indicates neither interest nor disinterest. However, Sumana is definitely interested in meeting the foreign nun.

"Lead the way," Sumana says, with perhaps more enthusiasm than he would wish to express.

The three of them leave the monastery together and walk along the main road through town. There are the typical rows of tightly packed small shops. Since Sumana can't handle money, he often ignores these little shops. The only ones that usually catch his attention are the casket-makers. In America, you only see a casket at an undertaker's establishment. Here in Sri Lanka, a casket shop is like any other. Seeing such a shop makes Sumana wonder if death is more prevalent here, a growing business, what with the constant civil war. As they pass the casket-maker's shop, Sumana stops to inspect the handy-work from a distance. The woods are beautifully hewn and lacquered. These are not shabby caskets, as one might see in newsreels on mass murders in Third World countries.

They turn onto a side street that takes them to a residential area. Kusala opens a gate leading to a two-storey house and they all follow him down a short path and then up the steps to the front door. He knocks at the door.

A thin older woman answers the door. She is a ten-precept nun — a woman who is not a bhikkuni, but is also not a laywoman. The order of bhikkunis disappeared from Sri Lanka, and the other Theravada countries, several centuries ago. Within the last few years, there have been attempts to reinstate it by way of Chinese Buddhism, which has maintained an order of bhikkunis up to the present. Instead of bhikkunis, the Theravadin countries have women who follow either eight or ten precepts, shave their heads, and wear robes, though not the same colors the monks wear. Many of these women live a life of poverty, as they do not receive the generous donations that monks do. They must also live in groups of at least two or more. Some of them become schoolteachers, while others live in rooms near or in a monastery, where they do chores and prepare meals.

When the nun sees the monks, she prostrates before them three times. Sumana is not comfortable with this display, hoping that she does not touch his feet, for if she does and he enjoys it even for a second, he would then have to confess it when he got back to the hermitage. He moves back a little. She rises and asks them if they would like to come in. Kusala asks her if the white-skinned nun lives here. She answers by motioning them into the living room. The two bhikkhus sit on a couch and Rahula sits on the floor.

Sumana waits nervously for the white-skinned nun to appear. He tries to recall if he has heard about her before, but can't recollect any mention of a foreign nun living in this part of the island. Perhaps they know some foreign monks in common. Sumana sees that subject as a good way to break the ice if nothing else does.

She enters the room. Her robes are bright yellow, and she wears a traditional blouse with tight sleeves that cover her arms down to her wrists. Her head is shaved clean. Her eyes are green and her features are very light and delicate. She moves gracefully towards them and pulls out a handkerchief, prostrating before them three times about a meter from their feet. She finishes bowing and rises, sitting on her knees, with her hands clasped in front of her in respect.

Sumana is transfixed by her face. She is quite young, probably about twenty. She was undeniably a beautiful woman before becoming a nun. Her face is thin, but that is because she has no hair. Unlike the nuns who have spent time in Thailand, she still has her eyebrows, which are reddish-brown. On further inspection, which is something Sumana is not aware he is doing, she has light freckles around her nose, creamy skin, and thin lips. She smiles, as if knowing she is being admired, and her teeth are white and even.

"I am Gotami," she says. "What are your names?"

"My name is Sumana, and the other monk is Kusala, while the young layman is Rahula."

"I am pleased that you have come to visit me. I didn't know that an American bhikkhu was staying here in town."

"I'm actually staying at Atakkachari Arañña. We just came for dana at the monastery."

"Oh, I see. So where are you from, Venerable Sumana?"

"I am from California."

"So am I. Whereabouts?"

"San Diego."

"San Diego! Why so am I!" she says, letting out a laugh. "What a coincidence! Did you meditate at the temple there?"

"No, not much. I mostly went to retreats in the Bay Area and then sat with a small group in Hillcrest."

"Funny, I never went to the Hillcrest group. I preferred the Buddhist temple. I was originally interested in Zen. But what I wanted was to see India. And so here I am."

Rahula and Kusala half listen to their conversation, putting more of their attention on Gotami's and Sumana's facial expressions. Rahula sees Sumana as reserved, while Gotami appears relaxed and at ease. Kusala finds Gotami's style of communication quite delightful and wishes he could join in, but he doesn't know enough English to have this kind of conversation.

"How long have you been in robes?" Sumana asks.

"Only about three months."

"How do you like it?"

"Frankly," she says, her expression changing towards displeasure, "I don't really like it here. I want to find a place where I can read and meditate and talk to monks about the Buddha's teaching."

"Can't you do that here?" Sumana asks.

"There are no books in English. It is also too noisy and busy around here to meditate. Besides, I have chores to do, and I am not allowed to go to the monastery alone. When I do visit there, the only one who will see me is Venerable Ananda. He's a nice monk, but he's very old and not such a great teacher."

"Well, maybe my teacher, Venerable Aggachitta, can be your teacher too. He's at the monastery now. He's the most famous meditation master in all of Sri Lanka."

"Really! That would be great!" She exclaims with far more enthusiasm than is comfortable for everyone.

Her exclamation apparently catches the ear of the senior nun who comes into the room and now stands at a distance, with an intimidating stare directed at Sumana. This makes Sumana even more uncomfortable, so he rises from the couch. The other two men also rise and all three of them proceed to walk out of the room. Near the front door, he notices that Gotami has gotten up and followed them. He turns around to face her.

She is only five or six inches shorter than he is. Her green eyes look right into his. Something in him turns to liquid. He loses his voice.

"Will you talk to your teacher for me?" she asks.

"Yes," Sumana says, looking directly into her eyes, and then through her eyes to what he imagines is behind them: a feeling, one that he believes is shared, of two lonely people taking leave of each other, dreading never having the chance to see each other again. As Sumana turns towards the door and walks out of the house, he warns himself that this is a dangerous feeling.

CHAPTER
19

Sumana, Rahula, and Kusala walk back to the monastery in town. Rahula and Kusala talk in Sinhala. Sumana ignores their conversation, since there is not much of it he can understand. His thoughts center around whether he had seen Gotami before at one of the Buddhist functions he went to in San Diego. He imagines that her hair was blonde like her eyebrows. It must have been straight, soft, and silky. It's a bit harder to picture the kind of clothes she would have worn. Though she certainly wasn't wearing bright yellow robes. Perhaps she wore blue jeans and a colored blouse. That's a safe assumption. She would have been very young then, perhaps only fourteen years old. In that case, it would seem impossible that he'd have ever met her, since an adolescent would never go to a Western Buddhist function, unless it was at her parent's house. Sumana was one of the youngest people at the Hillcrest group, and he was twenty-three.

Sumana becomes aware that they have arrived back at the monastery. Rahula says that he has to go in to get the food for Maggaphala and tell his uncle that they are going back to the hermitage. Sumana replies that he will wait outside for him. Rahula runs up the steps, leaving Kusala with Sumana.

Kusala stands next to Sumana, thinking of some way to start up a conversation. He finally lands on an idea.

"You are Aggachitta student, right?"

Sumana utters a distracted, "Yes."

"Is he arhat?"

Sumana returns to the present moment with that question.

"I don't know. He may be an arhat," he says, and then recalls the incident of Aggachitta shouting when splashed with water at the outhouse, "but I think he's not quite an arhat. Maybe he's an anagami."

"Why not arhat?" Kusala asks, curious as to whether Sumana has found out something secret about Aggachitta.

"It's nothing," Sumana says.

Kusala is now very interested in what Sumana might know.

"You see something?"

"Well, if you want to know, I'll tell you what happened."

Sumana goes on to relate the whole story of the outhouse incident.

Rahula goes back to the dining hall where he left the shopping bag. He picks up the bag and then goes down the hall to find his uncle. He asks a monk where Aggachitta is. The monk does not know, but does know whom to ask, leading him to Ananda's office.

Ananda is in his chair behind the desk. He asks Rahula to sit in one of the high-backed chairs facing him. He wants to know all about Rahula, where he was born, who his parents are, and is delighted to discover that Rahula is Venerable Aggachitta's nephew.

Now Rahula can get to the reason he is here.

"Bhante, do you know where my uncle is? I must inform him that I am going back to the hermitage."

"He is probably in the library, doing some important work. It is best we do not disturb him. I will be having tea with him shortly and will tell him for you."

"Thank you, Venerable Sir." Rahula gets up and bows to the elderly monk, hurrying out the door.

Rahula feels bad that he has kept Sumana waiting for so long and is somewhat relieved when he sees Sumana talking to Kusala, who is laughing at something Sumana is saying. Sumana is speaking in an animated way with many body gestures. Rahula sees Sumana act out an expression of being shocked by something, looking around himself frantically, and then scampering off. It is at that moment that Rahula approaches him and says, in a soft, dry voice, that they should get back to hermitage.

Sumana chuckles and Kusala laughs some more as they part. Rahula wonders what Sumana was telling him. Someday he will have to ask Sumana.

Aggachitta sits at a table in the study with several books spread out before him. He has been going from one book to another, jumping around a good deal, trying to collect all the relevant sutta passages on conditionality. Any lesser mind might jumble up the causes, the supports, the various sources of suffering and make a messy collage of conditionality. His mind orders all of these elements into a perfect structure, and when he sets a link in motion, it easily propels the next link and so on, like a row of dominoes.

His thoughts flow on. The force that propels is *sankhara*, the heart and soul of the Buddha's teaching on conditionality. Sankhara is the glue that holds the structures together. It is the craftsman, Vishvakarman, who molds the structures. Ignorance, the source of sankhara, is like Brahma, existing before all, giving life to the builder of the world, and then stepping aside, shrouded in eternal emptiness, emanating His realization, detached from His creation. It is the builder that we can only see when it lifts a fin above the muddy waters of consciousness, like some great whale in the ocean. We can never capture the beast that is sankhara. It swallows us whole every moment of every life, and we live in its belly, never knowing the world beyond.

Aggachitta is astonished by this mixture of metaphors from other major religions. He has always considered such allegorical language too imaginative, and therefore ambiguous, for serious philosophic research. Perhaps he has to exercise his intellect with such ways of thinking, to strengthen his mind for what lies ahead. For he knows he must soon leave the poetry and diversity of the suttas and enter the cool intellectual world of the *abhidharma*, where no word escapes exact definition, and all counter arguments are listed along with the ways to demolish them. From there, he must make a foray into the treacherous logic of Nagarjuna. Only after that will he attempt to understand the analytical brilliance of Vasubandhu and the logical precision of Dharmakirti. Then the repetitious reasoning of Buddhaghosa will be a walk in the park, though he fears that after all this careful examination, he may in the end find fault with Buddhaghosa. For a Theravadin scholar there is always danger in deviating from Buddhaghosa's point of view. It throws a good deal of the knowledge he has come to rely on into question. It turns the scholar into a rebel, and Aggachitta prefers to stay safely within the scope of orthodoxy. At least, that is how he has always thought of himself.

He leans back in his chair and closes his eyes. He wonders where this journey will take him.

CHAPTER
20

Sumana and Rahula make their way back to the hermitage in silence. Rahula is not completely familiar with the trails that lead through the jungle, so the two of them zigzag their way through the dense brush, heading generally in the right direction. Sumana can tell this by the position of the sun. Rahula knows by glancing around at the hills in the distance and the ones nearby. They arrive at the hill where the monument to Atakkachari is. Sumana fears that the cobra he saw yesterday is here waiting for him. He keeps an eye out for it.

As they pass the monument, they see Maggaphala coming up the path to greet them. He is in a bit of hurry.

"I am glad you have come back so early. I woke up and everyone was gone. I need to eat," he says looking at the shopping bag in Rahula's hand.

Rahula hands it to Maggaphala, who opens it and takes a whiff of its contents. They follow Maggaphala back to the dining hut. Sumana decides to go to his hut. He can't understand why Maggaphala, or any monk for that matter, would break the rule about not eating after noon. If he had bothered to ask Maggaphala, he would have found an acceptable reason, a loophole in the rule, which some believe to be a modern interpretation, which allows a monk to eat after noon for medical reasons. Maggaphala is a diabetic. He has to control his diet, which he does in a very limited way, avoiding sweets and eating a few times a day to keep his blood sugar constant.

Sumana's attention soon leaves thoughts of Maggaphala and follows images of Gotami. He keeps seeing her shiny white face and yellow-robed body, and replays her facial expressions, her exclamations, and her confession of not being happy. He imagines introducing her to Aggachitta so that she can start a consistent meditation practice. That reminds him that he has barely meditated at all today.

He approaches his hut with the determination to go inside and immediately sit down to meditate. As he nears his hut however, he hears sounds coming from inside it. Someone is moving the table. Who could it be? Sumana freezes. A scenario of calling the police forms in his mind. "There is someone in my quarters," he hears himself saying over the phone. When that scenario fades away, he is left standing in front the door, terrified at the prospect of having to open it.

Nonetheless, he turns the knob, opening it just a crack. He peers inside the small hut and sees the back of a short white-skinned monk. This monk is stubby — not fat, but chunky — moving about with a gleeful lilt in his steps. Sumana immediately recognizes who it is, without seeing his face. It is his old friend, his mentor if you will, Venerable Palaparuchi.

Now Palaparuchi has a long history as a bhikkhu. He would be a bhikkhu of over twenty years if he hadn't disrobed twice for a few months. Each of those times was for an extended stay in a psychiatric ward, the most recent one being seven years ago. His doctors have variously diagnosed him with manic-depression, schizophrenia, acute psychosis, paranoia, post-traumatic stress disorder, generalized anxiety, attention deficit disorder, and as being pathologically narcissistic. He has taken medication for most of these psychological conditions with little, if any, success. The Sinhalese doctors often give up on him and leave him to his own devices after a while. In a well-ordered monastery, where all the monks keep a daily routine, Palaparuchi functions without any significant problems. It is when he goes out into the world, or the jungle, that he tends to have his most severe psychotic episodes.

Sumana is largely unaware of the extent of his friend's psychological condition. He knows that Palaparuchi has a tendency to get a little crazy, but wouldn't anyone who has been cooped up in a monastery for several months? Sumana has learned a great deal from Palaparuchi, for he has meditated with many world-renowned meditation teachers and has used their ideas and beliefs to create imagined identities. These days Palaparuchi fancies himself as one who has arrived at the attainment of anagami through the fourth jhana, where the six psychic powers of the Buddhas are supposedly developed. One who attains an advanced stage of liberating wisdom through this jhana may possess one, three, or all six of these super-normal abilities. In Palaparuchi's estimation, he has three of these powers: the Divine Ear, which enables him to hear the gods and what others say at a distance, the Divine Eye, which enables him to see invisible beings, and the third one, which is the ability to know the thoughts of others. With these powers, just the other day, he goes on to explain, he saw his friend Sumana in this hermitage. He heard Sumana thinking that he needed his friend Palaparuchi by his side to cut away the remaining defilements of mind so that he may enter nibbana.

Palaparuchi finishes making a space for himself to sleep on the floor of Sumana's hut. He has been to this hermitage before, passing through on a holiday with a large group of monks and lay people, so he knows that there are only two poorly furnished huts for monks and which one is designated for the junior monk. However, he has never met Venerable Aggachitta, who was away at the time, said to be staying at the monastery in town for a few days.

Sumana goes up to Palaparuchi and bows to him. Palaparuchi turns and has a big grin on his round, chubby face.

Palaparuchi says, "Sumana, great things are happening. You are on the edge of crossing over, of reaching the final destination."

Sumana straightens up and is a good ten inches taller than Palaparuchi. He looks down into his face and says, "How do you know these things?"

"I can't say," he says, hinting at the reason behind his comment. For a bhikkhu may not speak openly about any attainment. If he did, he would have to confess it.

"What brings you here?" Sumana asks. "I thought you were going to stay at the International Meditation Center until the rainy season."

"I've done enough meditating for a while. Now I want to make use of what I've gained from it. That's why I'm here: to help you with my new gifts."

Sumana is not at all sure what his friend means. Palaparuchi is hinting at things that Sumana knows are not possible for him. Now if Aggachitta had hinted at these very same things, Sumana would have little difficulty believing him. But Palaparuchi! His mind is far too distracted and agitated to arrive at any semblance of sublime concentration and insight. What's going on here?

Yet Sumana soon forgets these thoughts and moves on to more congenial topics of conversation.

"I hope you had a pleasant journey."

Palaparuchi nods.

"Will this be comfortable for you, sleeping on the floor? I can let you have the mattress," Sumana says.

"You can!" Palaparuchi exclaims. "That's perfect! My back has been bothering me and sleeping on the floor will definitely aggravate it."

Sumana was not expecting Palaparuchi to accept his offer.

"How long do you plan on staying?"

"Well," Palaparuchi says, "that depends on how long it takes. For some people it happens in an instant. For others it can take lifetimes."

Sumana imagines living with Palaparuchi for the rest of his life in the little hut. It already feels too confining and too intense for him. What's this "it" he refers to? It couldn't be nibbana, could it? If it is, Sumana fears, we're looking at lifetimes together. That thought makes him queasy. He must get some air.

Palaparuchi interrupts his thoughts with a pressing concern.

"Where is the bathing bucket? I need to bathe and can't find one."

Sumana pulls out the old leaky bucket from under the table.

"I can't use that! It's full of holes!" Palaparuchi says. "Doesn't this place have a decent bucket?"

"There's the meditation master's bucket," Sumana says.

"Well, where does he keep it?"

"In his hut, I guess."

"Is he here?"

"No," Sumana says, "he's in town."

"Good, let's go get it. By the way, do you have towels and soap?"

"There's a towel on the clothesline out back, and here's a bar of soap," Sumana says holding the bar of soap he used yesterday, wrapped in its paper packaging.

"Don't you have a soap dish?" Palaparuchi asks, grimacing at the slimy yellow soap in his hand.

"No."

"Well, let's go then, and get the meditation master's bucket."

Maggaphala sits on the bench in the dining hut, with his large black alms bowl on his lap, and the shopping bag on the bench next to him. He reaches inside the bag and pulls out one newspaper-wrapped packet of food after another, emptying their contents into his bowl. Slowly the bottom of his bowl fills with rice, fish, and vegetables. He pauses for a moment to reflect on the generosity of those who have given him this food, and on Rahula for his thoughtfulness in bringing him back something to eat. He is grateful. This food will bring physical comfort to his body. He then places his right hand into his bowl and scoops out a large handful of rice, fish, and vegetables, stuffing it into his mouth. He chews slowly and pauses reflectively before reaching into his bowl for another handful of food.

Rahula watches Maggaphala eat as he waits for the water to boil. He is daydreaming as he half attends to the kettle of water, alert only to the sound of it boiling over, which it eventually does, spattering onto the kerosene flame. This startles him. He turns down the flame, adds tea to the kettle, and lets it simmer. He wants to get back to his daydream, but forgets what it was. He only knows it had something to do with a woman. Was it the white-skinned nun or the woman in the dunes? Both seem oddly like the same woman. A woman trapped in a house, out of reach, alone in a foreign world. These thoughts don't make sense to Rahula, and he wonders why he's having them.

He doesn't understand what a woman is. He's only seen the behavior of girls, his sisters, and from that limited knowledge he can't know the mystery of what a woman is. He's gotten the notion, from the bhikkhus he's known, that a woman is always an object of lust, a source of temptation, and so must never be allowed into one's heart. What he's beginning to imagine is that a woman brightens the world, offers a man kindness and affection not possible otherwise, raises him above his limitations, enables him to achieve his dreams and arrive at his true destiny. This is how he wants to see women, and now remembers that he was thinking about his girlfriend in Colombo, imagining her to be both the nun and the woman in the dunes, and from there he sees her as the woman of his dreams.

Maggaphala finishes eating and looks over at Rahula, noticing the young man's blank gaze at the tea bubbling in the kettle. He coughs twice to snap Rahula out of his trance. Rahula looks over at Maggaphala lazily, and then realizes that he must bring the monk water to wash his hands and bowl. He grabs a pitcher of water and goes over to Maggaphala, who holds out his right hand, encrusted with rice grains, pepper powder, and coconut sauce, over the spittoon, waiting for the cool water to flow over it. The water puddles on his palm and then flows over between his fingers, and he moves his hand so that it touches each fingertip and finally his thumb, rinsing away all the accumulated food particles.

"I'll have tea later," Maggaphala says. "Right now I'm ready to bathe and take a nap. Will you hold tea for me?"

"Yes," Rahula says, still pulled into his thoughts about women.

Maggaphala rises from his seat, taking his bowl into his arms. He stops a moment and says to Rahula, "If you don't mind, I would like to use the cave as my lodgings for my stay here."

"I don't mind," Rahula says, more out of a habit to please than from actually not minding. "I can sleep here in the dining hut."

"Thank you," Maggaphala says, smiling at the boy in a friendly and appreciative way.

Rahula smiles back, but instead of feeling anything for Maggaphala, he touches a feeling of longing for the woman he imagines in his daydreams.

Sumana takes the leaky old bucket and follows Palaparuchi out of the hut. They go around to the clothesline and take the two towels hanging there. One is a long bath towel and the other is a short hand towel. Sumana gets the short one.

They walk over towards the meditation master's hut. Palaparuchi, whose name aptly describes a prominent feature of his personality, meaning "someone who desires gossip," relates to Sumana some details of monks they both know. He speaks mostly about one of their friends, an Australian monk, who's laid up in the hospital after a hernia operation, for he just visited this monk yesterday. Sumana wants to interject that he met a foreign nun today, but Palaparuchi continues his flow of chatter. He wants Sumana to comprehend the suffering their fellow monk is going through, having to live in a crowded hospital ward, on a mostly liquid diet, exposed to the constant blare of radios, even though he is supposed to be in a ward reserved for monks.

Suddenly Palaparuchi stops talking and shushes Sumana, who's been completely silent. He kneels down behind some bushes a few yards from Aggachitta's hut and signals Sumana to get down and hide.

He sees Maggaphala exiting the meditation master's hut. He's carrying the new shiny bucket.

"Is that the bucket?" Palaparuchi whispers to Sumana.

Sumana nods that it is.

"What is that monk doing here? I know him!" Palaparuchi says.

Sumana is about to answer, but Palaparuchi puts an index finger to his own lips, "Shhh! We don't want him to hear us."

Maggaphala walks past the bushes where they're hiding. He looks over and spots their orange robes and white shaven heads. Instead of stopping, he just walks on.

When Maggaphala is out of view, Palaparuchi says, "That monk is evil. Now I see why I had to come here. He'll try to stop you on the path."

"Where do you know him from?" Sumana asks, since that's the only question — of the possible questions coming to mind — that seems easy to ask.

"My first teacher. He was there when I was first told."

"Told what?"

"I can't reveal it," Palaparuchi says, making a gesture that his lips are sealed. "This monk finds ways to discredit worthy monks. He's a yakkha, an evil spirit in a grotesque body. I must protect you from him."

Sumana thinks a moment about the discrediting of worthy monks. That's exactly what he feels Maggaphala did to him earlier in the day. He hasn't thought about that for a few hours, and now when it comes back to mind, it is less a thought and more a feeling of pure rage. He hates anyone who thinks he's better than everyone else.

"You're right, he's a mean and envious monk," Sumana says.

"Oh, he is much worse than that!" Palaparuchi exclaims. "He's Mara incarnate. He's the Evil One. He's out to destroy the great teaching of the Buddha's. He casts doubts and suspicions on those who truly see and know, turning the ignorant away from the wise, leading them further into delusion."

Palaparuchi's dramatic language has a strong effect on Sumana. It is initially what attracted Sumana to him, for it makes him sound very knowledgeable indeed. When Palaparuchi speaks this way, Sumana gets a feeling of being on the right side, with the right people.

"What do we do now?" Sumana asks.

"What do you mean?" Palaparuchi says with a quizzical expression.

"We can't go to the cistern, for this monk will be there."

"Oh, that. Well there is only one thing to do. Let's go get a cup of tea."

Rahula pours himself a cup of tea, mixes in some sugar, and then sips it slowly. Between sips, during the silence that follows upon swallowing, he hears the faint sounds of movement in the bushes not far from him. He looks up at the trail leading to the dining hut, but sees no one, and so goes back to drinking his tea. The sound appears closer, as if just outside the hut. He sets his cup of tea down on the ground and gets up to see what is making the noise.

He goes around the hut, enters some of the dense brush in the direction of the sound, and feels something grab hold of his ankles. His body trembles with fear. When he looks down and sees the soft, delicate brown arms embracing his legs, he recognizes a purple plastic bracelet on the slender woman's wrist. His fear quickly dissipates. She stands up to face him and look into his eyes. She's thin, with long straight black hair, light brown skin, and dark brown eyes.

"How did you get here?" Rahula asks her.

"I took a bus from Colombo and then walked the rest of the way. I had to see you. Your last letter sounded so desperate. I was afraid that you had already decided to become a monk."

"Does anyone know?"

"About us? Well, maybe my parents."

"Do they know you are here?"

She steps back, swaying a little as she thinks up an answer.

"They know I love you."

"I have been thinking about you," Rahula says, recalling his earlier daydreams.

"What have you decided?"

This question is far too direct for Rahula's comfort.

"I want to be with you, but I don't know what I am going to do with my life."

"That's what I want to hear," she says, excitedly embracing him.

This is the first time a woman has ever embraced him. Rahula is not sure what to do, whether to put his arms around her or leave them by his side. He decides to leave his arms at his side; and she quickly ends the embrace.

"We can be together now," she says, looking into his eyes.

"You mean marriage," Rahula says, not knowing what just mentioning that word means to her.

"Yes, of course."

Just then, Rahula hears a man talking loudly in English. He feels a strong impulse to go back to the dining hut. She feels him pull away emotionally.

"You don't want to marry me?"

"I must go and do my job. Wait for me here. I'll be right back."

"All right," she says, happy with the thought of his hasty return, making herself a place to sit on the ground.

Rahula leaves her and reaches the dining hut before Palaparuchi and Sumana.

Palaparuchi enters the dining hut, sits down on the bench, and snaps at Rahula to get him a cup of tea. Rahula likes this kind of directness and immediately admires this monk for knowing what he wants.

Sumana sits down quietly next to Palaparuchi. He's decided to listen to his friend's endless jabber and not mention anything about meeting Gotami after all. The fact that he's met, her has turned into something very private and personal.

Palaparuchi gets his cup of tea and looks around with a sly grin. He wants something to go with his tea, such as a piece of sweet treacle.

Rahula watches Palaparuchi, trying to anticipate his needs, but he can't read his expressions.

Finally, Palaparuchi asks if any sweetener was added to his tea, which of course is the case, since it is awfully sweet.

Rahula replies, "Do you need more sugar?"

"Is there anything else you have instead?"

Rahula hunts around some tins near the stove and finds a cube of treacle, which he then offers to Palaparuchi with both hands. Palaparuchi accepts it and smiles at him.

"So who are you?" Palaparuchi asks.

"I am Rahula."

"He is the meditation master's nephew," Sumana adds.

"So you are here to serve the Great Master till he finds you worthy to take vows and receive instruction. I commend you your determination at such a young age. You wouldn't have any catumadhu, would you?"

"We don't have any special sweets like that here."

"What a shame," Palaparuchi says, "catumadhu would go well with this tea. What does it matter, anyhow? All things are impermanent."

Palaparuchi looks at Sumana for some kind of confirmation.

"Right," Sumana says, "sweets are impermanent."

Palaparuchi glares at Sumana for getting it all wrong.

"What are you, some kind of idiot? I wasn't talking about sweets. I meant," He exclaims, with his finger in the air, "the absence of catumadhu is a condition for the knowledge of all things being impermanent!"

Sumana adjusts his posture, straightening his back. He now feels as though he must ponder his friend's words.

However, Palaparuchi won't keep quiet for that long, drawing his attention to something entirely unrelated.

"Did you know that an anagami doesn't need much sleep? I've slept two hours a night for the last four days. What's that noise? It sounds like a leopard in the bushes!" He says, jumping up from the bench.

Palaparuchi's sudden reaction startles Sumana, causing him to spill the remainder of his tea on his robes. Fortunately, it has cooled down.

"I don't hear anything," Sumana says, aware that he does hear his heart pounding violently in his chest.

"There it is. I hear it again."

Rahula is not alarmed by this, since he knows that it is not a leopard making the sound.

"We must leave," Palaparuchi says, "Leopards love the color of monk's robes. We are certain prey."

Palaparuchi runs from the dining hut and down the path, with Sumana jogging behind him, holding the bucket with towels and soap in the crook of his arm. They find themselves back at Aggachitta's hut and crouch down where they were hiding before. It is not long before Maggaphala walks along the path, swinging the meditation master's bucket by its handle. He looks refreshed and happy. What Palaparuchi sees, however, is something else.

"Mara returns from the realm of the devas to wreak havoc on those who seek liberation. He robs the worthy of their new bucket, steals their sunlight, and makes them hide in the bushes."

Sumana listens to Palaparuchi, chuckling at his use of imagery, as if Palaparuchi were talking about a play they are both watching.

"But no more," Palaparuchi announces. "It is time for us to rise and claim the prize. But wait, we must not give ourselves away, for doing battle with Mara before bathing dooms us to defeat. The Buddha could encounter the Evil One before bathing, but not mere disciples like us."

Maggaphala opens the door to the master's hut and goes inside. He sets the bucket down in the corner of the hut where he found it. He looks at the bed and contemplates taking a nap, but it just does not seem right to sleep in his old friend's bed. Instead, he sits down on the bed and begins to think. He wonders who the other white-skinned monk hiding in the bushes is. Then he tries to figure why they would be hiding for so long, for his bath must have taken nearly half an hour. "What do they want in this room?" He looks around the room, at the bookcase, the water dispenser, the shaving mirror, the desk, the kerosene lamp, and finally at the bucket. None of these things seems to be anything special for a monk, except perhaps the water dispenser. Maybe they just want a drink of purified water. But they could have done that while he bathed. It must be something else.

Maggaphala finds this puzzle entertaining and so sits on the bed, looking around, trying to figure out which article of the meditation master's meager possessions these two monks covet. Then he deduces that they must want something he took with him to the cistern. That could only be the shiny new bucket. He goes over, picks up the bucket, and carries it out the door. Once outside he looks directly at where Palaparuchi and Sumana are hiding.

"Is this what you are looking for?" He yells to them.

Palaparuchi remains crouching and whispers to Sumana, "This is a trick. He's trying to coax us out into the open."

"He seems harmless enough," Sumana says.

"That is Mara you are talking about. He can appear well meaning and courteous as a way to lure you into his trap. Just wait. He'll go back to his realm when he realizes he can't tempt us with this new bucket."

Maggaphala waits patiently for them to emerge from the bushes. He can hear their faint whispering, but can't make out what they're saying. He does sense however, that the other monk, whom he vaguely recognizes, is agitated and distressed. Since he would rather get back to the cave and take a nap than get involved in the juvenile antics of two foreign monks,

Maggaphala puts the bucket down in front of the door and follows the path leading back to the cave.

As he walks away, he pauses a moment to look back. He sees the other monk lift up the bucket, and then recognizes who that monk is.

"Oh, my God," he mutters, "the mad monk!"

CHAPTER
21

At approximately two o'clock, Ananda sends a samanera, a novice monk, over to the library to ask Aggachitta if he would like to join him in his office for tea. Aggachitta tells the teenage samanera that he will be there in a few minutes. The samanera goes goes back down the hall to Ananda's office and relays the message. Ananda then asks him to bring tea for two.

The tea arrives and still there is no sign of Aggachitta. Ananda sends the samanera back down the hall to look in on Aggachitta, but he is not to disturb the great scholar this time. Aggachitta is hunched over an open book, with a notebook near him, his right hand holding a pen poised ready to write something down. The samanera returns to Ananda and reports what he saw. Ananda sighs, takes a cup of tea for himself, and then asks the samanera to take the other cup of tea to Aggachitta.

Aggachitta barely glances up at the entrance of the samanera, and when he sees the teacup and saucer moving closer in his field of vision, he motions that it be placed down away from his books. The samanera does as directed, chuckling as sets the tea down. Aggachitta wonders what what could be so funny about setting down a cup of tea, but then attributes the teenage samanera's behavior to the silliness found in many young people in robes these days. The samanera blurts out a few laughs, though he tries to restrain himself, and then exits the room, closing the door behind him. Aggachitta can hear louder, unrestrained laughter from the other side of the door. He looks at his tea to see if some practical joke is being played on him. He is irritated by this intrusion. He doesn't have time for such nonsense. He tastes the tea. It tastes fine. What could be so funny?

Getting back to the subject at hand, he has tried to do in a matter of a few hours what he would really need several days to accomplish, skimming passages instead of reading them thoroughly. He has made notes on three of the most prominent chains of dependent arising and is now contemplating a fourth. This fourth one is a series of chains, branching from a single trunk, with no real logic holding them all together. That's because it is found in a poem, and as such is mostly disregarded by scholars. Why disregard something because it doesn't fit neatly into a schema? It is the lack of coherence, of neatness, that intrigues Aggachitta. He's attempting to go beyond neat formulations. He wants his work to be about something alive and dynamic, the great chain, and not about the standard set of ideas and assumptions. Maybe this poem will be his guide. It could very well be the earliest expression of conditionality in all of Buddhist literature.

He puts his pen to paper, writing these words in Pali, using the ornate Sinhalese script:

Sañña nidana hi papañca sankha

This states how delusion arises in the mind and then grows and spreads. It comes from some kind of faulty perception, a *sañña*. In addition, that perception, if one traces it back a few lines, is a misunderstanding of what liberated consciousness is. It is not ignorance, as in never knowing something to begin with, but rather a case of misapprehending states of mind that appear liberated on first encounter, though they are nothing more than delusions.

These few well-chosen words uttered by the Buddha two and half millennia ago shift the sense of ignorance from being the cause of delusion to being its effect.

He contemplates the idea that perhaps some people are trapped in samsara because they have deluded themselves into believing they are liberated when they are not. Maybe ignorance and delusion are the cause of each other. That is true dependent co-arising! The fantasies of a deluded mind foster ignorance, just as ignorance fosters deluded fantasies.

For a moment, Aggachitta understands something that is not logical, not formulaic. There is no escaping the interplay of delusion and ignorance when one is in it. That is the world. That is the self. Without it, what is there?

He wishes he had written all this down while he was thinking about it, for just as quickly as it arose, it vanishes, leaving only a sketchy memory. All that is left are the Pali words he scrawled on the piece of paper before him. Words he knows by heart and need not have written down in the first place.

CHAPTER
22

Sumana and Palaparuchi take the master's bucket and go to the cistern. Palaparuchi hurriedly takes off his outer robe, revealing a flabby distended belly, and yet he still has to tighten the fold on his under-robe so that it will not fall off during bathing. He picks up the master's bucket and lowers it down into the water with the rope tied to its handle. He kneels down and pushes away some leaves with his other hand and then pushes the rim of the bucket underwater, filling it up. He raises the bucket to where he now stands, but instead of setting it down on the ground, he grabs it in midair with both hands and lifts it up over his head, spilling the cool water over his head.

He does this a few times and then grabs the bar of soap. As he soaps up, he says to Sumana, "This is a great cistern! The water is fresh and cool. You really have it made here."

Sumana goes over to the bucket and lowers it into the water. He lets one or two leaves get in it, picking them out before he pours the water over his head and body. He raises the bucket, his whole body slightly trembling, pausing to get up the nerve to douse his body with cold water, and then he just lets go and dumps the water all over him. He imagines it to be a lot of water as it seems to keep on falling from the sky, running down his limbs and trunk. It is cooling, exhilarating. He knows what Palaparuchi means. This is a great cistern!

Sumana pours another bucketful over himself and then sets it down for Palaparuchi, who is covered in foamy white soap. Sumana would never be that indulgent with soap. He gently applies a thin lather to his trunk and belly, and then his arms and legs. He does not try to clean everywhere, doing just enough to eliminate odors and noticeable grime. Palaparuchi on the other hand is very thorough with his grooming. He douses water on every conceivable part of his body. He even asks Sumana to lather up his back. Sumana doesn't like to do this sort of thing for other monks. He prefers not to have any physical contact whatsoever. Life is simpler for him that way.

"Come on, Sumana, I want to get my back clean with the next bucket. I'm getting tired lifting water."

"You don't need your back lathered. It gets clean just from water."

"No, no, that isn't true. I can feel a layer of dried perspiration along my shoulder blades. Perspiration is water resistant, you know."

Sumana gives in to Palaparuchi's wishes as he has done all afternoon. He gets a lather going in his hands and then rubs the soap on Palaparuchi's back.

"Harder, Sumana, harder! You have to get into the skin to get the sweat out."

"I'm doing it as hard as I can!"

"There, that's good. Keep doing it like that."

"Isn't this enough yet?"

"No, just a little more there, and then go down to the small of my back."

"I'm not going to give you a back rub," Sumana says, defiantly.

"Okay, Okay, that's enough, now hand me the bucket so I can rinse off."

Sumana hands him the bucket. Meanwhile the soap he put on himself has dried and is beginning to itch. He scratches his belly and chest, leaving bright red lines across his skin. Palaparuchi takes one bucket after another, emptying them over the back of his head so the water flows down his back, clearing it of soap.

Sumana gets anxious about the soap drying too quickly. It would be disrespectful for him to ask a senior monk to hurry up. So he waits impatiently. Palaparuchi finally hands Sumana

CONSCIOUSNESS AND CONDITIONALITY

the bucket and goes over to where he put the large bath towel. Sumana frantically lowers the bucket and sets it down in front of him. He begins splashing water on his chest, legs and arms, and then dumps the remaining water on his head. He gets three more bucketfuls, in rapid succession, emptying them on his head. He then feels as though he got as much soap off as he could, but he still has the suspicion that he was too late and some parts of his skin are caked under a thin film of soapy residue, ready to break out in a rash later on in the day.

The two monks sit down together, and for the first time since Palaparuchi's arrival, they enjoy being silent and listening to the sounds of the birds of the jungle.

After the two white-skinned bhikkhus flee in fright, Rahula goes to find his girlfriend, Arati. She is standing in the small clearing where he had left her.

"I was getting tired of sitting, of waiting for you," Arati says. "Couldn't you hurry them along?"

"They thought you were a leopard," Rahula says, chuckling.

She laughs. Now she looks like the girl he remembers. Their initial meetings at the school library eventually led up to a sunrise walk on the beach in Mount Lavinia. They each told their parents they had to be at school early and rendezvoused at the rocks beneath the Mt. Lavinia Hotel. There was a group of soldiers in training jogging in formation along the shore, and Rahula thought for a moment that he could join the army if nothing else. A few of the soldiers looked over at Arati and smiled, obviously liking what they saw. Instead of being jealous, Rahula looked at her and marveled at his good fortune of having such a beautiful girlfriend. He put his right hand into her left hand. She giggled and smiled, flirting with him. It was a most exhilarating experience for him. As they neared the Dehiwala side of the beach, where there were more people sitting in beach chairs and milling about, he saw a couple out of the corner of his eye kissing. Suddenly his good mood deflated. He could never do that! When they reached the

Bambalapitiya end of the beach, Rahula knew it was time to say good-bye. He let go of her hand and turned to face her. She leaned her face towards his, not far from his mouth, and he felt embarrassed by the impulse to kiss her on the lips. He backed away and, averting his gaze to the ocean, said that he would write to her. The following week he would be leaving for the southern interior of the island, he went on to explain, where he would stay with his uncle, who is a bhikkhu, in the jungle. She was horrified by this news and scolded him for not telling her sooner. Rahula was hurt by her words and could not see the feelings for him that were behind them. He could barely muster up a good-bye. That was the last time he saw her.

"I'm so happy," she says. "When do you want to tell your parents and set the date?"

Rahula doesn't comprehend what she is talking about, and so, bewildered, asks, "What date?"

Arati frowns. She likes Rahula's dense and sometimes silly boyish ways most of the time, but not when discussing something serious. Still, she isn't averse to taking matters into her own hands to get what she wants.

"The date of our wedding."

Rahula backs away from her. He doesn't want to anger her, but he also doesn't want to commit his life to her just yet. He weighs these two options in his mind and convinces himself that he can give wedding date now and then change his mind later.

"It'll have to be after the rainy season, as I promised my uncle I'd be here to help the bhikkhus for the next five months," he says, lying about the rainy season obligation.

"Can't you take back your promise?" she says. "I traveled all this way to be with you. Isn't that a good reason?"

Rahula feels cornered, unable to think of a way out. If he agrees to take back a promise he never made but now wishes he had, he will be a married man in a matter of weeks, or even days. The only way out would be if he could be ordained as a samanera. How would he be able to explain to her a sudden need to be a samanera? He'd have to make something up. He could say that he's now a sotapanna, and therefore can't live as a householder, but a lie like that would certainly displease his uncle.

Then again, does he not want to marry her? She's pretty, lively, a little aggressive and pushy, but that can change over time. As a married couple, they would have to live with his parents, and he'd have to find a job to support them, and go to university to study for a profession. His indecision about what to do with his life would be over. However, it might just go into another phase, one where he has responsibility but is still without direction.

Arati sways in her light, flowing single-piece dress. She repeats her idea in the form of a plan for Rahula's future. "You can just tell your uncle you're sorry but you can't spend the next five months here in the jungle. You're not suited for it. You don't even have to mention me. Then you can come away with me to Colombo. We can get married and you can go to university to become a barrister, or minister, or something like that, and I can raise our children."

Rahula's feeling of being cornered intensifies. He remembers the woman in the dunes and the man trapped in the sunken house with her. The more ways he tries to escape, the harder he digs, the more trapped he realizes he is.

"I can't talk about this now. I must attend to the bhikkhus. We have three new bhikkhus at the hermitage, and they need to be looked after."

"But what about me?" she says angrily.

"I will return shortly and take you into town, where we can find you a place to spend the night."

"Can't I stay here?"

"No. Women are not allowed to stay overnight in the hermitage," Rahula says. "Stay right here. I will be back in a few minutes."

Rahula turns and walks away, not looking back at her. At first, he is preoccupied with urgent plans to get her out of the hermitage and back to Colombo. As he gains distance from her, he realizes that his real concern is her preoccupation with marriage.

CHAPTER
23

With the primary intention of returning Aggachitta's bucket, Sumana and Palaparuchi enter his hut. Palaparuchi holds the bucket by its handle and scans the room for a place to set it. Sumana stands in the doorway, looking in, but because it is so dim in the hut, he can't see much of anything. Palaparuchi goes over to the water dispenser and looks it over carefully. He opens the spigot and water gushes out onto the floor, and then he cups his hands under the spigot and sips some of the water before closing it.

"This is a good dispenser. You should have one like this."

"Let's just leave the bucket and get out of here," Sumana says.

Palaparuchi sets the bucket in the puddle of water on the floor, apparently trying to hide the spill with it.

"When will he come back?"

"I don't know," Sumana says. "He could be back any minute now."

Palaparuchi walks around the room and takes a quick inventory of Aggachitta's visible possessions. What he plans on doing with this information is anyone's guess.

"Let's go," Sumana says impatiently, with a hint of irritation in his voice.

"I'm coming," Palaparuchi replies as he lifts up a book on the table and reads its spine.

Sumana can't wait for his friend any longer. He begins walking back to his hut. He is fuming inside. Palaparuchi forces him to take too many risks, which may get him into trouble. He would never do the things Palaparuchi drags him into doing on his own. If Palaparuchi weren't here, Sumana would no doubt be meditating in his room. And that reminds him. He has only meditated once today and it is nearing sunset.

Palaparuchi catches up with him on the path to his hut.

"So what shall we do now?"

Sumana replies, "I have to meditate."

"Great! Where do you usually sit?"

"In my hut."

"There is no meditation hall here? Is there a building designated as the *sima* that we can use?" Palaparuchi asks.

"I don't know what we use for a sima."

"But we'll find out tomorrow," Palaparuchi says.

"Tomorrow?"

"It's the *uposatha*. Tonight the moon is almost full and so tomorrow is the fortnightly meeting of monks."

"Oh, that's right."

They reach Sumana's hut and go inside. Sumana pulls out his double robe and folds it up, placing it on the ground. Palaparuchi watches him do this and is aghast.

"How can you treat your double robe like that?"

"It's the only thing I have to sit on."

"That's just not right. You do need more guidance."

Palaparuchi goes over to his bags of possessions, which he neatly tucked in a corner. One of his bags is a bowl bag like Sumana's, while the other is a duffle bag. He reaches inside the duffle bag and pulls out a couple of robes, some towels, a blanket, and finally, at the bottom, two round stuffed black meditation cushions. He hands Sumana one of them and takes the other for himself.

Sumana sits on the ground with his rear on the hard black cushion, while Palaparuchi sits on the bed with his cushion wedged in behind his lower back, propping himself up against the wall.

"Who will keep time?"

Sumana replies, "I just glance at my watch on occasion."

"Good. Then you can keep time. Do you have a bell?"

"No," Sumana says.

"Then we will have to use mine."

Palaparuchi gets up off the bed and rummages around in his bowl bag, coming up with a tiny brass bowl with a miniature wooden striker. He taps the bowl bell once with the striker, smiling at the pleasant high-pitched ringing sound it makes.

"Maybe I should be timekeeper, since I have the bell."

"All right," Sumana says, and gets up and goes over to Palaparuchi, who is now getting comfortable on the bed, and gives him the watch.

"So how long do you want to sit for?"

"I don't know," Sumana says as he sits down again. "How about one hour?"

"How about we have two half-hour sittings?" Palaparuchi suggests.

"It doesn't matter to me."

"Good. Then I will ring the bell at 4:05, and then we will relax for five minutes, start another sitting at 4:10, and go till 4:40."

"Fine," Sumana says, "let's begin."

"Okay. The sitting begins now!"

Rahula walks past the dining hut, considering which bhikkhu to consult about his dilemma. If only uncle were here! He would approach him with this situation, this trap he finds himself in, and do whatever he advises. But, perhaps, it is fortunate that his uncle is not here, for he is certain that Aggachitta would advise him to become a samanera, which is a step, like marriage, that he's not ready to take. What he needs is someone with knowledge of the world. Sumana comes first to mind, and then Sumana's friend. Both of them know enough about living in the world, women, and the life of a bhikkhu to give him a clear perspective.

Rahula goes to the cistern to see if they are there, finds the bathing area empty, and then goes over to Sumana's hut. He steps up to the window of the hut and peers inside. It is very dark and he can only make out their forms. Palaparuchi is sitting on the bed opposite the window, while Sumana is on the ground. He sees Palaparuchi's head as it hangs with his chin almost touching his chest. He can only see the back of Sumana's head, which is slightly tilted to the right. He surmises that they're meditating and shouldn't be disturbed. Who can he consult now? He doesn't have much time, as Arati will soon grow impatient and start looking for him around the hermitage. He doesn't want that to happen, fearing that she might meet Aggachitta on his way back from town.

Rahula runs over to the cave, where he is sure to find Maggaphala. He recalls from this morning's conversation that Maggaphala is a Shakespeare scholar. Rahula surmises that he must know something about his kind of predicament from having studied Shakespeare. Didn't Shakespeare write that story about Romeo and Juliet?

Inside the cave, Rahula hears snoring. Maggaphala is asleep on his back on what was until now Rahula's bed. Rahula decides to wake him up, so he picks up a stack of books and drops them on the floor. The bang brings Maggaphala sharply awake.

"I'm sorry," Rahula says, making it appear that he dropped the books by accident.

"It's all right. I probably slept long enough. Have you come with my afternoon tea?"

"Oh, I forgot," Rahula says. "Do you want me to go and get it?"

"That's all right. I'll get up and walk with you to the dining hut."

Maggaphala slowly angles his girth into an upright posture on the bed. Once he's upright and has rubbed his eyes, Rahula speaks.

"I need your help on an important matter."

"Can't it wait until I have woken up completely?"

Rahula thinks a moment. "No. I need to get your advice now."

"Advice? Advice about what? I don't give advice. I'm the wrong person for you."

"No, you're not. You know Shakespeare."

"Oh, so now that you have read some modern existentialist literature you want to delve into the mysteries of the great master. I don't blame you. Which play would you like to begin with?"

"Romeo and Juliet."

Rahula says this dimly realizing that the story of Romeo and Juliet is far more complicated than his own dilemma, so he adds, "It's not the story I'm interested in, but the situation of the boy and girl."

"So you've read it. Why does it interest you?"

"I'm in a similar situation," Rahula reveals, astonished at his courage in telling his secret to a complete stranger.

"You have a young lady."

"Yes."

"I see. Tell me all about this girl."

Rahula relates what he clearly remembers about how they would meet in the library, their time on the beach, their letters, and her arrival at the hermitage.

"You mean to tell me she's here now!" Maggaphala exclaims. "Where is she?"

"I left her in the bushes not far from the dining hut."

"We must go find her. Is she all right?" Maggaphala says.

"She's fine, Venerable Sir. I told her to wait for me as I had some work to do."

"And telling me your predicament is the work you had to do?"

"Yes, you understand perfectly."

"All right," Maggaphala begins, with a plan in mind, "bring her up to the cave. We will both talk to her and figure out what is to be done."

Rahula is overjoyed that Maggaphala is willing to do this extra service.

As Rahula is about to cross the threshold of the cave, he hears Maggaphala say, "Be sure to bring back a thermos of tea. Milk tea, please."

Rahula goes down to the dining hut. There he finds Arati sitting in plain view on the bench reserved for bhikkhus.

"Do you have anything to eat?" She asks.

"I have to prepare some tea for Venerable Maggaphala. Would you care for some tea? Then we both can go visit him."

"Let's eat first!"

Rahula rummages about in some of the bags near the stove and comes up with two hard-boiled eggs and some pieces of white bread. He hands them to her and she begins to peel the eggs, dropping the eggshells into one of the spittoons. Rahula meanwhile ignores her and heats up the tea left in the kettle, and prepares some powdered milk, which he then pours into the simmering tea. As he lets the tea sit for a minute, he watches Arati eat another egg. She bites off the tip of the egg, revealing the grayish yellow yoke, and then she takes a bite of bread. She chews both egg and bread at the same time, her cheeks wide with food. Rahula brings his attention back to the tea, which is now ready. He unscrews the top of his uncle's favorite thermos, a big metallic one, and pours all of the milk tea into it. He seals the thermos and gets up, ready to go. Arati is chewing the last of her egg.

"Come on, let's go and visit the monk."

"I'm not finished yet. I need some water to wash my hands."

Rahula brings the water pitcher over and has her put her hands over the spittoon, where he then proceeds to rinse them. She has a delightful smile on her face as he does this. When he is done, he sets the pitcher down and gets her a towel.

She says, "No, not that towel, it's dirty. Can't you find a clean one?"

Rahula looks around and notices one of his uncle's orange towels hanging over the table. He must have left it there this morning. Rahula picks it up and hands it to her. She takes her time wiping her hands, getting in-between each finger.

"Now we must go and see the senior bhikkhu, before it gets too late," he says.

"Okay, I'm ready. Let's see this bhikkhu of yours."

She stands up and brushes off her dress, first in front and then behind. Rahula watches her pat the synthetic cloth along her belly, her thighs, her rear, and thinks to himself that maybe marriage would be much more exciting than staying in a forest hermitage with bhikkhus.

CHAPTER
24

Rahula and Arati go up to the cave together, with Rahula in the lead. She stops short of the entrance, extending her right arm towards him.

"Give me a hand. This hill is steep."

Rahula reaches down and puts his hand in hers. Her grip is tight. He pulls her up and they reach the entrance of the cave. He drops her hand and opens the cloth entrance for her. She smiles and slips right by him gracefully into the cave.

Maggaphala rises from the bed to stand up as a show of respect for the woman entering his room. He has lit the kerosene lamp and moved the two chairs to face him on the bed. He remains standing as Rahula comes into the cave. Rahula reminds Arati that she is in the presence of a bhikkhu. This has no meaning for her, so Rahula demonstrates what a lay person should do when seeing a bhikkhu by going over to Maggaphala and prostrating before him. He expects her to follow, but she just stands where she is, watching.

"Please, that isn't necessary," Maggaphala says. "Sit in these chairs. Do you have my tea?"

Rahula rises from the ground and goes back to the entrance of the cave where he laid down the thermos. He picks up the thermos and walks over to Maggaphala sitting on the bed, handing it to him with both hands.

"Did you bring a cup and saucer?"

"I completely forgot," Rahula says, ashamed that he could not even do this simple task right.

"Well, never mind, I found a glass on the floor. Will you clean it for me?" Maggaphala says pulling out a large drinking glass and handing it to Rahula.

"Just a minute," Rahula says, and goes back into the closet in the cave, where he pulls out an orange handkerchief and begins vigorously wiping the rim of the glass.

"There," he says, "it's all clean."

"Would you mind pouring me some tea before giving it back," Maggaphala says, handing over the thermos. Then on second thought he says, "Perhaps the lady would also care for a cup of tea."

"Yes, that would be nice," Arati says.

Rahula now has to find another cup. First, however, he pours Maggaphala a steaming cup of milk tea. He fills the tall glass up to just below the rim, leaving enough space for the monk to hold the glass near the rim and not be scalded by the heat of the tea. The delicate part then is handing the hot glass of tea to someone without spilling any. He holds the glass tightly between his right thumb and index finger as he walks over to Maggaphala, who then takes the glass in the middle. Rahula lets go of it, fearful that it will now drop, but Maggaphala adroitly lets the fluted glass slide down in his hand until he holds it by his thumb and index finger.

Maggaphala takes a tiny sip of the tea, realizes that it's still a little too hot, and so sets it down on the table near the bed. Rahula meanwhile looks for more tea glasses and comes up with two short glasses that will do. He pours Arati and himself a cup of tea, which just about empties the thermos. He hands Arati her cup, and then sits down in the chair next to her. They are now all facing each other, sipping hot cups of milk tea.

Maggaphala is the first to speak.

"This fine young man has told me the most pleasant story of how you two met."

Arati smiles and shoots a loving look at Rahula.

"Now he has related to me that you would like to embark on the state of matrimony. Is that so?" Oddly enough, as Maggaphala says this, he pictures himself more like a priest than a bhikkhu. This side of Christianity has always appealed to him, and if he could, he sometimes thinks he would rather be more like a priest than a bhikkhu. In his estimation a priest doesn't bear this whole burden of trying to become fully liberated and can be content just doing normal priestly things.

Arati says, "We would like to get married. That's true. I'm glad Rahula told you. Can you marry us?"

"No, no, certainly not! Bhikkhus don't perform marriage ceremonies."

Arati turns to Rahula and says, "Then why are we talking to this bhikkhu? I thought you brought me here to discuss our wedding!"

Rahula is baffled by Arati's assumption that he brought her to Maggaphala to discuss their wedding. He wanted to discuss marriage, but now he realizes the only thing she wants to discuss is the wedding. He has no idea how he's going to get out of this one. For a brief moment, he tries to convince himself that marrying her is the best thing to do right now, and then he starts to think of some way to get out of this predicament.

"Rahula is a good man, young lady. By the way, what is your name?"

"I am Arati."

Maggaphala pauses for a moment to consider how to comment on this unusual name.

"That is a beautiful name. Has anyone told you what it means?"

"My mother only said that she first named me Devi, but by the time I went to school, the name Arati seemed to fit me better, so she changed it."

"I see," Maggaphala says. "So you have no idea what it means?"

"My father says it means that I am a pain in the neck. He uses that expression a lot when he talks about me. I have always thought that he was joking. So what does it mean?"

Maggaphala pauses to think. He has to be diplomatic about this. He doesn't want to provoke the poor girl. What kind of father names his child after Mara's daughter, Arati?

"Your father is no Pali scholar. It simply refers to not being wholly satisfied with what one has."

"I don't understand! It means that I'm a bitch!" She exclaims, enraged.

"No, no, no, nothing of the sort," Maggaphala says, trying to calm her down.

Rahula is horrified by her use of such language in front of a bhikkhu, while Maggaphala feels distaste for the woman's rage and wishes Rahula would jump in and calm down his bride-to-be.

The three of them are silent for a while, letting the tension in the room clear. Arati pouts and then reaches over to hold Rahula's hand. He winces at this display of affection in front of a bhikkhu. She's not acting at all like someone who was brought up religiously. This gives Rahula an idea:

"Arati," he says.

"Don't call me that anymore!" She snaps. "I'm going to change my name back to Devi first chance I get. I'm no Arati!" She exclaims, glowering at Maggaphala.

"What I need to know," Rahula says softly, "is if you're Buddhist or not."

She takes a deep breath, trying to stifle her anger.

"I don't know why that would matter. My grandfather on my mother's side was Buddhist. My father is Christian and my mother used to believe in Lord Buddha. I was raised Protestant, but my mother taught us some of the Buddha's stories. So I guess I am both."

"I didn't know that before," Rahula says.

"What difference does it make?" she asks.

Rahula looks at Maggaphala for some help with his answer. Maggaphala sips his glass of tea, and is not interested in making eye contact. Rahula decides to take a bold step, for he wants both the option to marry her if he does not become a samanera and to become a samanera if he does not marry her.

"I'm not sure. I will need to talk it over with my parents."

"Good," she says, confident that his parents will like her and prefer him getting married to becoming a fat old bhikkhu like the one she sees before her.

"Let's go," she says, "I'm tired of this."

As they rise to leave, she has a brilliant idea.

"Why don't we go back to Colombo right now and get your parents' approval?"

Rahula acts as though he didn't hear her. He goes over to the entrance of the cave and passes through it to the outside. He then waits for Arati to follow. Her thin arm, with the purple plastic bracelet, emerges from behind the brown cloth covering the cave's entrance. Rahula stares at her hand groping in the air for his. Then she shouts to him to help her out. He reaches for her hand, grabbing her wrist tightly, pulling her up out of the cave. Her face, beaming with delight, appears first. Rahula, however, knows himself to be utterly lost now, under the sway of this young woman's will.

Maggaphala relaxes in the silence that follows. Near his bed is a copy of the Shakespeare's collected works. He picks up the book and moves over to one of the chairs, adjusting the light so that he may read. In Shakespeare, scenes between lovers are entertaining. In real life however, they are most unpleasant.

He opens to *A Midsummer Night's Dream* and begins reading. An atmosphere of delight arises in the cave as he immerses himself in another forest, in another time, where invisible beings roam the night, engaged in sport and wooing.

CHAPTER
25

Using a desk lamp, Aggachitta finds his eyes tire less than when he uses a kerosene lantern. However, when he looks up from his notes, he has difficulty focusing on any of the objects in the library. He wonders how late it is and so checks a watch he carries in an undershirt pocket. The watch says 5:38. The sun will set soon. If he wants to get back to the hermitage before nightfall, he must leave now.

He ponders if there is any pressing reason why he should return to the hermitage. He imagines Sumana sitting in meditation in his hut, probably a little upset that he did not have an interview today, but nonetheless content to keep on meditating. Rahula is probably reading his book and doing some of his chores. Aggachitta can spend the night here and get an early start in the morning on some of the books he has not been able to get to today. Then he can return to the hermitage after the morning meal.

Aggachitta turns off the lamp and sits in the dark. Now that he has decided to stay the night, he can slow down. He closes his eyes and straightens his back in the chair. An acute pain shoots up from his lower back. His shoulders feel stiff. He wiggles them a little to loosen them up and then stills his body.

Images of black ink on paper, words from the books he has read, flood his mind. The print is mostly Sinhalese, forming ornate patterns, creating combinations that produce words he does not recognize. The image quickly vanishes, leaving Aggachitta dazed. He opens his eyes and peers into the dark atmosphere of the room around him. With his eyes open, there are no more images, and he can feel his body in the chair, hear his breathing, and direct his thoughts. He doesn't like it when his mind just goes on its own without consulting him. He can brave it for a while, but does not care for it.

Nonetheless, he closes his eyes again. White blank pages appear, one brilliant white foolscap after another. Drawings begin to form on the successive pages and soon the notion of page, of surface, drops away, and there is just a three dimensional white light with swirls of color in the center. Zooming in closer, the swirls are yellow in the center with blue, green, and red layers appearing like a fan, spreading to the ends. As the colors spread, Aggachitta has the thought that this is the spreading of delusion born of ignorance. His attention returns to his body with a jolt. Pleasure flows through his arms and legs, and he draws it into his chest and lungs.

He wants to turn on the light and jot down this understanding, but decides to hold off. What if there is more to come? Instead of trying to stop the arising of visual images within his mind, he tries to coax them into coming. After a few minutes, when nothing happens, he gives up and turns on the light.

This time he writes down his ideas.

"*Papañca-sankha* is the spreading of delusions that come from misapprehending the true nature of things. As the spectrum of colors all exist in a single ray of sunlight, so all delusions exist within the ignorance of a single individual. Such a statement is not logical and cannot be proved, but nonetheless, in practice, delusions are plural and ignorance is singular. Consciousness is the medium of proliferation for all faulty perceptions and is inextricably conditioned by its reliance upon, and furtherance of, misapprehensions due to ignorance. There is no pure consciousness existing unaffected by this process as long as there is a consciousness that is. That is the fallacy of a higher self. In denying the existence of a higher self, consciousness is joined with ignorance for the generation and proliferation of delusions. It is never transcendent; it is always plain and simple. There's no ultimate truth to be found in consciousness, except the truth that suffering arises through conditions spawned by ignorance."

"That says it all," Aggachitta remarks to himself.

He rereads it, making a couple of minor changes. A knock at the door disturbs his concentration, but he feels he has reached a good place to stop for the night. He rises from his chair and goes over to the door, opening it slowly all the way. A samanera about Rahula's age and height is standing on the other side.

The samanera says, "Venerable Ananda invites you to spend the night here. We have a room prepared for you."

"Thank you," Aggachitta says, "that is very kind of him. Give me a moment to return these books to their shelves. And then I'll follow you to the room."

Sumana gets up from his meditation sitting and notices that the sun is setting. Palaparuchi never rang the bell. He is sound asleep, sitting hunched over on the bed. Sumana wonders if he didn't also fall asleep, since he can't remember much of his meditation sitting. It's only when he takes his watch back from Palaparuchi that he realizes almost two hours have passed since they began the sitting. Where was his mind all that time? He just can't remember. He recalls hearing some rustling in the bushes outside his hut early on in the sitting, and how he feared that it might be the leopard they had heard earlier, but soon after that, his mind just vanished and didn't return until a few minutes ago.

He makes his way outside, careful not to wake Palaparuchi. He walks a good distance from his hut, going in the direction of the cave. As he approaches the cave, he looks up into the sky and sees the full moon rising in the east. It is luminous and liquid in the clear sky, glowing orange. He stops and looks at the moon, marveling at its beauty, and soon he is thinking about Gotami.

While gazing at the moon, he tries to conjure up her image in his mind. Her robes appear amber, as does her face, round as the moon before his eyes. He then closes his eyes and imagines her walking towards him. She stops a few yards away. She holds out her right palm like the bodhisattva Padmapani, lightly gripping the stem of a purple flower between her left thumb and index finger.

This image hangs in his mind as the moon climbs into the sky, growing whiter as the world grows darker. Her image fades, and with its loss, words come into his mind instead. He regrets not letting her know that he too is lonely and isn't entirely happy. "If only I could have met her before becoming a monk," he says to himself.

There, he has thought the dreaded thought. That it is better to live as a layman and have real intimate relationships with people, instead of masquerading halfway around the world as some shaven-headed ascetic. What he wouldn't give right now to lose some of the restraint and formality and have real contact with a mature and thoughtful woman. It is not sex he hungers for, but the company of a woman who cares about him.

In truth, he has no idea if the real Gotami could become a good friend. She seems to be as taken with this life of renunciation as he is. She's definitely looking for the same thing, for liberation of mind, freedom from suffering, the attainment of nibbana, all that. It is serious stuff, almost too serious for someone like Sumana to take seriously all the time. Sometimes, like now, he wonders why he can't just take a weekend off, enjoy himself and relax a little, and then come back to work as a monk, a weekday monk. That would surely make his life a whole lot easier!

Sumana turns in the other direction and sees the last bit of purple and lavender fade in the evening sky. He looks down at the ground and realizes that he forgot to bring a flashlight, so he dashes back to his hut to get one.

Maggaphala has been reading *A Midsummer Night's Dream*, changing voices for each character in his head. Arati's voice comes in frequently for that of Helena and Rahula's for

Demetrius. When he reads Demetrius say, "You do impeach your modesty too much, to leave the city and commit yourself into the hands of one that loves you not," he recalls Rahula's and Arati's situation vividly and hopes that they can come to some resolution. And when he comes to where Helena says, "We can't fight for love as men may do; we should be wooed, and were not made to woo," he understands how ill-equipped Rahula is in the art of courting. If only they would read Shakespeare, it would become clear as day to them that they are not ready for courtship.

Then something he read a few pages back piques his curiosity. From the back of his mind, one of the major riddles about this play comes to the forefront. He skipped over Oberon's speech on the flower, because he never could make sense of it. Yet it is a crucial element of the play. The god of love, Cupid, is flying through the sky on a moonlit night. He aims an arrow at a virgin and lets it loose. Instead of hitting her in the heart, it goes wide of the mark and lands upon "a little western flower," which turns from white to purple. Maidens then call the purple flower "love-in-idleness." This purple flower is believed to contain some kind of juice that when placed on the eyelids of a sleeping person, causes him or her to fall in love with the first creature seen.

"Love-in-idleness," he murmurs. He recognizes it as a larger concept than he has acknowledged. Like most readers, he has focused on the popular notion of love potions turning the hearts of men and women to fancy those they otherwise would never notice. However, this is something different — grander and more mysterious — if one emphasizes idleness more than love. The characters in the play are essentially idle. They have no particular work or calling, and occupy themselves solely in the sphere of romance. They are mostly silly children puffing themselves up into being adults, having no knowledge as to what being an adult actually entails. The women are more determined to have the one they truly love, their hearts being truer to one person; while the two men, both succumbing to the effects of the purple flower, fight each other for a woman they both ignored before.

That brings Maggaphala back to the purple flower. He knows that scholars believe it to be St. John's Wort, which has a variety of medicinal qualities, but does not cause attraction to another person. Shakespeare is not speaking of a physical purple flower but a psychological one, he thinks, and becomes excited, as though he's pursuing some great understanding. Consciousness goes from white to purple when love's arrow strikes it. It becomes saturated with a strong tendency towards intense infatuation, and seeks a being to become infatuated with. This drives the person to fall in love with the next person he sees. The object of this infatuation does not see it coming, and so must flee the pursuer. However, if she wants to be loved by him but can't believe her eyes, she questions the truth of the very infatuation she is seeking.

Maggaphala experiences intense rapturous sensations coursing through his body. He has cracked another one of the great master's mysteries.

Sumana goes into his hut. It is very dark inside, so he goes over to where the kerosene lamp and matches are and lights the lamp, turning its wick up higher than usual, making the light bright for his eyes. Palaparuchi stirs awake, still seated on the bed. He opens his eyes and sees Sumana's form illuminated by the lamp. Palaparuchi fixes his attention on Sumana's profile, seeing his orange robes hanging on him like an evening gown, and for a moment, Palaparuchi sees a creature of androgynous sex, one that tickles certain delicious feelings. Palaparuchi is a master of suppression. He effortlessly drowns his feelings in a flood of ideas as to how to spend the evening hours.

Sumana remains standing, unaware of Palaparuchi's stare, the right half of his body illuminated by the lamplight, the left half in shadow. He tries to remember where he put his flashlight and begins looking around the room for it. At one point in his search, he notices Palaparuchi's face, catching the tail end of a grin.

"Do you have a flashlight?" he asks.

Palaparuchi jumps off the bed and goes over to his duffle bag. He reaches down inside to pull out one flashlight after another, three in all. He checks the batteries in each one by turning it on and shining the light into his eyes. All of them work.

"Which one do you want?"

"I'll take the metal one."

"That is an excellent choice! It has served me well over the years. So where are we going?"

Palaparuchi is now standing. He refolds his robes around his body, tightening them so there is no chance of them falling off.

Sumana says, "Just out for a walk."

Palaparuchi goes to the door, opens it, and steps outside. The moon has risen in the sky, illuminating the trees with a silvery luster. In front of the hut, the ground glows like mercury.

Palaparuchi looks back at Sumana through the open door of the hut and says, "We must go while there's still light! Come on, Sumana!"

Sumana puts out the lantern and follows Palaparuchi with the flashlight, for in his exuberance, Palaparuchi forgets to take one.

CHAPTER
26

Rahula and Arati (who now wishes to be called Devi) find themselves in an unfamiliar part of the jungle, with the moon rising off to their right. Rahula has a flashlight, but uses it sparingly as the batteries are dying. Devi stays close to his side, questioning him about what he plans to say to his parents when they get to Colombo. Rahula is trying to concentrate on the way out of the jungle, for he can't find certain landmarks he has relied on in the past. He must now navigate by the moon. He surmises that it is rising just south of the town, so if they head northeast they will eventually free themselves from the dense jungle and arrive at the coconut grove. Of course, he's not absolutely sure that northeast is precisely the right direction.

He doesn't let on to his confusion, for he's afraid Devi will become angry at him, making things worse, not better. She has no difficulty following by his side, and offers no help in choosing which direction to go, even though she made it to the hermitage without any apparent problems earlier that day. Rahula wonders how she managed to find him in the jungle; she may have a better sense of direction than he does. He tries to think up some way to phrase that question without giving her the impression that he thinks they are lost. No matter how he words it, he is certain he will either embarrass himself or anger her. He considers it better to stop than go any further.

They stop at a small clearing under a large tree. Rahula shines the yellow-orange light on the ground to see if there is a place for them to sit, and luckily, there are a couple of large smooth rocks at the base of the tree. He brushes off a rock for Devi, and then one for himself. They sit down facing each other, not more than a foot apart.

Rahula turns the flashlight off.

"Why did you do that?" She asks.

"We must conserve the batteries. Besides, we should adjust our vision to the moonlight. Then we may not need the flashlight at all."

"It certainly is bright. It must be full."

"Yes," Rahula says, "tomorrow is the *uposatha*."

"What's that?" She asks.

"It is the day when the bhikkhus recite their vows and confess their transgressions. Lay people come to the monasteries in great numbers to take the five precepts and hear the Buddha's teaching. I'm surprised you don't know about it."

"Like I said, I was brought up Protestant. My mother thought it would be disrespectful to my father if she took us to any Buddhist festivals."

"Then you are not really Buddhist," Rahula states, thinking that this is the best angle yet on getting a time extension for the biggest decision of his life.

"I am so! My mother is half Buddhist! Your parents will understand when you put it that way."

"I have never lied to my parents," Rahula says.

Devi looks at him wide-eyed.

"You don't expect me to believe that do you?" She says, nudging him.

Rahula feels caught in his own trap this time. Of course, he has lied to them. Everybody does at one time or another. It is whether the thing one is lying about is truly worth it that is the question here.

"You're trying to wriggle your way out of marrying me," she says. "I have heard enough about Sri Lankan men to know that's how they handle things. They say 'yes' meaning 'no' and 'no' meaning 'maybe' and 'maybe' meaning 'yes'."

"I never said 'yes'!" Rahula exclaims.

"But you've said 'maybe'!" Devi counters. "And I'm holding you to your word!"

"Did I really say 'maybe'?" Rahula asks, genuinely confused.

"That's all you say. Your letters are full of maybes. You want me and you want something else. Most of all, you want to please everyone. So maybe you do one thing to please me, something else to please your parents, and something else entirely different to please some old bhikkhu. I know you, Rahula. You are spineless, self-centered, and lovable all at the same time. That's why I must be the strong one here."

Her words do not offend him, but her frankness and the tone she takes with him make him feel weak and inferior. She is indeed the strong one here. He puts his head down in his palms and begins to cry softly. The leaves near him rustle and he feels a slender arm slide across his back. She lays her head on his shoulder and pats his back gently.

Sumana doesn't want to go near the monument to Atakkachari, though Palaparuchi is intrigued by the idea of visiting a monument that contains the bone relics of an arhat. Sumana persuades Palaparuchi to go with him to the top of the hill where the cave is, so that they may get an unobstructed view of the moon and perhaps of the town in the distance. As they head off in the direction of the cave, Palaparuchi prattles on about the magical qualities of bone relics, even though they have decided to save that adventure until daylight.

"A true bone relic of an arhat can levitate. That is one way to tell that it is from a real arhat. Another way to tell is to put it in water and see if it floats. That is, if you can get close enough to one to touch it. Usually they're buried in monuments or cemented into statues. I saw one once in a glass container. It hovered in the center, never touching the bottom or the sides."

Sumana imagines a human shinbone levitating in a vacuum-sealed container the size of an automobile.

"How big are these relics?" He asks.

"They are tiny, no bigger than a grain of rock salt."

"Oh," Sumana says, now picturing a salt crystal suspended in mid-air.

"Arhat relics can also act like talismans to ward off evil spirits."

"Is that a fact?" Sumana says, confused as to whether he believes in magic or not. He recalls hearing that the Buddha did not practice magic, but that does not mean he did not believe in it.

They arrive at the hill where the cave is. Palaparuchi looks up at the cave and sees the glow of lamplight on the cloth entrance.

"Does someone live in the cave?" He asks.

"Rahula, the temple boy."

"It must be nice in there. Do you think he would let me meditate there one night? I would stay up the whole night and battle Mara to the end if he did."

"I don't know," Sumana replies. "Let's just get to the top."

Sumana's words are terse. It's exasperating being Palaparuchi's friend. What he would really like to do right now is go back to his hut and spend some quiet moments alone.

They make their way up the path leading to the cave. Palaparuchi wants to peek inside the cave and get a look at what it's like inside, for he imagines it may be the place where he'll attain final liberation. They make such a racket that Maggaphala decides to leave off reading Shakespeare and find out what is going on outside.

Palaparuchi notices Maggaphala's menacing shadow grow bigger and bigger on the cloth covering the cave's entrance. This shadow of a bald head and bulky upper body appears to Palaparuchi as a monstrous demon, and has him shaking with fear. A fat arm pulls the cloth up from the bottom and hangs it over the back of his head. With his body lit from behind like this, Sumana and Palaparuchi can't make out the face, but they're sure it's not Rahula. Sumana turns his flashlight on and shines it into Maggaphala's face, blinding him.

Maggaphala puts a hand across his eyes and says, "Who are you? What are you doing here?"

Sumana recognizes the voice as the monk he met earlier in the day. Palaparuchi, on the other hand, jumps to his own conclusions.

"That is what we want to know of you, demon in monk's robes!"

"I am Maggaphala Thera," he says, incensed by being called a demon. "And who are you to treat a Thera with such disrespect?"

"I am a True Bhikkhu!" Palaparuchi asserts proudly.

"So am I!" Maggaphala states firmly.

Sumana interrupts in a lowered voice, saying, "Palaparuchi, this is the monk we saw using the master's bucket."

Palaparuchi turns to face Sumana and speaks to him in a quiet voice, "Ah, I see what you mean, Sumana. He looks like a bhikkhu. But I know better. With my powers of god-like vision, I can see through this human form and know what is truly there." Turning to face Maggaphala, he exclaims, "You are Mara! Those bhikkhu robes are but a poor disguise for who you truly are!"

Maggaphala not only recognizes Palaparuchi's voice, but this time also recalls the last time he saw him. This monk was so overtly hostile towards others, Maggaphala asked the head monk to evict him from the monastery. He never had any success talking sense with this mad monk, and now is not the time to try again.

Maggaphala inches back into the cave, making sure the curtain is closed tightly behind him. He walks over to the bed and lies down on his back. He can hear the two foreigners talking outside for a couple of minutes, with Palaparuchi using some choice expressions to describe his disgust at seeing Maggaphala. When they finally leave, they go upwards instead of down.

He relaxes his body, shuts his eyes, and feels a wave of humiliation come over him. Cruel words make him feel this way, but he interprets their behavior as the karmic fruit of his skepticism about the advanced attainments of others. Perhaps there has been one real sotapanna among all the fakes, and what he experiences at times like these is the bad karma from his blanket skepticism. Then again, this particular incident could be the karmic fruit of having Palaparuchi expelled from the monastery nearly two decades ago. How is he to know which it is, or if there are even more karmic conditions than he is aware of. It is too much to think about at this late hour, and since he is already quite exhausted from this long day, he decides to let himself go to sleep for the night. This is perhaps his most common way of dealing with the hurt, the humiliation, the depression — in short, the whole mass of emotional suffering he experiences in his life.

Palaparuchi and Sumana trudge up to the summit of the small hill. It is nice and flat, with a few large rocks to sit on. Sumana sits on a rock and looks eastward at the lights of the town. He points this out to Palaparuchi, who then comes near him and sits down on the same rock.

Sumana isn't comfortable with Palaparuchi sitting so close to him. He gets up and walks over to another rock, but Palaparuchi just follows him there. For some reason, Palaparuchi is trying to get next to Sumana, to have their bodies touch. Sumana doesn't want that to happen, so he moves from rock to rock, until finally he speaks up about it.

"Can't you give me some space?"

"I have to keep close to you. There's a yakkha on this hill: a fierce and terrible demon. I must be by your side to protect you."

"Stop the nonsense! That monk is not a demon! He's just an ordinary bhikkhu."

"It is not him I am talking about. You can't see the yakkha. Only I can. He's moving from tree to tree, walking across their branches, following each move you make," and then he turns to one of the three small trees on the summit and yells, "You will not eat us tonight, you fierce yakkha! I will slay you with my powers if you dare!"

Sumana looks at the tree, expecting to see something, since he can't believe his friend is hallucinating. He sees nothing. Then he hears a bird rustling in the inner branches out of view. Maybe that is Palaparuchi's yakkha.

"I think it's just a bird."

"No, that's just a disguise. Yakkhas can appear as all sorts of creatures to the eyes of an ordinary person. But for one who has god-like vision, the true form appears."

The bird flies up into the sky. They watch it soar and head past the moon.

"There, we have purged this hill of its yakkha," Palaparuchi says. And then in a completely different, more playful tone of voice, he says, "What shall we do now?"

"Let's go back," Sumana says.

"Do you have anything to read in your hut?"

"No," Sumana replies, "I'm here to meditate."

"I don't want to sit again tonight," Palaparuchi whines. "I dissolved enough defilements for today in that last sitting. I created a mind-made body and left my physical body behind...."

Palaparuchi continues to relate his out-of-body meditation to Sumana as they walk down the hill. He brushes against Sumana several times on the journey. Sumana just wants to be alone. If only Palaparuchi weren't senior to him. He would then be able to kick him out of his room.

Rahula and Devi break their embrace and look into each other's eyes. Rahula fears that she's going to kiss him. Then he fears that he's going to kiss her. Nothing of the sort happens. They stand up and brush themselves off. In the distance they both hear a car alarm go off. It is a loud whooping siren. They quickly head off in that direction and soon they are clear of the jungle and in the coconut plantation. From here, it's easy. Rahula wants to hug her, but restrains himself. He's not sure where any display of affection might lead. Right now, uppermost in his mind is finding her a place to stay for the night.

Rahula follows the same route he took earlier in the day, only because that is the only part of town he knows. She can't stay at the monastery. At first, that poses a problem. He doesn't want to ask her to find a room in a hotel, as he does not know if she has any money with her. Besides, what money she does have should be used for a bus ticket home. Where can she stay for free? Then he remembers visiting the nun earlier. Perhaps she could stay there.

He leads her to the house where the nuns live and goes up to the front door. The foreign nun, Gotami, answers the door, but she doesn't immediately recognize him.

"I was here with the white-skinned monk, Sumana Hamdaru."

"Oh, yes, I remember him. You were the layman with the two monks."

"Yes, that's correct," he says.

Devi, pushing Rahula aside, asks Gotami if she could come in and use the phone.

"We must call our parents in Colombo," she insists.

"I'll have to ask the landlady," Gotami says.

"Can you also find out if she can stay the night?" Rahula chimes in.

"All right, I don't see a problem with that. We have a couple of empty rooms."

She leaves the door wide open with Rahula and Devi waiting on the porch.

Rahula says to Devi, "It's too late for me to call my parents. I'll stay at the monastery nearby and call them first thing in the morning."

Devi smiles and says, "I thought you would say that. Never mind. I'll take care of everything."

Gotami returns with the landlady, who is a middle-aged Sinhalese widow, dressed in all white, with her hair tied up in a bun. She asks Rahula who he is and he tells her that he is the nephew of Venerable Aggachitta and that he is staying at the hermitage.

"Why, Venerable Aggachitta is a most austere and noble bhikkhu," the landlady says. "I'm sure his nephew is well brought up. And who is this?" She asks, pointing at Devi.

Devi curtsies, which is something she learned at finishing school, and gives the landlady a friendly smile with a generous display of perfectly white teeth.

"I am Devi," she says. "I have come to visit the hermitage for the uposatha, but I got the day wrong, you know, which day is really the full moon day, and so I arrived a day early. I only need to stay the night."

"Why of course, young child, you can stay the night and then we will all go to the hermitage for the uposatha. Maybe even Gotami will come with us. She has never been there."

Devi is led into the house. Rahula stays out on the porch and says good-bye. Once Devi is inside, she persuades the landlady to let her to use the phone. She calls not only her parents, but also Rahula's.

Rahula walks to the monastery where his uncle is. Podi Kusala recognizes him from earlier in the day and offers to lead him to his uncle, but he declines, choosing to sleep in the dining hall. Podi Kusala laughs whenever Rahula says his uncle's name, so Rahula wonders what is so funny about his uncle. Then Podi Kusala tells Rahula the story Sumana told him earlier this afternoon. Rahula laughs like he has never laughed before at the image of his uncle squatting in the latrine, surprised by a bucket of water thrown in his face.

Venerable Aggachitta lies down, but has a hard time trying to sleep. His mind is just too active. He gets up, turns on the room light, for there is no desk lamp, and takes out his notebook. Sitting cross-legged on the bed with his notebook in his lap, he begins to write.

He scrawls the heading, "A note on why I have deviated from my doctoral thesis."

Below that, he writes, "In my early days I primarily concerned myself with presenting the traditional Buddhaghosan viewpoint on the subject of conditionality. A belief in momentariness and constant flux formed the core of my dissertation, so I also conceded that the standard twelve-link chain of dependent co-arising described a past life, the present one, and the next one, and nothing else. Since then I have questioned both the doctrine of momentariness and the three-lifetime view. What I have concluded is this."

Here he stops writing, as he hasn't concluded anything yet. He's just getting started. He crosses out the last sentence and continues writing from there.

"The doctrine of momentariness involves a view of events occurring within such small units of time that one would be hard pressed to say they actually exist. While the three-lifetime view, by its very nature, involves looking at a prior existence that one may have no knowledge of, and a future one that may or may not occur. What these two views ignore is precisely what we can know about the conditionality of our current existence. We can observe dependent co-arising in our lives without taking up either the belief in rebirth or in an impercep-tible rapidly changing reality."

That's better, but where does it lead? Aggachitta would like to see it lead in the direction of explaining the true nature of delusion and ignorance, though he's not prepared to say that he fully understands what that is yet.

He pictures consciousness as an infinite flat panel of white light spreading in all directions. There are pools of color, like puddles of oil, here and there in the white light. Some of the puddles spread into each other, while others remain self-contained. There's nothing holding the panel of light, no projector, no strings from above. It is suspended in space, emanating from within itself.

Aggachitta writes, "The source of knowing remains unknown."

Part Three

Nibbana
and
Rebellion

CHAPTER
27

Aggachitta manages to sleep for about three hours before waking up. He becomes aware of the need to empty his bladder, and so gets out of bed and walks down the hall to the toilet. He turns on the light and squats squarely over the hole. A bhikkhu is not allowed to urinate while standing up, so he has no choice but to squat, even though it puts him in a vulnerable position. He fears that one of these immature samaneras will open the door and throw a bucket of water at him. That's not likely, as there's a spigot with a hose attached to it, which he uses to hose down the toilet after he is done. He then goes out to the washbasin to wash his hands and face, dousing the top of his head with water as well.

On his way back to his room, he checks to see whether he's still sleepy or wide awake. He decides that he's wide awake. He feels energy surge into his trunk and head. He goes to his room to get his notebook and then heads off to the library.

The monastery is deathly quiet at this hour, which must be around midnight. It dawns on him that it would be a perfect time to meditate, but meditation may take away valuable time that would be better used for research and contemplation. He wonders where to put his mind, and so rummages through what he remembers of his earlier thoughts, looking for what is missing in them. He hasn't looked at nibbana yet. His attention has been solely on the chains of dependent co-arising and has not lighted on what happens when the chain breaks apart and ceases. What is missing is the unconditioned.

Then an utterly strange new idea occurs to him, one that stops him in his tracks as he reaches the door of the library. He opens the door, turns on a light, and sits down, opening his notebook on the table before him. He begins writing.

"Constructed nibbana: the idea of what nibbana is displaces nibbana. The ancient bhikkhus versed in the abhidharma, who came up with the notion of *nibbanadhatu*, the element of nibbana, turned nibbana into a concept. They conceived of it in such a way that they made it into something they could describe. It became the words that described it. There became only one right way to look at it, to define it, and to realize it. What is real nibbana?"

Aggachitta doesn't like asking himself that question, for he believes he should know the answer if he has truly attained some stage of noble understanding, such as sotapanna or beyond. Instead, he sees that his thoughts about nibbana are also constructed, and not the real thing. Does this mean that his experiences are also invalid? Are they constructed too? Here he tries to remember the last time he has known nibbana, or better yet, *nirodha samapatti*, for that is all he could really know with any certainty if he were still not an arhat. Now nirodha, how can that be constructed? It is when the mind is perfectly empty. Is the emptiness Aggachitta has known the same nirodha that the Buddha knew?

He decides to look up some sutta passages to give him guidance in this matter. He is about to follow through, but hesitates. Is looking in the suttas the right place to resolve such a question? Perhaps meditation is a better place to explore this question. However, if he meditates and nothing comes of it, he would have lost valuable research time. Which is it going to be?

Aggachitta ponders these two options. Through meditation, he would be using the raft, so to speak, on the river of consciousness as a vehicle to solve the riddle of nibbana. While with research, he would use analytic insight to discern the meaning of certain passages, and then apply that knowledge to his current understanding of nibbana. Both ways involve his mind. And if his mind has delusion in it, grounded in ignorance, then it can only lead to an erroneous conclusion. How can such a mind know nibbana?

Here he sees some light. Of course, that mind can't know nibbana. How does he know that the only consciousness that arises in his stream of consciousness is ignorant? There could be moments of consciousness that have an understanding of nibbana, or how else could he even consider the possibility of attaining nibbana in this life?

The only way to find out would be to meditate and notice each consciousness that arises. That is what his Burmese teachers would advise, believing that only with such constant awareness can nirodha be discerned.

He goes over to the couch and sits down on it. He closes his eyes, with his hands on his lap and his feet touching the floor, and turns his mind within. All is quiet for a moment.

Gotami has decided to do some preparatory reading for her meeting with Venerable Aggachitta. She sits cross-legged on her bed with a book in her lap. It is unusual for her, or for any bhikkhu or nun, to stay up late. The Buddha recommended sleeping during the middle of the night. She can't sleep, no matter how hard she tries, for she's awfully excited about having found a teacher at last.

To Gotami's way of seeing things, a teacher is the end of searching, the end of being isolated, the beginning of finding the true path to liberation. He's the embodiment of all the qualities of the Buddha — kindness, wisdom, compassion, tranquility, skillful means. With his superior guidance, she will overcome all impediments, all self-inflicted doubts and worries, and all defilements of mind. He offers the cure to what ails her and all of humankind. In brief, the teacher is an all-knowing, fully awakened meditation master.

She reads a few pages of the book on her lap, and then skips ahead to another chapter. She's reading *Living Buddhist Masters*, a book compiled by Jack Kornfield, a former monk. It contains the writings of certain highly regarded Theravadin meditation teachers, along with biographical sketches of each one. What she likes most are not the ideas of the teachers (some of them are far too technical for a novice), but the stories of these masters. Her favorite is the story of Sunlun Sayadaw.

Sunlun lived in a village in Burma and was a farmer with a wife and family. He was largely uneducated and had little religious training. He began meditating, observing his breath at the nostrils. His breathing soon became rapid and loud, like some kind of heavy machinery. He would breathe like this for an hour or more, and then his breathing would slow down. Sometimes it would stop altogether for a few minutes. He is believed to have purged himself of defilements of mind through entering exalted states of consciousness. He continued meditating on his own, finding it almost impossible to work and live as a husband to his wife, and so he became a bhikkhu. Scholarly monks who then came in contact with him asked him about his experiences and understandings, determining from his answers that he was possibly an arhat. A meditation center was formed around his rapid breathing practice, and the author of *Living Buddhist Masters* had spent some months there.

Gotami wishes she could go to Burma and study with a Burmese master. However, Burma is politically unstable and it is hard to get long-term visas, even for bhikkhus. While Sri Lanka allows her to stay for a year, it does not have any great meditation masters, at least not any listed in Mr. Kornfield's book, which contains only Burmese and Thai masters. In fact, Sri Lanka has only a handful of bhikkhus who even practice meditation, much less teach it. There may be only a couple meditation masters on the whole island, and she's fortunate enough to find one of them.

She does not know what, or how, Venerable Aggachitta teaches, but she is sure that it will be as good as what she would get in Burma. He must teach one of the Burmese methods, the one he used to attain nibbana. That's what she really wants: a teacher who has attained some noble stage of awakening, at the very lowest an anagami. She's certain he will know what she must do in order to become a sotapanna in this very life. With that thought, she puts the book away, turns off the light, and slips under the covers.

After she closes her eyes, she takes refuge in the Buddha, dharma, and sangha, and then recites the ten precepts she has undertaken as a nun. Firm in her resolve, she can now go to sleep.

Palaparuchi vows not to sleep at all that night. The full moon night of the uposatha is reason enough. There are particular monks who try to spend the whole moonlit night in meditation, seeking final liberation as did the Buddha, seated under the Bodhi tree, over twenty-five hundred years ago. There is no Bodhi tree to speak of at the hermitage, an oversight of the lay founders. There are many other trees, however, and all Palaparuchi has to do is pick one. He needs Sumana's help.

Sumana is trying to sleep, but it is hard for him to get comfortable on the floor of his hut. His double robe is simply not enough padding against the hard ground. He tosses and turns, and when he drifts off for a few moments, some noise coming from the bed usually wakes him. He wonders what Palaparuchi could be doing, but never opens his eyes to find out.

Palaparuchi lights the lamp at around one. Sumana is awake, lying on his back.

"Sumana, I need your help."

"What is it? Can't you see I'm trying to sleep?"

"I need to find the right place to meditate for the rest of the night. If you help me find it, then you can have the bed."

Sumana considers whether getting up and walking around the hermitage in the middle of night with Palaparuchi on some kind of mad quest is worth having the bed. He imagines being in the bed, experiencing the firmness of the mattress holding his body and the softness of the pillow under his head. He's up and ready in no time.

Palaparuchi and Sumana go outside, each with his own flashlight. The moon is very bright, but the light is so diffuse that it is sometimes hard to see details, especially when something moves. Sumana walks a few paces behind Palaparuchi as they follow the footpath to the cistern. They stop at the outhouse. Palaparuchi goes inside. Sumana waits outside. Palaparuchi talks to him from within the outhouse.

"Do you know the official story of the Buddha's attainment? He had been starving himself for years trying to find liberation and one day found that he was too weak to do anything. So he decided to eat a regular meal. Just the thought of eating real food turned his five fellow ascetics against him, so they left. They left the future Buddha because he wanted a decent meal. Do you believe that? I don't. Anyhow, the Buddha was very thin and terribly weak, but he was determined to attain nibbana that night. All he needed was some food. Out in the jungle, where was he to find something ready to eat?"

Palaparuchi pauses in his narrative, giving Sumana a chance to imagine what it would have been like for the Buddha to be a hundred times hungrier than he is now, faced with the hopelessness of finding food in the jungle. Sumana would have given up a long time ago and gone into town, where food is plentiful.

"Can you refill the water tin for me?" Palaparuchi asks, pushing the outhouse door ajar, still squatting inside, with the empty cocoa tin in his outstretched hand.

Sumana takes the tin and goes over to the cistern. He recalls having heard this story before, but not as Palaparuchi is telling it. He doesn't know how factual his friend's storytelling is, though he finds it the most enjoyable part of being with him.

At the cistern, he holds the tin underwater, filling it up absent-mindedly, while thinking about the Buddha knowing hunger before knowing nibbana. The Buddha satisfied his hunger first, attained final liberation after. One did lead to the other.

Sumana brings the full tin of water back to the outhouse and hands it to Palaparuchi through the slim opening in the door. Palaparuchi makes immediate use of it and hands it back to Sumana.

"You should have a bucket in here, or, at least a larger tin. Can you fill it up again for me?"

Sumana takes the tin and walks back to the cistern. He's ashamed of being hungry at night. The Buddha must have eaten late in the day when he attained nibbana. Otherwise, he would have been hungry that night. He ate at night and it didn't stop him from attaining nibbana.

Sumana returns with a tin of water. Palaparuchi is standing at the door to the outhouse waiting for him. Sumana gives him the tin to place in the outhouse for the next person. It suddenly occurs to Sumana that he neglected to do that the other day when he doused the meditation master with a bucket of water. He felt what it must have been like for the master to sit with his robes drenched and his face dripping with water, with no water in the tin to wash up with afterwards. What suffering and humiliation to go through! Maybe Aggachitta is an arhat after all.

Palaparuchi continues his story as he leads Sumana in the direction of the dining hut.

"As the Buddha wandered in the jungle, he came across a girl who was herding cattle. She had with her some rice mixed with cow's milk and offered it to the Buddha. He accepted her offering, ate the porridge, and then sat under the Bodhi tree. The rest is history."

Sumana becomes conscious of how sane Palaparuchi is sounding. He's not the same monk he knew earlier in the day. He's closer to how Sumana mostly remembers him. This change is inexplicable; but then, so are Palaparuchi's sudden transitions into madness.

Sumana wants to comment on Palaparuchi's saneness, but doesn't know how to state this observation without risking an outburst. The safest thing to do is stay with Palaparuchi's current theme.

"So the Buddha attained nibbana after eating a meal?" Sumana asks.

"It wasn't much of a meal. You and I would never be satisfied with a bowl of milk and rice porridge. It was more like a snack, an energy bar, before the final battle with Mara."

"What happened next?"

"You know what happened," Palaparuchi says. "Mara sent his daughters to tempt him and his army to deter him from his resolve. The Buddha fought them off. Then his consciousness was free to know every one of his past lives and see into the nature of existence. He knew samsara, and was able to pull the plug on it. That is how you arrive at nibbana."

As they near the dining hut and Palaparuchi turns his flashlight on, shining it from top to bottom, corner to corner, making sure no one is there. Sumana follows right behind him. Palaparuchi goes over to the tins near the stove and opens one after another, looking for something. He turns to Sumana.

"All they keep here is tea. Where's the leftover dana kept?"

"In the cave," Sumana answers.

"Where in the cave?"

"There's a cabinet near the entrance. It has supplies as well. What are you planning to do? You know we can't eat till daybreak."

Palaparuchi looks up at Sumana, his eyes bright with some mysterious force behind them.

"This is no time to obey mindless rules. I must eat so I can sit under a Bodhi tree and attain final nibbana before dawn. That is my destiny. Are you coming with me? You will be my Sujata, the one who fed the Buddha porridge before his awakening. You'll gain a mountain of merit for this act."

"But I don't want to break the rule! I don't want to go up to the cave either. I just want to go back to sleep," Sumana whines.

"Good! Sleep then. Miss this opportunity for merit. It will be bandied about that you slept while I attained nibbana. Everyone will know you as a lazy monk. No one will give you alms. You will have no supporters, no friends. If that is how you want it, then go, go back to your fiber mattress and cotton pillow, and spend the night dreaming while I break the chain that binds me to renewed existence."

Sumana is shocked that Palaparuchi actually believes that he could attain nibbana if he meditated through the night. He has heard enough, gone through enough inconvenience, and wasted enough time today.

"I've given it some thought," Sumana says, "and I have decided not to go any further. Do what you have to do, but leave me out of it. I'm satisfied with just being the meditation master's student and following his instructions for however long it takes. So I'm going to bed."

Palaparuchi is stunned. Perhaps his friend is right about sticking with the meditation master and attaining nibbana through persistent effort for the rest of his life. That is not Palaparuchi's way. He believes that he will make an end to suffering at a predestined time. If that is tonight, then this is what he must do.

Sumana leaves Palaparuchi alone in the dining hut. On his way back to his hut, he wonders if he's doing the right thing. The thought of Palaparuchi attaining nibbana tonight briefly crosses his mind, but it takes only a few seconds for the absurdity of it to set in. By the time he reaches his hut, he can barely contain his laughter. He stumbles inside and plops down on the bed. Laughter, like hiccups, comes and goes, rocking his body, making it hard to fall asleep, even though he's extremely tired.

CHAPTER
28

Gotami is too agitated to sleep. All she can think about is meeting the meditation master. She worries about whether he will like her or just ignore her. If he ignores her, that is not a bad sign, for that is how bhikkhus often relate to women. However, if he likes her, then maybe she can go to him for instruction every day. If he ignores her and yet likes her, which is the most likely scenario, maybe he will teach her once every two or three days. Then a more serious concern occurs to her. What will she do if he does not think much of her meditation practice?

This thought increases her anxiety. He might not find her worthy. Then she will have to be content with Ananda or any other less enlightened teacher who happens to be in the vicinity. She will never get anywhere on this noble path if that is her lot.

Now she knows what she must do. She has to meditate. She must put her best foot forward. She sits up in bed and assumes a cross-legged posture, straightening her back. She pictures her bodily form in her mind, and it looks good. The master will certainly approve. Then she considers which technique to use, trying to figure out which one the meditation master would approve of most. She weighs awareness of the breath at the nostrils against awareness at the abdomen. She goes with the abdomen. If she does that, then she should include noting rise/fall. She adds that to her list. Is there anything else? Oh yes! There is noting "thinking, thinking."

Now she is ready to begin. She takes refuge three times, skips over the ten precepts, and jumps into a recitation of the qualities of the Buddha, dharma, and sangha. Now she's sure her mind is properly directed. She places her attention on her abdomen. It is barely moving. She's thinking about it not moving, and so notes "thinking, thinking." This is going well so far, she thinks, and then notes "thinking, thinking" again. Her abdomen still isn't moving much, though she does hear her stomach rumble, and so notes "hearing, hearing." I'm being very mindful, she thinks, and then notes "thinking, thinking." She wishes her abdomen was moving more so she could be noting "rising, rising" and "falling, falling" instead of "thinking, thinking" all the time. That is what happens when you are aware, she tells herself, inserting a quick "thinking, thinking" after that thought.

She breathes faster so as to feel her abdomen. As she does so, she recalls what she read earlier about Sunlun Sayadaw. He didn't do this noting technique and he became an arhat. All he did was breathe fast. Why not switch techniques? This thought is followed by a hurried "thinking, thinking." Oh, shut up! The response is a loud, imperious "thinking, thinking!" Her breathing gets even faster, and she forcefully plants her attention on both nostrils. Thoughts come with the occasional "thinking, thinking" appended to them, but she now pushes them both away, drowning thinker and commentator in the roar of her breathing.

She breathes like a steam-driven locomotive for several minutes. Dots of light pop up and vanish within the black space of her mind. White, red, yellow, blue balls surge and burst here and there. It's like a fireworks display. Her body sparkles with crisp sensations of joy. Her heart feels cool and delicious. Her breathing is unstoppable. It's like riding a galloping horse and trying to keep hold of the reins. She's tossed about, her body swirling in her seat, jerking in the shoulders and neck. Her breathing gets stronger and stronger, completely overtaking her. She feels an explosion rising up from within. Her body freezes, as though paralyzed. A strong, brilliant bright white light bursts up from her spine and into the very center of her brain.

"This is it," a voice within her says, calm and unruffled, her body light and without tension, her mind completely still, floating on a translucent plane of infinite whiteness.

Aggachitta sits on the couch, his back hunched over a little and his breathing shallow. The first few minutes are filled with thoughts about constructed nibbana, and he outlines an argument supporting it that he plans to include in his article. Then comes a few minutes of less interesting thoughts, as he tries to let go of his tendency to direct his mind in meditation. These mundane thoughts annoy him at first, but he soon becomes patient with them, noticing them to consist of ideas on how to avoid anticipated problems. Part of him always has to be prepared for any eventuality. It's the same part that began a term paper on the very day it was assigned, finishing it at least a week before it was due. When he recognizes the student in him within these thoughts, he experiences compassion for that young man. As a student, he worked so hard to memorize, analyze, and eventually express his ideas, he seldom thought about anything outside of his studies.

This train of thought softens the pressure to be aware of every little thing, which he felt at the beginning of the sitting. For it is not possible to be that aware during periods of contemplation, worry, and recollection. When he experiences some compassion for himself, something falls away from his consciousness and he can step back a little and shine some awareness on what arises. What emerges is a sense of relief at being able to have his mind do nothing. He has always worked his mind too hard; now it can rest. Soon enough, he feels compelled to explore this state of restfulness.

Consciousness is present, but not acting as it usually does. Certain sankhara — mental activities — do not push to the surface, propelling things into action. Not even the thoughts around this lack of activity produce activity, for he sees how his mind generates activity so as not to rest too deeply.

He begins to notice each thought without giving it any ground to land on. Spaces form between thoughts, and when thoughts come, they dissolve as soon as they are noticed. The spaces grow longer and longer, and what was before called rest now merges into a state that is as still as his mind has ever been. For several seconds his consciousness is totally still, yet also awake and aware. Then a thought floats to the surface, is known, then is gone. The stillness returns, though he is not sure if it ever left. He does not know what to call it. Words can't survive here, and meanings seem to be as empty as their evanescent shells. In the blink of an eye, he's hunched over, breathing slowly and calmly, his mind empty, unaware that this is so.

Sumana can't get to sleep. The moonlight that now illuminates the interior of his hut makes him uncomfortable in his own skin. He keeps telling himself to settle down and go to sleep, but he doesn't follow his own orders. It occurs to him that the only thing to do is to get calm through meditation and see if that will help him get to sleep. He decides to sit on the bed this time as a way to remind himself that once he feels sleepy in the meditation sitting, he will lie down and go to sleep.

He brings his attention to his sitting posture. His legs are crossed, though that will change once he starts to feel tired. He can feel the buoyancy of the mattress beneath him and decides to bounce a little on the bed. It feels good to go up and down like that. Then he stops. He's having too much fun. That thought makes him giggle, and he recalls some of the silly things which happened during the day. Palaparuchi is like a little kid sometimes, he thinks, and so is he when he is with him. He recollects all the talk about Mara and yakkhas, chuckling to himself at the craziness of it all.

He realizes that this isn't going to help him get to sleep. It's too stimulating. Anything he puts his attention on is too stimulating. Gotami, Aggachitta, Maggaphala, Rahula, the monks at the village temple, are each in their own way exciting thought objects for him.

Palaparuchi, he is so sly, he thinks, especially the way he rationalized eating in the middle of the night. His imagination kicks in and he sees Palaparuchi sitting under a tree eating a sandwich in the thick moonlight. He watches Palaparuchi take huge bites, chewing with his mouth closed, his cheeks bulging. There is something sinister in this image. It is as though Palaparuchi has taken food from starving children to feed his greedy gullet.

Sumana breaks off this scenario, realizing that this is just his hunger speaking. He briefly wishes he went with Palaparuchi to raid the food cabinet, as he imagines his body getting up and joining his fellow monk. He stays put however, reminding himself that he desires sleep right now, not food. Still he tells himself that there will be food in the morning.

Sumana feels comforted by knowing that tomorrow will certainly bring new adventures in eating. It is the uposatha, and many laypeople will be coming with baskets full of the best dishes they can afford. They will even come shortly after daybreak with a ten-course breakfast, and he will be served milk coffee, and will have fried sweetbreads for dessert. That is far better than day-old white bread and marmite, which is what Palaparuchi has most likely found to eat.

The images of food calm his mind, and soon he finds himself dreaming about a large banquet held in his honor. He's above the huge spread, looking down on it, as if he were an invisible being in the room, naming each delectable dish as he scans it. His body slumps and he forgets to lie down before entering into a deep sleep.

CHAPTER
29

Gotami's consciousness returns from being submerged in inner white light. It is largely unchanged. That is the first thing she notices. The next thing that enters her mind is the decision to tell the meditation master about this extraordinary experience. It will give her something to talk about and it may impress him. She's so happy that it happened at this particular moment. It must be auspicious. With that thought, she decides to recite the *Mangala Sutta*, and so opens her chanting book to that sutta.

Devi, who's sleeping in the room next door, is woken up by the sound of Gotami's chanting. At first she doesn't recognize it as words, reaching her as a ghostly whisper. As she strains to listen, she can hear separate words, but she can't understand them. She gets up out of bed and straightens her dress. She regrets not having packed a bag of clothes and taking along a comb and toothbrush.

She wonders what time it is and so opens the door to search the house for a clock. She goes into the living room and then down a hall leading to the kitchen. In the kitchen, she turns on a light and sees a clock on the wall. The hands on the clock point to about half past one. She wonders why this nun would be chanting at this late hour.

She has not really thought about the nun until now. She just saw her as a bald woman in yellow. Now she wonders what this woman's story is. She's only a little older than Devi. She's not ugly, or apparently stupid, so Devi can't figure out why she would decide to become a nun. She's actually quite attractive, and Devi produces a scenario of a young white woman fleeing a jealous lover, as she has seen on imported soap operas from America. This scenario provides the only logical explanation why a woman like this would become a nun. She has the urge to ask Gotami about her lover in America and why she has to hide from him in Sri Lanka. Isn't being halfway around the world enough?

Devi opens the refrigerator and finds some milk and fruit. She pours herself a glass of milk and peels a banana. She sips the milk and chews bites of banana as she embellishes her story of the nun's life. This nun must come from a wealthy family to have such a jealous boyfriend. Her family is also looking for her and has traced her to Sri Lanka, so she has had to shave her head and wear yellow robes, and thus assume a new identity in order to hide from them and avoid being sent back home to marry the man her parents have in mind for her. It's her angry parents, and not the jealous boyfriend, who are at this very moment roaming the streets of Colombo, going from hotel to hotel, trying to find her. That is why she is a nun!

She finishes her milk and banana, leaving the unwashed glass in the sink and the peel on the table. She decides to go back to her room, but if she hears the nun chanting again, she's definitely going to approach her. She will then use the excuse of being kept awake because of the nun's late night chanting to probe for details of her life.

Instead of following her own plan, she alters it by stopping outside the nun's door and putting her ear against it. She doesn't hear any sounds coming from the room. Could she have imagined the chanting? With that thought, which does not dispel her belief in what she has truly imagined about Gotami, she returns to her room.

Lying in bed, she tries to picture what it would be like to be a nun. Ghastly!

Palaparuchi sits in the dining hut drinking a hot cup of milk tea that he has made for himself. He reworks his latest scheme. The food is in the cave, the one Mara occupies. If he enters the

cave, Mara is sure to wake up. Then he would have to do battle
with the Evil One in order to get the nourishment needed to
become strong enough to fight Mara's army and resist the
temptations of his daughters. That was not how the Buddha
did it. He tries to figure out a way to get into the cave and get
food without Mara waking up, but he knows he does not have
the necessary magical powers, such as being invisible and
walking through walls. He now wishes he had acquired the full
six superpowers instead of the three he believes he has. He
can't pick up the other three without first becoming an arhat.
He has to become an arhat before getting the nourishment so
that he may defeat Mara, which he must do in order to become
an arhat.

After he finishes his cup of milk tea, he goes over to the
pitcher of water to wash his cup. The pitcher is practically
empty. The temple boy must have forgotten to refill it. Besides,
where is the temple boy? Shouldn't he be sleeping here in the
dining hut? And for that matter, where is the meditation
master? Has Mara taken them prisoner?

Palaparuchi is torn between a fantasy of fighting Mara for
the release of the meditation master and the temple boy and the
reality of going to the cistern to fill the pitcher with water.
Then he remembers that the meditation master has a water
filter in his hut. Since Mara is holding the master hostage, he
will not be in his hut. Palaparuchi decides to bring the pitcher
to the master's water filter, fill it, and then use the master's
bucket to get more water for the filter.

He takes care of all this as planned, but while he's in the
master's hut, he gives into a sudden urge to sweep and dust the
room, and organize the master's possessions. This takes him an
hour or so. Then he goes back to the dining hut and proceeds
to clean it as well, and puts the tins, utensils, and pots in some
kind of order. When that is done, he picks up a rake and, in the
twilight before dawn, rakes around the master's hut, the dining
hut, and finally Sumana's hut.

As the colors of the new dawn appear in the sky,
Palaparuchi quietly enters Sumana's hut to get his alms bowl.

He then walks through the jungle, determined to arrive at one of his favorite monasteries in time for morning alms. During his walk, Palaparuchi becomes aware of a feeling of sadness. He tries to locate the source of it and discovers that he feels hurt by how Sumana has treated him.

He was excited about seeing Sumana. He had hoped that Sumana would be happy to see him, which he was in a way, but Palaparuchi sensed that Sumana perceived him as an intrusion, and perhaps even as a burden. He intended to rekindle the bond he felt with Sumana, but instead he now feels rejected by his friend.

This rejection hurts deeply. Palaparuchi traces his current hurt feelings back to earlier in the day at all the times Sumana pushed him away or refused to do something for him. Then he got a brilliant idea as to how to win Sumana's favor by treating his friend to a midnight snack. He was certain Sumana would welcome that. He carefully presented his gift so that Sumana would feel comfortable breaking the rule of not eating between noon and daybreak. He was dismayed when his plan backfired and Sumana retreated to his hut.

This sadness is an old enemy he has feuded with over the years. As he walks through the coconut plantation, he feels the energy drain from his limbs and torso, and his mind begins to get numb. He walks on automatic pilot. He dreads going back on antidepressants. He just wants to get some nutritious food in him, have another cup of tea, and engage in some light conversation with other monks.

As he leaves the plantation and sets foot on the dirt road, the sun rises above the hills in the east. Palaparuchi reinvents himself for this sojourn into town. He's no longer an anagami with psychic powers. He's just an ordinary bhikkhu passing through town, stopping for morning alms at the nearest monastery.

Rahula hears people washing pots and pans in the small kitchen adjacent to the monastery's dining hall. He slept the night on the floor of the dining hall, with only a blanket and a pillow. He's a bit groggy, but manages to quickly dress himself and go off to the lavatory. When he's washed up, he makes his way out of the monastery, not saying good-bye to anyone.

As he walks down the steps to the street, his mind begins to work on various plans for the day. First, he has to get back to the hermitage before his uncle returns. Then he has to find a solution to the girlfriend problem. After that, he can put his attention on his various chores and responsibilities.

The entanglement with Devi fills him with apprehension. He knows she's going to push him towards marriage. He half surrenders to the idea, and thinks it will not be so bad. Then, as he turns the corner to the road leading to the coconut plantation, he pauses to consider what it would be like if he could just say "I won't marry you" and be done with it. That thought makes him feel better than the idea of marrying her does. Then he imagines her response to it, and he feels much worse. It's intolerable for Rahula to feel the pain of being hated by someone, anyone. He pulls his mind out of that imagined scenario and replaces it with one of him agreeing to marry her on his terms. That makes him feel more confident. What are his terms? He hasn't any. All he really has is a way of operating that so far has protected him from being the object of anyone's hatred. Perhaps those are his terms: he'll do what she wants so that she doesn't hate him.

Nearing the coconut plantation, he sees a bhikkhu walking in his direction. It's the other white-skinned monk. The bhikkhu gazes at the ground in front of him. He carries his alms bowl tightly in the crook of his right arm. His body is very tense. He walks right past Rahula without even recognizing him.

Rahula stands for a moment, watching the back of the bhikkhu as he goes down the road. He admires the bhikkhu. He does what Rahula can't. He just does what he wants.

Mrs. Jayatilaka, Gotami's landlady, rises at the crack of dawn. She does her morning chanting along with offering a plate of flower petals to the small Buddha statue in her room, and then goes downstairs to the kitchen to make breakfast. She turns on the kitchen light and is struck by the sight of a banana peel on the dining table. It wasn't there when she went to bed. She's sure of that. She picks it up and takes it over to the garbage can, which is under the sink, and notices an unwashed glass, once containing milk, in the basin. She throws away the banana peel and then scrubs the dirty glass.

She wonders who had this midnight snack. Her mind latches onto Gotami, since she can't imagine the senior nun doing such a thing and the white-skinned nun is basically an unknown to her. She has never spent much time with foreign women. Her only real exposure to them has been through movies and old television shows, so her opinion of them is not very high. They have loose morals and no spiritual direction. She had hoped that this nun would be different, but she is proving to be like the celluloid women Mrs. Jayatilaka knows intimately.

She realizes that she can't say anything about this to the nun, for that would be disrespectful. However, she can talk about this behind the nun's back with her superiors. That would be the proper thing to do. Now all she has to do is find the right opportunity to bring the subject up.

Meanwhile, Gotami is getting ready in the bathroom. She first shaves her head, then washes her face and brushes her teeth. It is much easier shaving with running water and a wall mirror. She straightens her robes and takes a long look at herself in the mirror, seeing if there are any smudges on her clothes, or missed hairs on her head. Devi is waiting outside the bathroom, and knocks on the door. Gotami takes a couple of minutes to finish up before opening the bathroom door.

Devi looks her in the eye. She wants to ask her a question, but is concerned that the nun's answer will take too long, and she can't afford to wait any longer. Gotami passes by her wondering why this wiry girl is here. She too has questions she would like to ask.

Gotami goes to the kitchen. Mrs. Jayatilaka makes half an attempt to bow to her, and then goes back to brewing tea and

frying eggs. Gotami senses that her landlady is not happy with
her. She wants to ask if anything is the matter, as she would
have done with her own mother in a similar morning situation,
but she knows that it would be disrespectful. Sinhalese women
generally do not like intimate conversations. They perceive
such talk as embarrassing and distasteful. They would rather
have a pleasant enough conversation with you and then
disparage you behind your back. Well, that's human nature for
the most part when heart-to-heart conversations are not
allowed in one's life.

That's something Gotami truly misses in the nun's life. At
the dining table, waiting for her breakfast, she suddenly feels a
sense of loss. She misses her mother and her close friends, with
whom she would have the chance to talk honestly about her
feelings. Perhaps more than a great teacher, what she needs
now is a trustworthy friend. The same person can't be both.
She's reminded of the monk she met yesterday. Sumana was
his name. A pleasant name and he seemed really sincere and
kind.

Mrs. Jayatilaka brings a plate of eggs and toast and a cup
of tea to the table, setting them down in front of Gotami.
Gotami smiles up at her and Mrs. Jayatilaka returns her smile
curtly before turning around and walking away, leaving
Gotami alone in the kitchen.

Gotami minces the eggs on her plate with a fork. Devi
enters the kitchen and sits down at the table across from her.
She stares at the nun lifting tiny pieces of fried egg to her
mouth, chewing, swallowing, an endless repetitive cycle, or so
it seems this early in the morning. Devi is not particularly
hungry or thirsty. Her mind is running over one scheme after
another, and sometimes two at a time. She wonders when her
parents will arrive, and if they will take the same bus as
Rahula's parents. If they do arrive alone, how will she be sure
that they can find the forest hermitage? She forgot to give
them directions, though that would have been difficult, since
there is not a well-marked trail through the jungle. Those plans
and concerns then give way to a more immediate scheme to

learn more about the nun. She begins searching for the right
questions to ask. Her English is not that good. When she
speaks English, she feels less in control of things.

"You like Sri Lanka?" Devi asks, the pitch of her voice
rises appreciably when she says the name of her country.

Gotami finishes chewing before replying, though she only
says, "Yes."

"Why?"

"It's beautiful, warm, and I can stay here as long as I
want."

"America, it is not good?"

Gotami considers for a moment what this girl is asking her.
Is she asking for her opinion about America or is she asking a
personal question about why she left America?

"America is good for many things. It's not the best place to
practice the Buddha's teaching," she replies.

"Oh," Devi says, she thinks a moment. Then she boldly
asks, "Good for boyfriends?"

Gotami blushes at this question. She hasn't thought about
any of her old boyfriends for several weeks. She wishes she
could enlighten this young woman on the painful and unsatis-
factory aspects of dating and long-term relationships. That's
probably not what the woman wants to hear. Not if the boy she
was with last night is her boyfriend.

"You can find a boyfriend anywhere. Even here in Sri
Lanka. But that is not for me."

Devi looks at her intently, and says, "Why?"

"Because I'm a nun! We don't have boyfriends any more."

Devi considers what it would be like not to have a
boyfriend. Without Rahula, her vision of the future becomes
dark, vague. Anything could happen, and it may not be what
she would want.

"Look," Gotami says, reaching across the table to touch
Devi's hand, "If you find happiness with a boyfriend, then
that's a good thing. May you be happy."

Devi is startled, confused, uncomfortable, and angry. This
nun should not be touching her hand. She should be more

respectful and polite. Devi pulls her hand away and places her hands in her lap. She looks down at them for a moment and then raises her head to speak to the nun. She wishes she could just slip into Sinhalese and speak her thoughts with ease.

"You don't understand us! We have nothing. I want to have something. The only way to get it is marriage."

Gotami is struck by this frank statement. She chastises herself for being so ignorant of the condition of most Sri Lankan women.

"Yes," Devi continues, speaking animatedly, "I want to be happy, but not just happy. I want a good life. And you, you, you had a good life and now you don't. That is what I see."

Gotami doesn't like what she's hearing. She can't imagine Devi having the faintest clue what her life was like before. While at the same time she hopes Devi doesn't think she was spoiled, envied, had it all, like some kind of princess.

"I'm not much different from you," Gotami says. "Only I wanted something else out of life. I want to put an end to suffering and become fully liberated."

Devi doesn't know what to do with this information. It sounds to her as if the nun is chasing a dream and throwing her life away. Devi wants what is real, concrete, lasting.

There seems to be no way for them to bridge this gap of misunderstanding, so they sit quietly until the senior nun and the landlady call for them. It is time to go to the hermitage.

CHAPTER
30

A loud knocking on the door awakens Aggachitta. He was sound asleep, dreaming. He was at the forest hermitage, though it was not the hermitage as it is now. This one had several cement huts, a large whitewashed dining hall, and a circular wooden structure that served as a meditation hall. There were many lay people and several bhikkhus wandering around the premises, taking tours of the new buildings, including a new lavatory with running water. Aggachitta was outside of all this activity, observing it moving around from place to place, as if he were an invisible being. Then one of the laymen recognized him and came over to him. "Your good work has made all this possible," the layman said to him. "This can't be my doing," Aggachitta responded, and then was about to explain why when the first loud knock woke him up.

Aggachitta gets up slowly and goes over to the door. On the other side of the door is a samanera, who was told to wake Aggachitta before breakfast. Aggachitta picks up his notebook and alms bowl, so that he'll be ready to leave right after eating, and then he makes his way to the dining hall.

This time Aggachitta finds a place to sit on the bench with the other bhikkhus, near the head of the line, only a couple of people shy from being the most senior. There are long tables in front of the forty or so bhikkhus and ten samaneras, where plates of food and cups of tea are placed. In a couple of minutes, after everyone has a plate of food in front of him, the senior-most bhikkhu begins eating, and all the others follow suit.

As Aggachitta eats his breakfast of cold vermicelli noodles, chickpeas, and shredded coconut, he takes a couple of glances down the row of bhikkhus seated near him, for there was a bhikkhu who caught his attention when he walked in. It is a white-skinned bhikkhu, though not his new student. After he gets a good look at this bhikkhu, who is short and stubby with thick black nubs on his face and head, he loses his curiosity, concluding that this monk is probably just passing through town and is not seeking meditation instruction from him.

Aggachitta tries to bring his attention back to his thoughts of the night before, wanting to pick up where he left off when he went to sleep. He was seeking to understand what nibbana is. Once again, he focuses his thoughts on this subject: it is perfect stillness with the highest level of animated intelligence. It is the unparalleled calm of having all desires never needing to be satisfied, resting where they are spawned, curling up and dying in their beds. It is the beacon in the darkest night of longing and despair, the shore upon which all burdens are discarded. There's no arriving at it, or leaving from it. There's no being in it, no being of it. It is what it is. Consciousness ceases its endless and unstoppable production of-self and its creations and no longer is consciousness. Without the knowing mind, nibbana is known. Now the riddles make sense. Language only creates confusion here. Only nibbana knows what it is.

Nibbana knows. That is the most interesting proposition in Aggachitta's current thought process. All the rest preceding it, except for the initial idea of an animated intelligence combined with perfect stillness, was derivative in some way. Nibbana lives. That is what he is saying.

Aggachitta continues this line of thought as he slowly chews his food. Nibbana sees, hears, touches, tastes, smells, and thinks, but without creating any desire, suffering, or renewed and unique forms of existence. It's nibbana that eats food for the arhat. It's nibbana that moves the limbs, decides when to bathe, when to sleep, and it's nibbana that shines through the eyes and utters words. That's why the Buddha stated that he was not distinct from nibbana.

Aggachitta's mind pulls itself out of this train of thought with the wish to write everything down, which is certainly not possible at this moment. As he continues eating, he sits with the urgency to write, but by the time he has finished eating, his urge has dissipated into a contented feeling, for he knows he will remember these ideas as long as he lives. Now nibbana makes perfect sense.

Sumana, like many people in the early morning hours, falls into a sleep cycle of intense dreaming. He's a monk in this dream, but that gives him little comfort, for he's a monk living the life of a layman. That's the worst kind of monk. None of his fellow monks knows he has a wife, children, a large house, and a big, fancy car. He smokes cigarettes and drinks hard liquor. He's in a haze of smoke, sipping a Bloody Mary, as he sits in an outdoor chair near his swimming pool. He watches his wife swim in the water. She's a beautiful woman with long reddish hair that sticks to her head and back as she swims butterfly across the pool. He admires her curves as she swims. He feels a tightening around his groin. The splashes made by her butterfly strokes get louder, and he senses himself rising out of this dream world, his mind no longer translating the knocking on his door into splashes. He opens his eyes and is initially confounded. He's surprised to find out that this is his true life and the other was just a dream.

He sits up in bed and looks around. The knocking continues outside. He wonders if it is a woodpecker, though he has never seen one in Sri Lanka. Then he surmises that someone must be outside his door wanting his attention. It couldn't be Palaparuchi, for he would just walk right in. Who could it be?

"Who's there?" He shouts.

A muffled voice replies, "It is me, Rahula. I need to talk to you."

"I'm just getting up," Sumana says. "Give me a minute to get dressed."

Sumana looks down at his under-robe to see if it is wet from this morning's dream. It looks dry, though a bit wrinkled from sleeping in it. He stands up and loosens the fold that holds the cloth on his hips and refolds the robe tightly. He grabs a yellow rope used as a belt and ties it under the fold around his waist to keep the under-robe securely in place. Now he is ready for his outer robe. He has only two such robes. One is orange and the other is brown. Orange is for the city, brown for the forest. He dons the brown one. He sits down on his bed and shouts to Rahula to come in.

Rahula enters the hut sheepishly. He goes over to Sumana, bows before him, and then sits on the floor. He looks up into Sumana's eyes. He's obviously distressed.

"I need your help," Rahula says.

"What is it about? Have you gotten into some kind of trouble?" Sumana asks.

"You can say it is trouble," Rahula replies.

Sumana realizes that this is a serious matter. He would rather not discuss anything serious before breakfast, or even afterwards for that matter. Now he has no choice, so he dives in.

"What kind of trouble are you in?"

"Well, you know, I have this problem, well, with a girlfriend."

Rahula looks up at Sumana to see if he understands without saying more. Sumana's expression is blank, giving no hint of knowing more than what Rahula has just told him.

Rahula continues, "She wants me to marry her."

Sumana, with as much tact as he can muster, asks, "She's not going to have a baby?"

"No! It's nothing like that," Rahula snaps back. This mistimed remark on Sumana's part touches some kind of feeling in Rahula, giving him a burst of energy. "I don't even want to! I don't know what I'm going to do. I wish I didn't have to make this decision."

"What decision?"

"Should I marry her?"

"You can just tell her you are too young to get married," Sumana suggests, recalling his first year of college, when his girlfriend mentioned cementing their relationship.

"Do you think that would work?"

"Sure, why not? You can even say something about all the things you have to do before you can get married. You can tell her that you have to finish college first. Or, you can push it back even further by saying that you would like first to get established in a career before having a family."

"Do you think that will work?"

"Yes, of course," Sumana says, tempted to tell Rahula that he said these very same words to a girlfriend once, and look at him now, he's not married. "She will think you're making a mature, adult decision. Women like that."

"Good," Rahula says, his mood cheering up. "She should be here soon. Will you help me talk to her?"

Sumana would like to say no, but when he looks into Rahula's pleading eyes, he feels compelled to say yes.

"Okay. I'll just be around, standing in the background, when you talk to her."

"She doesn't speak English very well," Rahula says, perceiving a future communication problem.

"I can manage a little Sinhala," Sumana says, aware that he is unable to understand complex sentences in that language.

Sumana and Rahula get up to leave the hut.

Once outside, Sumana asks, "Have you seen Venerable Palaparuchi?"

"He's in town," Rahula informs him.

"Oh," Sumana says, conjuring up an image his friend dining at the four-star monastery he ate at yesterday. He then imagines that he is in store for a bland, simple Sri Lankan breakfast. Before he fully believes that scenario, he remembers that today is the uposatha, and so this morning's meal could be as sumptuous as what he would get in town.

Maggaphala rises from sleep to the sound of voices outside his cave. He is at first apprehensive about it being the mad monk, but once he recognizes the unaccented Sinhala, he knows that's not the case. He gets up and puts on an outer robe so that he is presentable. Someone lifts the cloth to the cave and peers inside. It is an old man, who obviously can't see in the dark. Maggaphala approaches him, seeing his features well enough in the dim light. The man winces at the sound of Maggaphala's steps, and then pulls his head out of the cave. There's a hurried discussion between three men outside the cave. Maggaphala makes out that they believe there's a leopard inside, so he rushes to the entrance and throws open the cloth to show them that a man is living here. The three laymen are frightened by the cloth opening upwards, but when they see Maggaphala's face emerge from behind it, their fears are put to rest.

"Bhante," one of the men says, "you scared us. We thought there was a leopard in there. We're happy it was only you."

Maggaphala steps out of the opening and onto the rock used as a step to the cave. The three laymen bow before him with hands clasped. They are eager to tell him why they have come to the hermitage.

"Bhante, Venerable?" the one who speaks for all of them says.

"My name is Maggaphala Thera."

"Venerable Maggaphala Thera, we are here for the uposatha. Give us the Ten Precepts so we may purify our conduct for this one day."

"Why certainly," Maggaphala says.

The three men sit on their knees before Maggaphala as he recites the Triple Gem. He chants it quickly, running the words together, but still delivering the proper rhythm and feeling. Then he jumps into the Ten Precepts without any preamble and does not wait for the laymen to finish reciting each one after him, hurrying on to the next one before they have a chance to say samadiyami (I undertake) at the end of each precept. He wraps up the Ten Precepts and it takes the laymen several seconds to catch up and finish saying the last one.

They rise and face Maggaphala. Maggaphala looks at them for a moment and then walks down the hill with the three laymen following him, as bhikkhus always walk ahead of laypeople. He goes straight to the dining hut, where he expects to find a multi-coursed breakfast and a hot cup of milk tea waiting for him.

The first thing he notices is that the dining hut has been swept and all the tins and pots have been neatly stacked and organized. It wasn't this way last night. He's surprised that these three laymen would do this. It's certainly not customary.

He looks around for any sign of morning alms or a cup of tea, but there's nothing. The laymen catch up to him in the dining hut. One of them informs him that their wives and daughters are coming with breakfast and had to wait for the market stalls to open in order to buy certain delicacies. Maggaphala does not mind waiting for delicacies. Now if they can only get the hint to brew him a cup of tea. He would do it himself, but laypeople usually don't like it when bhikkhus do things for themselves.

Maggaphala sits down on the bench. The three laymen stand around, doing nothing. They're all waiting for something. Then one of the laymen, the one who spoke at the cave, asks Maggaphala a question.

"Can you give us meditation instruction?"

Maggaphala looks across at the man and beckons him to be seated. He sits on the ground in front of Maggaphala, and the other two men sit behind him.

Maggaphala says, "Meditation is an art. By art, I mean that its success relies chiefly on one's talent for it. If you have a gift for meditation, you need no instruction. It just unfolds before you. If you're not gifted, no matter what instruction you receive you'll make the same mistakes. I can instruct you to observe your breath at your nostrils, but you will fail at it unless you are truly gifted. Better not to start meditation unless you're ready to take it to its end."

The man says, "I have never meditated before. How would I know if I'm gifted?"

Maggaphala replies, "Well, then, let's see if you are. Go to a secluded place, sit with your back upright, but not rigidly so, and place your attention on the front of your face. This instruction comes directly from the *Mahasatipatthana Sutta*."

"And what about noticing the breath?" Another man asks.

"Don't worry about that. With your attention on the front of your face you will become aware of your breath," Maggaphala says.

"Is that all we have to do?" the first man asks.

"Yes. Just try not to move too much. I doubt you will think too much. But if you do, it makes more sense to be kind to your thoughts than to hate them."

The three men get up and go off to find a place to meditate, leaving Maggaphala. He's not alone for long, as his wish is answered after a few minutes when he hears female voices approaching the dining hut.

Maggaphala remains seated as four women enter the dining hut. Two of them are nuns and the other two are laywomen. He recognizes Devi from the previous day, but shows no familiarity. The two nuns approach and prostrate before him, and then the older laywoman does the same. Devi remains standing.

The older laywoman gets up and goes to the stove, lights it, and sets a pot of water on it. The two nuns look up at Maggaphala, waiting for him to tell them what to do. Instead, he watches the laywoman rummage around the tins for tea, milk, and sugar. He's glad she has arrived. Then he brings his attention to the two nuns in front of him.

One of them is a foreigner. He's surprised at her youth, placing her as the same age as Devi, who has wandered off, perhaps in search of her boyfriend. Just thinking about Rahula and Devi gives Maggaphala a feeling of impending tragedy. "They are the tragic characters in this play," he thinks, moving his lips.

"Did you say something, Bhante?" The foreign nun asks him. Her voice is sweet and soft, startling Maggaphala with its pleasantness.

"I was just thinking out loud," Maggaphala says, charmed into honesty by her voice. "So you have come for the uposatha?"

"Well, I have come for meditation instruction," Gotami says.

The laywoman at the stove turns around upon hearing this and says, "This bhikkhu is not the meditation master."

"You're not?" Gotami asks him, embarrassed by her mistake.

"I'm Maggaphala, a bhikkhu of twenty-five rains. I'm no meditation master, but I give instruction on occasion."

"Was the meditation master your teacher?"

"No, we're just old friends."

"Perhaps then you could tell me what he teaches?" Gotami asks.

"To tell you the truth, I have no idea. I hadn't seen him for over two years until yesterday. We only talked a short while. He left for town while I was taking a nap. He should be back soon."

The laywoman brings a big porcelain bowl of milk tea over to Maggaphala. That is how she has seen it done at the monastery in town. The bhikkhus and samaneras who live there take their tea in large cereal bowls, holding it with both hands as they sip.

Maggaphala likes his milk tea this way. As he drinks it, the two nuns also drink tea, except they have to drink out of small orange juice glasses. Everyone is drinking tea when Sumana appears.

Sumana sits down on the bench next to Maggaphala. The laywoman immediately prepares him a bowl of tea and brings it to him. When she hands him the tea, he accepts it with both hands, but it is very hot. He anxiously looks around for a place to put it. Gotami gets up, pushes past the laywoman, who is bowing to Sumana, and takes the tea out of his hands, setting it down on the bench next to him. Sumana blows on his hands to cool them down as Gotami sits down on the ground near him. During all of this, Sumana forgot to notice if Gotami touched his hands or not. If she had, and he enjoyed it, he must confess it. If not, then nothing happened. However, if she did touch his fingers, considering his feelings for her, he could have experienced a mind-moment of joy without being aware of it. He makes a mental note to ask her if she touched his hand before the *patimokkha* ceremony this afternoon, which is when he would have to confess it.

Sumana is a little timid about picking up the bowl of tea again. He pokes it lightly with a fingernail to gauge its heat. Gotami and the other nun both drink down their tea, while Maggaphala relishes each drop, drinking it slowly. Sumana finally takes his first sip. It's good, very good, and just the right temperature, he thinks to himself. Then he takes another sip, and another, soon drinking all of it down.

When he's finished, Gotami speaks to him. "Venerable Sumana, can you tell me what the meditation master teaches?"

All eyes are on Sumana. He doesn't know if he can explain Aggachitta's instructions well enough at this point, but he's willing to give it a try.

"Venerable Aggachitta has you start with the instruction to just sit." he says. "You don't do anything in the meditation except become aware of sitting. From that everything follows."

"That's not much different from my instructions," Maggaphala says, pleased that his instructions are much the same.

Gotami asks, "What technique is this? Where did he learn it?"

"It is not a technique," Sumana replies. "He studied in Burma, but I do not think he learned it there. He may have discovered it."

"No, that's not the case," Maggaphala interjects. "It's right there in the *Mahasatipatthana Sutta*, in the *iriyapatha* section, the chapter on awareness of posture, where it says, "When sitting, he knows he is sitting." And then in the instruction on awareness of the in and out breath, the Buddha first says to be aware of the body sitting, with a straight back, and one's attention on the front of the face."

Maggaphala is happy to have made this point. He's no expert on the suttas, or on meditation for that matter, but he has come to certain conclusions about meditation over the years. One of those conclusions is that if the instruction does not come from the *Mahasatipatthana Sutta*, then it's not a Theravadin practice. The second main conclusion is that if the instruction comes from a later school of Buddhism, then it has been modified by that school. He feels great confidence in himself and in his old friend Aggachitta for keeping their meditation instructions firmly rooted in the four areas of awareness found in the *Mahasatipatthana Sutta*.

"But I have never heard this instruction anywhere!" Gotami exclaims.

"And I never received it until I came here," Sumana concurs.

"That may very well be true," Maggaphala says. "You see, the simplest and surest instruction is the hardest to find."

"Why is that?" Gotami asks.

Maggaphala replies, "Ask those who write the books on meditation and teach to crowds, who have big centers and wealthy organizations, who do missionary work under the guise of giving people the true teaching of the Buddha, and who make a mockery of the noble path by granting attainments to practically every student who comes their way."

Sumana puts his head in his hands, and Gotami wears a frown on her face. In the silence that follows, all of them sit still for several minutes. The spell is broken by a group of Sri Lankan women entering the dining hut and creating a commotion, one that can only mean breakfast for everyone.

CHAPTER
31

Rahula decides to go to the cave instead of the dining hut. He wants to change his clothes. Perhaps today, when everyone has left, he will do some laundry. His clean clothes consist of only one pair of pants, a tank top T-shirt, and a sarong. He puts on the pants and T-shirt and collects his other clothes into a dirty sarong, tying it up in a bundle and stashing it in the cave.

As he leaves the cave, he looks down the hill and sees Devi approaching. She shouts to him to stay where he is. He waits for her.

"We need to talk before everyone comes," she says.

"We can go inside the cave. No one is here," Rahula says.

"I know," she says. "I saw the fat bhikkhu down there."

They both go inside the cave. Devi sits on the bed, while Rahula sits in one of the chairs. They can barely see each other in the dim light. Devi reaches out her right hand for Rahula to hold. Rahula moves his chair closer and clasps both of his hands around hers.

"I wanted to see you so badly this morning," she says.

Silence follows as Rahula tries to conjure up something to say.

"I enjoyed seeing you," Rahula says, "but wouldn't it be better for you to return home."

"You want to get rid of me!" She exclaims.

"No, that's not it, exactly. I'm worried about you."

"That's sweet," she says. "I do plan on going home later today. First, we must get ready for people coming. Then we need to figure out what we're going to say."

"That sounds like a good idea," he says.

"Good. I will need to bathe. Where is the shower in this place?"

"We don't have one."

"Then how do you get clean?"

"We have a cistern."

"What is a cistern?" She asks.

"It's a pool of water. We use buckets to bathe with."

"It must be outdoors then," she says. "Then how do you bathe. You can't take off all of your clothes in the open air."

"We wear a sarong."

"You'll have to show me how."

Rahula gets up and goes over to where he put his clean folded up sarong and brings it over to the bed. He stands in front of her and unfolds it. Then he wraps it around his chest and folds it tight so it won't fall off.

"This is how women should wear it for bathing."

"Can I try?" She says. On further reflection, after he hands her the sarong, she says, "Could you step outside while I put this on?"

Rahula does as she asks. He waits patiently just outside the entrance to the cave.

Devi emerges from the cave, wearing the brightly colored sarong tied tightly under her armpits and snug around her chest and back. She is holding her dress crumpled up in one hand with her underwear. Apparently, she intends to wash her clothes as well.

"Let's go to this cistern," she says excitedly.

"First we have to get a bucket, some towels, and a bar of soap. Please wait a moment. I have towels and soap in the cave." Rahula goes in and gets them, though he forgets his bundle of laundry.

They walk down the hill to the meditation master's hut, where the good bucket is. She has one hand on the top of the sarong, making sure it does not slip down as she walks. They make it to Aggachitta's hut without incident. Rahula goes inside and, not finding the bucket in the usual place, looks around for it. It is right in plain view, under the water dispenser. He grabs it and goes outside. Devi walks behind him to the cistern. She is completely quiet, which surprises Rahula. In fact, he realizes that she has not said much all morning. Then he recalls she said something about people coming. She must mean people coming for the uposatha.

At the cistern, Rahula strips down to his bathing trunks, folding up his pants and shirt and setting them on the bench. Devi immediately takes the bucket and goes over to cistern. She places her clothes in a small pile on the cement ground. She lowers the bucket into the water and hoists it back up. She lifts up the bucket and pours all the water over her clothes. Then she takes the bar of soap and rubs it against the wet clothes, producing a rich lather. She takes the ball of clothes and kneads it with both hands, pounding it violently against the ground after every few kneads. When she's satisfied that her clothes are sufficiently saturated and pummeled, she gets a couple more bucketfuls of water and rinses them on the ground. Then she gets a bucketful of clean water and puts her clothes into the bucket, swishing them around in the cramped space. She empties the soapy water from the bucket and sets it down. She walks over to the clothes line, unraveling her underwear from her dress as she does, carefully hanging each individual article of clothing on the line in the brilliant morning sunlight.

Rahula is glad that she's finished washing her clothes so he can now use the bucket. He is able to get in three bucketfuls of water, just enough to create several beads of water over most of his body, when Devi wants it back. Rahula hands it to her. He picks up the bar of soap she used to clean her clothes and begins to lather his chest, arms, and legs. Devi lowers the bucket back into the cistern, only half-filling it, and raises it above her head, letting it pour slowly over her face. The water dribbles down her face and barely touches the sarong wrapped tightly around her chest. She grabs the bar of soap and washes her face. Rahula realizes that she will not be able to see well enough to get a bucket of water to rinse the soap off her face, so he takes the bucket and fills it from the cistern, placing it down in front of her. She smiles at this considerate gesture, and, with both hands in the bucket of water, she splashes her face free of soap. Rahula then takes the rest of the water and pours it over the soap that is now sticking to his torso. The soap flows down his flat abdomen and collects around the elastic band of his bathing trunks.

Devi asks for the bucket back and proceeds to fill it with water. This time she dumps a bucketful of water over her head, getting her hair completely wet, the water splattering down on her sarong, dampening it in places, leaving it dry elsewhere. Rahula takes the bucket back and proceeds to get some more bucketfuls to rinse off the remaining soap. Devi starts to soap up her long, stringy hair, rubbing the bright yellow bar of soap against her head. Then she sets the soap down and digs into her scalp with her fingernails, swirling up a rich white lather. The top of her head is crowned in this white foam as she waits for Rahula to finish dowsing himself. She says nothing as she admires Rahula's young, smooth, blemish-free body, glistening in the sunlight.

Rahula is unaware that she is observing him, and so, without being conscious of her presence, he lifts the band of his trunks, as he always does, and applies soap to his genital area. He looks down into his trunks to get a good lather everywhere. Then he lets go of the band of his trunks. It snaps back to his tight abdomen with a thud. This jars him a little and he becomes aware in the periphery of his vision that Devi is standing just over to his left, her head adorned in foam. He wonders if she saw him washing himself. She's looking away when he turns his head to see her, and so he assumes she didn't see anything. He lowers the bucket into the cistern and pulls up a bucketful of water. Before pouring the water over himself, he turns to face the other direction, where Devi can't see what he is doing, and lifts the band of his trunks again, slowly pouring the cool water over himself, rinsing that area completely. He is surprised that Devi is not complaining about the soap drying on her head.

After he finishes, for that is the final part of bathing, he gets Devi a bucket of water and sets the bucket down in front of her. He tells her that he will be sitting on the bench drying off. She smiles up at him in a sweet, loving way.

As Rahula dries himself with a towel, he sneaks glances at Devi in the process of bathing. She quickly and efficiently rinses her head free of all soap, taking only three successive bucketfuls to do so. Rahula wonders if that is enough water to rid that much hair of soap, but from where he sits, it seems to have done the job. Devi gets another bucketful from the cistern and sets it down on the ground. She squats on her haunches in front of it and splashes some water on her armpits and shoulders. Then she rubs the bar of soap under each armpit and moves the lather over her shoulders and down her arms. She rinses immediately, cupping one hand and filling it with water and then carefully dowsing the opposite armpit. This appears to Rahula as a slow, inefficient way of washing, but he says nothing. He's entranced by her bathing this way, though he won't allow himself to watch her for any more than a few seconds before looking elsewhere, so she doesn't catch him watching her.

With her arms cleansed of soap and grime, Devi lowers the bucket and fills it again, setting it down in front of her. This time she is standing. She loosens the fold of the sarong around her chest, giving the fabric some play. With one hand holding the sarong above her breasts, she kneels down and picks up the bucket with the other hand. She lifts it up to her chest. It is heavy and she becomes unsteady, her back and arm muscles tightening. Rahula is tempted to run over to help her, but then she would know that he was watching her, so he stays put, watching her more intently, now sure that she can't turn around to catch him in the act.

She pours the water slowly over the front of her body, keeping the sarong in place. The cool water feels good sliding down her breasts and belly, curling around her legs on the way down. She closes her eyes for a moment and thinks of nothing but of that feeling, almost swooning in the curls of it. She sets the bucket down and picks up the bar of soap, which she then applies to her skin under the sarong, reaching in first from the top and then from down below.

Rahula turns away as she soaps up, but in his imagination, he can see what she is doing all too clearly. The heat of the sun, which was pleasantly drying his hair a moment before, is now much too hot for him. A faint tingling erupts in his chest and spreads down to his thighs. He closes his eyes and knows not only that feeling, but also the unrest behind it. He can't sit still. He can't do what his body wants to do. He can only clench his fists against the agitation within.

Devi finishes rinsing herself. She stands with her back to Rahula. She undoes the fold that keeps the sarong snug against her chest, and, with both arms, she stretches out the cloth behind her, like a bird spreading its wings, and through the diaphanous weave, Rahula can see her shoulders, the curve of her torso, and the budding roundness of her hips. Just as quickly as she draped this cloth over her feminine form, she draws it around her again, tightening the sarong over her chest and back, turning the fabric back into clothing.

She turns around to face Rahula, and with a delighted smile, says, "That was fun. Do you bathe like this all the time?"

Rahula acts as though he was looking elsewhere until he heard her question, trying to appear as if he didn't look at her once through all of this. He can only think of one thing to say.

"Yes."

CHAPTER
32

Aggachitta decides to visit the library after breakfast. As he walks down the hallway, further reflections on the great chain of dependent arising occur to him. He has to deal with the problem of *upadana*, which normally gets translated as grasping, clinging, or attachment. He doesn't particularly care for any of these definitions, and yet he can't find one more to his liking.

Once inside the library, Aggachitta sits down at the table, with a pen and notepad in front of him. He ponders the question of upadana in the chain of dependent arising. He remembers learning as a young student that the verb form of upadana, *upadiyati*, simply means, "takes."

From there, he considers it further, writing down his thoughts as they come to him. "If it is not grasping, not attachment, what is it? Is it the impulse to quench one's thirst? Is it the type of taking involved in merely taking a drink? Thus dependent on thirst is the taking of a drink of water. If one does not take a drink, then one is always thirsty. Not taking a drink only continues the unfavorable condition of thirst, aggravating it beyond one's tolerance, bringing one to a serious state of dehydration and eventual death.

"But upadana is probably not the drinking of the liquid, which comes later down the chain, probably at the point of *jati* (birth). That is two links away. So perhaps upadana does not refer to the taking of liquid but of the need to drink in order to eliminate thirst. Thus from thirst is taken up the only way one knows how to quench thirst. Upadana limits one's choice in the matter to that which one has taken countless times before without thinking. It's attachment is to what has been done before in the same situation; it's grasping at what one has learned to do. Thirst is then merely the basis for one doing what one has always done before, trapped in eternal repetition, making the same choices and performing the same actions as always."

As Aggachitta reads these thoughts over, he feels a sense of misgiving. His ideas are jumbled, raw, riddled with holes. Any reasonably informed person could see the weaknesses in his current way of thinking. He's just playing with generalizations. There's no real world these ideas relate to. When he pauses a moment and turns his attention within, he finds a sickening feeling around his thirsts. He picks one out for closer examination. It is his thirst to make a contribution to Pali scholarship by writing down his ideas and putting them into a book that will be printed and sent all over the world to be read by everyone interested in this subject. This daydream does not excite him. It does not come with a tickle in his chest or a surge of energy, but rather carries with it a dull ache, indigestion, and nausea. The thirst itself is like an illness, a disease of his body and mind. It squirms there in his head, twisting his throat, tightening his belly, and locking his limbs in its clamp-like clutches. It's like a parasite that has gotten hold of his body and is eating him from within. It numbs his mind with its poison.

"This is upadana," he tells himself, and, when he utters these words, they come out in a chilling whisper.

All his symptoms suddenly vanish and his mind is light and spacious. In that moment, he knows what upadana is not. Attachment, grasping, taking up are all wrong. This he now knows for sure. The right idea is not an idea at all.

He leans back in the chair, dropping the pen on the notepad in front of him. He closes his eyes and puts his hands in his lap.

A string of words enters his mind like a banner across the sky:

It is not established in any way, not set in motion, not supported by views and concepts. It is simply the end of suffering.

When the words fade, he is left with a void that does not immediately refill with thought.

CHAPTER
33

After breakfast, Sumana is anxious about what to do next. He would like to spend more time with Gotami, though he would also like to rest after eating and get in a couple of meditation sittings before seeing Venerable Aggachitta. He sits in silence pondering whether to stay for a few minutes, just in case Gotami seeks him out, or retreat to his hut.

Gotami seems preoccupied with cleaning up the plates, cups, and pans after breakfast. She has a stack of dirty dishes on the table. She looks over at Sumana and asks him where she can wash them.

"We get all of our water from the cistern," Sumana replies.

"Can you show me where the cistern is?"

"Let me help you," Sumana offers, jumping up from his seat and going over to the table.

He ends up carrying the metal pans, while Gotami balances a stack of plates and cups in both hands, which rattle and occasionally chime as they walk down the dirt path to the cistern. Sumana is conscious that he is alone with her. He wonders if he will confess this offense this afternoon. It does not feel like an offense, though it does have the quality of doing something forbidden, something dangerous.

As they arrive at the cistern, Sumana catches Rahula and Devi in the corner of his eye taking the other trail leading to the cave. He notices that Devi's hair is wet, and she's wearing a sarong instead of a dress. He surmises that the two young people must have been at the cistern bathing while he was eating breakfast. A picture forms in his mind of Rahula and

Devi together, naked, lathering each other up with soap and then pouring buckets of water over each other's body. With this image a faint tension arises, one that makes Sumana lower his head with shame, filling his chest with trepidation.

Gotami sets her stack of plates on the rocks near the cistern's edge. Sumana arrives a moment later, setting the metal pans down next to them.

"Do you have a bucket?" She asks.

"I'll go get one. Wait here," Sumana replies.

"And also bring some soap and a scrubbing pad," she says to his back as he walks away.

Without turning, he says, "Yes."

It's not what is said between them, for it is banal and practical, but the tone of familiarity penetrates his heart. It makes him feel closer to her every moment they are together. They are like brother and sister. There's no difficulty speaking to each other, no words go misunderstood, nothing breaks their bond.

A kind of sweetness forms in his mind that he can't quite identify. He has affection for her, but it goes much deeper than that. He conceives of them as being two halves of a whole, each incomplete without the other. He belongs to her and she belongs to him in an exquisite way. Theirs is a spiritual union. Their physical bodies never need touch and yet they will remain entwined forever. He pictures two vapors, one blue and the other red, rising together sinuously in space, wisps of blue and red, lightly curling around each other, slowly blending together where they touch.

Sumana arrives at his hut and immediately snaps out of his daydream. He must find his bucket. It is not where he put it last. Palaparuchi must have moved it. He could not have taken it with him. Sumana looks everywhere in the small hut, but he still can't find it. Oh well, he thinks, that old bucket would have been an embarrassment anyhow. He decides to go get the master's bucket, sure that it will impress her.

Sumana knocks at the door to Aggachitta's hut in case he has returned. When he doesn't hear an answer, he nudges the door open a crack and peers inside. The hut is dark. There's nothing to indicate that anyone is about. He enters cautiously. He looks around the hut but doesn't see the bucket where Palaparuchi left it. Then he remembers seeing a glint of metal-reflected sunlight at the level of Rahula's thigh as he and Devi were leaving the cistern.

As he climbs the hill up to the cave, he catches his breath and puts a hand over his belly. He usually does not exert himself this much after breakfast. He pauses for a moment. He looks up into the sky, remembering that he's in Sri Lanka, that this is a wild and exotic country, with all sorts of dangerous animals and crazy individuals. He feels a strong urge to go back to the cistern and be with Gotami, even without the bucket. Then he feels another kind of shame, one that follows upon failure. No, he must not return without the bucket.

He reaches the cloth opening of the cave and is about to announce himself to its occupants, but restrains himself. They could be making love. He would not want to barge in on that. He puts his ear to the cloth and tries to hear what sounds there may be. He hears two people talking softly in Sinhala, a man and a woman. He can't make out what they are saying, but pictures them lying in bed together, naked under the sheets, speaking in whispers. He then pictures the conversation as after-sex talk and so walks away from the cloth, taking a few steps down the hill. But he can't go back to the cistern without a bucket. Where could his bucket be?

Just then the cloth of the cave opens and Rahula's face appears.

"I thought I heard someone out here," he says.

"I don't want to disturb you," Sumana says, "but could you loan me the bucket?"

"Yes," Rahula says, and then darts back into the cave to get it.

Sumana walks up to the entrance and is tempted to peek inside. Rahula emerges shortly with the bucket in hand.

"When you're finished, can you return it to my uncle's hut?"

"Certainly."

Sumana wants to ask him what's going on between him and the young woman, confused as to the correct phrasing of the question for a Sri Lankan youth. He hangs about, not saying anything, much too long.

"You need something else?" Rahula says, assuming that Sumana is dallying because he needs something from the cabinet, such as flashlight batteries, a notebook, or even a towel.

"Oh, yes," Sumana says, "I need some detergent and a scrubbing pad for washing dishes?"

"I'll get them for you," Rahula says, ducking back inside.

Gotami sorts out the pans, plates and cups. While she waits for Sumana to fetch a bucket and dish-washing soap she decides to go back to the dining hut to see if there are more things to be washed. Since breakfast, the dining hut has filled with people, mostly elderly women and their husbands. The table is covered with packages containing food, soap, robes, towels, and other supplies for the bhikkhus. Gotami is struck by the abundant gifts, since nuns generally receive very little in the way of requisites.

Maggaphala is sitting on the bench, drinking another cup of tea, engaged in a conversation with a small, thin, gray-haired gentleman wearing a light cotton dress-shirt and a pair of tan slacks. Gotami notices their conversation more than the others, for theirs is the only one in English. She then remembers her purpose for returning and combs the hut for anything that may need cleaning. She finds a couple of cloth napkins, a few towels, the kettle and tea strainer, and two large metal serving bowls. She gathers them up, neatly stuffing them into the serving bowls. Maggaphala notices her as she makes her way out.

"Young sister!" he shouts.

She is unclear if he is referring to her, so she stops and looks across the room at Maggaphala in confusion.

"Gotami! I would like you to meet someone!" Maggaphala says loudly.

She weaves her way past several people the few yards to where Maggaphala and the gentleman are sitting. The man rises from his seat on the ground and clasps his hands in front of his chest, showing respect to Gotami, which surprises her greatly. She smiles and looks over at Maggaphala, who says, "This is Dr. Perrera. He's the head of the board of donors of Atakkachari Arañña. He's a very influential man. He can help you if you have any problems while you are here."

"That's very nice of you," she says to Dr. Perrera, who smiles back while moving his head back and forth in excited affirmations.

Dr. Perrera replies, "I'm pleased to meet you. I had heard that a foreign nun was staying in town, but I didn't know that she also sought meditation instruction from Venerable Aggachitta. Is that why you came here?"

She assumes that by "here" he means Sri Lanka, insinuating that the whole purpose of her coming to this country and becoming a nun was just for the chance to study with Venerable Aggachitta. As a nun, she can no longer let herself slip in a little white lie for convenience sake, but feels she must always set the record straight, avoid any unintentional deception, if that were ever possible.

"I just heard about Venerable Aggachitta for the first time yesterday."

Dr. Perrera is deflated by his well-defined illusion of her being pierced so abruptly. Now he flips the other way and sees her more as an opportunist.

"So any teacher would do, and you just happened to hear that such a great and renowned teacher lived in the vicinity?"

"No, not exactly. I've been praying for a great teacher and yesterday by chance I was visited by Venerable Aggachitta's student, Sumana, and was told that I could arrange to get instruction. I am extremely grateful for this once-in-a-lifetime opportunity, and so have come here today for an interview with the great meditation master."

This story sounds wonderful to Dr. Perrera's ears, much richer and more captivating than any story he could have created on his own. The smile returns to his face, as does the excited head shaking.

"Where are you off to now?" Maggaphala asks.

"As you see," she says, holding up the two large serving bowls with their overflowing contents, "I am about to go to the cistern to clean up after breakfast."

"You need not do that!" Maggaphala exclaims. "There are several women here who can do that for you."

Dr. Perrera then goes over to a group of women and gives them orders. Four of the women go over to Gotami and take the bowls from her. Before they leave, Gotami tells Maggaphala that she left pans, plates, and towels at the cistern, and that Sumana went to get a bucket and some detergent. Maggaphala translates this to the women, who then leave.

"Please sit with us," Maggaphala says. "When Venerable Aggachitta arrives, I will introduce you."

Sumana carries the shiny new bucket with a container of dishwashing powder and two scouring pads in it. Though it took longer than he expected, he succeeded. He wears a smile of success, anticipating Gotami's appreciation when he enters the bathing area. Instead, he sees four Sri Lankan women bending over the pans and plates, rubbing them with rough twisted rope, without the use of soap or water. He goes over to them, sets down the bucket, and removes the detergent and pads from it, setting them down on the ground. They stop what they are doing and prostrate down before him. He gives them a blessing and tells them in broken Sinhala to use the bucket and soap powder and return the bucket to the cave when they are finished. One of the women appears to understand him, shaking her head back and forth at each thing he tells her to do.

Then he leaves. He wonders where Gotami could be. As he thinks about her, his heart feels heavy. The sense of her loss pierces through him. He feels distraught and anxious. He doesn't want to see her feeling the way he does now. He changes course from heading towards the dining hut to going to his hut. He has the urge to lie down. Another voice, filled with more agitation than despair, tells him he must meditate. When he enters his hut, he's torn between lying down and meditating. He eventually settles on meditating while lying down.

Lying on his back on the fiber mattress, he brings his attention to his body touching the bed. His attention then moves from his back against the mattress to hearing his breathing. He then includes feeling his chest heaving under his breathing; and, when pulsating colors appear behind his eyelids, instead of becoming calm and serene, he experiences a stabbing sensation of incredible anguish in his chest. His mind is flooded with a feeling of failure, coated in a glistening blackness, which submerges the tiny voice that he identifies him as himself into a hole resembling a house sunk thirty feet below the surface of a sand dune.

Tears begin to well up from the sunken house, slowly pulled up to the surface like a bucket of water, which is tossed with force out of his eyes, running in torrents down his cheeks. He can't remember ever feeling as sad as this. Simon the child comes to mind, crying to his mother, a constant of his early years. Maybe he was mostly the emotion of sadness before he could speak. That thought fascinates him with its bald truth, so he enlarges on it, thinking that perhaps everyone greets sadness before becoming conscious of having a self.

The sad feeling pounds against his temples and forehead, wanting to be released, not analyzed. His mind flashes to Gotami and he sees her form, like a phantom, moving toward him in the dark space in front of him, slipping gracefully through his skin and into his mind. She swims in his consciousness as a separate entity, and then — adapting to his own vibrations — merges with his being.

He opens his eyes. His breathing has slowed down. The sadness appears to have dissipated. What has changed? He listens for a feeling to arise to tell him the answer. All that he is aware of is that, in a subtle way, the rough surface of his consciousness feels as if it has been sanded down, leaving his mind smooth and shiny.

CHAPTER
34

Aggachitta's consciousness returns first to an awareness of his body, then of a short inhalation, and finally to an awareness of being Aggachitta again. Yet his mind does not stop there. Thoughts about being Aggachitta rise to consciousness and dominate his attention. He feels propelled forward in time. He finds himself in a scenario of being at the hermitage and seeing his friend Maggaphala. He then remembers that he forgot to see his student, Sumana, for an interview yesterday. His nephew, Rahula, then comes to mind, and he imagines him having read several more chapters of the book about a man trapped with a woman in a house built beneath a mountain of sand. This image brings with it a sensation of sand blown in waves across his brain, as if his thoughts were sand and thinking was the wind. The image of blowing sand soon vanishes, and is replaced by inward swirls of colors, drawing his mind up into strands of color, releasing it in a moment of bliss.

Now he believes he's fully awake, for his mind is indeed alert, present, and vibrantly alive. One moment he's aware of being and then is aware of not being. Then there's being again. Wakefully sitting, his mind is drawn in again, this time to a dot of blue light, leading him down a dark tunnel until he's smaller than the dot of light. In it — at the very heart of its blueness — he experiences a dissolving feeling followed by an extremely pleasurable sensation bursting forth over his whole body. He is again aware of being and then aware of not being. He returns, however, when he realizes he has been absent in his own consciousness. He clings to this consciousness as his own. He's once again aware of being Aggachitta.

He tell himself that he must get up, rousing his mind to snap out of this loop so he can regain control of his mind and body. He opens his eyes, which helps considerably. He rises from the chair, goes over to the light switch, and turns it on. The room appears flooded with light from the overhead incandescent bulb. Everything looks unreal to him as his eyes adjust. It occurs to him that the world of the mind is vastly different from that of the senses, which some believe it imitates. In truth, the mind has its expanses where the senses can never go. Thus, he puts this recent meditative experience in the category of going beyond the kamaloka (the realm of sense desire) and entering the realm of subtle form.

Moved to philosophize about this experience in writing, he sits down at the table again. Then he remembers that he must return to his hermitage. A dislike of having to do things he doesn't wish to rises up. He wants to rebel against returning to the hermitage, but there's nothing to fight except his desire to be seen as a responsible person. He holds the pen in his hand with the notepad beneath it, waiting for the victor in this internal conflict to tell him what to do.

A moment later, he is writing feverishly all that comes to him without caring where he should be and what other things he should be doing.

Palaparuchi walks briskly down the paved road towards the dirt path that leads back to the hermitage. Just ahead of him is a group of laypeople. He lowers his eyes to ignore them as he hastens past them, but one of the men speaks to him.

He is of average height, with a dark complexion, portly and balding. He asks in good English, "Venerable sir, do you know the way to Atakkachari Arañña? I have been there once, but have forgotten the exact turn off."

Palaparuchi stops in the middle of the man's question and turns to face the group. They appear to be two separate families. He can't tell who the three girls and one boy belong

to, but the two couples are easy to discern. The tall thin woman
wearing the flowery dress with her hair in a bun goes with the
man who asked the question, while the shorter, heavier woman
wearing the plain skirt and blouse belongs with the tallish
athletic man who remains silent and in the back of the group.

"It's not far from here," Palaparuchi replies matter-of-
factly.

"Are you going there?" the man asks.

"Yes. You may follow me if you wish."

"That would be splendid," he says, and then turns to the
whole group to translate into Sinhala what just transpired.

Palaparuchi does not wait for the man to finish talking to
the others before setting off in the direction of the path to the
hermitage. They keep a respectful distance from the fast
walking bhikkhu, but not so far back that Palaparuchi can't
hear what they're talking about. Since he's quite familiar with
conversational Sinhala, Palaparuchi has no difficulty following
their conversation. However, since he can't see who is talking
behind him, he has to guess, and at times wonders if he has the
correct image of the person who is talking.

The shorter woman — who has a round smooth face, with
a smallish attractive nose and bright white teeth — speaks in
one rapid sentence after another, sounding defensive. She says,
"My Arati would never come up with such a notion on her
own. It could not have been her idea to run away like this.
Your son is to blame!"

"Our son has been staying with his uncle in the jungle and
could not have initiated this!" the first man replies.

"We have letters," the other man says.

"What letters?" asks the woman who is with the first man.
Her thin, tightly drawn features loom large and haunt
Palaparuchi's mind.

"These!" the other woman says, pulling out a stack of
letters, or so Palaparuchi imagines without deviating from his
downward gaze on the dirt path before him.

"Letters don't mean a thing," the first man says, his voice
growing irritated, hostile. "Our son loves to write about his

experiences when he's away. These letters are no doubt harmless."

"You're mistaken about your son," the other man says. Everyone appears to have stopped behind Palaparuchi.

When the man resumes, his voice seems more distant than before. "We have read his letters. He speaks of being in love with our daughter."

"Let me see these letters," the tallish thin woman demands.

Then a girl speaks up in a loud shrill voice. "We must hurry! The white-skinned bhikkhu is far ahead of us!"

Palaparuchi stops and turns around. He sees the men and the women gesticulating wildly at each other, their bodies and faces contorted by rage. A strange thought comes unbidden into his consciousness: nothing makes sense except that everything is absurd. As this realization grabs hold of him, he begins laughing uncontrollably. He tends not to form delusions from such verbal realizations, since he does not attribute a high attainment to them. In his hierarchy of understandings, he considers them inferior insights. All he has understood here is an idea about reality, not true reality itself.

The children make a game out of catching up with Palaparuchi. They agree on the terms of the game: everyone runs up to him and the first one to circle him wins. Palaparuchi is laughing so heartily, he does not see the three girls and the boy run as fast as they can towards him. One of the girls, a tall lanky twelve-year old, is in the lead. As she closes in on him, Palaparuchi notices her out of the corner of his eye. His laughter suddenly vanishes and is replaced by apprehensive thoughts of the girl running into him and thereby touching him, which is an offense he might have to confess. He turns around, with his back facing the oncoming children, and stands as still as he can, shutting his eyes in anticipation of contact. He can feel the wind the girl stirs up as she circles him. The hem of his robes slap against his ankles and a chilly breeze caresses his bared shoulder and neck. He pictures in his mind a dark female phantom whirring about him. When the breeze subsides, he opens his eyes and sees a young girl panting in front of him. Then a running child slams into his back. He balances himself and turns round, scowling at the boy stumbling before him. The two younger girls finally arrive out of breath.

Soon Palaparuchi is standing in the center of a circle of kids, not knowing what to say or do, barely conscious of his anger at being pushed, completely unaware of how he is glaring at them. Then the two couples reach them, each of them scolding their children for behaving so badly towards a bhikkhu. Now Palaparuchi can tell that the boy belongs to the couple with the athletic quiet man and the shorter woman, while the three girls belong to the heavy balding man and his tall thin wife.

When the parents finally feel satisfied with their admonition of their children, they look to Palaparuchi for him to say something about what just happened. He remains silent on the subject, for his mind has journeyed into the future. He's picturing himself sitting down to be served one tasty dish after another, conjuring up the rapturous sensations that follow upon such taste experiences, going through something akin to an erotic fantasy, which is cut short when he notices everyone staring at him.

"Let's not waste any more time," he says. "We're not far from the hermitage. It is through the jungle here about a quarter of a mile. Follow me."

He starts with long strides and a fast pace, but once he reaches the denser brush of the jungle, he slows down and walks more carefully. Everyone is silent behind him. He imagines himself to be a jungle guide, leading a group of big game hunters in search of an elusive leopard. In his fantasy, his alms bowl becomes a magic weapon, a metal wheel out of Hindu mythology, which can be flung at one's enemies with deadly force and precision. Following on his heels are brave hunters, with rifles, pistols, and shotguns, ready to watch his back in case the leopard attacks.

He is submerged in this scenario, gaining some kind of joy out of it. It adds a grandiose quality to the mundane, which he

244

SEEKING NIBBANA IN SRI LANKA

has come to require with greater frequency like some kind of opiate.

Then, from behind him, the shorter woman begins talking loudly, breaking the spell, causing him to fume within. He wants to turn around and silence her with the meanest look he can muster, and it requires great restraint on his part not to do so. She keeps on talking about how the other couple's son lured her daughter into this jungle and has done god knows what to her. Palaparuchi finally has had enough and yells, "Won't you shut up! The leopard will hear us!"

"Leopard?" the portly man exclaims, clutching his two younger daughters close to him.

"There is a leopard in this jungle?" the other man asks.

"Shush! Be quiet. We can make it to camp without startling him if you can only be quiet."

They hold their children's hands, huddled together, moving slowly and cautiously behind Palaparuchi. Now they are acting properly. Palaparuchi takes small steps forward, pushing away a branch here and there, mindfully placing his feet, careful not to disturb anything or make any noise. Those behind him begin to follow his lead, moving almost as slowly and mindfully as he does, keeping their fear in check, regretting that they ever made this journey. The children too are quiet, but whereas their parents move mindfully out of fear, they do it as a game, competing with each other as to who can be the lightest on her feet and make the least noise.

Their progress is slow, but within twenty minutes, they enter the clearing near the monument to Atakkachari. Palaparuchi stops in his tracks, straightens up, and turns around to address them.

"We have made it safely. I commend you on a job well done." Then he turns around in the direction of his destination, the dining hut, and resumes his journey. The two families remain where they are for a few moments. The parents are baffled by his statement, ascribing it to his being a Western monk and therefore highly eccentric, while the children smile at each other over how well they played the game.

Sumana opens his eyes after his long meditation sitting. It must have been close to two hours, which means that it's nearing time for dana. The thought of being late for dana follows naturally. It gives him a burst of anxious energy as he quickly wraps his robe around his body and takes a moment to look at his face in the handheld mirror. He is satisfied that he looks neat and clean. He opens the door of his hut and is blinded by the brightness of the sunlight outside. This further brings home the point that it must be nearing time for dana. He sees colored dots and holds one hand over his brow, shading his eyes from the sun, as he makes his way to the dining hut.

He remembers that Gotami may still be here, sitting in the dining hut waiting for the meditation master to arrive. He reflects on looking at his face in the mirror, wondering if in the back of his mind he wanted to make sure he looked good for her, even though he had not thought about her while doing it. From this, he contemplates whether his mind can know something without him being aware of it.

There's no simple and easy way to put this thought into language. The word "intuition" is used so often and clumsily these days that he is hard put to say what it means and whether what he knows is indeed intuitive. Then he becomes aware that he has allowed such a contemplation to continue. He has tried to be aware only of the present moment and thinking is not being aware, as he has understood it. Now, however, thinking about the subtle nature of awareness creates a chain of thought on knowing what awareness is and what it is not. It is and is not intuitive. According to his previous teachers, knowing the past and the future has had no place in the knowing of the present moment. Is that true? Is it possible to extract the present moment from the past and the future? Isn't the current present moment the future of a previous present moment and the past of a future one?

He arrives at the dining hut to find it crammed with people. Around the monks' bench are Maggaphala, Gotami, the elderly nun, and a well-dressed gentleman. Surrounding the table are several women and a couple of men arranging bowls of food. On the far side of the hut is a group of men, women and children. They are talking the loudest. Sumana feels someone's finger touch his bared shoulder. It is Palaparuchi.

"What is going on here?" Sumana asks.

"A three-ring circus," Palaparuchi answers.

"Are all these people here for dana?"

"I'm sure we'll have enough to eat. Don't worry," Palaparuchi says.

Out of the corner of his eye, Sumana notices Rahula and Devi enter the dining hut. They don't see him, but are instantly spotted by the group of men, women, and children, who call their names and motion to them. Now Sumana watches the group. Palaparuchi also trains his attention in that direction.

"Those people were talking about the strangest thing on the way here," Palaparuchi says in a low voice.

"What?"

"I thought they were mistaken about a girl being here at the hermitage, but there she is."

"What are you talking about?"

"Venerable Aggachitta's nephew lured that young girl into the jungle with love letters."

"No, that's not true," Sumana says, defending Rahula.

"Oh?"

Sumana is self-conscious talking about what Rahula has told him and so lowers his voice even more.

"She has come here with designs on Rahula. He doesn't want to marry her, but she wants to marry him."

"If he marries her," Palaparuchi whispers, "then he can't become a monk!"

"But he doesn't know if he wants to become a monk."

"What? That's crazy!" Palaparuchi exclaims in a loud voice.

Gotami and Maggaphala stop their conversation and look in Palaparuchi's direction. She asks Maggaphala who the other foreign monk is. Sumana watches her, hoping to catch her eye the next time she looks over his way. Her eyes bulge as she

listens to Maggaphala's account of Palaparuchi. She looks over at Sumana, catches his eye, and gestures for him to come over and join them, moving her lips at the same time to say, "Do not bring that other monk with you." Sumana is not good at reading lips and so just walks over to her with Palaparuchi right behind him.

Gotami kneels on the ground to bow to Sumana. She need not do this for his sake, as he wishes she would just treat him as an ordinary person. Palaparuchi, on the other hand, relishes the thought of the young white-skinned nun bowing to him. However, she turns away from Palaparuchi as he approaches her, instead fixing her gaze on the scene developing across the room. Sumana sits down on the bench next to Maggaphala, while Palaparuchi remains standing. All of them become transfixed on what is going on between Rahula, Devi, and their respective families. Gotami asks Maggaphala to translate what they are saying.

"The tall woman, who I believe is Rahula's mother, is shouting at her son that he should never have kept a secret from them," Maggaphala says. "If he was interested in this girl, he should have at least told his father so that he could speak to the girl's parents. 'Now look at the mess you have caused!' She says to him."

"Rahula seems sad," Gotami says. "What's he saying?"

"I can't make it out. The other woman, Devi's mother I presume, is saying something about making things respectable. Devi agrees with her, saying that there's no point in discussing what's past when there's a wedding to plan."

"So they're going to get married?" Gotami exclaims with genuine surprise.

Sumana adds, "I know Rahula doesn't want to marry her just yet. Let's wait and see."

"Neither does Rahula's father," says Maggaphala. "He's saying that his son is too young for marriage and must go to university before doing anything of the sort. He's adamant, but he's meeting strong resistance from the girl and her mother, who are both saying, or shouting rather, 'This isn't your concern! Let Rahula decide for himself! He's an adult.' That's news to me."

"Rahula looks even sadder," Gotami says, with a tear rolling down her cheek.

"How else should he look?" Sumana asks. She looks at him not comprehending what he's saying. "I mean," Sumana stammers, "everyone is trying to tell him what to do, what his life should be about, and he hasn't the faintest clue. I looked sad then too."

"You went through something like this yourself?" Gotami asks, now including Sumana in her feelings of sympathy for Rahula.

"Yes, like this, but certainly not this."

"Hush," Maggaphala says to them. "You're missing the decisive moment here. Devi's father has calmed everyone down and is now making a proposal. He suggests that they start over as if nothing has happened. The two families can get together and discuss the union of Rahula and Devi, while the two lovers should be given more time to get to know each other so they can be sure they're making the right choice. This idea is a truly modern solution. This suggestion is greeted by the women as unnecessary, since if they love each other, what is the point of further discussion. I can see Rahula's father is amenable to this. In fact, the three men are breaking away from the women and are coming in our direction."

No sooner has Maggaphala said this than the two fathers and Rahula come up to Sumana and Maggaphala, who are still seated on the bench. In order to avoid being stepped on, Gotami moves over closer to Sumana.

Rahula's father begins to speak in English, but before he actually starts, he bows once to Maggaphala and rises with his hands clasped in front of him. "Venerable sir, do you know where my brother, Venerable Aggachitta, is at this moment?"

"I don't believe he is here," Maggaphala replies.

"He stayed overnight at the monastery in town," Rahula says.

"Then are you the senior monk here?"

Maggaphala looks over at Palaparuchi standing silently off to the side and then back at Rahula's father. "Yes, I guess I am."

"What is your name?"

"Maggaphala Maha Thera."

"I am Suriya. My colleagues refer to me as Suri," Rahula's father says by way of an introduction, obviously trying to establish an alliance with Maggaphala.

"You may have overheard some of our discussion. What I would like to know, Venerable Sir, is in your esteemed opinion, should these two young people be hastily married, or should they be given time to come to a reasonable decision on this matter?"

"Well, I'm not the sort of bhikkhu who meddles in the affairs of others and gives unwanted advice, but since you have asked me for my opinion, I would refer you to the works of the great master of the human condition, Shakespeare. Don't scoff at this suggestion, as ridiculous as it may sound, for the bard of Stratford has often written of youth falling in love against their parents' wishes and ignoring sound advice."

"That is a very noble suggestion," Suriya says. Devi's father agrees and asks Maggaphala to enlarge upon this topic.

"It is the mark of youth to rush into love, to surrender to it, and pay no heed to those who have had the experience of youthful love and know how it colors the senses. Speak to your son and daughter from having known firsthand what love is and how to tend its growth. Let them not fear the passing of love, but rather embrace its powers of survival through adversity."

"You speak with elegance," Devi's father says. "Have you studied drama?"

"Studied it?" Maggaphala says grandly, "I acted in plays all through my university years."

"So, getting back to the point," Suriya interrupts. "What course of action should we take?"

"Educate them about life, and trust them to come to their own decision."

"That sounds very good indeed!" Suriya exclaims.

"Good," Maggaphala says looking around at Sumana, Palaparuchi, and Gotami, which reminds him of something important.

"You know," he says in a lowered voice to both men, "monks have to eat before noon and like to begin eating by eleven, especially on days when there are so many people bringing offerings."

Aggachitta puts down his pen and slumps back in the chair. He is exhausted from having written several pages in a new and unfamiliar style. He is quite convinced that it is incomprehensible. He feels it would be unwise for him to show this notebook to anyone. A picture forms in his mind of the reader he's addressing in his writing, an imagined expert Buddhist scholar, whose background exceeds his own and whose critical judgment instantly detects any flaw in research, any error in reasoning.

Here before him are pages that contain passages of an intensely personal nature, of trains of thought that violate the laws of logic, and translations of the Buddha's words that are original and therefore unorthodox. He feels the urge to tear up the notebook and burn it. As he pictures a fire consuming his labors, he feels the sorrow of monumental loss and wishes to save these writings from the flames and preserve them for posterity, even if no one will ever read them.

What is so revolutionary in what he's written here? He can't find a convincing answer, but what he does do is think more deeply about what he has written. Without being fully aware of it, he turns back a couple of pages and begins reading.

"Inner experience is extremely varied. I no longer believe that it can be reduced and summed up. It's because of the varied and confusing nature of inner experience that the Buddhist scholastics had to simplify and reify what can only be deemed as indefinable, indescribable. Therefore, they put forth the concept of *nibbana-dhatu*, the element of the unconditioned, itself a contradiction in terms. Then they had to find an experience that represented the unconditioned. It could not be a jhana, for those states of mind are believed to be conditioned, though they may fool those of other persuasions, such as believers in Vedanta, as being unconditioned. It had to belong to the same family of inner experience, namely, those experiences that exhibit a higher, if not altered, state of consciousness. There it was, standing right in front of them, the experience of attainment that was like a jhana but not a jhana, the knower of which can then be said to have had a glimpse of nibbana. However, the experience was not supposed to be taken as nibbana, just as an analogous, congruent state of mind, equally unconditioned, but still not the final, highest unconditioned reality. This jhana which is not a jhana became known as nibbana though it is not nibbana. It is given another name: *nirodha*. It is given a special designation: *nirodha-samapatti*, labeling it thus as an attainment. Its original designation gets lost, or rather, misplaced, in its new found home as the representative of nibbana.

"*Sañña-vedayita-nirodha* is what it was called before. *Sañña* means perception, *vedayitam* means experience, and *nirodha* means the ceasing of. It is a state of mind where experience stops, perception stops, but consciousness remains. Instead, it has been interpreted as a moment in one's train of inner experience where a gap occurs — a moment of nothing at all — and then a returning to consciousness. That is what I have always taken nirodha to mean. A gap could be just a gap, however, indicating nothing.

"If I separate nirodha from the knowledge of nibbana, and just look at nirodha as the ceasing of experience and perception with consciousness remaining, then there can be those brief periods where one's mind is clear of everything except the knowing of being clear of everything. It is not a gap, not a loss of consciousness, but a clear space of knowing the act of knowing."

Aggachitta pauses here to ponder this last line. He understands what the inner experience is he is referring to. It contains neither experience nor perception, and is thus indescribable. The act of referring to it is truly misleading because there are no experiences and perceptions. The nature of absence in such states of mind would naturally lead someone to believe that they were indeed empty, devoid of everything, and hence a gap between two periods of being conscious. However, that does not get at what sañña-vedayita-nirodha is: a clear space of knowing the act of knowing.

How else could he put it? The larger question then looms. If nibbana is not represented by nirodha, then how is it represented? Can someone arrive at nibbana and yet have nothing to hold onto as nibbana? The act of holding onto something is indeed fleeting, though the thing held onto may be permanent.

Aggachitta turns his notebook to the last few clean pages and begins writing down this last train of thought. He has lost track of time. When he hears a knock at the library door, he looks up to see a teenage samanera peering in and announcing that dana is to be served shortly.

CHAPTER 35

As the laypeople put together the final touches for the main meal, Gotami, Sumana and Palaparuchi stand around just outside the dining hut, where they can talk among themselves without being interrupted or overheard. Gotami doesn't feel comfortable around Palaparuchi, who hovers too close to her and persistently asks her questions about her past. Sumana tries to answer as many of these questions for her as he can, but there are several things he still doesn't know about her.

"What would you have done if you hadn't decided to become a nun?" Palaparuchi asks her.

Gotami lowers her head and looks away, wondering what she should reveal about herself. She would like Sumana to know these things about her, but not this strange, dark, disturbing monk.

"I probably would have completed college."

"What did you want to be?" Palaparuchi asks. "I wanted to be the CEO of a large corporation."

"I thought about…" she hesitates, looking over at Sumana on her right, trying to ascertain if he is listening closely enough to this, "I thought about becoming a school teacher. I like children. I worked as a tutor for a young Latina girl. She was the younger sister I never had. I still write to her."

Palaparuchi alternates between being captivated by Gotami's sweetness and innocence, and feeling revulsion for her. He thinks that Sumana is taken in by her. He, of course, is impervious to her feminine snares.

"I didn't know you were a tutor," Sumana says. "I had thought of doing that in high school, but I got so wrapped up in thinking that life was meaningless that I never did anything for anyone else."

"Of course life is meaningless," Palaparuchi interjects. "You just accept it and leave it at that and go on living. That's my philosophy."

"How can you both think that way?" Gotami exclaims. "The Noble Eight-fold Path is the meaning of life. When I was tutoring Maria I knew I was giving her what no one else could, not her parents, not her teachers, nobody in her life. I cared about her life by caring about her English pronunciation and comprehension. It wasn't going to change the world or make anyone enlightened, but something changed in me that gave me meaning. Not life — but my living this life — has meaning.

"When I went to the Zen center and began sitting, I saw that I wanted to live my life to the fullest potential and become fully liberated. It was either continue studying to become a teacher or take up a lifelong dharma practice. The two are not mutually exclusive, but they were vastly different pursuits.

"Now," she says, looking over at Sumana, meeting his anxious eyes, "what is your story? How did you become a monk?"

Sumana is thrown into turmoil by this question. He realizes that he would rather give her one answer and Palaparuchi another, but since he can't, he has to choose which one of them he is going to please. In a momentary flash of bravery, he chooses to open up to Gotami.

"I have always told my story through external events. I would always say that I became a monk because I went to that retreat and sat with that teacher and through doing this and that practice I could only conclude that the way to become fully liberated was to become a monk and so here I am."

Sumana pauses to catch his breath after such a long run-on sentence, and then continues, "But my heart tells another story." He lets out a sigh. "I didn't have a future. I didn't want to become my parents, and I didn't know what else I could become instead. In a way, my situation wasn't much different than poor Rahula's, except no woman was after me to marry her, which I saw as a good thing. Perhaps that just meant that I was unlovable and destined to be alone."

Now he feels that he has revealed too much and wishes he could retract this last statement. The silence of his two listeners unnerves him, but he pushes through the shadow his shame has cast over his words, and, struggling with his emotions of sadness and fear, he continues.

"I just didn't know what else to do, so I became a monk. I keep telling myself that this is the right choice, the only choice for me, but I feel in the back of my mind that it was the only choice I was willing to make, not the only one I had. Like Rahula, I saw my life as consisting of two choices, neither one I liked, and so I jumped at a third choice that was neither of the two and obliterated any need for me to choose again — unless I choose not to remain a monk for the rest of my life. That's the beauty of our situation. The issue as to what we will do for the rest of our lives does not come up unless we contemplate leaving the order."

Gotami has been listening with a mixture of her own sadness and feelings of pity. Whereas Sumana feels uplifted, she feels depressed and drained. Palaparuchi, as may well have been expected, tuned out most of what Sumana was saying and pursued a fantasy of his own. In his mind, Sumana is like Prince Siddhartha, finding no satisfaction in the world and so left it to find liberation, which is precisely what Sumana would want his friend to have heard.

"You're not fully committed to this way of life then?" Gotami asks.

"I wouldn't say that. I may have chosen the monks' life for the wrong reasons, but who doesn't have some wrong thinking in their life decisions. Right now, today, I can say that I'm progressing in my practice with the help of my teacher. All I really needed was to find the right teacher."

"That's all I need too," she sighs.

"You will," Sumana says softly.

Meanwhile, inside the dining hut, all of the lay people, including Rahula's and Devi's parents and siblings, are seated on the hard ground facing Maggaphala, who is seated on the bench. Their hands are clasped in front of their chests as they await Maggaphala's talk on the virtues of giving, of keeping the precepts, of having faith in the Buddha's teaching. That is what they are accustomed to hearing. However, Maggaphala does not give the usual kind of dharma talk, as one might well expect from him.

He speaks in Sinhala. His voice commands the attention of all, even the young ones, though they await his words with less eagerness than the adults seated around them do.

"The story of Meghiya will be the theme of this talk," he announces. "Meghiya was the Buddha's first full-time attendant. Before there was Ananda, there was Meghiya. One day, Meghiya asked the Buddha if he could go to a village near where they were staying for alms. The Buddha gave him permission and so Meghiya went into the village, received alms, and took his bowl of offerings to the bank of a nearby river, where he planned to eat his food. There he saw a beautiful mango grove, which captivated his mind with its loveliness. He then went to the Buddha to get permission to meditate in that grove, for he believed he would find true and complete liberation of mind meditating there. The Buddha didn't grant his first request, or his second one, but on the third try, he gave in to Meghiya's request, telling him that he could do as he saw fit. Meghiya then went to the mango grove and sat in meditation. During meditation, his mind was filled with thoughts of violence, of lust, of all sorts of despicable things not worthy of a bhikkhu. His mind was so overwhelmed by these thoughts that he could not meditate in that beautiful grove, and so returned to the Buddha. The Buddha was then able to teach him the necessary conditions for liberation.

"The story of Meghiya is about the major obstructions to hearing the Buddha's teaching and learning from it. Meghiya believed that by going to a beautiful place, his mind would become quiet and focused, but that's not always so. In a beautiful place, such as this hermitage, a person whose mind is turbulent and under the sway of destructive and unethical forces may still not find inner peace.

"When the Buddha spoke to Meghiya about what he needed for his own liberation, the first thing he mentioned was a kalyanamitta, a good friend. That good friend gives the necessary help and support, becoming the guiding presence in one's practice of the Noble Path. He (or she) can be your teacher, or just a fellow monk or nun or lay disciple. What sets the good friend apart from all others you will meet on this path comes out of what the Buddha next said to Meghiya. The good friend is pure in conduct, pure in speech, pure in effort, and pure in wisdom. He's not perfect, only pure. There is only one Perfected One and that is the Buddha, which we worship today with many various and wonderful offerings."

His speech concluded, Maggaphala motions to Mrs. Jayatilaka and the elderly nun to present the offerings of flowers, food, tobacco, and other items to the Buddha statue placed on a pedestal in the dining hut for this occasion. Everyone watches the two women bring the tray of offerings to the statue and set it down in front of it. The whole group then chants the qualities of the Buddha, dharma, and sangha, and a sharing of merit. When they are finished, Dr. Perrera rings a metal gong three times and everyone then rises to their feet.

Sumana and Palaparuchi straighten up upon hearing the gong, forming a two-man line with Palaparuchi in front. Sumana follows Palaparuchi into the dining hut and over towards the bench where Maggaphala is sitting. Palaparuchi refuses to sit down next to Maggaphala. Sumana might have sat down on the bench next to Maggaphala, but that's not permitted since he was ordained after Palaparuchi. They both stand near the bench, saying nothing. Dr. Perrera comes over and asks them if they need assistance. Palaparuchi tells him that he would like to sit in a chair. Dr. Perrera is perplexed by this request and has no idea where a chair for this white-skinned bhikkhu is to be found.

Maggaphala says, "There are two chairs in the cave, which can be brought here for these bhikkhus."

Dr. Perrera speaks hurriedly in Sinhala to several laymen standing around him, urging them to make haste and bring back the two chairs. He then apologizes to Palaparuchi and Sumana for not being prepared for them. Palaparuchi accepts his apology and remains standing, while Sumana, tired of standing around, wanting to rest his legs, sits down next to Maggaphala on the bench. "Just temporarily," he tells everyone.

No one, at first, seems to be paying any attention to Gotami as she slips past Palaparuchi and sits down on the ground several feet from the bench but in direct line with it, on a spot that she calculates would be after the two chairs. The elderly nun is the first to notice, and so she tells Mrs. Jayatilaka to go over to her, which she does. Mrs. Jayatilaka informs Gotami that she can't sit there, but must sit on the other side of the hut with the lay people. Gotami does not understand why she can't sit in the same row as the monks and asks Maggaphala to explain this to her.

"I take it that this is your first dana with monks," Maggaphala says.

"No, I have eaten with monks before. In town, I sit at the same table with the young boy monks, at the very end."

"Well, they don't observe the rules for monks as strictly in town as we do here in the forest. Everyone here expects the monks to obey every rule to the letter. Some laypeople even believe that we are all arhats." Maggaphala chuckles at this digression. Palaparuchi throws him a menacing look.

"So, to put it simply, we have to act with more rectitude here, which means for you, unfortunately, that you will have to sit with the laypeople. You can eat at the same time as the monks, so you can keep the precept of eating before noon."

"But I'm a nun!" Gotami says in her defense.

"Not quite," Maggaphala replies. "And it's that fact that your senior nun wants you to submit to. We'll talk later, after dana."

Gotami gets up and goes across the room, sitting down on the ground near Rahula's and Devi's group, who have been completely quiet since Maggaphala's talk. Rahula's three sisters and Devi's brother are content doing nothing as they sit. The children don't talk to each other, nor do they seem bored. They awaken Gotami's curiosity as she now sits observing them. She wishes she knew enough Sinhala to talk to them.

The two chairs arrive and are placed down next to the bench. Palaparuchi sits down in the one nearest the bench and Sumana sits down in the other one. The chairs are straight-backed wooden dining chairs with hard seats and backs. They are more comfortable than the bench. Sumana also likes the feeling of having his own private seat. His black alms bowl is securely placed in his lap ready and waiting to be filled with a wide variety of delicious and satisfying taste sensations. Out of his left eye he can see the arms ladling food into the black bowls of the two senior monks. A surge of impatience grips his frame, tightening his features, and he notices not hunger, but fear, the primal feeling of being overlooked, left out, forgotten, starved to death by neglect. Why would such a feeling arise now? The answer his mind gives him is swift and exact: because of desire.

He has no time to absorb this idea, his mind having been drawn into the realm of sight and the world of reactions related to that sense. He smiles and licks his lips at the breaded fish fillet dropped deftly into his bowl. Then comes one visual treat after another, and he conjures up the tastes to follow. He can't yet touch and taste the food in his bowl, but that doesn't distress him, for he can imagine clearly a precise taste for each morsel. A new world waiting to be born is lying there in his bowl, in mounds of color and form, to be translated into more palpable sensations, to merge his being in the sensual sphere, where heaven is found in the flavors of well-seasoned meats, beans, and vegetables.

On Sumana's left — in the periphery of his vision at first, but being so important right now that he turns his head to get a full look — Palaparuchi tentatively touches and moves some food in his bowl with his right hand. Maggaphala has yet to begin eating, waiting for the last two lay people to put their contributions into his bowl. Sumana can feel the tension of waiting for the starting sign, his eyes firmly fixed on Maggaphala's right hand resting on the rim of his black bowl.

Maggaphala coughs and a layman comes over to him, asking if he needs water. He says he does. Even after the last serving person finishes adding to Sumana's bowl, he still can't eat. The pressure is unbearable. Maggaphala takes two large gulps of water, and then a final sip. Then he has to wipe his mouth with his handkerchief. He looks over at Palaparuchi and Sumana, catching Sumana's eye, smiles at him in a friendly way, which Sumana takes as just wasting more time, and then faces the group of lay people standing around the table, some with serving dishes still in their hands. He can't thank them for the food, according to the rules of discipline, so instead he just smiles at them. To Sumana all this is unnecessary, just for show, but to Maggaphala it's his way of expressing heartfelt appreciation.

Then, before digging in, Maggaphala remembers something and motions Dr. Perrera, who Sumana recalls was the one serving the fish fillets, and whispers something to him. Dr. Perrera goes back to the others and tells them what Maggaphala said. They then go over to the elderly nun and Gotami sitting on the ground across from the monks and begin serving them. Sumana hopes — no prays — that Maggaphala will not wait until the nuns have been served before beginning to eat. His prayers are answered, as Maggaphala then puts his right hand in his bowl and brings a hard-boiled egg up out of it and towards his mouth. Sumana watches as Maggaphala's lips touch the egg, his mouth opens slowly, and in goes the whole egg. Dana has officially started.

The three monks and two nuns eat while those who are serving stand around waiting for the cue to start serving second helpings. Some people are talking among themselves, especially where Gotami and the elderly nun are sitting, which is particularly distracting for Gotami. She eats slowly, taking only small amounts of food from her plate. As a nun, she can't use a monk's black alms bowl for eating, but must use a plate. She has grown accustomed to eating with her hands, though at times such as now, she wishes she could just use a fork. Her fingertips are covered with sauce and particles of food.

Just as second helpings are being served, Aggachitta enters the dining hut. He sets his bowl down on the bench and adjusts his robe. He picks up his bowl and sits down next to Maggaphala, who looks over at him and smiles. A crowd of laypeople with serving dishes quickly gathers in front of him. They excitedly ladle food into his bowl, sometimes two at a time. When they finish serving him, they move back to the table, making room for other laypeople to bow before Venerable Aggachitta and receive his blessing. Sumana is glad that he is sitting away from all this commotion and is left alone to concentrate on the remaining clumps of rice, potato, chickpeas, and fish in his bowl.

Aggachitta can finally begin eating. He takes a look around at all the lay people gathered here and notices the two nuns. The elderly one he has seen before at a function in town, but the white-skinned nun is new to him. Then he thinks nothing more about them as he begins eating, for his mind shifts to wondering why his brother and his family are here. There has been no correspondence to that effect, so it must have something to do with Rahula. Then he shelves that thought for later, putting his full attention on eating.

Dana goes smoothly from this point on. When the monks have finished with the main meal, laymen come around with a pitcher of water to rinse their hands and bowls, and laywomen collect the plates from the nuns, who have to rise and go over to a spittoon placed for them near the stove in order to have the debris on their hands rinsed off. Once the nuns return to their seats on the ground, and the monks have wiped their hands and faces with their handkerchiefs, dessert is served on metal plates and each monk and nun receives a bowl of vanilla ice cream. After dessert, Sumana and Palaparuchi rise from their chairs and excuse themselves. Sumana heads off in the direction of his hut to nap, while Palaparuchi hovers about the dining hut, figuring out what he will do next.

Dr. Perrera requests that Aggachitta give a dharma talk before the laypeople eat. Maggaphala tells his friend that he already gave a talk on the Meghiya Sutta.

"That's a fine sutta," Aggachitta says. "What do you recommend I say? I don't give the most popular talks and these are not the kind of people who would be interested in my scholarly work."

"Try talking about something simple, such as the importance of keeping the five precepts."

"Why don't you give the talk instead of me? You know what they want to hear."

"I have already addressed them. They want you. They think highly of you. All you have to do is say a few things they can understand and one or two things beyond their comprehension."

Uncertain as to what he is going say, Aggachitta clears his throat as if to begin. He has spoken to such groups on several occasions, using a stock lecture on the merits of giving to the monks and keeping the five precepts. Now, with his mind having engaged far more relevant topics, which he would be more than happy to present to an educated audience, he's torn between going the well-trodden route and the new path.

People are waiting for him to speak, even Gotami, though she knows she won't be able to understand anything in Sinhala. She just wants to hear his voice, get a sense of his nature, and feel his presence. However, her mind is not just content with that, as she starts planning on how to approach him for an interview afterwards.

Aggachitta says, by way of both an introduction and an apology, "I have been away from the hermitage and have only just now returned. During my time in town, I had the opportunity to read, meditate, and reflect on many important parts of the Buddha's Teaching. I don't want to bore you with my research and reflections, for they are of a more scholarly nature, but I do want to convey what I see as the essence of the Buddha's path.

"The Buddha's teaching is about nibbana and nothing less than the true attainment of nibbana. All that we do in the name of the Buddha is about nibbana. The Buddha is nibbana. Practicing generosity, following the precepts, sitting in meditation, being kind and friendly to oneself and others, are nibbana — not just activities beneficial to the attainment of nibbana. Only we do not know nibbana, we do not see the Buddha, in these actions. Why? It is because our eyes are covered with dust, with the dust of ignorance. We follow ignorance and thus do not know nibbana in the here and now.

"I'm not saying that nibbana and samsara are the same, nor that nibbana exists underneath a veil of illusion, or any such philosophical notion. What I'm saying is that nibbana is the path to its attainment, and by knowing that, we know nibbana in the precepts, in our generosity, in our friendliness, in our minds in meditation. Nibbana is of the path, but the path is not always of nibbana. The path is not always pure, not always practiced in accordance with nibbana, but it moves towards nibbana, partaking of the purity of nibbana."

Aggachitta is silent for a few moments, letting his ideas circulate in his consciousness, feeling his dissatisfaction with his expression, while at the same time being satisfied with the understanding he has tried to express imperfectly. He waits for doubt to arise, as it habitually does when he expresses a conviction, and is comforted by its apparent absence.

Part Four

Path
and
Fruit

CHAPTER 36

Now that dana is over for the bhikkhus and the nuns, the lay people can eat. Gotami gets to her feet and quickly makes her way over to Venerable Aggachitta. She wants to get to talk to him before anyone else does, as she suspects that the elderly nun and Mrs. Jayatilaka will want to leave soon, seeing as they would have no reason to stay past lunch. She weaves past one person after another in the short distance from one end of the dining hut to the other, bumping into one gentleman, who scowls at her, making her feel bad about herself for a moment, full of greed as she is to get to talk to the man she must have for her teacher. Once in front of Venerable Aggachitta, she prostrates three times before him and asks for compassion. When she rises to meet his eyes, she finds that Suriya, Aggachitta's brother, is leaning over Aggachitta, whispering in his ear.

Aggachitta rises from the bench and goes with him, leaving the dining hut. Gotami is startled by his sudden departure and has the impulse to chase after him, but checks herself, telling herself that it would be improper to run after him. She will just have wait here until he returns.

What is she to do now? She looks back at the bench where Aggachitta was sitting and her eyes meet Maggaphala's gaze. She has spent much of the morning chatting with this monk, and though he does possess some kind of worldly wisdom, she seriously questions his abilities as a meditation teacher. Her judgment of him as a potential teacher almost entirely rests on what he told her about his encounter with the three men when they returned from having tried his instructions.

The three laymen had come back for additional instruction, doing what Maggaphala told them to do for a good two hours. One of them claimed to have seen bright lights and colors, while another said that he was not aware of anything for long periods of time, and the last one stated simply that his back hurt all the time. Each of them waited for Maggaphala to comment on their experiences and tell them other things they could try, but Maggaphala only said, "That's good. Just continue," and left it at that.

Gotami wonders what kind of teacher always says, "Just continue." To her, such a response would mean that he's not listening to a word she's saying, or — what she has come to conclude about Maggaphala — that he doesn't know anything beyond the initial instruction. It's hard to believe that is the case for a monk of over twenty rains in robes, but it explains why he had no advice to offer the three laymen. However, she can still acknowledge him as a kind and well-meaning monk, even though he could never be her teacher.

She wants a teacher who can see into her mind — who knows exactly what instruction she needs to arrive at the path to nibbana. That's why she's so distressed by Aggachitta being ushered away. It now seems that she won't get the teacher she deserves and may have to settle for the Anandas and Maggaphalas of the world.

"He'll return. Please, sit. We can chat some more," Maggaphala says.

She sits down listlessly on the ground in front of him. The last thing she wants is to have another conversation with Maggaphala. She would rather just feel sorry for herself, for the life she has chosen, where others don't trust her to be an upright and ethical person, and she has to continually subordinate herself to those around her who are not worthy to be her superiors. If she could only put the right words to these feelings, she would love to complain about this to someone, but not the elderly nun or Mrs. Jayatilaka. They would probably see her as ungrateful, resentful, and arrogant.

"I see you're not interested in conversation," Maggaphala says to her.

"I'm tired of talking," she says. "I just want to meet Venerable Aggachitta and become his student, like Sumana."

"Ah, but Sumana is a bhikkhu."

"So?"

"For him it's easy. He can stay here at the hermitage for as long as he likes. Aggachitta will not refuse him an interview and will be able to observe his progress closely. There are no complications regarding the teaching of a monk by another monk, but when it comes to teaching a woman, the whole thing becomes terribly complex and unmanageable. Even if Aggachitta does decide to teach you meditation, it will be very difficult for you to see him regularly and for him to spend enough time with you. You'll get much less instruction than Sumana with far more trouble."

"So I should just give up and not pursue this any further?"

"No, don't give up! It's going to be difficult, that's all. But it'll only happen if you don't give up."

"I see. Do I have your word on that?" she says with a budding smile.

"I'll do all I can," Maggaphala replies.

Gotami feels relieved. Even if she has to leave early with the other women, she'll have yet another opportunity to meet Venerable Aggachitta. Having Maggaphala and Sumana as allies seems to be all she really needs, but that still doesn't give her the level of certainty and comfort she requires.

Aggachitta is aware that his hut is not as he had left it. Someone was in it while he was away. He has to push that thought to the back of his mind, because his brother, whom he hasn't seen for a few years, has a pressing concern.

Aggachitta sits on his bed and his brother sits on the floor in front of him. He waits calmly for his brother to begin.

"May I speak now?" he brother asks.

"Yes, begin."

"Your dharma talk was interesting. I can see why people say the things they do about you. From such a vantage point, the problems, the hopes and joys, the miseries and defeats, of us worldly people must seem inconsequential. We do not concern ourselves with nibbana. It is something I don't understand, and perhaps never will."

Aggachitta is baffled by his brother's words. Aggachitta has always thought that his brother was sympathetic to his way of life. If he understands Suriya's beliefs correctly, he seems to regard Aggachitta's beliefs as inconsequential in light of his own.

"This relates to my son, Rahula," Suriya continues. "When we entrusted him to your care, we only wanted two things to happen. One was that he would be safe from the violence in the cities and villages. The other was that he would think seriously about his life and be able to make a responsible choice about how to live it. We feared that he might decide to become a monk, but we never dreamed that he would get mixed up with a girl and consider marriage at such a young age."

"I did not know," Aggachitta interjects, truly surprised to hear that Rahula is involved with a woman without him knowing about.

"It's been going on for some time. Did you not know that he has been writing letters to her?"

"He would go to the post office every time we went on alms round in town, but I had no idea he was writing to a young woman. I assumed he was writing to you."

"And yesterday," Suriya continues, pursuing his case against his brother, "while you were away, the girl came here to the hermitage. Who knows what went on between them! With you gone, surely there was no supervision. Now she wants to marry him. That is not the future we had in mind for our son! He must first finish university before we'll allow a marriage to take place."

"Ah, I see," Aggachitta says. "You're upset with me because Rahula may not fulfill your ambitions for his life. What if he decides not to get married and became a bhikkhu instead? You've not thought of that possibility have you?"

Suriya is enraged by Aggachitta's comments. He stands up and raises his voice to his brother. "You thief! You scoundrel! You can't take our only son! How could you betray your own brother like this?"

"First of all," Aggachitta says, his voice rising in volume with a touch of aggression behind it, "I have done nothing of the sort. Your son hasn't decided to become a bhikkhu, though he may at some point."

"Then he must leave this hermitage! I will not have him join the sangha!"

"You think that'll turn him into the son you want? He'll just rebel in another way. Perhaps he'll run off with the girl instead!"

"I should have known that you would try to influence my son. I did not listen to my suspicion, and now it's too late. Now he also has the idea lodged in his young mind that he can leave the world like his uncle. That's not what I sent him here for!"

"Fine. If that is truly how you see things. Please do not take him yet."

"Why?"

Aggachitta pauses for a while, not knowing how to present the practical side of Rahula's being here. If Rahula goes away, then who will store food for the bhikkhus, who will handle money for them, who will clean up after meals and serve them tea? Temple boys, especially for a forest hermitage like this one, are hard to find.

"He is helpful."

Suriya takes a moment to absorb the full meaning of Aggachitta's response.

"You make that sound as though he's your servant. Is that what your nephew is to you? What a mistake it was to send him here! I thought he would learn from you how to become a responsible and thoughtful adult, and now I see that all you had to offer him was menial labor."

"He has been studying," Aggachitta states in his defense.

"What has he been studying?" Suriya inquires. "Has he been studying how to be a bhikkhu? What the rules are? How to get everything you need given to you?"

"In fact, that hasn't been his current area of study. He's been reading existentialist literature."

"Existentialist literature?" Suriya exclaims with disbelief, and then with laughter. "You must be joking?"

"It's serious literature."

"It's depressing, dry, and highly overrated. What do you think he'll learn from it? That life is so lacking in value and meaning that it's better to commit suicide? Better yet, join the sangha and live your life in a fantasy world!"

"Is that what you think of my life?" Aggachitta exclaims, a reservoir of rage rising to the surface.

"Look, Brother," Suriya says sternly, "I never understood why you acquired your doctoral degree in philosophy only to become a hermit in the jungle. You could have had a fine, rewarding career, a loving wife and family, and still have made a great contribution in your field. Instead, you take these twenty-five hundred year old sayings to heart and go off in search of something that may not exist. You sacrificed a perfectly good life. I will not have my son making the same mistake."

Suriya stands up and stomps out of the hut. Aggachitta feels tears well up and sting his eyes, eventually rolling down his cheeks. He half believes his brother is right. He pictures a life he could have had. He sees the wife and children he does not have, the office with his nameplate on the desk, the volumes of his writings on the bookshelves, and a write-up of his achievements in a prestigious journal in his hands. He laments not having that life. When it passes, he feels deceived, manipulated, and used. Who took this life away from him? His Burmese meditation teacher comes immediately to mind, the one who indicated to him that he is a sotapanna. It was because of him he chose this life.

He sits in silence, his mind going through the life he has lived, bringing it up to the last twenty-four hours, and he concludes that, yes, he originally went in search of something that did not exist for him. Now, he is absolutely certain that it does. He gently confirms to himself that he knows nibbana is not a myth nor an idle pursuit, but a living reality. With that certainty, he draws his attention within, and soon transcends the worldly feelings of remorse, hatred, and sorrow. He abides in a tranquil state of mind that enables him to explore the conditionality of these feelings without taking them up. Today, he does this instead of taking a nap.

CHAPTER
37

Rahula and Devi excuse themselves from the others saying they would like to take a walk after eating. They walk towards the cave, climb the hill, and go up past the cave to the top of the hill. Devi wants to talk to him in private, and without the possibility of intrusion, about what just happened with their parents.

"I knew your parents didn't want us to get married," Devi says.

"They didn't say that," Rahula replies, defending them while knowing that she's right.

"They didn't have to. They know that I can't wait forever. They're just waiting for me to give up on you and go find someone else. By then, I will have wasted the good years of my life as your girlfriend."

"That's not how I see it," Rahula says, though that's exactly how he sees it.

"Well, then, how do you see our future?" Devi asks, surprised at herself for asking him to relate his thoughts on the matter.

"I can't see into the future," he says. The way she shakes her head conveys her dissatisfaction with this answer. "All right, I see us going out on dates," he continues, "having dinner with our families, sharing our secrets with each other, doing that for awhile, and then, when I've graduated, we can start planning our future together."

"That doesn't sound like your plans, but your parents' plans for you."

"No, that is exactly what I want!" Rahula says, trying to put some conviction in his voice.

"Well, I don't want that!" Devi shouts, thereby gaining the upper hand. "That's not love! If you want me, you'll have to risk everything for me! Your parents, your future, your life! That's love! That's what I want!"

Rahula feels as though he's being coerced into doing something he's afraid to do. He doesn't understand what she means by love. It sounds too dangerous and daring for the likes of him. He thought love was quiet, reserved, soft and gentle, not destructive and reckless as she makes it out to be.

"I guess I don't understand what love is," he replies.

"Well, if you don't love me, then there's nothing more to be said."

"But I do love you!" he exclaims.

"I don't see it."

Rahula — on the brink of tears at the thought of losing her — wonders how he can show her that he loves her. This may be the right time to kiss her, except he knows he's not capable of that just yet. He then tries to figure out if there's anything else he could do to convince her that he loves her.

"All right, all right," he says, "let's elope."

Devi jumps into his arms, pressing her body tightly against his, kissing him full on the lips. Rahula can feel a kind of electric vibration coming from her that is funneled through her lips and into his body. When the embrace is over, he feels oddly electrified, disoriented, and more trapped than ever before.

Palaparuchi has only one thing on his mind. He arrived too late to bathe before dana, so he now needs to get the master's bucket and retrieve his toiletries. It is risky bathing after dana, especially when there are laypeople around. Some of them get the same idea, as if bathing is part of the visit to a forest hermitage. Palaparuchi wants to finish bathing before any laypeople show up, so he hurries to the the cave, finds the bucket, and then goes to Sumana's hut, where Sumana is lying

down on the bed, awake with his eyes closed. He ignores
Sumana and rummages through his duffle bag for soap, a
towel, and a back-scrubber. He gathers everything up and
rushes out the door.

No one is at the cistern when Palaparuchi arrives. He
quickly takes off his outer robe and sets it on the clothesline
with his towel. He takes the bucket with his soap dish and
back-scrubber over to the edge of the cistern. He carefully
opens the soap dish, setting it down not far from the edge,
placing his back-scrubber next to it. Then he proceeds to fill
and empty three bucketfuls over his head in rapid succession.
Some water gets into his soap dish, making the surface of the
bar of soap slippery, and thus easier to lather. He first rubs the
bar of soap over his trunk, arms and legs and then across the
bristle brush of his back-scrubber. He returns the soap to the
dish and begins scrubbing his back. He enjoys the sensations
created around his scapula by the bristles, when he glimpses a
small figure run past him and pick up the bucket. It's the
youngest of Rahula's sisters. Right behind her are the other
two girls, who take the bucket from the little one and lower it
into the cistern together. The boy is standing off to the side,
watching the whole thing. Then the two women appear and
move closer to the cistern, scolding the girls for having taken
the monk's bucket. Everything happens so fast that
Palaparuchi doubts it is real. One of the women, Rahula's
mother, he thinks, hands him the bucket.

Palaparuchi realizes that this is a delicate situation. Him, a
full-fledged bhikkhu observing two hundred twenty-seven
major and minor rules, here bathing out in the open with two
adult women, three girls, and a young boy. "Well, the boy is all
right," he says to himself. He hopes he wasn't overheard
speaking to himself. But the women and girls, they pose a
problem of which there's only one solution.

"Women, may I have your attention," he says in Sinhala.
"You can't be here while I bathe. Please go away and come
back when I'm gone."

"Venerable sir," Rahula's mother says, "we've only come to wash up after eating. If you allow us the use of your bucket, we'll be finished in no time."

Palaparuchi lowers the bucket into the cistern as she speaks, half-listening to her request, and then dumps a cool bucketful of water over his soaped up body. He does this two more times, then sets the bucket on the ground, and walks over to where his robe and towel are hanging.

"Thank you," both women say in unison, as do the girls after them like an echo.

Palaparuchi ignores them as best he can. He reasons that if he successfully blocks women out of his mind, then he need not confess any infractions that might have occurred.

The two women are aware that he's ignoring them as they wash up, so they decide to ignore him as well, and begin talking as if he were not within earshot.

"What do you think of the monk's proposal?" Rahula's mother asks Devi's mother.

"He obviously never had a daughter of his own. Our Arati is certainly headstrong. We know that, but we love her dearly. She won't wait around. Your Rahula had better move fast or he'll lose her."

Rahula's mother is taken aback by these remarks. Perhaps she's not sure if she wants a girl like this as her daughter-in-law, or maybe she finds fault in talking so candidly about one's own children.

She replies, "Rahula is a sensible young man. I am sure he won't act impulsively. He will be a good influence for your daughter."

Devi's mother openly laughs at these remarks, offending Rahula's mother. They finish washing up in silence, taking turns with the bucket instead of sharing the water in it.

Maggaphala considers whether it's time to leave the dining hut and go to the cave for his after-lunch nap, or, if there's some reason to remain. Before he can decide, however, Devi's father approaches him. Instead of bowing and sitting on the ground, he moves the chair Palaparuchi sat on during dana over in front of Maggaphala and sits down in it. He looks Maggaphala directly in the face and says, "I've read a good deal of Shakespeare and wonder what plays you were referring to when you made the comment about love surviving through adversity."

"I wasn't thinking of any one play in particular."

"That's what I thought!" Devi's father says. "As I recall, in many of Shakespeare's plays lovers tend to act rashly, as if the love they feel at the moment is all that there is. They dread losing their true love, and have no confidence love's endurance and strength."

"That's an astute observation," Maggaphala says. "May I ask what you do?"

"I'm a filmmaker," he replies. "You may have heard of me. Hari Lal Vijayanayaka. I've made an award-winning feature film and several documentaries."

"I can't say that I watch movies," Maggaphala says, chuckling at the thought of bhikkhus sitting in a cinema, eating popcorn, engrossed in a silly film. "I do read drama and literature."

"But you have naive ideas about how the world works," Hari Lal states bluntly.

Maggaphala briefly considers whether to challenge that remark or just let it pass, deciding to challenge it in a passive sort of way.

"I only know a small part of the world."

"You don't know young lovers."

"Tell me then, what is it I should know?" Maggaphala asks.

"They don't obey their parents. They must rebel at all costs. They fight for the freedom to love each other as they want to. Interfering in their affair will only incite rebellion."

"So you know then what your daughter will do?"

"I'm not like my wife or Rahula's parents, or your average Sri Lankan middle-aged man. I don't want to control anyone, least of all my strong-willed daughter. She's very clever, that girl."

"I've seen that for myself," Maggaphala replies.

"Then you must know that your advice will have the opposite effect."

"It was the only advice I could give."

"Yes, you monks always try to be high-minded about things."

"And you are not being high-minded with your laissez-faire philosophy of life."

Hari Lal considers that comment briefly, finding it not worthy of a reply.

"That's not what I want to talk to you about. As I said, my daughter's life is her own. What interests me is if you would consider acting in a film I'm making."

"Me? Act? I haven't been on the stage for over twenty-five years!"

"You have a majesty about you that would fit perfectly in my next movie."

"I'm sorry. It would be unbecoming for a bhikkhu."

"Please consider it further. Here's my card."

Maggaphala takes his business card. He looks it over, reading it carefully. This man is a real filmmaker. It says so on his card. Maggaphala feels a certain pride rise up — maybe he could realize the ambition he cherished in his youth to become an actor. But he would have to limit himself to only playing roles as a monk. He could confess the infraction and not be in any danger of expulsion from the order if that were the case.

"What role do you have in mind for me?"

"The priest, naturally."

"Splendid."

Gotami follows along behind the elderly nun, with Mrs. Jayatilaka on her heels, as they walk through the jungle on their way home. She thinks about what Maggaphala said to her. Though it makes sense to wait for the right time, she's concerned about missing her only opportunity to become the master's student. She recalls having heard how Zen masters would let students sit out in the snow, not allowing them into the monastery until they have endured enough to prove their sincerity in wanting to learn meditation from the master. Today could require a similar test of her resolve. By going back home sheepishly like this, isn't she giving up?

"I'm not going back to the house just yet," Gotami says to Mrs. Jayatilaka behind her.

"What do you mean, dear?" Mrs. Jayatilaka asks, genuinely confused.

"I'm going back to the hermitage to speak with Venerable Aggachitta."

"Don't disturb Venerable Aggachitta. He has many things to take care of now that he is back at the hermitage. Besides, it's the uposatha. The bhikkhus have to come together to recite the patimokkha and confess their transgressions. Who knows how long that can take?"

"I don't care!" she says. "I will stay there until Venerable Aggachitta accepts me as his pupil."

"It isn't necessary for you to do this," Mrs. Jayatilaka says. She wishes the elderly nun could enter the conversation and dissuade the poor girl from this impulsive act, but the nun can only speak a little English and barely understands a quarter of the words they're using. She then speaks to the elderly nun in Sinhala, explaining the situation, translating her reply for Gotami.

"Your sister here wholeheartedly agrees with me. She says you'll embarrass yourself. It's not proper for a young nun to approach a revered Thera such as Venerable Aggachitta and present him with this kind of request. She also says," pausing a moment to let the old nun say more, "if you disobey, you'll have to find somewhere else to live."

Gotami is on the verge of tears, but beneath the hurt is rage, and that's what she wants to express right now. It would be highly irregular and completely inappropriate for a nun to yell at her superiors, so she keeps her anger in check, which just produces tears. Struggle as she may with her own feelings at the hard hearts of others, she manages to calm herself enough to say, "I'm going back. That's it!"

"Then you will have to find someone to take you in," Mrs. Jayatilaka says, and then adds, "I would let you remain at my house, but the other nun would not allow it. What can I do?"

"Nothing, I suppose. I will be back later to pick up my belongings."

"Where will you stay?"

"I don't know," Gotami says, but in the back of her mind, she thinks that she can stay at the hermitage with the monks. She can't think of any reason why they would not put her up, as they're kind people, unlike the elderly nun. Unfortunately, Gotami doesn't know enough about the rules of discipline, and how inflexible those rules are concerning women. If she did, she would realize she's entertaining a hopeless fantasy.

CHAPTER 38

Palaparuchi makes quite a racket getting dressed and packing his belongings, waking Sumana up and then making it impossible for him to get back to sleep. Sumana lies with his eyes closed listening to his friend sort through his possessions, redistributing them in his duffle bag, which Sumana hopes is a sign that Palaparuchi will be leaving today. He gets up and puts on his outer robe, and then speaks to Palaparuchi.

"The patimokkha is soon?"

"Probably, yes," Palaparuchi says distractedly, as he concentrates intently on which items to stuff into his alms bowl, taking into account the bowl's flat metal lid.

"I'm going to find out where it's going to be," Sumana says as he walks over to the door.

"Good, I should be packed by then," Palaparuchi replies.

Sumana walks down the path to the dining hut, thinking over the events of the last two days. He's glad Palaparuchi is leaving the hermitage, but he also feels some kind of feeling that he just can't name. As he walks, he thinks that maybe this feeling doesn't have a name, but surely all feelings must have been named by now. This one may just be new to him. He probes the sensations in his chest, cross-referencing with known feeling states. He rules out anger, disappointment, sadness, fear, joy, remorse, and envy, though envy brings him closer to it than any of the others. He stays with the sensation, holding the thought that it is like envy, but not exactly.

He stops under a tree, stands in the shade, and gives himself all the time he needs. An image forms in his mind of a perfectly happy bhikkhu, living alone, who goes through the day calm and contented, never troubled, never bored, always in a peaceful, blissful state of mind. He measures himself by that image. Envying an ideal being is the idea of the feeling, but it's not the feeling itself. For that, he must know this feeling as though it were the center of his whole being, the fulcrum of his present existence. It comes up, touching his chest like the sharp point of a pin, pricking once, and then subsiding. He names the sensation, capturing the emotion cloaked within it: desolation.

Sumana resumes his walk, somewhat uplifted by this moment of self-knowledge, his mind less bound up with worries and concerns, ready to face whatever may arise. As he nears the dining hut, he recalls how just an hour before there were crowds of people, and now it appears empty, except for the outline of a lone person sitting on the ground.

He enters the hut and looks down at the person sitting there. It is Gotami. He is both shocked and delighted to see her, but his face only expresses the shock.

Gotami begins to bow to him and he stops her. "You have already paid respect to me enough times today."

"I thought I had to bow every time I saw a monk."

"The Sinhalese like it done that way, but it's not necessary for me. I'm going to sit over there in one of the chairs. Would like to join me?"

Gotami rises from the ground and follows Sumana over to the two chairs. He sits in one and she immediately seats herself on the ground.

Sumana says, "You don't have to sit on the ground. Why not sit in this chair?"

"You're a bhikkhu," she says. "Laypeople have to sit lower than you."

"Look, no one is around," Sumana replies.

"But if someone should come in on us, they would see a monk alone with a woman sitting in a chair as his equal."

"I'm the one who is breaking the rules by having you sit in a chair. I'm the one who has to confess it, not you. I'd rather break that rule and confess it than treat you with disrespect."

"Fine, then, I'll sit in the chair, but I'll move it so that I face you and there's no possibility of any accidental contact."

Sumana gets up and moves the chair for her, setting it down facing his with about three meters between them. It looks odd for two people to be sitting that far apart without a table in the center. If a bhikkhu is to break the rule about being alone with a woman in a building, it's the desired impression to give anyone who may walk in on them.

They sit in silence for a couple of minutes, each looking down at the ground separating them.

Sumana breaks the silence with a question, "I thought you would have left by now?"

"I did leave, but I came back," she says, sounding low.

"What happened?" Sumana asks, concerned.

"I argued with the other two women. But that is not why I came back. I need a teacher! No just anyone. I want Aggachitta to accept me as his student, even if it's hard for me."

"I don't see why it would be hard," he says, trying to be encouraging.

"Because you don't know how hard it is being a nun!"

Gotami's face reddens and tears start to flow from her eyes. She tries to ignore her emotions, for she believes she should be able to be unaffected by them, but that's not possible. Soon she starts sobbing, covering her face with both hands, trying to hide her shameful behavior from Sumana.

Her sobbing touches Sumana in a way he doesn't expect. He's not sorry for her, but rather disgusted at himself for being so inert, so incapable of offering solace.

"Is there anything I can do?" he manages to say.

"No nothing," she says, uncovering her face, which is damp from crying.

Sumana pulls out his handkerchief and hands it to her. To do so however, he must rise from his chair and walk a few steps over to her. Just being that much closer to her somehow makes him resonate with her feelings more intensely. They could also be his own feelings, becoming more intense as he bridges the distance between their two worlds. When he sits back down in his chair however, he notices that instead of feeling her sadness, he feels numb.

"Is there any way I can stay here?" she asks, sending her desperation straight across the divide between them.

"I don't know. We can try. Maybe if Rahula leaves you can stay in the cave. You will have to ask Venerable Aggachitta. I can't promise anything," Sumana replies anxiously.

"Thank you, thank you," she says, her hands on her lap, a smile peeking out from behind the ruddy wetness of her lips.

"I'll see what I can do," Sumana says.

Now he's taken responsibility for her welfare. The last thing in the world he would want to do is fail her in a way that would lead to being separated from her.

At the bus station in town, Rahula and Devi wait with their families for the next bus to Colombo. It is an open air station that resembles a parking lot, with merchant stalls lining one end of it. The Colombo buses are supposed to stop near the bench they all sit on, near the stalls. It is hard for Rahula to stay with his own thoughts without overhearing his father talking with Devi's parents and the incessant arguing and periodic crying episodes of his younger sisters. In this noisy, overly turbulent environment — what with the added intrusion of blaring radios and big diesel buses — Rahula tries to recall where he left off in *The Woman in the Dunes*. He knows he didn't finish it, though he knows the ending, at least what is written of the ending in the beginning of the book, where the man is never found. He either lives out his life with the woman or perishes in the dunes.

This reflection doesn't seem to help him with his situation one bit. He was hoping to be consoled by the man's plight, for his own is not so bad. He has decided to run away with Devi. The plan is that they'll meet at Pettah bus station in Colombo the next morning and travel together to Kandy. From there they can travel to a small town in the central mountains and find work. It would take their parents some time to find them. By the time they're discovered, they'll already be married. The plan is mostly Devi's.

A large old bus pulls into the station and up to the bench where they sit. It reads "kolamba" in Sinhalese script on its destination plate. Devi boards the bus first, followed by her parents, Rahula's sisters and her brother, and then Rahula's father and mother. Rahula hesitates before boarding. He could just let the door close, run back to the hermitage, and forget this ever happened. But he can't. It's real now. He's going back home to become an adult. He's made his choice.

Once on the bus he sits in the window seat next to Devi. She reaches over to hold his hand. It is limp in her hand. His eyes stare vacantly out the window as the bus turns onto the street and begins its journey northwards to Colombo.

Gotami decides to make a large pot of tea for the monks, anticipating the arrival of Maggaphala and Palaparuchi, who come from separate directions at about the same time. Palaparuchi brings his duffle bag and alms bowl with him, setting them down on the table.

Palaparuchi and Sumana sit in chairs now facing Maggaphala sitting on the bench.

"Where do we hold the patimokkha in this hermitage?" Palaparuchi asks Sumana.

"I have never been here for the patimokkha," he replies. "Your guess is as good as mine."

"Shouldn't someone get the head monk!" Palaparuchi says.

"I'll go ask him after tea," Maggaphala volunteers.

Maggaphala realizes it's not possible to sit in silence with Palaparuchi around, as he will continue to ask Sumana questions or begin some long unendurable story or tirade. Maggaphala decides to initiate a conversation with Sumana, one that should last to the end of tea time.

"When I went up to the cave to lie down after dana," Maggaphala begins, "I found Rahula there packing."

"Rahula's gone?" Sumana asks, his voice betraying an inner agony, one that is far more poignant and easier to identify than the vague feeling he experienced earlier.

"I know you were fond of him," Maggaphala says.

"How could he do that?" Sumana exclaims.

"I don't understand it myself," Maggaphala replies. "I fear the young man is making a tremendous mistake."

"She got him," Sumana says softly, hoping that Gotami doesn't overhear him say that, which in all likelihood she did not, as she was near the stove preparing tea as he said it. She brings over a tray containing four glasses of black tea. Maggaphala takes his cup first, then Palaparuchi, followed by Sumana and Gotami, who sets the tray down on the table, pushing Palaparuchi's duffle bag to the table's edge to make room for it. She then returns to sit on the ground a few feet from the bhikkhus.

Maggaphala's mind is pulled back to his earlier conversation with Devi's father, Hari Lal. In particular, he ruminates on Hari Lal's remark that he has a naïve understanding of young people in love. It is true that Maggaphala has never fallen in love with anyone, though he fantasized about women when he was a young man. His limited understanding in this area rests solely on what he has read, fantasized, or heard from others. He's curious about what those who've had real relationships might say about love, but isn't sure how to bring that up in this mixed company of foreigners who have left that life behind them.

Gotami sips her tea quietly, but is not too comfortable with the silence, especially with Palaparuchi staring at her between his sips of tea.

She directs her attention to Maggaphala, asking, "What were you talking about while I was making tea?"

"We were talking about Rahula and Devi," Maggaphala says. "You know that Rahula has left the hermitage to marry her?"

"That can't be so!" Gotami exclaims. "He seemed so happy here. Weren't they going to wait until he graduated from college?"

"They may still wait," Maggaphala replies, "but it seems that the poor boy's fate is sealed."

"Relationships aren't as permanent as they used to be," she says, adding her own bit of wisdom. "Devi could easily find another man and rope him into a relationship. Why does it have to be Rahula?"

Sumana, who has been listening the two of them talk, now feels that he and Gotami agree, and so offers his thoughts on the matter. "It's like the story that Rahula is reading, *The Woman in the Dunes* — the woman accepts the man who's trapped with her. Rahula is trapped with Devi, so Devi wants to marry him."

"You mean," Gotami says, "because Rahula and Devi have some kind of history that binds them together, they should get married. If that were the case, I would have married my former boyfriend."

Palaparuchi suddenly takes an interest in the conversation. "Why didn't you just get married instead of becoming a nun? It would have been a lot easier."

Gotami glowers at him, and then responds with a tinge of remorse, "Sometimes I wish I'd just stayed at home, gone to college, and found a decent boyfriend. You're right. That would have been the easy way for me. But then I'd feel trapped in a life that wasn't my own, which I'd then have to deceive myself into believing was the life I wanted. At least now, even with all of the hardship and neglect I experience, I'm creating my own life."

"I have never looked at it quite that way," Sumana says. "We haven't left the world by taking robes, but rather have entered into a world where we can create a life for ourselves, one which is grounded in the path." Sumana is a bit flustered, feeling as though he hasn't been making sense, and so tries to say the same thing from another angle.

"What I mean is that the freedom of the bhikkhu's life lies in the responsibility we have to use our time to the best of all possible uses, seeking nibbana."

Still, he feels he hasn't quite gotten the idea across. Just then, Gotami interjects her thoughts from what he has said.

"You're onto something here, Sumana," she begins. "Why else would the Buddha teach that one who has realized complete nibbana must leave the lay life behind?"

Maggaphala decides this is a good place to add his thoughts on the subject. "The question here isn't whether the bhikkhu's life or the lay life is better for one's progress on the path leading to nibbana, but whether the path one treads actually does lead to nibbana."

Palaparuchi downs the remainder of his tea in one large gulp before jumping in with some thoughts that pour out of his mouth. "All this talk of nibbana is just rubbish! You just practice the path and sooner or later you find nibbana."

All three of them look at Palaparuchi in astonishment. On one level, which none of them is ready to admit, he makes good sense. On another level, which each of them is more than willing to acknowledge, the mad monk is deluding himself once again that he knows nibbana and the path leading to it.

Maggaphala is half-tempted to engage Palaparuchi on this subject, but decides he'd better not. The patimokkha ceremony should begin soon and he wonders why Venerable Aggachitta hasn't come to join them. He finishes his cup of tea and rises from the bench. "I'll be back soon with Venerable Aggachitta," he announces.

Once Maggaphala leaves, Palaparuchi resumes the conversation. He speaks in an animated manner, using hand gestures and much lengthier sentences, now that Maggaphala is gone. He believes he is expressing himself freely and clearly on a subject most dear to him.

"What most *putthujanas* — ordinary people," he adds for Gotami's benefit, in case she does not know what a *putthujana* is, "don't understand about the path is that it involves nothing more than going up the *ñanas* — the sixteen knowledges leading to Path and Fruit. One goes from one path moment to the next, until final nibbana is reached — it's that simple! That's why all you have to do is stick with the practice that leads you up the ñanas. That's the only true practice!"

"I've never heard that before," Gotami says, not at all convinced by what Palaparuchi is asserting. "I've heard there are many practices that lead to nibbana."

"Oh, that's a very dangerous view," Palaparuchi says. "Most practices just lead to more delusion. When you've arrived at the knowledge of what is the path and what is not the path, then you'll understand what I mean."

"And this practice of knowledges doesn't lead to delusion?" She asks, clearly signaling her disbelief in Palaparuchi's pretence of being free from delusion about nibbana and the path leading to it. She's more inclined to believe that the path of knowledges is more deluded than any other right now, for the very reason that Palaparuchi — whom she sees as being deluded — believes that it's free of delusion.

Sumana would like to interject something here, just to smooth out the tension between Gotami and Palaparuchi, but he doesn't know which line to take, whether he's for or against the path of knowledges. In a way, the whole discussion seems absurd to him, as it has nothing to do with personal experience and thus seems abstract and off the point.

Palaparuchi comes to his own defense. "This practice of the ñanas has produced many arhats and countless sotapannas over the past several decades. They'd never lie about their attainments."

A thought suddenly occurs to Sumana, so he asks, "How do we know they have attained when it is against the rules to speak of such attainments? And, if they broke the rule about revealing their attainments to others, then they're not bhikkhus who keep the rules, so they probably haven't attained at all."

Palaparuchi has obviously heard this argument before, for he answers without a moment's hesitation. "It's their teachers who indicate they're sotapannas."

"Then," Gotami chimes in, "how do the teachers know they've attained?"

Palaparuchi is exasperated by this line of questioning. It's too much doubt for him to endure on this matter. He must have complete certainty in it if he is truly what he thinks himself to be, that is, an anagami — one who has attained the third path and fruit, just one path and fruit shy of complete nibbana.

"The teachers observe the students going up the ñanas in the course of a meditation retreat," he retorts. "And when a student has the right experience at the right time in the sequence of ñanas, then it's determined that he's attained the first path and fruit, that of a sotapanna. This is a precise science. To be sure that the teacher is correct, the student is not told about his attainment. Instead, he is given a set of meditation instructions, which, if he does correctly, will prove that he is a sotapanna."

Palaparuchi is very satisfied with this explanation. No one could have put it better. He just hopes the questions will stop and that the senior bhikkhus will return so they can get on with the patimokkha ceremony. It's already getting late, and he wants to catch a bus to Colombo to arrive before nightfall.

Sumana, however, mulls over what his friend has said, comparing it with what he heard from Maggaphala the day before. It occurs to Sumana that perhaps his first teacher was wrong about him being a sotapanna, for it sounds as though his teacher used this very same system of knowledges. His own skepticism about being a sotapanna is not as painful as when Maggaphala cast doubt on it, though who knows if he could have questioned it like this without first having someone else question it for him. He hopes that this doesn't happen to him again — that Aggachitta has gone beyond this system of knowledges and has enough integrity not to impute to a student an attainment he may not actually have.

Gotami also takes time to reflect on the conversation, surprised that she has actually learned some new and valuable information from such a disturbing person as Palaparuchi. She just wants a teacher to give her a practice that will lead her to nibbana, and hasn't considered the possibility that she might get told she's a sotapanna when she's not one. It puts a damper on the whole enterprise. She believes wholeheartedly that entering the stream is possible in this lifetime, and is now dismayed by the idea that it's also possible to be deceived by one's teacher that one has entered it. Who can she trust in all this? She too hopes that Venerable Aggachitta is not one of those teachers who chart their students' progress through the sixteen knowledges and then drops hints that they have attained when they haven't.

They sit in silence for several minutes, immersed in their own reflections. Palaparuchi contemplates his attainments, as he prepares to share with the others what he sees as proof that the sixteen knowledges correctly plot a meditator's path to nibbana.

Palaparuchi breaks the silence to relate the story of his supposed attainments. "Before I became a monk and started meditating seriously about twenty-five years ago, I was a fairly well-adjusted, average sort of guy. My life wasn't very exciting. I was in business school and could only think about making a lot of money and living the good life. Meditation changed all that!" He exclaims with a hint of resentment. He settles down and begins again. "When I became a monk I began to have incredible meditation sittings. Sometimes I would leave my body and fly around in the god realms. Sometimes I would visit the hell realms and experience the suffering of tortured beings. Sometimes my mind would just go blank for several minutes at a time, and when I would return, I would feel great rushes of energy. This is how I knew the three characteristics of existence: impermanence, suffering, and no-self." He lists them for Gotami's sake, confident that Sumana has been taught the three seals of existence.

Sumana and Gotami only partly attend to Palaparuchi's story, though he imagines them to be listening with rapt attention. "So I would go up the ñanas regularly and have an experience of my consciousness vanishing. I've gone through these sixteen knowledges so many times I could be an arhat several times over. But it doesn't work that way. There's a special hitch to it. You can go up the ñanas at will as often as you want after you've attained a particular path and fruit as long as you don't enter upon the set of ñanas for the next path and fruit. The ñanas of the next path and fruit will be much more difficult than they were for the previous one. That's how you know the difference, I guess."

Here Palaparuchi is puzzled. How indeed does he know the difference between the experience of knowledges he has willed, and thus created, and those which have arisen for him as the next series of knowledges leading to the next path and fruit? He now tries to answer that question in his narrative.

"There are three ñanas in the middle of the whole thing which are always painful whenever I experience them. So when I pass through them I feel much better and have more energy and mental power. These three are fear, danger, and disgust. Fear comes from the dissolution of the self. Then from knowing that the self is impermanent, one sees the danger in self-existence, which creates disgust for renewed existence. Usually when this happens, I feel *domanassa* — the Pali word for depression. If I keep going up the ñanas, the depression gives way to energy and mental clarity. When my mind experiences a moment of emptiness, I attain the next path and fruit. It's that simple!" he says with a wide grin that turns into a self-satisfied smile.

Sumana gets an insight into how Palaparuchi can believe he's more advanced than he really is. It's a well-worn groove for Palaparuchi to go into a depression and emerge from it into some kind of revitalized state. It sounds like something Sumana heard years ago when he was a layman. A friend of a friend was said to have bipolar disorder. He then wonders if Palaparuchi sees his mood swings as indications of moving through this system of ñanas. It occurs to him that Palaparuchi could have turned his bipolar disorder into the path leading to nibbana. No wonder Palaparuchi seems so deluded about himself.

"I don't know, Palaparuchi," Sumana says. "Have you considered that you might be bipolar?"

Palaparuchi smiles and says, "Of course! I have been diagnosed as manic-depressive by a few psychiatrists. The medication doesn't seem to work, so I stop taking it. Why do you ask?"

"No particular reason," Sumana says, backing down from saying anything that might antagonize or hurt his friend.

"You think I'm crazy," Palaparuchi says. "But a crazy person can still go through the sixteen ñanas and arrive at nibbana. I'm proof of that!"

Sumana now wonders why his friend keeps claiming an attainment when the monastic rules of discipline strictly forbid it.

Gotami feels that the conversation between Palaparuchi and Sumana has become too personal. It's between two friends, so she should just remain silent. The idea that Palaparuchi is bipolar makes sense to her, and she can regard his estimation of himself as indicating mental illness rather than someone who is just a little crazy. Still, she has no compassion for him, finding him just as disturbing and disagreeable as before.

Palaparuchi doesn't care for the silence that follows his declaration of being proof that a crazy person can go through the ñanas and arrive at nibbana.

"You don't seem to understand how the mind works in the dharma," he says to Sumana. "When the mind touches upon the truth of things and experiences a moment of emptiness, knowing that moment to be nibbana, then that is a path moment, which is then immediately followed by a moment of fruition. One's mind cannot go back from there. It cannot be taken away. It doesn't matter if one is mentally unstable; the experience of nibbana is the same."

"I get it, Palaparuchi. You can be crazy and enlightened at the same time," Sumana says.

"No, not exactly. In the mind stream of the sotapanna there are moments of nibbana and there are moments of samsara. They don't arise together. There's no question of being liberated and crazy at the same time. One can't coexist with the other."

For Sumana, Palaparuchi seems crazy whenever he thinks he's liberated. It certainly seems as though both arise together. When Palaparuchi doesn't think he's liberated, he's not so crazy.

Gotami says, "This sounds a bit like crazy wisdom."

"There, you understand me correctly," Palaparuchi says.

"But with crazy wisdom, the emphasis is on wisdom, not on craziness," she says. "One is wise and acts crazy as a way to teach others who are stuck in conventional ways of being."

"That's exactly what I do," Palaparuchi says, putting an index finger in the air with a twinkle in his eyes.

Sumana now thinks that Gotami is feeding Palaparuchi's delusions, and wishes that she would stop.

"Now I can see my life more clearly," Palaparuchi says to Gotami. "Thank you, young sister. You have put my life purpose into greater perspective. I must use my craziness to teach the dharma."

Gotami now wishes she could take back what she said about crazy wisdom.

Maggaphala finds Aggachitta in his hut, sitting on his bed, having just come out of a meditation sitting. Maggaphala pulls up a chair facing him, his gaze directed towards the ground. Aggachitta wonders whether something is bothering his friend or if Maggaphala has some kind of major offense to confess in private before the patimokkha ceremony.

After a few moments of silence between them, Maggaphala raises his head to speak. He says, "There are some things I need to tell you about the foreign bhikkhu. Not your student, but the other one. I don't like to speak of anyone behind his back, but in this case I must."

"As long as it is not gossip or a lie," Aggachitta says, "I will hear it."

Maggaphala breathes a sigh of relief, as he was not sure whether Aggachitta would be willing to hear what he fears may sound like a string of complaints.

"I knew this foreign bhikkhu when he first ordained. We both had the same teacher, Venerable Ñanaphala Thera."

"Yes, I know him," Aggachitta says. "He also studied in Burma. Wasn't he one of those teachers who would hand out attainments?"

Maggaphala perks up at this remark. He had no idea that his friend knew what other teachers were doing. Maybe he can be more candid about the practice of teachers lying to students.

"Yes, that's one of his major failings," Maggaphala says. "But he's not alone in that."

"Sadly, no."

"So it would not surprise you that Venerable Ñanaphala told this foreign bhikkhu he was a sotapanna. At the time, I couldn't believe that such a crazy, inconsiderate, and egotistical person could be a sotapanna. It destroyed any faith I had in Ñanaphala as a teacher, and started me on a path of doubting the supposed attainments of others."

Aggachitta reflects on what his friend is saying. He lets his mind work on this topic with the complexity and subtlety it deserves. When a teacher believes he has eliminated a view of self, and yet attributes selfhood to others — as in telling them that they are sotapannas — that act itself indicates that he still has a view of self. That's how views operate, as opposed to explicitly stated beliefs. A view is a way of seeing things. It acts upon one's perceptions and concepts, and thus becomes embedded in an individual's consciousness. Knowingly or unknowingly, he's then bound to see and act accordingly. A belief, on the other hand, is a public statement of one's position, one's attitude, one's orientation, or one's allegiance. These teachers who believe in no-self may do so without realizing they still view themselves and others as selves."

Aggachitta then says, "It is your knowledge of no-self that creates the doubt regarding views of self that you hear. Your teacher may not have had such knowledge of no-self, so he attributed selfhood to others." Then, with a slight chuckle, he adds, "Without realizing it, such teachers are giving students a new identity as someone who has seen into the delusion of selfhood. It's a blatant contradiction."

"Precisely! And then look what happens. A mentally disturbed individual, such as Palaparuchi, thinks he's a sotapanna, and lives believing he's something he's not. He finds a home in the community of bhikkhus, where he considers himself superior to those who have not attained, and acts in ways that are disrespectful and harmful, damaging the reputation of the sangha."

"In that case," Aggachitta says, "he should not participate in our patimokkha ceremony today."

"I agree," Maggaphala says. "But how are we to get rid of him?"

"I don't know. I'm hoping you can come up with a plan."

"Before we do that," Maggaphala says, "there is another matter to discuss."

"What's that?"

"The young nun," Maggaphala says. "She wants to be your student."

"I see," Aggachitta says before moving into a pensive silence. He sees the difficulties involved in teaching a woman out here in the jungle. In forest hermitages throughout Sri Lanka, there has been a policy of discouraging women from seeking instruction from bhikkhus, because they might distract them from earnestly seeking nibbana. The urban monasteries are different in this respect, as the bhikkhus are studying the Buddha's teaching, performing rituals and ceremonies, and doing service work in their communities. Thus, they generally have contact with women. Having Gotami come out to the hermitage on a regular basis could stir up a lot of gossip among the laypeople and the bhikkhus in town, leading to insinuations of improper conduct, even if nothing of the sort happens. The only way to circumvent some of the inevitable gossip is to have her come to the hermitage with the group of laypeople offering dana on that day. She can then stay through the meal and have an interview right after eating. That will cut into Aggachitta's nap, but that's a sacrifice he's willing to make for an earnest meditation student.

"I think we can manage it," Aggachitta says. "I'll talk to her after the patimokkha."

Maggaphala feels relieved that his friend will teach Gotami, for he was dreading letting her down. With that taken care of, the two bhikkhus can put their attention on how to get Palaparuchi to leave before the patimokkha.

CHAPTER
39

Maggaphala enters the dining hut and then steps aside
Aggachitta, who stands looking at the foreign mor
and nun with a look of dismay. Sumana and Palaparuchi
over and prostrate before Aggachitta, who says a sh
blessing. When they get up from the ground, Gotami is rig
behind them, prostrating also to Aggachitta. They are now
standing, waiting for Aggachitta to tell them what to do.

Aggachitta decides to address Gotami first. "Maggapha
has told me that you wish to study meditation. We don't hav
time to talk about that now, but wait here until we'v
completed the patimokkha, and we'll try to find some arrange
ment for you."

Gotami is elated at how well things seem to be working
out for her. Sumana is also happy, though he keeps his smile i
check, afraid what the other monks might think of him if th
knew the way he feels towards Gotami.

"Now," Aggachitta begins, "since we have no sima here
which is a long story, since that should be the first thing bu
when constructing a monastery — we have to use the piece
land where the sima will someday be built."

"I don't understand," Sumana says. "Why can't th
patimokkha be done anywhere?"

"It just isn't done that way," Maggaphala answers.

"I am not an expert on the Vinaya," Aggachitta says. "M
understanding is that when there's a sima — or in our cas
land consecrated as a sima — that's where it is to be held."

"What do you do when you are the only monk?" Palaparuchi asks.

Aggachitta can readily see that Palaparuchi, if given the opportunity, would distract and annoy him with one question after another. He decides to give him short answers meant to stop all further discussion.

"I go to the monastery in town. This is the first time we've had more than one monk here for a long time. Follow me."

They walk out of the dining hut forming a line in the order of their ordination. Aggachitta is in front, Maggaphala is a few paces behind him, Palaparuchi is several paces behind Maggaphala, and Sumana is right behind Palaparuchi as they all walk in the direction of the monument to the hermitage's founder, Venerable Atakkachari. Once they reach the monument, Aggachitta points out where the four corners of the sima will be built, which is in a flat area overgrown with bushes, but with relatively few trees. Sumana believes he understands why the sima has not been built yet, since just clearing the land and preparing it for a structure would take considerable labor, not to mention money. Sumana does not quite understand what is being asked of him and the other bhikkhus when he sees Aggachitta walking through the dense brush to where the sima will eventually stand.

"You'll have to follow me," Aggachitta says.

"But there's a cobra in there," Sumana says to Maggaphala and Palaparuchi.

"I'm not going then," Palaparuchi says.

Maggaphala, on the other hand, ignores Sumana's comment and wades through the bushes to where Aggachitta is.

"Come now," Aggachitta says to the two white-skinned monks. When Maggaphala reaches him, he tells him what Sumana said. Aggachitta then addresses the two white-skinned monks, "There are no cobras here. It's safe!"

"I saw one here the other day!" Sumana shouts back to him.

"He was probably just passing through. No cobras live here. Come!" Maggaphala shouts back.

Sumana doesn't want to disobey his teacher and so steels his nerves with the thought that if he is bitten by a cobra and dies, he'll have done so while having obeyed his teacher. This thought, which he believes should give him courage, fails to do so as he nervously makes his way through the brush.

Palaparuchi on the other hand refuses to join the others. He says, "I will confess my transgressions and listen to the patimokkha from here."

"That is not good enough!" Maggaphala says to him, half in jest.

"Then I am leaving!"

"Good!" Maggaphala replies.

Sumana is confused by what's going on. It's as though Maggaphala is trying to get rid of Palaparuchi.

"Sumana!" Palaparuchi calls to him, "I'll see you again at some other monastery!"

The three remaining bhikkhus stand in silence for a couple of minutes before Aggachitta and Maggaphala start speaking to each other in Sinhala. Sumana is surprised to see the meditation master chuckle, though it's much more subdued than Maggaphala's loud laugh.

Maggaphala then speaks to Sumana. "Venerable Aggachitta and I felt it necessary to purge ourselves of your friend before going through with the patimokkha. See, there really isn't any reason why we can't use another building on the hermitage grounds, except for the cave, as our sima, but we had to find a way to get Palaparuchi to leave and not partici-pate in our patimokkha ceremony, because he doesn't take the rules to heart."

"But," Sumana says as a way to defend his friend, though it comes out as an accusation directed at Maggaphala, "you also break some rules, such as eating after noon."

"That's due to physical illness. It's not of the same gravity. The rules he breaks are the ones that keep the sangha a worthy and venerable institution."

"Let's get out of here," Aggachitta says. "Just in case Sumana is right about the cobra."

"That was a brilliant touch," Maggaphala adds.

Aggachitta walks back to the monument, followed by Maggaphala and Sumana. They head back to the hermitage, passing the dining hut, where Maggaphala looks in on Gotami, assuring her that they'll be back in an hour.

Aggachitta leads them to his hut. Once inside, the three bhikkhus adjust their robes to cover both shoulders and then kneel next to each other on the floor.

Aggachitta says, "Maggaphala will confess to me, and then I to him. After that, Sumana will confess to me. Then I will recite the patimokkha."

Maggaphala and Aggachitta huddle close together on the floor. Maggaphala begins by telling Aggachitta his transgressions, in Sinhalese and Pali. Sumana can only make out the one about eating after noon. Aggachitta listens patiently. When Maggaphala is finished, Aggachitta recites the customary words of compassion for one's faults. Maggaphala listens to Aggachitta, who says only a couple of things Sumana can make out. Then it is Sumana's turn. He walks on his knees closer to Aggachitta, their bodies nearly touching. Sumana speaks slowly into Aggachitta's ear.

"I have been touched by a woman on the hand and foot, and have been alone with a woman, a different woman, but was not touched by her."

"Are these your only transgressions?" Aggachitta asks in a formal impersonal way.

"Yes, as far as I know."

"Then ask for compassion for all transgressions."

Sumana then recites the necessary words in Pali to request that his teacher have compassion for his transgressions. Aggachitta grants Sumana's request. He is sincerely compassionate toward him, which immediately sends waves of relief through Sumana's nerve-racked body.

Sumana then sits cross-legged with his hands clasped in reverence, as does Maggaphala, both facing Aggachitta. Aggachitta begins reciting the patimokkha by heart.

Sumana is thankful that the patimokkha is being recited in Pali, for whenever he hears it in English, he dreads whether he has committed one offense or another unknowingly. He has read the patimokkha once and consulted it on three occasions during the two years of his having become a fully ordained bhikkhu. At times like this, he wishes he had remained a samanera, for those first three years were far less stressful than the last two. Yet he believes that living according to the rules of the vinaya (which are in the patimokkha) is more conducive to the attainment of nibbana. The rules are much fewer for a samanera and there's no need to confess and endure the punishment of certain offenses. A significant part of his life would be easier if he returned to being a samanera. However, he would look like a failure, as if he'd broken a major rule and was stripped of the right to be a bhikkhu, rather than it being a choice to make his life as a monk less self-conscious.

As he continues to listen to Aggachitta recite one rule after another, not understanding any of the Pali, he fears he has broken many of them unwittingly, knowing that ignorance of a particular rule is not an excuse for breaking it. He has heard that a true bhikkhu is so aware that he does not break a single rule. That's the ideal. Some bhikkhus believe that by not breaking any of the rules a bhikkhu doesn't create karma and thus becomes like an arhat. To such bhikkhus, adhering to all of the rules flawlessly is as close to being fully liberated as a person can hope to get.

Aggachitta finishes reciting the entire patimokkha. He pauses for a moment to collect his thoughts and then addresses Sumana in English.

"The Buddha framed the rules in the patimokkha to meet situations that arose. He didn't compose it as the supreme set of rules to be followed in order to attain final liberation. The patimokkha was an afterthought, coming about in response to the behavior of certain bhikkhus and how they were perceived by the laity. What is important in all of this is that you're a good person, not some kind of perfect bhikkhu. The rules are meant to guide your intentions on how to do things without incurring blame and criticism, but if your intentions come from a heart filled with lust, ill-will, and conceit, then all the guidance the patimokkha gives still can't turn you into an arhat."

Aggachitta and Maggaphala rise and adjust their robes back to the one-shoulder-bared fold. Sumana does the same, following them out of the hut. Sumana now feels somehow better about himself. He can be a good person. Even Aggachitta is not perfect, Sumana thinks, considering the ruse he played on Palaparuchi. Then again, there probably was no other way to stop Palaparuchi from attending the patimokkha, as he would be obliged to come to it. If Aggachitta and Maggaphala had consulted him beforehand, he would have told them that all they had to do was wait another hour or so and Palaparuchi would have grown impatient and left of his own accord.

Aggachitta and Maggaphala walk towards the dining hut, while Sumana, feeling an urge to be alone, goes off to his hut. It occurs to him that Aggachitta may not be a true bhikkhu either. As this thought percolates, Sumana begins to like him more and more. He's a real human being after all.

CHAPTER
40

After the bhikkhus leave to conduct their private ceremony, Gotami decides to use the time for meditation. She's beginning to feel quite calm and peaceful when Maggaphala breaks her concentration by approaching her to tell her that they will be finished in less than an hour. His well-meaning intrusion annoys her and she can't get back into the calm state of mind she was enjoying. Instead, she begins thinking, which then leads to thinking a lot. She doesn't want to be thinking, but then she thinks she might as well let the thinking go on if that is what her mind wants to do.

At first, her thoughts don't seem productive. There's a desperation accompanied by a fear of loss and failure. The desperation hovers around her chest while the fear of loss lodges around her eyes. She tries to figure out how to prevent loss from happening again. As she projects into the future, she becomes more acutely aware of how she has now lost her lodgings, her prized living situation, which made being at the hermitage today possible. What else can she lose? She can lose the chance to be Aggachitta's student, lose her newfound friends, and forfeit what she came here to do in the first place. She could fail as a nun and have to return home, to the lay life, in shame.

She projects even further into the future, building upon the theme of returning home to the lay life. There she is, years from now, living an ordinary life in San Diego, going to school to become a schoolteacher, having to support herself with a part-time job, with no time to meditate. There is something comforting in this imaginary future: her life is her own. She doesn't have to please people in order to find a place to live. She can take care of herself, live as a private citizen, use money to secure lodgings and purchase food. That world seems stagnant, unable to sustain something in her that has been growing ever since she started meditating and became interested in Buddhism. She can't put a finger on what this something is that has drawn her to this island country, a life of renunciation, a forest hermitage where she believes her search for a teacher has ended.

What's her motivation? She recalls hearing this question prescribed by one of her previous Zen teachers. Is it to become awakened? If not, is it just to be a nun? That doesn't sound right to her. This is not a choice between two directions. She's sure she became a nun for the right reasons — to live the only life she's aware of that's conducive to finding true liberation of mind as the Buddha taught. She has faith in the Buddha. If he teaches that liberation is more naturally arrived at as a monk or nun, then that's what she must do.

This line of thinking directs her attention to the issue of faith. She hasn't considered that her choice to become a nun was motivated by faith in the Buddha. Faith feels good, but is it enough for her to commit to a whole life as a nun? She could end up wasting her life because of faith.

The feelings of desperation and loss have long evaporated in the flow of her thoughts, and so when her attention returns to her body, and then to her feelings, she notices that there's an excitement — an ardor in her heart — that's connected with this faith she has touched within herself. Faith is stimulating. It's far more energizing, much more nourishing than rational thought. If she'd relied on rational thinking, she'd never have chosen this way of life. All along, she has believed that her faith in the Buddha was somehow reasoned. Maybe instead of reason being the basis, it has been meditation —— the practice, as everyone seems to call it — that has supported and informed her decision. Her meditation practice is what gives her faith in the Buddha's teaching.

Now she has come full circle. She's here in Sri Lanka because of her faith-inspiring meditative experiences, which have led her to become a nun to purify her conduct and become worthy of receiving instruction from a meditation master who is nothing less than the Buddha who inspires her with faith.

She lets out a sigh. Her life makes sense again, which settles her mind, and for one brief interval, it seems to her that this life she calls her own, believed to be hers to make with it what she will, is nothing more than a temporary home.

Whereas Maggaphala sees white-skinned monks as embodiments of Henry V, he sees white-skinned nuns as Hamlet's Ophelia. She is sometimes considered weak because she commits suicide, but in truth, she's a strong female character, going against the wishes of her father in pursuit of Hamlet. Her heart is torn between filial and romantic love. Foreign nuns appear to be docile and compliant, while underneath they harbor an intense aggressiveness, a contradiction that he finds captivating. He can easily imagine them succumbing to madness.

On the way to the dining hut, Maggaphala relates to Aggachitta some of his observations and insights about Gotami, but he doesn't talk about her in this way, for these are his private thoughts, which he shares with no one. Instead, he tells his friend that she is highly motivated, intelligent, and dedicated to this way of life.

Aggachitta and Maggaphala both sit down on the bench and Gotami bows to both monks before sitting with her legs tucked under her on the ground.

Aggachitta asks, "What meditation practices have you done?"

Gotami pauses before she answers. "I have practiced vipassana and Zen."

Maggaphala chuckles at her response. Aggachitta becomes more stern and serious.

"There are many forms of vipassana," he says. "Which type of vipassana have you practiced?"

"Oh, now I see what you are asking," Gotami says, hoping her previous answer hasn't created a bad impression. "I have practiced noting, mindfulness of breathing, and body scanning. And last night I tried Sunlun Sayadaw's method of rapid breathing."

Aggachitta silently considers her reply for a few moments.

"Oh! And one more thing," she adds, "I just sat using the instruction you gave Sumana: the instruction to just sit."

"What happened when you tried it?" Aggachitta asks.

"I had a lot of thinking," she says.

"Well, that's to be expected. Through these other practices thinking has been suppressed. When you just sit, the mechanism of suppression no longer controls your sitting and the thoughts that were always there, always willing to come up, start to come into the foreground. What kind of thoughts were you having?"

Gotami is baffled by this question. No teacher has ever asked her what she was thinking about in a meditation sitting, and when she would volunteer such information, she was often told that her story was unimportant and what was important was whether she was aware of each breath, or noted every sensation and sense impression. The invitation to share her thoughts makes her uneasy as well; she doesn't know what is proper to reveal to one's teacher.

"I was planning."

"You were thinking about where you might stay?"

"No, not that kind of planning," she says, and then takes a deep breath, steeling herself to reveal more intimate details. "Maybe it wasn't planning. It was a mixture of past, present, and future." That is how vipassana teachers seem to like thoughts organized, though it really says nothing about what she was thinking. She now knows she's going to have to reveal what was actually going on in her mind. Can she do this without becoming emotional? Teachers don't like emotional female students. She makes a determination not to get emotional before she resumes.

"I thought about my faith in the Buddha."

"That's good, very good," Aggachitta says, and Maggaphala, sitting beside him and listening all the while, · nods and smiles at Gotami.

All right, it seems like these two bhikkhus are kind men and will not judge her harshly, so she trusts that she can speak openly and honestly.

"I was thinking about how I made the decision to pursue liberation because of my faith in the Buddha. I could have made other choices, such as finishing school and becoming a teacher, but I saw that way of life as leading to stagnation. That's only part of it. I believe that meditating under the guidance of the right teacher will bring about liberation of mind. But I only have my faith, and it's very lonely, not wholly satisfying, and I wonder if I'm strong enough for this."

She's on the verge of tears and so looks away from the two bhikkhus.

Maggaphala whispers something to Aggachitta who replies in Sinhala. Maggaphala then addresses her.

"You have nothing to be ashamed of," he says, and when she looks up at him, his eyes are moist as well, but not as wet as hers. "This is a hard life. The Buddha's teaching is a difficult path. All of us have felt the way you feel, but few have the courage to admit it. We choose this path out of faith, trusting in someone other than ourselves — the Buddha, our teachers, our fellow monks — only to find that such faith isn't enough to dispel all doubts about the practice, the path we've chosen."

Aggachitta contemplates that when it comes down to it, faith is the key, just as it is in any religion. Here, however, it is not faith in God, sacred scriptures, or holy men. It is faith in something that is possible for one to attain because someone once, long ago, attained it. What that something is, no one can know with just faith. To know it, to fully know and enter into nibbana, one must go beyond faith while still having faith. There's a passage from the *Magandiya Sutta* that he would like to quote here, but such an austere intellectual reference seems out of place right now.

"I'm not alone in this?" Gotami asks, exhibiting a childlike vulnerability.

"No, certainly not alone," Maggaphala says and then looks over at Aggachitta for his input.

"Oh, yes," Aggachitta says, aware of his friend's glance, "most yogis feel this way at one point or another in their practice."

"See!" Maggaphala says to Gotami.

Maggaphala and Gotami wait for Aggachitta to speak, as if he has some great wisdom to impart. This expectation irritates Aggachitta, for he really has no wisdom to impart here, and would rather just resume the interview by asking Gotami more questions about her meditation sittings.

"The thoughts you are having," Aggachitta begins, giving in halfway to their unspoken request, "are purposeful. They lead to a contemplation of the teaching and the path. They can give you an idea of what is in excess in your practice and what is deficient. You have excessive faith, which is quite understandable, and you are deficient in the other four faculties."

"What are the other four faculties?" Gotami asks, wiping her eyes, her emotional period over and done with for now.

"They are awareness, tranquility, effort, and wisdom."

"What am I lacking in most?" she asks.

"That's hard to say," Aggachitta replies, wishing he hadn't gone into the five faculties with her. He can't seem to help it. It occurs to him that this view of meditation — trying to get these five faculties to be in some kind of harmony — is markedly formulaic and simplistic. What other approach can he use? Just two days ago, when thinking about how he told Sumana about the five faculties, he came up with another, more sensible way of going about this. What was it? Why didn't he write it down? He now recalls that it had something to do with listening closely to what a student says about her meditative experiences instead of interpreting them according to a conceptual model.

"I need to know more about your sittings before I make such an assessment. Besides, the five faculties are just handy measuring tools. You can do this practice without bothering to take measurements."

"I don't understand," Gotami says.

"Rather than focusing on where you are in your meditation practice by trying to ascertain how much faith or courage or wisdom is in it, let's just focus on what is actually happening when you meditate. Instead of measuring, which only indicates a quantity, we should be describing, which reveals far more of the quality of your meditation practice."

"Oh, I see," she says. "It's something like *Zen and the Art of Motorcycle Maintenance*."

Aggachitta and Maggaphala do not know what to make of this reference, never having heard of it.

"I don't know what you mean," Maggaphala says.

"Oh, you never read the book," Gotami says.

"No, I didn't know there was such a book."

"It is about Greek philosophy and how we've gone in the direction of quantifying experience and have ignored the insights that can be gained from seeing the quality of experience."

"That sounds like a fascinating thesis," Aggachitta says, distracted for the moment by thinking of the difference between these two lines of thinking.

"It helped me a lot," Gotami says, "except the story of the guy who wrote it is really tragic and depressing. All his thinking in the book just ended up making him insane."

"Thinking can do that," Aggachitta says, somewhat absent-mindedly as he goes through his memories of studying Greek philosophy, searching for quotes that corroborate this Western author's ideas. In this recollection, he comes upon what he believes makes Greek philosophy wholly different from Buddhist philosophy. The Greeks focused on the external world, trying to understand its laws, and then brought their attention to the human world. For the purpose of liberating the mind, the Buddha stressed understanding the laws of consciousness, not of matter. Somewhere in the history of Buddhist philosophy, however, the laws of the internal world were embellished to apply to the external world. It's as if the Buddha's teaching was westernized by Greek philosophy early on and has to this day been adapted to Western views, theories, and discoveries. The notion that all this quantifying in Buddhism may come from the Greeks is somehow comforting. It means that all the measuring, comparing, and concretizing in Theravada Buddhism could be weeded out, and something closer to the original intent of the Buddha could be cultivated in its place.

"Venerable Aggachitta," Maggaphala says to him, aware that his friend has been silent for a couple of minutes.

"Oh, yes, where were we?" Aggachitta says, wrenching his attention free from his compelling thoughts.

"You were asking me to describe my experiences," Gotami says.

"Yes, let's begin doing that tomorrow," Aggachitta says, feeling a great need to be in his hut writing down his thoughts.

"But where will I stay?"

"I have a place for you," Aggachitta replies. "It's the home of a laywoman. No one else lives there as far as I know. She's a former student of mine, when I was a teacher of Buddhist philosophy at the University. Currently she works as a psychiatrist for the regional hospital. Her name is Lily Perrera. She's Dr. Perrera's sister."

"Where does she live?"

"If Rahula were here, I would have him take you there. Perhaps Venerable Maggaphala can show you the house. It's not far from the monastery in town."

"I'm sorry," Maggaphala says, "but I must take my afternoon nap."

"I can find it on my own," Gotami says. "Just write down directions, please. And could you also write me a letter of recommendation?"

Aggachitta feels put upon by her requests, for if he were to write anything, he would prefer to write down his more profound thoughts. However, he feels an obligation to her, and so gets up and goes to his hut, telling her that he shall return shortly with her letter. Maggaphala also rises and says good-bye to her, heading off in the direction of the cave.

Gotami is left alone with her thoughts, but not for long.

Sumana enters the dining area to find Gotami sitting alone on the ground, with her head bent, her eyes staring at the uneven earth under the bench. Sumana goes over to the bench and sits down, accidentally placing his feet in her line of vision. When she looks up at him, he can see that she's been crying. He wants to know what happened, but is afraid to ask. It may be too presumptuous of him. They only met yesterday.

Gotami is the first one to speak.

"I just had my first interview with Venerable Aggachitta."

"How did it go?" Sumana asks.

"It went well. He's different than I expected."

"Yeah, he surprised me too."

"Why, what did he say to you?" she asks, before remembering the unspoken rule that you never ask another student what the teacher has said to him. Because, if you do, you might hear an instruction that is too advanced for you or you may begin to compare yourself with others.

"He talked about the five faculties, how I lacked awareness and effort and needed to build up those faculties."

"He mentioned the faculties to me too. He only said that my faith was high."

"He said my samadhi was high," Sumana chimes in.

"What did he tell you to do? I mean, what instructions did he give you?"

"Nothing new. That was all he said."

"He didn't give me anything new either."

They both sit silently pursuing their own thoughts. Perhaps Aggachitta is a great meditation master, but not such a great teacher, Gotami muses. Sumana wonders whether

Aggachitta is an arhat or not. If he is, then he may not be one who can teach. It may better for him not to be an arhat, but a partially liberated monk who can teach others.

"Maybe he only gives more advanced instructions after the first week or so," Sumana says, "and he's waiting for us to show our commitment and determination in the practice."

"You're probably right," she says, smiling up at him, relieved at his interpretation of the situation.

"Did he find you a place to stay?" Sumana asks, hopeful that he has, for he grows fonder of her by the minute.

"I can stay at the home of a laywoman. A psychiatrist," she answers.

"That's handy," Sumana replies.

"What?"

"In case you go crazy," Sumana says, thinking of his friend Palaparuchi. "It does happen. You know, Palaparuchi wasn't always like he is now. I think intensive meditation practice, and living as a bhikkhu for so long, did it to him."

"That's not what Maggaphala says," Gotami says.

"Why, what does he know about Palaparuchi's past?"

"Just that his teacher told Palaparuchi that he was a sotapanna and from then on he has suffered from delusions."

"Oh, I didn't know that."

"I had no idea until Maggaphala said that some vipassana teachers, even highly venerated monks, tell their students they've become a sotapanna when they really haven't. Did you know that?"

Sumana swallows slowly, anxious about what he might say. He can't lie to her, but he also can't reveal that his teacher told him he is a sotapanna. He wants her to see him as an open and honest person, someone she can trust, but he can't bring himself to disclose anything about his own experience. He can generalize about the experiences of others however.

"I've been aware of it. It's not all deception. Some people who are told actually have attained."

"How do you know that? Venerable Maggaphala says it is not possible for another person to tell if someone has attained or not."

"I'm not sure," Sumana says, withholding what little he has heard on the subject. "Perhaps you have to ask someone like Venerable Aggachitta that question. I'm sure he knows."

"I hope so," she says, thinking ahead to when she may be near the end of her training and in need of someone to confirm whether she is a sotapanna or not.

"I hope so too," Sumana concurs, projecting into the future where he imagines himself approaching Venerable Aggachitta with a particular meditative experience that he believes to be nibbana.

They sit in silence waiting for Aggachitta to return. When Aggachitta finally returns to the dining hut, he finds Sumana and Gotami sitting with their eyes closed. They look so peaceful and innocent to the middle-aged monk that he stops to consider how it has come to be that he has two earnest students at the same time. It's never happened to him before.

CHAPTER
41

Sumana opens his eyes and sees Aggachitta standing and looking down at him. He stands up and offers the bench to Aggachitta. Gotami also opens her eyes, but remains seated on the ground. Aggachitta approaches her first and hands her a folded up piece of paper. She takes the piece of paper and unfolds it. Aggachitta sits down on the bench and Sumana sits on the ground in front of him, next to Gotami, who jumps to her feet.

Gotami walks outside the dining hut into the sunlight to read what Aggachitta has written. One question after another pops into her head about his directions, but she restrains herself from asking him anything. She's happy enough to have this piece of paper. It's like a passport, and she folds it up and puts it in a special inner pocket next to her real passport. Aggachitta remarks that he will see her tomorrow. She affirms that she will come back then. Then she bows once to Sumana and once again to Aggachitta before departing.

Aggachitta looks across at Sumana and says, "We didn't get a chance to talk yesterday. I hope you meditated all right without our interview. Shall we begin with yesterday's sittings?"

Sumana considers Aggachitta's request for a moment. He hasn't reviewed his sittings from yesterday, and as he recalls, there were only two sittings, one with Palaparuchi and one without. Does he want to go through all the work to rehash these old sittings? What is the use of that? Instead, he wants to ask Aggachitta some questions of his own.

"Venerable Aggachitta," Sumana begins, "I wonder if I could ask you a question first."

"I may not be able to answer it until I hear your sittings," Aggachitta replies.

"It's a general question about meditation. I don't think it has anything to do with my sittings."

"Well then, what is it?"

"You believe very much in the instruction to just sit. Where does this instruction lead? How does purification — liberation of mind — come about by just sitting? I mean, the instructions other teachers have given me I could see leading somewhere, but this seems to lead nowhere."

Aggachitta takes Sumana's questions seriously. The instruction to just sit is extremely passive. That is the beauty of it. There is minimal intention in it. He could just say that, though that's not what Sumana is looking for. What is Sumana looking for?

Aggachitta says, "You seem to want meditation to lead you somewhere."

"Yes, of course, everybody does," Sumana says.

"That's how it's mostly taught," Aggachitta says, "as a means toward a particular end. The instruction to just sit is not a means to an end. It's a beginning that is at first a metaphor for an end and then slowly becomes its own end. At least it's not a harmful instruction, a purely theoretical instruction, or a perfectly meaningless instruction. It's a real meditation instruction, based on the one truth of meditation: the body sits and the mind moves. When the mind sits still, an end has been reached, the stilling of all activities."

"But, if I may disagree," Sumana says, not clear as to why he's taking this risk, "I have much more thinking when I meditate this way."

"But has your mind found stillness?"

Sumana pauses to reflect on his sittings before answering.

"Today, while I was meditating lying down," Sumana relates, "I had a moment when all inner conflict stopped. My mind was still then."

"That's good," Aggachitta says, smiling. "You knew inner peace through the absence of inner turmoil. That's very good indeed. What other kinds of things have you understood in your sittings?"

Sumana doesn't like to be asked questions about what he's understood. They always seem like trick questions, inviting wrong or inadequate answers. He wishes Aggachitta would just ask him to talk about experiences he has had, not understandings. He fishes around in his memory of meditation sittings for something he has understood.

"In that same sitting," he begins, "I was thinking about being born with sadness, how sadness has always been with me, coming before there was a self to feel sad."

"That's interesting," Aggachitta says. "Did that come before the understanding of inner peace?"

"Yes," Sumana replies.

Aggachitta makes a familiar association of suffering preceding a moment of freedom from suffering, which can be interpreted as a glimpse of nibbana and thus an attainment of path and fruit. Not that he thinks such a thing has happened to Sumana, but it's still possible for him to think this way even though he has thoroughly broken down the concepts supporting this interpretation. What he's missing now is some way of seeing understandings in meditation that would replace this old formulaic way of thinking. It dawns on him that it doesn't matter what he thinks about Sumana's understandings. These are personal experiences to be examined and penetrated by the person who has them, not by someone else who thinks he knows what they are.

Aggachitta asks, "I would like to know if these understandings have had any effect on you since then?"

Sumana shrugs. "Not that I can tell."

"They don't provide a key for further investigation?"

"I don't know what you are asking."

"I'm not sure myself," Aggachitta admits.

Sumana doesn't like hearing that Aggachitta isn't sure about something he's asking about. It makes Sumana feel like an idiot.

"What I meant was this," Aggachitta backpedals. "Your mind could have taken these understandings further, either in the sitting or outside of the sitting."

"To be honest, I forgot what I'd understood until just now."

"At least you are conscious of that now."

"But what good does that do?"

Aggachitta replies, "Being conscious of one's mind is like just sitting. It's good in itself, even if you don't see it leading anywhere."

"Is it like being mindful?"

"It's what is meant by being mindful."

They sit in silence for a moment. Maggaphala, who has just arisen from a short nap, enters the dining hut for a cup of tea.

Maggaphala lights the kerosene stove. He looks over at Aggachitta and Sumana and says, "Please don't let me disturb you. Would you like a cup of tea?"

"Yes, please," Sumana says.

"Well, where were we?" Aggachitta says to Sumana as an invitation to pick up where they left off.

"You were telling me what mindfulness is. I would like to hear more."

"Let's start by not translating *sati* as mindfulness. Sati actually means memory, recollection, calling back to mind, not mindfulness. Recollection is foremost an act of becoming more conscious. What is the difference between the two, you ask? Being mindful does mean being conscious, but only within a limited, specific range of awareness. One is mindful of something, such as one's speech, the feelings of others, or of doing right or wrong. Being mindful is thus a kind of focused attention that suppresses unwanted elements, so that one can then act in a wholesome manner."

Maggaphala interrupts. "That sounds in accordance with the Buddha's teaching on good conduct and right effort. I don't see what's wrong with it."

"It's phony," Aggachitta says, surprised at his choice of words. "A person who practices mindfulness in this way tries to become what he is not by suppressing and disavowing what he has become. He becomes mindful of the feelings of others so as not to hurt their feelings and thus be liked by them. If he were truly conscious of his own feelings, he'd learn that he can't act only in ways that don't hurt others' feelings. A conscious person hurts others and himself, learning from those experiences how hurtful thoughts, speech, and actions come about and create misery in this world for one's self and others."

"You're saying that the conscious person acts without being mindful at times, learning from those lapses through recalling them back to mind," Maggaphala says.

"In a way, that's what I'm saying. A conscious person is not always mindful in the present moment, for to be mindful is to be false. A conscious person doesn't hide from himself. He knows the imperfections within him. He knows how they arise and what conditions support and feed them. He knows the actions that come from them and the harm they cause. He knows the suffering inherent in selfishness, in pride, in all unwholesome states, and he doesn't simply disavow them, but owns them as the very activities that tie him to samsara. A conscious person knows the bonds of the world. A fully conscious person knows how to break those bonds."

"But, but," Sumana stammers, "isn't being mindful a good practice?"

"Mindfulness, as it is practiced, is good for one thing. It creates order. One can meditate without difficulty in an orderly world. Now can one see deeply within oneself and penetrate the truths of existence in an orderly world? I ask you, can one who isn't conscious of being trapped, knowing there's no conceivable way of escape, find the imperative within himself to become fully liberated? While those dedicated to mindfulness note and note, those dedicated to finding liberation become conscious of what keeps them mired in samsara and seek the proper means to abandon it."

"Well said! Well said!" Maggaphala chimes in. "Would anyone like tea? It's ready!"

Maggaphala brings a cup of tea for his friend and superior, Aggachitta, along with his own cup, over to the bench, handing both of them to Aggachitta so that he can sit down. Sumana gets up, goes over to the stove, and pours himself a cup of tea. He then takes his cup of tea to his hut, where he can enjoy it in solitude.

Maggaphala turns to Aggachitta. "If you feel so strongly about how mindfulness is construed in the Burmese method, I wonder if you share some of my feelings on the questionable practices of some vipassana teachers in that tradition."

"I do not know what you mean."

"I'm referring to the progressive stages of knowledge that supposedly lead to attaining the path and the fruit and how that system has led to teachers declaring students to be sotapannas when they can't possibly be."

"Are these your ideas?" Aggachitta asks.

"I'm not the only one who thinks this way, if that's what you're asking."

"No, I'm just curious how you know for a fact that those vipassana teachers you speak of are mistaken."

"By getting to know people who've been told they've attained."

"So your method is to observe those you believe were told they had attained and find out things about them that inform you that they have not attained?"

"Yes, that is what I have done."

Aggachitta says, "I don't know how reliable that is. One's own biases can easily enter into such observation."

Maggaphala replies defensively, "But I'm referring only to those people who are obviously mistaken about their attainment, such as that white-skinned monk who was here earlier."

"Well, in that case your method applies," Aggachitta admits without reservation. "But what about a more difficult case, where a person is told he has attained and for all appearances has undergone a vast transformation, which in many respects tallies with what the Buddha says about a sotapanna?"

"You're right in that kind of instance. My type of observation would probably not be of much use. Then what do you suggest?"

Aggachitta replies, "My way of looking at this is different. I have a philosophical bent, though at times I am a bit of an empiricist. Anyway, I would put the person to a test on the Buddha's philosophy as long as everything else lines up — his character is good, his mind clear and concentrated, and he's a conscious, well-intentioned individual."

"What kind of test would this be — multiple-choice, single-word answers, essays? How would you go about it?" Maggaphala asks, half-jokingly.

Aggachitta is wholly serious. He says, "I'd ask the person who believes he has attained the first path and fruit what his understanding of the Buddha's teaching is."

"Say he hasn't studied any Buddhist philosophy? Many of those told they have attained know very little about the Buddha's teaching."

"Then I'd keep the inquiry focused on the basic questions regarding the nature of existence," Aggachitta replies.

"But then, couldn't someone just happen to answer questions about existence as though he's attained the understanding of a sotapanna without having really attained it? Doesn't your approach give too much weight to the intellect and not enough to what the person has cultivated within himself through his practice?"

Aggachitta thinks a moment, agreeing with his friend as he does. There's really no way around this issue — no way to prove whether someone is a sotapanna or not. The progression of knowledges, which vipassana teachers rely on as the way to ascertain whether someone has become a sotapanna, is so remarkably elegant and convincing, it's no wonder they use it. All the teacher has to do is ask the meditator certain questions at each interview, and judging by the responses to these questions, he can pass the student through to the next stage of knowledge or keep her in that stage until she delivers a correct answer to the questions of that particular stage. The teacher then can mark her progress through the various stages, pushing her ahead or holding her back, until the day comes when the she reports to the teacher an experience which can be interpreted as the path and the fruit.

"You know, dear friend, there's a great deal to be said in favor of the system of knowledges in this regard," Aggachitta says.

"Oh?"

"It provides a clear and easy-to-apply model to assess a student's progress. If only it were not an illusion."

"What's left then?" Maggaphala asks.

"There is really only one way to know if one has known nibbana."

"And what is that?"

"One recognizes one has known nibbana through honest and thorough self-examination." Aggachitta pauses for a moment to let another train of thought into his response. "Nibbana is not one's concept of it, one's feeling of it, or one sensing of it. So how is it known?" He pauses again. "It is known without holding onto views."

Maggaphala is puzzled by this last remark; he was expecting something different. But he's willing to consider what his friend has said, even though it confuses him. He clasps his hands in respect to the meditation master, signaling the end of this auspicious meeting.

CHAPTER
42

Gotami follows Aggachitta's written directions as best she can. He seems not to know street names, but has a good memory for landmarks, even though they're odd ones. Aggachitta considers the coffin shop a landmark for the street she's to turn right on, and after that, a papaya tree as the landmark for the house Dr. Lily Perrera lives in. The house is quite a landmark in itself — the largest house Gotami has seen in this town. It's white, three-storied, with a cement deck on the second storey. It has what looks like a separate guest house with its own stairs on the third floor. Gotami is delighted by the size of the house. When she goes through the gate and past the garden, she hopes that it's the right house, for she can already picture herself living here.

She knocks on the door and notes that the porch is also quite pleasant and roomy — she can even imagine herself meditating there. A young woman opens the door and politely invites her into the house without asking her name or why she is here.

"Dr. Perrera will be with you shortly," the young woman says in English.

Gotami waits standing in the hallway. She looks at the pictures in frames on the walls. Some are photos of Buddhist statues and holy places, while others are reproductions of European paintings. There are no family pictures.

Dr. Lily Perrera enters the hallway from what appears to be a large library. She is a tall thin woman in her late forties. She wears slacks and a blouse, and her thin black hair is tied in a bun around the crown of her head. She smiles at Gotami with a full set of white teeth.

"My brother called to tell me he met you at the hermitage and hinted that I might be seeing you. You need a place to live, don't you?"

"Why, yes, how did your brother know?"

"He said you wouldn't last long with Mrs. Jayatilaka and her nun.'"

"He saw that?"

"Anyone could see that," Lily says. "I'm surprised you lasted as long as you did with those two women."

Gotami wonders what these Dr. Perreras know that she doesn't. Do they have inside knowledge on everyone in this town? Venerable Aggachitta did say that she's a psychiatrist. Maybe that's how. She hears everyone's secrets.

"Come and join me for tea," Lily says to her, and then asks the servant to prepare tea for them.

They go into the living room where there are three large white sofas positioned around the fireplace, with a square glass coffee table in the middle. The sofas, the other furniture, and the whole decor of the living room strike Gotami as being affluent for Sri Lanka, but middle-class for San Diego.

Gotami sits down across from the fireplace and Lily sits down on the sofa to her right.

"Please tell me something about your life," Lily says.

"First," Gotami says, "Can I ask about staying here?"

"You're welcome to stay here as long as you like."

"Where will I be staying?"

"You can have the upstairs cottage," Lily replies. "Do you want to see it?"

Gotami is so overjoyed that she will be staying in the cute guest house she saw that she does not have the breath to answer just yet.

Lily can see the elation on the young woman's face, and says, "After tea I'll take you up to your room. It has its own bathroom and a small kitchen."

Tea arrives on a tray in a formal porcelain tea set. There's also a selection of cookies and pastries, which tempt Gotami, though she restrains herself from having any, not wanting to break the vow of not eating after noon.

Lily pours her a cup of tea. The two women each take a sip and then set their cups down on the saucers placed on the glass table in front of them.

"So," Lily says, "you're an American who has become a nun in Sri Lanka. Tell me a little about yourself. I'd like us to get acquainted since you will be living here."

Gotami says, "I've only been a nun for a few months. I studied with Venerable Ananda, and now Venerable Aggachitta is my teacher."

"That's wonderful!" Lily exclaims, smiling and touching Gotami lightly on the knee. "He was my professor when I was an undergraduate. Back then he was quite the scholar. I wonder what he is like as a monk."

"Haven't you seen him?" Gotami asks.

"No, no, that wouldn't be proper," Lily says.

Gotami wonders what she means by not being proper, and would like to ask her that, but she fears the question would be construed as disrespectful. Fortunately, Lily chooses to elaborate.

"Before he went to Burma, he was a different man. He had no intention of becoming a monk. I doubt the thought ever crossed his mind, especially since he looked down on monks for being mostly ignorant of philosophy. He was a dynamic speaker, truly impassioned. You could feel the ardor in his words. We met often and talked about his ideas. But that's all in the past."

Lily's body tenses up and Gotami senses she's about to cry. But she holds herself back and refills her cup of tea absent-mindedly, spilling some on the saucer below.

"Well, that's my story," Lily says, wiping her face with a handkerchief. "Now, why don't you tell me yours?"

Rahula says good-bye to Devi at the central bus stand for
Colombo, which is in an area known as Pettah. Their families
take separate minibuses home. Rahula lives near the coast in a
section of Colombo called Bambalapitiya, while Devi lives only
a mile from Pettah. Their parents have agreed to meet and talk
about the young couple, while the young couple has made a
secret agreement to meet at the Pettah bus stand again at seven
the next morning.

Having finally separated himself from Devi, Rahula can
think more independently about his situation. His parents'
attention is taken up with his sisters, who are tired and cranky
after two long bus rides and their journey to the forest
hermitage. Only Rahula seems awake, though he wishes he
could somehow go off into a sleep that would obliterate the
events of the last twenty-four hours, from which he would
wake up back in the cave at the hermitage. He didn't anticipate
that he would feel such loss at leaving his uncle's hermitage.
He's surprised at himself for thinking of the hermitage as his
home. And when his thoughts go out into the future and hover
around the plan to elope the next day, he feels a stranglehold
around his chest and a swell of anxiety. So he tries not to think
about it, telling himself that he must keep his word to her and
just go along with the plan.

When they arrive at their second-storey apartment,
Rahula's mother immediately gets to work putting together
some food for dinner. Rahula's oldest sister helps her while the
other two go to their room for a nap. This leaves Rahula alone
with his father. They sit in the living room, his father on the
couch and Rahula in a padded chair. His father has not said
much to him after their conversation at the hermitage, and
Rahula wonders what his father truly thinks of his situation.

"Well son," his father says, "I hope this is what you want."

"It's not so bad," Rahula says, trying to get his father to
say more about what he thinks.

"It is not exactly what I had in mind for you," his father
says. "Marrying this young woman complicates everything. I
waited until I graduated and became a teacher before I

married your mother. We could have married younger, but we waited. We wanted to pursue our individual career choices before having children. What's wrong with that?"

Rahula considers what he's being asked, taking it more as an abstract question than one that pertains directly to him, as he has no thought of having children any time soon.

"It's a good idea," Rahula says, "but what would you want me to do?"

Rahula's father likes it when is son defers to him and asks for advice in this way. It makes him feel like he is being a true father.

"I want you to take things slowly. Don't get her pregnant. Go to university and study hard and earn your degree first. Then, if she's still the one you want to marry, go ahead and marry her."

"Wouldn't I be deceiving her then?"

"No, no, you misunderstand."

"I can't break my word,"

"You have the right to change your mind," Rahula's father replies. "You can decide to do anything with your life. That's how we raised you. You can choose whatever you would like to study as your career. We're modern parents. You can also choose the woman you would like to marry."

Being told that he can make all these choices on his own when he feels incapable of doing so, coupled with not wanting to make a choice that his parents would disapprove of, makes it very uncomfortable for Rahula to listen to his father right now. His father has never told him he has the freedom to choose a way of life that is unacceptable to both of his parents. He can't tell them of a choice he would make that they would not like and so could only conceive of acting on such a choice behind their backs. That's where eloping with Devi comes in, as well as another choice that is dimly edging its way into the foreground of his consciousness.

"The trouble is," Rahula says, being as honest and blunt as he is able to with his father, "I don't know what to choose."

"That's what I am here for," his father says. "I will help you choose."

Rahula sighs and becomes silent. He realizes that he will lose if he allows his father to choose for him. His father's philosophy is right, to a degree. Rahula knows he must come to a decision himself, but he needs something, some kind of self-knowledge he does not yet possess to make that decision. Where will such knowledge come from?

Rahula excuses himself and goes off to his bedroom. Instead of lying down, he decides to sit in meditation. He wishes he'd meditated more often at the hermitage so he would know how to do it better when he needs it. Like right now. Seated on the cool hard floor, he folds his legs, places his left hand in his lap and his right hand on top of it, and closes his eyes.

His mind is first receptive to memories of the day, then of the day before, and the day before that, going sequentially backwards in time. His attention grabs hold of the conversation he had with his uncle regarding making a choice about his life and he remembers how the choice to follow in his uncle's path came into the conversation. He begins to wonder what his life would be like if he decided to become a monk.

He can't visualize himself with a shaven head and so drops that contemplation. He puts his attention back on his body sitting, as his uncle has instructed him to do, and feels the beating of his heart. His heartbeat slows down as he focuses on it, as does his breathing, and he becomes noticeably calmer. An orange light forms somewhere in front of him and simultaneously he hears the sounds of plates being set down on the kitchen table not far from his small bedroom. The plates have a ringing sound when placed on the wooden table. The ringing is of a very high pitch, adding ripples to the orange light in his mind. The light is not rippling, he realizes, but rather, his mind is made up of these ripples visible in the orange light. All of a sudden, he sees a picture of himself, dressed in orange, with his head shaven. "That's it!" He hears a voice within him exclaim. He opens his eyes, exhilarated, full of energy, knowing exactly what he is going to do with his life.

Palaparuchi also traveled to Bambalapitiya, finding lodgings at a monastery not far from Rahula's house. During his bus ride to Colombo, Palaparuchi worked on elaborate fantasies based on his short stay at the hermitage. He has these fictions in his mind when he goes up to the head monk of the temple to offer his respects. He tells this monk, whom he barely knows, a couple of things about his adventures in the forest, such as meeting a real live arhat.

"There are no arhats," the head monk replies.

"He's an arhat, I am sure of it," Palaparuchi replies, trying to be convincing.

"We better not talk about such things," the head monk says. "You can sleep in the room at the end of the hall on your right."

Palaparuchi rises and gets his duffle bag, carrying it on his shoulder down the hall to his room. It's a private room next to the toilets. That's why it's empty. Palaparuchi is at first dismayed by this lack of respect, but soon recovers his sense of enthusiasm as he unpacks his belongings and spreads them out on the bed. He takes inventory of what he has and makes a mental note of what he needs. When he's finished going through his possessions, he decides to take a walk through the monastery and see who the other monks are, and possibly gain access to the room where all the gifts are stored, so that he can stock up on missing essentials.

He finds the other monks gathered together for their evening ritual of chanting and offering flowers to the Buddha statue. There are some laypeople dressed in white, left over from the uposatha day crowd, sitting in the back rows behind the monks, reciting the suttas along with them. Palaparuchi makes his way through the laypeople sitting on the ground to where the monks are and sits down near a group of teenage monks.

Palaparuchi clasps his hands in front of his chest and joins in the chanting. He mumbles the words, not knowing the suttas well enough to keep up with the others. He feels nothing and becomes aware of how he's just going through the motions.

He thinks that everyone here is just going through the motions and that no one has genuine feelings for the Buddha, the dharma, and the sangha. They are all chanting these suttas without comprehension, doing it mechanically in a sing-a-long fashion. This emptiness within, this apathy, this lack of devotional spirit, this deadness of soul is not something that he takes as a sign of enlightenment, for it is not an energizing state of mind, but rather a depressive one. When he is aware of depression like this, he feels compelled to change his state of mind. He gets up and walks out of the room.

Palaparuchi continues walking, going out the front door of the monastery, down the front steps and out onto the sidewalk. Monks are rarely ever seen walking around at night, as it's not considered proper, and there may even be a rule about it. Palaparuchi doesn't care about how he appears or if he's breaking some obscure, senseless rule. He only cares about eliminating the sad, dead feeling. The only way he knows how to do this, at least temporarily, is to find a situation — one that involves another person who can play along — and build an energetic self-sustaining fantasy world around that situation.

He goes out into the street and walks down towards Galle Road, the highway that runs along the coast, which is a bustling business district. He submerges himself in the crowds of people on the sidewalks, walking past street vendors and shop fronts, careful not to step on any beggars sitting on the cement with aluminum cups in their hands, asking him, a bhikkhu, for small coins.

"Don't you know I can't handle money?" Palaparuchi shouts in Sinhala at one of them, and continues on his journey down the strip southwards toward the Mt. Lavinia Hotel. His actual destination isn't the hotel, but that's as far as he's willing to walk before he finds what he's looking for. There are many distractions offered for the ordinary person on this boulevard, such as movies, restaurants, bars, and dance clubs, but nothing for him. What would be a suitable distraction, a possible entertainment, for a monk? He looks around at the nightlife on the streets and notices a man standing on a box talking at the top of his lungs to a small group of people standing around him. It strikes him that this would be an entertaining thing to do. He looks around him to see if there's something to stand on, a platform or a bench that would raise him above the crowd. He spots a store that's closed with steps leading up to it, and decides to make that his soapbox.

He starts shouting in Sinhala about the wiles of Mara, the greatness of the Buddha and living arhats, and extols the restraint of the monks' life, sounding like some sort of evangelical preacher, for that is how he pictures himself. Only a few passersby can understand his Sinhala. Soon his vocabulary and grammar begin to fail the expansiveness of his thoughts, so he shifts to English, shouting at the top of his lungs, grabbing the attention of many onlookers, and soon, much to his surprise, two police officers approach him and take him by the arms off the steps. Palaparuchi imagines they are protecting him from a bomb that is about to explode in the shop behind him.

Hours later, he wakes up in a hospital ward. His wrists and ankles are tied to the bed frame. He struggles for a moment, and then relaxes as he remembers this hospital from before. He recalls that they treated him well here, and last time he had a lot of fun during the first half of his stay. A mischievous chuckle takes hold of him, and, before it fades away altogether, another fantasy life arises from up within him, one that will not only fill his time in the psychiatric ward, but most likely will also extend his stay indefinitely.

Rahula rises before dawn after a long and peaceful night's sleep. His bag is still packed from the hermitage. He turns on a lamp and writes his father a note, saying that he has made his own choice, he will contact them, and they should not worry about him. He makes his way quietly through the apartment's living room and out the front door.

The air is cool. Rahula has always liked early morning best in Colombo. Some of the street lamps are still burning. There are very few people out at this hour, and few cars on the streets. He passes by the neighborhood monastery on his way to Galle Road to catch a bus to Pettah. He's half-tempted to step inside and say hello to the monks, stopping at the steps to the front door. Then he realizes that if he stops there, he may be late.

Rahula arrives at Pettah just before seven in the morning. The bus station is beginning to get active, with vendors setting up and a few buses arriving. He purchases his ticket, and then walks around the station looking for Devi, not seeing her anywhere. He goes over to where the bus to Kandy is supposed to leave from and keeps an eye out for her.

One bus comes, is boarded by the passengers around him, and leaves without him. She still has not come. To distract himself from waiting he goes inside the bus station to check on the time and get something to eat. It is seven-thirty. He gets a small bag of fried cashews and eats them one at a time as he walks back to where he is supposed to meet her. A bus has pulled in and is already boarding passengers.

As he waits for her, chewing the last of his cashews, out of the corner of his eye, a man who he vaguely recognizes approaches him. It is Devi's father, Hari Lal.

Hari Lal stops in front of Rahula. He looks angry, which frightens Rahula.

"She said you were to meet here and elope," he says.

Rahula, too frightened to speak, shakes his head in confirmation.

"You are not honorable!" Hari Lal accuses Rahula. "After what we agreed on yesterday, you would take my daughter from me without asking for my permission?"

"I, I, I'm innocent!" Rahula finally blurts out.

"What are you innocent of? Of stealing my daughter, betraying my trust? What is it that makes you innocent?"

"I changed my mind," Rahula says.

Hari Lal is thrown off guard by this remark. The young man isn't making any sense.

"Last night," Rahula explains, "I saw my future clearly. I'm going to become a samanera. I am returning to my uncle's hermitage."

"You're deserting my daughter!" Hari Lal exclaims.

"Isn't that what you want?" Rahula lamely asks.

"No, no, you have me all wrong," he says. "I object to your eloping with Devi, not to your being engaged to her. When I caught her trying to sneak out this morning with a suitcase and an overnight bag, I knew what was afoot without having to ask her. I came down here to give you a piece of my mind. I was outraged that the both of you would lie to us and try to sneak away behind our backs."

"You're right," Rahula admits. "It's a shameful way to behave."

"She's going to be furious!" Hari Lal says.

"Are you going to tell her for me?" Rahula asks, dreading the prospect of doing it himself.

"You better do that yourself. Come with me. She's at home. Afterwards, do whatever you must. I assume you have informed your parents of your plans."

Rahula follows Hari Lal out of the bus station. Hari Lal hails a taxi and they sit in the back seat together.

As Rahula sits in the cab, he thinks about his current predicament. It reminds him of *The Woman in the Dunes*. The man just can't find a way out. When he thinks he has a strategy that will work, it always fails and he's back with the woman. Rahula wishes that he'd finished the book before leaving the hermitage. He only knows that the man is never seen again in the outside world. But, what happens to him in the world of the dunes? Does he still live there with the woman or does he kill himself? Those are the only endings he can imagine.

They arrive at Hari Lal's house, which is a small single-storey house on a quiet side street. They get out of the cab. Hari Lal pays the driver and then walks up to the front door with Rahula behind him. Devi's mother is standing behind the screen door, throwing it open for her husband and Rahula to enter. The door opens directly onto the living room, which is small and square with one couch and a few straight-backed wooden chairs.

Devi is sitting on the couch sobbing. She looks up at Rahula as he enters. He keeps his eyes lowered and sits down in the chair furthest from her. Hari Lal and his wife sit down on two chairs directly in front of their daughter.

Hari Lal says, "Rahula has something to tell you."

Rahula is suddenly terrified. He doesn't like being put on the spot, but that's not wholly it. He can't bring himself to say something that would hurt another human being.

"What does Rahula have to tell her?" Hari Lal's wife asks him.

"Sssh! Let him tell you for himself. Rahula, this is your opportunity."

Rahula has a hard time getting his tongue and lips to move, not realizing that the problem is not physical, but mental, in that he must say something he would never dream of saying to anyone.

"All right, Devi," Rahula says, straightening up in his chair.

"Yes," she murmurs, her tear-drenched eyes peering at him.

"I saw my future," he says, realizing that this is the best way to say it, the best opening line he could possibly use.

"Yes, what did you see?"

"I saw myself in orange robes with my head shaved."

Devi starts sobbing hysterically. Her mother goes over to her on the couch and comforts her. She struggles against her mother's embrace and manages to stand up. She stares down at a terrified Rahula and yells, "You cheat! Liar! Fraud! How could you do this to me?" She begins sobbing again and, instead of sitting down, she runs out of the room. Rahula is afraid that she might come back even angrier than before, so he gets up, quickly says good-bye, remarking that he has a bus to catch, and runs out the door. By the time Devi returns with the packet of letters he wrote, which she intends to throw at him along with some choice invectives, he is a good block and a half away. He hails a cab and gets in, for it is worth the extra rupees to make a fast getaway. Besides, once he's a samanera, he will have no need of money.

CHAPTER
43

Sumana wakes up at dawn and sits up in bed. He closes his eyes and brings himself back within himself, but now it's not a sleep where his mind is imprisoned, but rather a waking meditative world where his mind can roam free. He knows he's not dreaming because he's hearing real sounds, though the colorful pictures his mind conjures up have a dreamlike quality, and they appear vividly real to him. A picture of burning logs comes into view, slides through his field of inner vision, and then vanishes. His mind is picture-less for a few seconds and then his attention follows a fireball shooting across a pitch-black sky.

The main thing that tells him he's awake and not dreaming is that he can feel and hear each breath going in and going out. If he were sleeping, he wouldn't be aware of his breath at all. His breath brings him into the world. It is the world. An in-breath becomes a picture of streaks of red paint across a white canvas, and an out-breath brings with it streaks of blue. Red streaks pass by, then blue streaks, not erasing or covering each other, but each in their own space on an expansive white background. His attention follows a red streak, tapering down into an arrow, the tip of which glistens for a moment. His mind shines brilliantly, blissfully, his body tingling all over in its wake. His mind rests, basking in its self-created happiness. A blue streak starts up quickly and then slows down as it too tapers off into an arrow with a shiny steel tip. The sharpness of the tip, magnified several times, reveals a beveled edge, perfectly honed, clean and pure, radiant and brilliant, and for an instant so is his consciousness. Blissfully, his body tingles all over, waves upon waves of the sweetest, most delightful sensations.

Sumana pulls himself back to his breathing, breaking the state of mind that produces such experiences. He knows with certainty what just happened. His mind arrived at some important state of consciousness. He attained something, but not nibbana. He is sure of that. He continues to ponder this experience for a while, then gets up, and goes out to wash up and get ready for breakfast.

Maggaphala rises after dawn, robes himself, and walks from the cave to the dining hut. He's not fully awake, a little groggy from sleep, more tired than usual after a full night's rest, which he attributes to the long and busy day he had yesterday. The first thing he does when he gets to the dining hut is light the stove and boil some water for tea. He goes over to the bench to sit awhile before checking on the pot of water. He looks around the hut, remarking to himself about the poverty of the place. Why don't these devout lay Buddhists do something about it? They can start by building a new dining facility.

On further reflection, Maggaphala concedes that a whitewashed concrete dining hall would detract from the forest hermitage ambiance, so necessary in keeping this place alive. This is a magical place. Many strange and wondrous things have happened here. As he tries to pinpoint examples of the magic of Atakkachari Arañña, he comes up short. Maybe that's just how he would like to see it. What it is in reality is perhaps closer to what most people would dread about such a place. It's not remote, but it's lonely here when no one is around. There's really nothing to do except eat, sleep, bathe, meditate, read and talk to others. This morning, for the first time, Maggaphala is beginning to see where he has landed.

The water begins to boil out of the top of the pot, pulling Maggaphala out of his reverie. He gets up and goes over to the pot, pulls out a handkerchief to take it off the stove and set it down on the ground. He then opens the tin of tea. He reaches inside it, his fat fingers almost getting stuck, as he pulls out a clump of black stringy tea leaves. It's not enough tea for his taste, but he settles for that amount, since he doesn't want to hurt his hand by reaching into the tin again. He opens the top of the pot with his other hand and dumps the tea inside. He takes the spoon and stirs the tea. Then he puts the pot back on the stove, with the flame turned low, and lets the boiling water further cook the tea. He regrets that there's no powdered milk to be found, wishing that Rahula was here to look for some milk and mix it for him.

He turns off the stove and pours himself a bowl of tea, holding a tea strainer over the bowl with one hand and getting the stream of tea to pass only through its basket. The bowl fills with tea, taking about half of the pot. Maggaphala sets the pot down on the stove. Then he takes his bowl of tea over to the bench and sets it down next to him to cool a little.

He notices a couple of new mosquito bites on his arms and legs, by sensation only. He keeps his gaze directed in front of him, as he enters into a kind of trance. There's no energy in his mind that he can detect, nothing pushing his thoughts. Instead, there is a heavy, mud-like feeling in his mind, and when an idea surfaces it doesn't move anywhere, doesn't trigger anything. It just sinks back down into the mud. He turns his head and looks down at his bowl of tea. He slowly reaches for it, thinking that the caffeine will have a stimulating effect on his mind, though he regrets he could not make the tea as strong as he would like.

As Maggaphala sips his tea, he does notice his mind perk up a bit, but his thoughts don't lead him as they usually do. Instead, they hold a mirror up for him to see his mind. As he peers into this mirror, a three-dimensional understanding of something about himself comes into focus. He is unhappy. He is not suffering, not terminally ill, not in pain, just not happy. The word "unfulfilled" comes readily to mind. Yes, that is it! He's unfulfilled in this life.

He recalls that yesterday, for a moment, something unexpected happened that promised a release from this overall feeling of being unhappy in his chosen way of life. He scolds himself for not pursuing the opportunity further. He feels it's now imperative to contact Hari Lal and accept his offer to act in his movie. The thought of fame and immortality on the screen pleases him greatly. When it passes, leaving in its wake this pervasive unfulfilled void within him, he realizes that it's all a fantasy. He has chosen to be a bhikkhu and so must find fulfillment as a bhikkhu. That's his life's challenge. That means, like his friend Aggachitta, he too must arrive at nibbana. Only in that way will his life have meaning.

Now that he has his bearings again, he finishes drinking down his bowl of tea. He sets the empty bowl down next to him. His eyes close almost of their own volition, shutting out the rays of the morning sun. There is light, however, one that glows a creamy white, spreading in all directions.

Aggachitta wakes up with the sun streaming down on his face from his eastward facing window. It must be after eight in the morning for the sun to reach this far. He does not know how he could have slept in like this. He must have been very tired from the events of the last couple of days. That is the only way he can justify this apparent indolence.

He dresses quickly and heads directly to the dining hut. He arrives at the entrance to the hut at the same time as Sumana. They stop and face each other.

"Bhante, I had an extraordinary meditation sitting this morning. I need to talk to you about it," Sumana says.

Aggachitta looks at him, still not fully awake, though his mind and senses are alert. "After breakfast."

"Good," Sumana says, eagerly. Sumana stands aside for Aggachitta to enter the hut.

"Has breakfast been served yet?" Aggachitta asks Maggaphala.

"There is no one here to serve it," Maggaphala replies. It's true that bhikkhus can't get food and serve it to each other. They need someone who's not a bhikkhu to handle the food and serve it to them. One of Rahula's many necessary functions.

"What did you do before Rahula?" Sumana asks Venerable Aggachitta.

"I would walk into town if I wanted to eat in the morning," Aggachitta says.

"Would you go to the monastery or on alms rounds?" Maggaphala asks.

"Sometimes one, sometimes the other," Aggachitta replies, "but it's not necessary for three monks to go out on alms round together. And it's too late for breakfast at the monastery."

"So what should we do?" Sumana says, suddenly alarmed by the situation, disheartened by the prospect of not getting anything to eat for breakfast.

"There's another way," Aggachitta says. "One of us goes into town on alms round and brings food back for the rest of us. By dana time there's bound to be a layperson here to prepare leftovers from yesterday."

"So who will it be?" Maggaphala asks. All three of them already know the answer to that one. It will be the junior monk, Sumana.

"But can't I have some tea and talk to you about my meditation sitting first?" Sumana says to Aggachitta with a slight whine in his voice.

"It's already getting late." Aggachitta replies. "We have ample time to talk about your meditation experiences today right after you get back and we eat."

Sumana refolds his robes so that both of his shoulders are covered. He picks up his black alms bowl and is ready to go on alms round. He has only gone on *pindapata* a few times and has not found it satisfying. He has heard from other foreign monks that you can get much better food going on alms round than you can sitting around at a monastery, but his experience has been that there is much one is given that is uneatable by his standards and just gets thrown out. He doesn't like shouldering the responsibility of bringing back food for his superiors. What happens if he brings back disagreeable alms? What he would like to do is just go to a restaurant and order some takeout, but that's not allowed. He can't even go to the local market or to outdoor vendors for food. He must go to people's houses and stand outside their front doors until they come out with food. This is far too much stress for him this early in the morning. He bows to the other monks before setting off on his mission.

Maggaphala goes over and fixes his friend a cup of tea. He brings it over to Aggachitta, who is now seated on the bench, and hands it to him. Instead of sitting down next to his friend, Maggaphala sits down on the ground in front of him cross-legged.

"Why not sit on the bench?" Aggachitta asks him.

"It would not be proper for me considering what it is I am about to ask of you," Maggaphala replies.

Aggachitta is poised on the edge of the bench, his curiosity aroused, waiting for Maggaphala to speak.

"I'm ready to rekindle my meditation practice and would like you to be my teacher."

Aggachitta is a bit unsettled by his friend's request. He regards Maggaphala as a colleague and is initially averse to the idea of him as a student. For a student, in Aggachitta's mind, is someone who knows very little and needs a great deal of education, but a colleague is someone who knows a good deal, with perhaps some of it wrong or misinformed, and is most likely unable to learn anything other than what he knows. To have a colleague thus become a student changes the way of teaching. At first, this thought discourages Aggachitta, but after warming to the idea of changing his way of teaching, which he is doing anyhow with his new students, he starts to see this as a splendid opportunity for both himself and his old friend.

"All right, I will accept you as my student."

Maggaphala is a bit uneasy at the suddenness of this change of roles. He would have liked a smoother transition from being a colleague to being a subordinate. If that's what he has to do now to make something meaningful out of his life as a bhikkhu, then he's more than willing to make that sacrifice.

"When do we begin?" he asks.

"We can meet here for tea this afternoon," Aggachitta replies.

"Splendid," Maggaphala says, with a broad smile. "That gives me time to meditate before dana," he adds, rising from the bench.

"You know what to do?" Aggachitta asks, half in jest.

Maggaphala stands for a moment, contemplating a witty reply, but then opts for an honest one.

"Just sit."

CHAPTER
44

Rahula feels a certain elation come over him in the cab, a sense of freedom. "I have escaped the woman in the dunes!" he whispers to himself. Yet, in the back of his mind, he knows he has chosen the village over the woman, the hermitage over the university, monk's robes over suits and ties, and the comparisons go on and on in his mind as part of his joyful mood.

At the bus station his mood fades, for he has to find the right bus and get on the first one he sees, which at nine o'clock could be difficult, as the station is twice as crowded as it was just an hour ago. Fortunately, a bus is waiting for him, practically all full, with one lone aisle seat in the back next to an old man. The bus leaves the bus stand and takes the road leading east out of town, where it will turn onto the highway and head south to the town near the hermitage.

Just outside of Colombo, the bus comes to a roadblock on the highway. Cars are allowed to pass, but all buses and trucks must stop. It takes about five minutes for the bus to pull up to where the troops are. It's stopped and boarded by three soldiers, all carrying machine guns and wearing belts with grenades and ammunition clips. They are young men, not much older than Rahula.

As the first soldier walks down the aisle to the back of the bus, Rahula thinks about what it would be like to be a soldier. He quickly dismisses the prospect as being too dangerous, and besides, he could never bring himself to kill another human being. The soldier stops at the man in the seat in front of

Rahula, peering at what looks like a leather satchel next to him. The soldier asks the man to hand him the satchel. The soldier sets the satchel on the ground, opens it, and fishes around for something he does not find. When the soldier stands to hand the satchel back to the man, one of the grenades in his belt touches the metal bottom of the seat the man is sitting on and is knocked loose out of the soldier's belt. Rahula watches the grenade fall to the ground in front of him and keeps his eyes on it as it rolls down the aisle of the bus slowly, threateningly. Rahula's heart beats faster and faster, as he imagines that the grenade could go off at any moment. He glances at the old man next to him, and nervously tells him that a grenade is rolling down the aisle, thinking that perhaps for an old man a quick death would not be such a bad thing after all. The soldier in the middle of the bus eyes the grenade rolling towards him and bends down to gently stop it. He picks it up. He yells at the other soldier for being such an idiot as to allow this to happen. The three soldiers stop their searching and all leave, one yelling at the other, continuing their argument outside the bus.

The bus continues on its southeastward journey. Rahula is in a state of disbelief for a few minutes. The reality of possibly dying right then and there sinks in. Never has death come so close before. He tries to imagine what nonexistence would be like, but he can't picture it. Instead, he begins to value his life as never before. He sees all his indecisiveness — his willingness to have others choose for him, his allowing people to manipulate his need to please — as not valuing life. There has to be more to existence than that. That is a much better reason to enter the monastic life. With that thought he is even more certain of his decision.

Gotami rises around nine o'clock, her room atop the house ablaze with sunlight. The walls are white, everything is fresh and clean, and she feels completely renewed. She gets up and changes out of one set of robes and into another. She likes having her own bathroom, and spends more time than usual grooming herself this morning, clipping her nails, shaving her head, flossing her teeth, applying lotion to her face, hands, and feet. Once she is all ready, she opens her door, remembering to lock it behind her, and goes out onto the deck and then down the stairs leading from the second-storey to the ground floor. The stairs come out just to the left of the front door. This is how she must enter the house. She knocks on the front door. The young female servant opens it, ushering her inside.

"Dr. Perrera has left for work," the young woman informs her. "She has instructed me to prepare a light breakfast for you and give you food to take to the hermitage."

"Oh, that is very kind of her."

She leads Gotami into the kitchen, which faces east, its white walls lit up brilliantly by sunlight entering from a wall of glass looking out onto a splendid garden. Gotami is elated that this is not a dream. She has landed the best living situation possible for her.

She sits down at the kitchen table where a place setting is there for her. There is a cup of coffee, a glass of orange juice, and the young woman sets down a plate of scrambled eggs and toast. She sips the coffee first, drinking it down half-way before moving on to the food. She then gingerly eats the eggs, finishing the meal off with toast. She leaves the orange juice untouched, not realizing what a rarity orange juice is in Sri Lanka, doing so because of some dietary belief that citrus should not be mixed with starches.

She wipes her lips with a large cloth napkin. "This is like living at a five-star hotel," she says to herself.

The young woman lifts a big, heavy plastic cooler and carries it with both hands over to Gotami, setting it on the floor near her. Gotami takes one look at it and is immediately intimidated by its size and apparent weight. She does not believe she can carry it all the way to the hermitage herself. She wonders if the young woman can find some man, a young strong one preferably, to haul this cooler for her. The woman knows of no one offhand.

Gotami tries to pick up the cooler with her right hand and finds it too heavy. Perhaps she can lighten it a bit so that she can carry it. The young woman sees her about to open it and stops her, saying that Dr. Perrera insisted that everything in the cooler must be taken to the hermitage today. Gotami then asks the young woman to accompany her, so both of them can carry the it together. The young woman has to stay in the house, Dr. Perrera's rules.

Gotami sighs and tries to lift the cooler with both hands. She can get it above her ankles and move, shuffling her feet a few meters before having to set it down on the ground. Then she takes a moment to catch her breath and give her muscles a rest. She carries it to the front door on the first go around, and out the door and to the front gate on the second. She is already perspiring heavily and regrets having applied lotion. She looks around to see if there are any men walking around who could carry this for her, but she does not know enough Sinhala to frame such a request even if she found someone.

It takes her about twenty minutes to get as far as the town's monastery. Her robes are soaked around her armpits and her face is dripping with perspiration. She is convinced that everyone who has passed by her has noticed her unseemly appearance, even the two young men whom she asked to help her during one of her several rest stops.

She sits down on the monastery steps. Maybe one of the monks will come out and offer to help her. As she sits, she is reminded that Aggachitta will want to know about her meditation sittings. Her attention then does not go to her sittings, but to her thoughts about Aggachitta. He was in love once. She pictures how sad Dr. Lily Perrera was after telling her that. He was truly and deeply loved. Gotami feels differently about Aggachitta now. He must have loved her too, and chose to pursue something higher and nobler instead.

Gotami becomes aware of someone standing a couple of feet from her, sensing his presence first, and then seeing the hem of his robes hanging around his white ankles.

"Good morning!" Sumana says, genuinely happy to see her.

"Good morning," she musters.

"What do you have in the cooler?"

"Food."

"That's great!" Sumana exclaims. "I have been sent on alms round to bring back food, even though there are leftovers in the cave. But being as we're bhikkhus we can't offer that food to ourselves."

Gotami is dimly aware of the rule he's referring to, wondering what he is trying to say with this unnecessary explanation.

"Will you carry this cooler for me?" she asks. "It is quite heavy," she adds as he bends down to pick it up.

"You're right," Sumana says, lifting the cooler with both hands up to his waist. "It must be packed. Do you know what's inside?"

"I am not supposed to look," she says.

"Oh."

"Let's go," she says, "I don't want to be late for my interview."

They walk together. Sumana carries the cooler with both hands, only stopping to rest when they reach the dirt path through the coconut plantation. For the first half of their journey, they are silent, thinking to themselves, wondering what the other is thinking at times, but not asking.

During the rest stop, Sumana places the cooler on the ground and stands next to it. Gotami squats on her haunches a few feet away from him.

Sumana says, "I had a most amazing sitting this morning."

She says, "Go on, tell me about it."

"We're really not supposed to talk about our meditation sittings, except with our teacher," Sumana says, as he was just trying to make conversation, and not intending to say more about his meditation sitting.

"What's going to happen if you tell me about it?"

"You may become envious."

She looks at him with disbelief mixed with outrage.

"I doubt it," she says. "Why would I want your meditation sittings?"

"I don't know," he replies. "My old teacher told me that if I talked about my sittings with another meditator, that person would want to have my experiences and become discouraged if that did not happen."

"That's not going to happen with me," she says. "I'm pleased with my own sittings and wouldn't trade them for anything in the world. So go ahead, tell me if you like."

Sumana notices how relaxed he now feels around her. He wants to tell her about more than just his sittings. He would like her to know how he feels around her, how he has thought about her, what she is beginning to mean to him, if those are things that he can get past the internal censor, the head monk in his skull. Perhaps he should just stick to telling her his sitting, for that is the most harmless thing he can relate right now.

"I wanted to talk to Venerable Aggachitta about it first, but maybe it will help I relate it to you first."

"All right, I'm listening," she says, straightening up slowly and then walking over to the cooler. She unfolds her handker-chief and lays it across part of the flat plastic lid, smoothing it out before she sits down.

Sumana walks over to where she was squatting earlier and, without a thought about getting his robes dirty, sits down on the ground. This strikes Gotami as very odd, for it's not proper for her, as a woman, a layperson, and a nun, to sit in a higher seat than a bhikkhu, even if that seat is just a rectan-gular cooler. This seating arrangement does somehow suit the situation, where the one seated higher listens compassionately to one seated lower.

Sumana relates, "I was aware of each breath going in and out, seeing a red streak for the in-breath and a blue streak for the out breath, and all of a sudden, I saw the end point of the red streak and my mind was sucked up into it. It was so blissful! It then happened on the end point of the blue streak, which was like the sharp point of a knife. I saw it so clearly."

Gotami does not know what to make of Sumana's experi-ence. In one respect, it doesn't sound at all extraordinary, while in another, it sounds to her like a special experience, one that she has yet to have. She can see why a teacher would think envy would arise upon hearing of such experiences, but she does not covet Sumana's experience. She just admires it and wonders what it could be.

"You will definitely have to ask Venerable Aggachitta about it," she replies.

"I plan to as soon as we get back," he says.

This comment bothers her. Sumana has all the time in the world to meet with Aggachitta.

She keeps this to herself as they rise from their respective seats and continue their journey through the coconut grove. Sumana becomes more and more conscious of how quiet she has become since he told her about his sitting. Maybe his old teacher was right about not talking about these things with others. He wants to make up to her, to undo whatever he said that has made her sullen and detached, if only he could know what it was without having to ask her about it.

Before they get to the last part of the journey, the remaining quarter mile through dense jungle, Sumana stops to rest. He can't tolerate her silence any longer and picks up the courage to speak to her.

"Why are you so quiet all of a sudden?"

She pauses a moment and says, "You can see Aggachitta whenever you want. I can only see him for a little while in the morning. Do you understand?"

"Yes, I'll have my interview after you leave. Is that what upsets you?"

"Thank you for understanding," she says in reply.

They resume their journey. This time there should be nothing in the air to bar them from having a conversation. Sumana feels an urge to talk about anything with her, while Gotami would rather save her breath and energy for when she gets to the hermitage. Sumana's desire to speak turns into anxiety as he remains silent, for he hopes that she will begin a conversation with him since he was so considerate. He walks uneasily in front of her, thinking of one thing after another to say to her, and then it occurs to him that all these little phrases and questions that come into his mind are completely irrelevant and annoying. He can't give voice to his true feelings about her. That is taboo. Instead, he brings his awareness to those feelings, and, where he expects to find some kind of sexual tension — a desire for her female body stripped of all that makes her a person — he finds in its place an aspiration to know her, Gotami the person, more completely.

This is *nama-rupa*, he thinks to himself. In the West we call it mind and body, but in the East, it has always been name and form, *nama* and *rupa*. Name is the person, while form is the body of the person. They can't be divided. He has heard that several times in dharma talks. We tend to see them as divided, and from that division lust for the body arises.

That is an important insight for Sumana, and he carries it with him, along with the cooler, the rest of the way through the jungle and into the dining hut.

Sumana sets the cooler on the table. Gotami goes over and prostrates in front of Aggachitta. Sumana's focus quickly returns to the contents of the cooler however. He is terribly hungry. He hasn't gone so long without eating as far back as he can remember. Besides, he has worked up an appetite with all the exercise he has gotten this morning.

Gotami rises and waits for Aggachitta to speak to her. Instead, Aggachitta looks over at Sumana standing near the table and says, "We can talk before dana."

"I'll help with dana," Gotami offers, rising from the ground, hiding her mild resentment at Sumana going first, even though they had discussed it. "I can take the things out of the cooler and set them on the table," she says, realizing that she's doing her teacher and the other bhikkhus a service by doing so. If she isn't going to get meditation instruction first, at least she can earn some merit by setting out lunch for the bhikkhus and offering the food to them. This thought pleases her more and more as she opens up the cooler.

Sumana approaches Aggachitta on the bench and whispers to him. "Can we talk in private?"

"Certainly," Aggachitta says. "We can go to my hut."

As Sumana leaves, he glances over at Gotami, trying to catch her eye, so that she can see the apologetic expression on his face. Unfortunately, she's busy pulling one ceramic bowl after another out of the cooler and setting them down carefully on the table. She does not pause to look up at Sumana, her thoughts elsewhere. Her attention soon leaves the repetitive task and goes to her meditation sitting last night. She was generally composing letters in her meditation sitting, telling everyone she knew about her new home. She described her lodgings in detail to her parents, confident that they'd be glad she's safe and comfortable. She went on and on about finding a teacher in a letter to a girlfriend of hers who shares her interest in Buddhism. For the first time in a while, she thought of an old boyfriend who was a self-proclaimed Buddhist, more interested in the martial arts than in serenity and simple living, thanking him in her thoughts for introducing her to the Zen Center where she started meditating. It all began there. In remembering her first teacher, she was filled with gratitude.

What about the periods in her sitting where there was little or no thought? She abruptly answers her own question. There were no periods like that last night. All she was doing was going over her life, which is something she could do anytime. How is this meditation? It's not Zen, not vipassana. It allows too much mind wandering. It doesn't rely on observing the breath. Aggachitta doesn't speak of emptiness or no-self. There are no mantras of impermanence. There seems to be nothing to hold onto, nothing to call it.

Fear catches her by surprise. What has she fallen into here?

Sumana and Aggachitta go directly to Aggachitta's hut. Once inside, Aggachitta pulls up a chair and motions Sumana to sit on the bed.

"So, tell me about this meditation experience you had," Aggachitta says.

"I was watching my breath, and when there was an in-breath I saw a red streak across a white background. I watched the red streak to its end, which was an arrow. I was pulled rapidly to the tip of the arrow and then it vanished and I was filled with bliss."

"Did you feel the bliss throughout your body?"

"Yes, I felt it all the way down to my feet and hands."

"Well then, the red streak was a sign," Aggachitta says, looking at Sumana's uncomprehending expression. "By sign I do not mean omen or symbol or anything like that. A sign is a visual image the mind creates when it is fully concentrated on something. You were concentrating on the breath and so your mind created a visual picture of the breath, the red streak, and your attention stayed on that instead of remaining on your breath. As your attention clung to the image, your mind altered it in a way that would draw your focus completely into it. The moment of your mind being completely in it was a moment of *jhana*, of complete unification of mind around that image."

"A jhana?" Sumana asks, recalling that he has heard the word before in reference to a higher meditative state of consciousness. And now, his teacher is using the same word to describe an experience he has had. This is truly startling to him.

"Yes that's right, a jhana. You entered the first jhana for a moment. It will happen again and again in your sittings now that it has happened once."

"Is it some kind of attainment?" Sumana asks, hoping that it is, for that would mean that he may have reached what he was after by going into the jungle and could now return to his home monastery, where meals are served on time.

"It is and it isn't," Aggachitta replies. "It's a momentary state of liberation from the *kamaloka*, the realm of sense pleasures, and can be used as a basis for gaining true liberating knowledge. Thus it is an attainment, but it's not the kind of attainment that we're seeking. It's helpful on the path, and can be developed over time, though it can also lead one astray."

Sumana is both comforted and disturbed by Aggachitta's statements. He's glad he has made it to this point, where on occasion he can feel some kind of liberation of mind, but he's also dissatisfied with himself for not finding true liberation of mind in his meditation sittings. Perhaps that would be asking too much of himself right now, but that was not the case with his old teacher, who often told him that he was close to being fully liberated. All he had to do was sit, restrain his senses, and live a quiet life in a secluded place.

"Just continue meditating as you have been," Aggachitta counsels him. "If this happens again in your sittings, take a moment afterwards to recall the experience and see its main characteristics. Then, if it happens again, you will be more aware of it. By becoming aware of these jhanas over time, you will learn how to master them."

"How long will that take?"

"Months, years, who knows?"

Sumana is a bit confused. His new teacher doesn't believe that he's as close to being an arhat as he had thought. No one has ever told him that it may take years just to master something that is not even true liberation of mind. He had not bargained to spend the rest of his life out in the jungle. He had assumed that with the right teacher it would only be a matter of weeks, a few months at the most. This thought is most disheartening.

Aggachitta does not know what to make of the young monk's sudden drop in enthusiasm.

"This is a good development," he says, trying to cheer Sumana up. "It's a precious gift. Not all meditators have samadhi as good as yours."

Sumana's face brightens at this compliment. He wants to know more about this gift for samadhi he did not know he had until recently. There will be time for that. He feels absolutely committed to living here and meditating under Aggachitta's guidance for as long as it takes.

"By the way," Aggachitta says, "did you walk all the way from town with the nun?"

"Yes," Sumana says, surprised by this question seemingly coming out of nowhere.

"Next time," Aggachitta cautions, "have a layman present. You do not want people seeing you alone with her. There will be rumors and gossip, and some concerned layperson will hear of it and come to me asking me to do something about it. We don't want that to happen."

"I understand," Sumana says.

"Good, then let's go to dana. We can talk about your other sittings later."

As they walk to the dining hut, Aggachitta thinks not about Sumana's meditative experience, for that is clear-cut and taken care of, but of the imminent need for a temple boy to replace Rahula. A hermitage such as this one can't run efficiently, the monks can't act as blamelessly, without one. Although, it does occur to him, when he sees Gotami next to the table with the contents of the cooler all laid out in plain view, that a laywoman or nun coming to the hermitage on occasion might work just as well as having a temple boy.

Maggaphala enters the dining hut soon after Aggachitta and Sumana, carrying a smaller cooler containing leftovers from the day before. He was not able to get settled in his meditation sitting, as his mind went constantly to thoughts about food, and so after about ten minutes he got up and went over to where the food is stored and began sorting through the packets of leftovers, putting the more desirable ones in the portable cooler.

He walks over to the table where Gotami is standing next to all of the bowls laid out upon it, leaving little room for the cooler or the newspaper wrapped packets of food it contains, so he sets the cooler down on the ground. He looks over the dishes on the table, hovering over today's offerings of rice, broiled cubes of fish, lentils, gotu kola salad, curried vegetables, fried cashew curry, and potatoes in coconut sauce. He is captivated by the different odors coming from the food, which at one moment is appetizing and at the next not so appetizing. He tries to figure out, using his sense of sight, which dish is unappetizing, but can't quite place the particular unpleasant smell with the dish it belongs to. After a couple of minutes of puzzling over this, he decides that it must be the curried vegetables and so makes a mental note not to eat any.

Maggaphala then asks Gotami to lift one bowl at a time a few inches off the table so that he may touch each one lightly with the fingertips of both hands. This is the customary way of offering food to the bhikkhu sangha, and once it is done, all of the bhikkhus can get their food buffet style. Maggaphala and Gotami then gather what spoons and ladles are to be found. Maggaphala puts the serving utensils into the dishes, and then motions to Aggachitta to come over and begin serving food into his bowl. Maggaphala follows behind his friend, ladling large spoonfuls of everything, except the curried vegetables, into his large black alms bowl. Sumana follows close behind him, elated that he can serve himself this way, for he can pick and choose what he would like to eat and gets to decide how much to put in his bowl. When all the bhikkhus have finished filling their alms bowls, Gotami can do the same with an ordinary plate. Once Gotami has taken a dish however, it is no longer offered to the bhikkhus, and so if any of them wants second helpings, Gotami, or some other layperson, has to serve them.

Aggachitta, Maggaphala, and Sumana all three squeeze together on the bench, the two chairs having been returned to the cave. Maggaphala has the hardest time eating since he is sitting in the middle and his right arm keeps rubbing up against Sumana's left side. Sumana moves down more and more until he is only half sitting on the bench. He then turns his body around on the bench and sits on the edge, no longer facing in the same direction as the other two monks. Maggaphala can eat without difficulty now and Sumana can eat without being nudged repeatedly by his fellow monk.

Gotami sits across from the three monks on her spot of ground. She has all the room she needs and no one to disturb her eating.

Maggaphala finishes first and asks Venerable Aggachitta if he's going to get additional food or not, which he declines, thereby allowing Maggaphala to get second helpings without waiting for his friend. To do this however, Gotami would have to stop eating and serve the seated bhikkhus. She is so engrossed in her own thoughts while she eats, she does not look up at Maggaphala, and now Sumana, who are both looking at her to get her attention. Fortunately, for everyone concerned, Rahula makes his entrance.

Aggachitta notices him first, exclaiming, "Rahula! You're back!"

Everyone looks over at Rahula, surprised and elated to see him.

"Rahula," Sumana says, "you have arrived just in time."

"I can see that," Rahula says. He goes over to the table, picks up the bowl of cashew curry, and brings it over to his uncle, who accepts a small amount in his bowl. He then ladles larger portions into Maggaphala's and Sumana's bowls. He then brings one dish after another over to the bhikkhus, who each accept Rahula's offerings, even if it is a dish that one of them does not particularly want, such as the curried vegetables in Maggaphala's case, for they are all overjoyed at Rahula's reappearance in their world. Rahula then goes over to Gotami and asks her if there is anything she would like. She points to the table and asks him to bring only the lentils and the curried vegetables. He brings her one dish at a time, placing generous helpings on her plate.

"You may serve yourself now, Rahula," Aggachitta says. "You must be hungry after your long journey."

"I certainly am," he replies and quickly grabs a plate, taking helpings from what is left.

A mood of contentment settles over everyone. For a moment, but not at the exact same time, each of them has the thought:

This is the life!

CHAPTER
45

Aggachitta returns to his hut after Gotami's interview. She asked him some difficult questions, much like Sumana the day before, which makes him wonder if the two of them are not somehow comparing notes on what he has been teaching. For the first time, he is beginning to realize that he is teaching a new form of meditation, which he can no longer call *vipassana*. That was the essence of Gotami's questions to him. "What do you call this kind of meditation? Has anyone written a book on it? Where does it come from and where does it lead?"

Aggachitta goes to his desk and picks up the exercise book where he has been jotting down his recent thoughts. He flips through it to see if he may have written something in the last few days on this new approach to meditation, but all he finds are his philosophical musings. The musings are what his mind does to articulate certain kinds of understandings, but they do not speak of a practice, or of a path. He wrote at length about the path, though he never described how meditation fits in with it. To correct this omission, he intends to write something about it.

He picks up his notebook and flips it open to the page where he wrote:

"It is not a gap, not a loss of consciousness, but a clear space of knowing the act of knowing."

When he wrote that sentence, he was conceiving of a pure consciousness that knows the process of knowing. From his current perspective, he was describing an ideal state of consciousness, one that he would now attribute a temporary existence to, rather than as something eternal and absolute. He now wonders if indeed such an ideal, pure consciousness can exist at all, and if it is just a habit of mind for him to conceive of such a consciousness. What would his experience of "a clear space of knowing the act of knowing" be if knowing the act of knowing was just another mentally fabricated concept? If that were the case, then the knowing he had considered to be pure would have perception and experience in it, and so it would not be nirodha, where perception and experience ceases, leaving only consciousness. Just as there is no separation of knowing from the known, there can be no higher knowing that exists without perception and experience.

Then his mind flashes to nirodha thus being impossible. Then, because of that, nibbana does not exist. And then, as a crescendo, a realization that all concepts have no reality other than their mental existence, and therefore all he knows about nibbana and the path is not real, a figment, a mirage. After a second of utter despair at there being nothing salvageable from these realizations, a marvelous and sublime understanding occurs to him:

Samsara is such.
Nibbana is the final knowing of that.

Why this has not occurred to him before is the first thought that occurs to him now. The answer is clear. His view of consciousness, despite all he believed about its emptiness, impermanence, no-self, and suffering, was still conceptual. As much as he would like to contemplate this further, he knows that whatever it was he understood is now past, and beyond retrieval.

THE END